ON THE RUN

"No one's offered to help us in a very long time. Thank you."

The tightness returned to his chest. "Nothing to thank me for yet. I'll see you at supper."

Glad to get away from his unfamiliar emotions, Josh walked out of the bedroom. He didn't know how it had happened, but he had a woman and a kid in his life—the last thing he needed. A woman and a child with a threat hanging over their heads.

A woman he wanted and couldn't have.

He wondered if things could get any worse.

And knew damn well they could.

Also by Kat Martin

BEYOND CONTROL

KAT MARTIN

ZEBRA BOOKS
KENSINGTON PUBLISHING CORP.
http://www.kensingtonbooks.com

ZEBRA BOOKS are published by

Kensington Publishing Corp.
119 West 40th Street
New York, NY 10018

All Kensington titles, imprints, and distributed lines are available at special quantity discounts for bulk purchases for sales promotion, premiums, fund-raising, educational, or institutional use.

Special book excerpts or customized printings can also be created to fit specific needs. For details, write or phone the office of the Kensington Sales Manager: Attn.: Sales Department. Kensington Publishing Corp., 119 West 40th Street, New York, NY 10018. Phone: 1-800-221-2647.

Zebra and the Z logo Reg. U.S. Pat. & TM Off.

First Printing: June 2018
ISBN-13: 978-1-4201-4319-5
ISBN-10: 1-4201-4319-0

eISBN-13: 978-1-4201-4320-1
eISBN-10: 1-4201-4320-4

10 9 8 7 6 5 4 3 2 1

Printed in the United States of America

Chapter One

Dear God, he was supposed to be gone! The sound of the front door opening and closing, familiar heavy footfalls in the entry sent shock waves through her body. It was almost midnight. Damon should have been in Los Angeles attending a three-day business conference with his father.

Tory glanced wildly around the bedroom. She had nearly finished packing, just a couple more boxes to fill, then first thing in the morning she was leaving. She had rented an apartment on the other side of Phoenix, a fresh start for her and Ivy, her four-year-old daughter.

A noise, Damon bumping into the coffee table in the living room, pushed her nerves up another notch. Her heart set up a murderous clatter as a chair tipped over and crashed to the floor. Damon swore foully.

He was drunk. Again. Her heart jerked, speeded. Lord, what was he doing here? Why was he still in Phoenix?

She swallowed, tried to focus, think what to do. He must have missed his flight, had probably gone out with his sycophant buddies, guys who enjoyed the free booze and the women, the expensive nightclubs and strip joints, all paid for by Damon Bridger from the trust fund his father provided.

Four months ago, when she had first met him, he had been different. They had crossed paths at a nightclub called the Peacock, a loud sort of place she rarely frequented, a place she had gone with her best friend, Lisa Shane, to celebrate Lisa's birthday.

With his jet-black hair and golden brown eyes, Damon was amazingly handsome, like Johnny Depp, Lisa had said. The attraction had been instant and amazing, or at least so it seemed.

He'd called the next day and immediately begun his pursuit. Back then, his gifts had been simple but expensive presents for her and Ivy. Presents chosen especially for the two of them, a tiny hummingbird pendant because she loved birds. A small silver princess ring for Ivy with the little girl's name engraved on it.

She'd thought he was special, that he would make the perfect father for her daughter, someone to end the last four lonely years since her husband had died.

She had lulled herself into believing the handsome man who was courting her would make her happy.

Tory glanced at the glowing red numbers on the clock on the nightstand: 12:01 A.M. Ivy was asleep in her room at the opposite end of the hall. Damon had changed so much that lately she had begun to worry he might hurt her little girl.

She swallowed. The tread of heavy, uneven footfalls coming down the hall sent a trickle of fear down her spine. Week after week, he'd grown more and more antagonistic, and more and more violent. He had pushed her, had slapped her once, but each time he had apologized and begged her forgiveness. Last week he had hit her with his fist.

It was the end, as far as Tory was concerned. She was moving out, the sooner the better. His trip to LA should have provided the perfect opportunity.

Tory closed her eyes as the door swung open and Damon staggered into the bedroom. A cold smile stretched over his handsome face. "Nice of you to wait up," he said.

She forced herself not to run, to keep her spine straight and not flinch. "I thought you were in LA with your dad."

Instead of answering, his gaze swept around the bedroom, taking in the open suitcases, the boxes she hadn't yet loaded into the trunk of her car. "Where do you think you're going?"

She took a deep breath. No way to avoid a confrontation now. "I'm leaving, Damon. I'm taking Ivy and moving out. I told you it wasn't working. I've got a place of my own." There was no waiting till morning now. She had to leave before something bad happened. "I'll come back and pick up the rest of my things over the weekend."

The beautiful diamond engagement ring he'd bought her glittered in its blue velvet box on the dresser. She had planned to leave a note with the ring when she moved out of his condo.

She started for the door, praying he wouldn't try to stop her, but Damon stepped in front of her, blocking her way. His mouth thinned into a hard, unforgiving line.

"You aren't going anywhere. You're staying right here where you belong. You're mine, Tory. I keep what belongs to me. Surely you know that by now."

She kept her chin high, though she was trembling inside. "I'm going, Damon. I'm taking Ivy and leaving. Get out of my way." She took a step forward, but he shoved her back, hard enough she stumbled.

"You're my fiancée. You're not leaving this house." He gripped her wrist and dragged her over to the big king-size bed. "Take off your clothes. You're gonna put out. I gave you that fancy diamond—now you're gonna pay for it."

Fury swamped her, making her reckless. With her red hair and fair complexion, there was no way to hide the angry color in her cheeks. "What, you didn't get laid while you were out with your friends?"

Damon backhanded her across the face, splitting her lip, sending her sprawling onto the mattress. A spray of blood flew across the pillow and she bit back a moan.

"What I do or don't do is none of your business. Not since you slept with that guy in your office—what was his name? Oh yeah, *Clark*."

She wiped the blood from her mouth with a trembling hand. "I didn't sleep with Clark. I told you, it was raining. My car wouldn't start so he gave me a ride home. That's all it was." But his jealousy had grown along with his temper.

"You're a slut, just like the rest of them. For a while you had me fooled, but not anymore."

"Fine, if that's what you think, just let me leave and you'll be rid of me." She came up from the bed and started for the door, but Damon shoved her back against the wall.

"You'll leave when I say, not before." He caught her wrist and dragged her forward. She cried out as he slapped her again, hard enough to knock her to the floor. When he kicked her, Tory drew herself into a ball and put her arms over her head. She didn't dare fight him, not with Ivy just down the hall.

"You little bitch." Damon grabbed a handful of her T-shirt and hauled her to her feet. "You need a lesson on how to behave and I'm gonna give you one."

Tory muffled a cry as he drew back his fist and punched her, her jaw exploding in pain as she hit the floor.

She put her hand up to protect herself. "Stop it, Damon! I'll do whatever you want!"

"Oh, you're gonna do what I want, all right, you little whore." He dragged her up by the hair and slapped her, punched her again, knocking her into the dresser, banging her head so hard she saw stars and landed on the floor.

He was leaving her no choice; she had to fight back or he was going to kill her.

Tory shot to her feet and charged forward, punching him

with her fists, kicking him, doing her best to hurt him. He was over six feet tall and muscular, an invincible wall of meanness and determination.

The last thing she remembered was trying to dodge the blow as his fist shot toward her, her body flying backward, slamming into the wall. His boot crashed into her ribs and pain shot through her. Then she felt nothing at all.

Victoria Bradford woke up the following morning in a Scottsdale Memorial hospital bed, one of her eyes swollen shut, with a concussion, four broken ribs, a punctured lung, and her entire body black-and-blue and covered with cuts and abrasions.

Through her one good eye, she spotted a nurse walking into the room. "My . . . my daughter . . ." She moistened her lips. "Where's . . . Ivy?"

The nurse looked at her with pity. "Your little girl is fine. She's staying with your friend Lisa."

Relief filtered through her. *Lisa. Thank God.* Lisa would take care of Ivy. Tory didn't ask about Damon. She didn't want to know. She was simply grateful to be alive. At least she and Ivy were safe.

Then the unwanted thought occurred. They were safe. But for exactly how long?

Chapter Two

Iron River Ranch, Iron Springs, Texas,
Four Months Later

Joshua Cain shoved back his chair and rose from the round oak table in his kitchen. Next to the empty plate of overcooked eggs and slightly burned toast, the Iron Springs *Gazette* lay open on the table.

The headline read *Lone Wolf Terror Attack in Austin.* Below was the story of an Islamic extremist who had attacked a man with a butcher knife. Fortunately, the victim, a former police officer, had fought off the attacker and killed him. According to Homeland Security, the threat was over.

Josh didn't read more. He'd left the war behind when he'd left the Middle East. He had come home to Texas to forget about fighting and terrorism and good men dying, and that was exactly what he intended to do.

Crossing the living room, he pushed open the front door and stepped out on the porch beneath the overhanging roof that ran the length of the two-story ranch house.

The sun was out this early April morning, the temperature warm, the sky a clear robin's-egg blue. The year was beginning to heat up, but the Texas temperatures wouldn't be unbearable for at least another two months.

Josh didn't mind the heat. He'd spent the last four years fighting in the blistering deserts of Iraq and the barren mountains of Afghanistan. The hot, damp climate on this side of Texas, along with the wide-open spaces and deep green grasslands, suited him just fine.

Refusing to think of the war, Josh tugged his battered straw cowboy hat a little lower across his forehead and started across the open space between the forty-year-old house he was remodeling and the barn he had just finished rebuilding. A dilapidated old cow barn sat in the field beyond, one of his next projects.

He'd been back in Texas since December when he'd officially left the marines, two months after he'd run into enemy gunfire, been shot three times, taken a load of shrapnel, and nearly died.

He'd spent the following months in the hospital in Landstuhl, Germany, before returning to Texas to live in a double-wide trailer on his brother Linc's twenty-five-hundred-acre property seventy miles east of Dallas, Blackland Ranch.

Linc had insisted he take some time, finish healing, try to figure out what the hell he wanted to do with his life. Grateful for his half brother's help, Josh had accepted the offer, then been surprised to discover that finding out what he wanted didn't take as long as he'd thought.

As a kid, he'd loved country living, loved horses, wrangled cattle every summer and dreamed of owning his own place someday. But he'd had to work from the age of twelve to help support himself and his mother, living barely above subsistence level; it had been little more than a pipe dream back then.

Now he was the proud owner—along with the bank that held the mortgage—of the Iron River Ranch, a two-thousand-acre spread along the northern boundary of his brother's property.

The ranch had come with fifteen head of Black Angus cattle and thirty head of horses. He had kept seven geldings— good, reliable cow ponies—sold and traded the rest for brood-mares and colts he chose himself. He was looking to buy a stallion, had his eye on a registered quarter horse named Handley's Pride.

He'd always had a way with animals, planned to raise a few cows but focus on breeding, training, and selling horses.

He glanced up at a noise in the barn, the sound of hooves pounding against the stall. Satan was at it again. He started walking. Damned horse would be the death of him—or somebody else.

The animal probably should have been put down, and he might have done it if it hadn't been for his sixty-seven-year-old neighbor, Clara Thompson. The woman was convinced Josh could save the stallion if he was patient enough, and he was dumb enough to give it a try.

"Señor Cain! Señor Cain!" His latest hire came racing out of the barn, the jet-black stallion hard on his heels. Josh ran toward them, flapping his hat and shouting, driving the great black beast off in another direction.

"I quit!" Ramirez stomped toward him. "I am through with this place and that crazy horse!"

"Take it easy, Diego. I'll take care of the stallion."

"He nearly killed me! I am finished. I have a better job offer, one where I do not have to risk my life."

Josh didn't try to talk him out of it. He had a feeling the stable hand was partly to blame for the animal's foul temper, at least this morning. He had a hunch Ramirez had been an-tagonizing the stallion. There were guys who liked the control, liked lording it over what they considered a dumb beast, and Josh had a feeling Ramirez was one of them.

Josh watched the man grab his rope, halter, saddle, and bridle and toss them into the back of his old brown pickup. The engine fired up and the pickup shot backward, spun, and roared off down the dirt road toward the two-lane highway that led to Iron Springs.

Josh sighed as he crossed the stable yard and went into the barn for a bucket of grain. When he came out, the big black stallion tossed its head and snorted as it trotted back and forth along the fence line.

Sonofabitch. Another half hour shot to hell trying to coax the horse into the pasture. And now he'd have to drive into town, post some notices, and put an ad in the paper for another stable hand.

He had two full-time ranch hands lined up, due to start in a couple of days, but they would be mending fences, helping him rebuild the cow barn, and doing deferred maintenance the property desperately needed, the reason he had bought it for such a reasonable sum.

The life of a rancher was never easy, and yet Josh loved every minute. He relished the solitude, the time it gave him to deal with the past and come to grips with the present, think a little about the future.

Grabbing the bucket of oats, he went after the cantankerous horse.

It was hard to believe four months had passed since Tory had left Phoenix. After the attack, she had moved to Houston, taken a high-paying job as an executive secretary, assistant to the president of Huntley Drilling, a small oil company. She'd liked the work, which paid well and was less stressful than her former job as an advertising executive with the Elwin Davis Group, the top marketing agency in Phoenix.

But she had gone to a headhunter to find the job so it hadn't taken Damon long to track her down. The harassment had started right away, with him showing up at her apartment, at work, making threats, scaring Ivy. Demanding Tory return with him to Phoenix.

She'd called the police and they had done their best to help, but in Texas, the restraining order she'd gotten in Phoenix had to be updated to be valid. That meant her abuser had to be notified and given a chance to argue his side of the case in court.

She didn't have the money for more attorney fees, and the restraining order she'd gotten after the attack hadn't really done any good. In Houston, when the neighbor's kitten had turned up with a wire around its neck, strangled and bloody, dead in front of her apartment door, it had been time to move on.

New Mexico sounded good. She'd taken an interim job at a dry-cleaning store in Albuquerque just to earn some money. But the first day of work, the owner had cornered her in the garment racks and suggested her job could be a lot easier if she provided a few fringe benefits. She had quit the same day.

She'd been lucky. By the end of the week, she'd found a job over the Internet, office manager of Dominion Potash, a potassium mining company in Carlsbad. She'd liked the challenge of organizing the office and keeping the company running; she'd liked the small, high desert community famous for its world-famous caverns.

After two months with no sign of Damon, she had finally begun to settle in. She'd even allowed herself to make a few friends, relax enough to leave Ivy with a sitter once in a while and go out to a show or dinner in the evenings.

But every day she worried.

Every night, she lay awake, straining to hear the sound of an intruder. Tonight, as she lay in the darkness and listened to the heavy footfalls outside her bedroom door, she knew Damon had found her again.

Cold fear slid through her. It was as if her worst nightmare had come to life and she had to live it all over again.

Only this time, she was prepared.

Her heart slammed like a hammer against the wall of her

chest as he shoved open the bedroom door. She had no idea how he had gotten inside, but she knew him well enough to know if he wanted in, nothing was going to stop him.

There was no time to pick up the phone and dial 9-1-1. Help wouldn't arrive in time if she did. Instead she summoned her courage and forced down her fear.

"What are you doing here, Damon?" Glad for the white cotton nightgown she'd started wearing after the beating, she sat up in bed, her eyes on the man who had just stepped into her bedroom.

She knew exactly what to do. In her mind, she had rehearsed this scenario a hundred times. The knowledge calmed her a little. "Get out before I call the police."

He just laughed. "You think I'm leaving? It's taken me months to find you. When I leave, sweetheart, you're going with me."

Like hell I am. "What happened to you, Damon? You never used to be like this."

"You don't think so?" He propped a thick shoulder against the wall and crossed his arms over his chest. "I finally accepted who I am—that's what happened. Sooner or later, you will, too."

She was shaking inside. She didn't dare let him see how terrified she really was. "I'm not going with you, Damon. Not now or anytime in the future." She was ready for this, she reminded herself. She just needed him to come a little closer. "I'm warning you. I'm calling the police. This is your last chance."

"You little bitch. You think you scare me? You've belonged to me since the day you put my ring on your finger. That isn't going to change. It's time you accepted it and I plan to see that you do." A hard smile curved his lips. "First, I'm going to punish you, give you the beating you deserve; then we're leaving. And there isn't a damn thing you can do."

Wait, Tory warned herself. She swallowed a fresh rush of

fear as Damon shoved away from the wall and started toward her. *You'll only get one chance*. The eyes she saw in her nightmares were dark with a combination of barely suppressed rage and anticipation. His hands fisted as he stalked across the room, around to the side of the bed.

The stun gun was in her hand before he reached her. She swung her arm toward him so fast he didn't see it coming, the stun gun making contact—right in the middle of Damon's chest.

A gurgling sound came from his throat. His eyes shot wide open and his teeth clenched into a frozen snarl. His muscles contracted. His head jerked back and forth before she hit him again and he crashed to the floor beside the bed.

Tory shot off the mattress. With shaking hands, she pulled open the top drawer in the nightstand and grabbed a couple of nylon zip ties from the bag she had bought at Home Depot to prepare for exactly this. Dragging Damon's limp arms behind his back, she looped a tie around his wrists and cinched it tight. She did the same with his feet, pulling the tie tightly together around his ankles.

She hit him again with the stun gun to be sure he wouldn't struggle while she stuffed a washcloth into his mouth and tied a scarf around his head to hold it in place.

Dressing quickly in jeans and a short-sleeved sweatshirt, she opened the closet door and grabbed the go-bags she kept packed for her and Ivy, snatched her purse, stunned him again just because he deserved it, and ran down the hall.

She shook the little blond girl's shoulder. "Get up, sweetheart, we have to leave."

Ivy was wide-awake in an instant. "Is it him? Is he here?" Her daughter was terrified of Damon, and she had every right to be.

"He's tied up in the bedroom. We need to leave. We have to hurry."

Dressed in her unicorn pajamas, Ivy grabbed Pansy, her

brown velvet stuffed pony, and raced down the hall to the living room.

She slid to a stop in front of the door. "Where are we going?" She looked frantically back over her small shoulder, her face pale with fear.

"Someplace safe. Someplace Damon won't find us."

Ivy's blue eyes filled with tears. "There's no such place, Mama." She started crying. "There's no place safe from Damon."

Tory jerked the door open and urged Ivy out into the night. "There *is* a place, honey. This time we won't stop until we find it."

Tory and Ivy raced for the car.

Chapter Three

Three weeks passed. Three weeks since Ramirez had quit and left the ranch, and Josh still hadn't found a reliable stable hand. He'd hired a kid just out of high school but the boy had quit after shoveling manure only a couple of days.

Like a lot of kids today, Chris expected to start as foreman instead of working his way up from the lowest job on the ranch, or at least that's the way it looked to Josh.

He'd had to fire the second guy for stealing.

"You're finished, Randy," he'd said. "Get your stuff and get out of here."

The lanky black-haired teen clamped his hands on his skinny hips. "Man, you gotta be kidding! You're gonna fire me for taking a five-gallon can of gas? I had to drive out here, didn't I? That ought to be worth something."

"You wanted the gas, you should have asked. Take a hike and don't come back."

"Screw you, dude."

The kid grumbled all the way to his car, then shot Josh the bird as he roared off down the dirt road to the highway.

So Josh was back to shoveling the stalls himself. With so

many people looking for work, it should have been easy to hire someone, and he could afford to pay for the help.

In high school, he'd been dirt poor, working two jobs to help his single mother feed and clothe them. His life had changed course when his mother had told him about his half brother, a son his no-good father had sired by a previous wife before Josh was born.

Lincoln Cain, a man who'd spent two years in prison for attempted robbery, had become a mega-successful entrepreneur. Linc had turned his life around and was now co-owner of Texas American Enterprises, a billion-dollar corporation.

His brother's success had motivated Josh to rethink his own potential. It made him believe he could make a better life for himself.

Over that summer, he'd set some goals, met them, set new goals and achieved those, too. The summer after graduation, his mom, a smoker, had died of lung cancer, which had sent him into a tailspin for a while, but at least she was finally free of the drunken wife-beater who had been Josh and Linc's dad.

Josh had put himself through community college, then enlisted in the marines. He'd gone on to become a special operations sniper, but the smartest thing he'd done was invest in his brother's company.

Every extra dime he earned, every penny he could get his hands on, went into Tex/Am stock. Being in Afghanistan made saving easy. The stock he bought went up, split, went up, split, and went up again.

Josh wasn't the multimillionaire his brother was, but he wasn't poor, either. Buying the ranch had set him back a little, but the mortgage was the only money he owed. He still had plenty in the bank, enough to live the way he wanted and make the ranch a success.

The trick was finding decent help. He had a couple of good wranglers, but there were other jobs he needed them to do. He'd keep looking. He had a couple of ideas that might pan out. The hands lived in town. He had moved the double-wide he'd been living in onto the Iron River Ranch, but it was empty now that he'd moved into the remodeled house.

He'd decided to put an ad in the newspaper offering the use of the trailer along with the job. Might get someone more reliable.

In the meantime, he had plenty of work to do.

Josh grabbed a shovel and a wheelbarrow and headed for the horse barn.

Tory drove the old blue Chevy Malibu along the two-lane road. Up ahead, a sign hung above a narrow dirt track running off to the west, IRON RIVER RANCH.

"Are we there yet, Mama?" Ivy had asked at least a dozen times since they'd left the Walmart parking lot in Iron Springs. The ten-mile drive didn't take long, but to a four-year-old who'd been in the car for days, they couldn't reach their destination soon enough.

"We're very close, sweetheart. This is the turn, right here." Tory checked the gas gauge as the wheels left the pavement and started rumbling over the bumpy dirt road. Less than an eighth of a tank. She hoped the ranch wasn't much farther.

More than that, she prayed the job hadn't already been filled.

She sighed as the aging Malibu rolled along. She was basically in bumfrick Egypt, ten miles north of Nowhere Springs, almost out of gas, with twenty-three dollars and thirty-three cents in her wallet.

Last night, without enough money for a hotel room and afraid to use her credit cards for fear Damon would some-how track her, they'd slept in the car in the Walmart parking lot. As soon as the McDonald's was open, she had pulled through the drive-thru and bought a cheap breakfast, then started driving out to the ranch to somehow convince the owner to hire a woman with a daughter and no actual ranching experience.

She thought of the ad in the paper she had spotted last night on the counter in the Iron Springs Café. If she somehow managed to get the job, it would be perfect. Besides a steady paycheck and the ranch being way off the grid, the position included the use of a double-wide trailer.

After being on the road for the past three weeks, living out of hotel rooms and suitcases, the trailer sounded like a palace.

Ivy pointed toward the cluster of buildings up ahead: a couple of barns, several fenced training arenas, and a two-story home with dormer windows and a covered porch running the length out in front. A double-wide sat fifty yards away.

Vast stretches of open green pastureland surrounded the complex, where horses and cattle grazed, and there were ponds and woodlands in the distance, a few dense clusters of trees.

The Chevy bumped over the last patch of road, pulled up in front of the house, and Tory quickly turned off the engine. No use wasting what little gas she had left.

"Mama, there's a man over there by the barn."

Her gaze swung in that direction. There was, indeed, a man. The noisy buzz of a saw covered the sound of their arrival, giving her time to assess him.

Shirtless, he was working with his back to them, broad, tanned, and muscled above a narrow waist that disappeared into a pair of faded jeans. The jeans hugged a round behind and long, powerful legs.

He was tall, she saw when he straightened away from his work and walked into the barn, with medium brown hair cut short. She got her first look at his face when he walked back out: handsome, with masculine features, at least three days' growth of whiskers along a solid jaw. The front of him was just as impressive as the back, a broad chest with solid pecs, muscular biceps, and six-pack abs.

Unease filtered through her. This was a strong, powerful male. She knew firsthand what a man like that could do to a woman.

Tory shoved the notion away. Not all men were like Damon. Before she'd met him, she had been married to a good and decent man, the father of her child. Jamie Bradford, her high school sweetheart, was one of the gentlest people she'd ever known. Her father had been a good man, before he'd fallen in love with his secretary and divorced her mother, leaving the two of them alone.

Tory took a courage-building breath. "Stay here, sweetheart." Cracking open the car door, she slid out from behind the wheel. "Don't worry, sweetie. Everything's going to be okay."

She hoped.

Ivy sank down in her booster seat, trying to make herself invisible. Tory had survived the fights, arguments, and finally the brutal beating Damon had given her that had put her in the hospital. Though he had never hurt Ivy, the little girl had seen the results of his mistreatment, leaving her with an unnatural fear of men.

Tory glanced at the big, thick-chested male striding toward her, shrugging into a blue denim shirt. Ivy would be terrified of him. If there was any other way, she would climb back in the car and just drive off.

There wasn't. Tory started walking, meeting the man halfway. She glanced around but didn't see a soul besides the big man in front of her. Her uneasiness returned.

"May I help you?" he asked, and she thought that at least he was polite.

"My name is Tory Ford. I'm looking for Joshua Cain. Is

that you?" He had blue eyes and a cleft in his chin. From a purely physical standpoint, the man was flat-out hot.

"I'm Josh Cain. What can I do for you?"

"I saw your ad in the Iron Springs *Gazette*. You're looking for a stable hand. I'm here to apply for the job."

He just shook his head. "I'm afraid it's a man's job, Ms. Ford. Mucking out stalls and cleaning tack, feeding the livestock. It isn't something you'd want to do."

"Work isn't supposed to be fun, Mr. Cain. That's why they call it work. I can muck out stalls, clean tack, and feed stock as well as anyone else."

"Sorry. I'm looking for a man. I appreciate you're coming out, but—"

"There are laws, Mr. Cain. Equal rights for women. Have you never heard of that? Lawsuits against discrimination?"

His jaw hardened. His eyebrows came down in a frown. "Are you kidding me? You're going to sue me because I won't hire you to shovel horseshit out of the barn?"

She could feel the heat creeping into her cheeks. With her fair skin, there was no way to hide her embarrassment.

She looked him straight in the face. "I need this job, Mr. Cain. I need the house that comes with it." She forced herself to smile. "Why don't we compromise? You give me three days to prove I'm up to the job. If I'm not, I won't give you any more trouble. Three days. If you don't think I can handle the work, I'll leave. I won't argue, I'll just go."

A muscle jerked in his cheek. He didn't like being pressured. He looked at her hard, and then those condemning blue eyes traveled over her shoulder to something behind her.

"Who is *that*?"

She didn't have to turn to know Ivy had climbed out of the car. Like Tory, she was small for her age, but her hair was blond instead of red, and her eyes were blue instead of green.

"That's my daughter. She's only four." Desperate now, she

could feel her heart throbbing softly inside her ribs. "We need a place, Mr. Cain. I'll work hard. I'll do whatever you need done. Just give me a chance."

He swore the F-word under his breath, not loud enough for Ivy to hear. Damon wouldn't have cared. She clung to the hope that fostered.

"What do you plan to do with your daughter while you're working? You can't leave her in the house alone."

Tory glanced around wildly. She had known this would be a problem. Before, she'd had money enough to hire a sitter or there was day care for employees' kids.

She looked at the fenced yard off to the side in front of the trailer. The grass was sparse and in need of a trim. Maybe he'd had a dog or something, but it was clean and empty now. The weather was still good and there was a little gazebo with a table and benches in the middle. She'd be able to keep an eye on Ivy while she was working.

"She could play in the yard. She likes to color and she already reads kids' books. She wouldn't be any trouble. If this works out, I'll have money to pay for a sitter."

Cain looked at Ivy, paced away then back. "Dammit."

"It's just three days. If I do a good job, you won't have to search for someone else."

He ran a hand over his short brown hair. "Did you sleep in your car last night?"

She refused to answer. She didn't want charity from Cain or anyone else.

"Fine," he said. "You've got three days. But I'm not cutting you any slack. You do a man's job for a man's pay. If you can't hack it, you're out of here."

And from the look on his face, he was clearly hoping she would fail. Hell, maybe she would.

She managed a fake smile. "Okay, it's a deal." She stuck out her hand to seal the bargain, for a moment didn't think he was going to shake. Then he sighed and took hold of her hand, not too hard, just firm enough to let her know he was in charge.

"You start tomorrow morning. Six A.M. sharp. There's enough food in the trailer to last a few days. I'll bring you a quart of milk. After that, board's on you. If you're still here, you'll need to make a trip into town for groceries."

Relief filtered through her, so strong it made her head swim. She had a place to stay where no one would look for her. She had a job, which meant food and money for necessities. If he kept her on, she'd find a sitter to watch Ivy. She'd have time to figure things out, make a new plan.

She took a step back, set an arm around her little girl's shoulders, and drew her forward. "This is my daughter, Ivy. Ivy, this is Mr. Cain."

"Hello, Ivy," he said. He had an unusual voice, deep and resonant, but at the same time soft and oddly compelling.

Ivy shrank back.

"Say hello, honey," Tory said.

"I don't want to stay. I want to go." Clinging to Tory's waist, she burrowed into her.

"She's shy," Tory said.

"The trailer's unlocked," Cain said. "It's clean and ready to go."

"Thank you."

He turned and started striding back to the barn. She probably should have been at least a little afraid of him. Oddly, she wasn't.

Then again, she hadn't been afraid of Damon, either.

At six A.M. the next morning, Josh checked his watch. Time to go to work and no sign of the woman.

Hell, he was an idiot. Now he had a woman and her kid

living in his trailer. No way could he expect her to do a man's work. She could stay a couple of days; then she had to go.

He just hoped to hell she kept her word and left without giving him any more trouble.

Carrying his empty plate of bacon and overcooked eggs to the sink, he turned on the water and rinsed off the plate and his utensils as heavy footfalls sounded on the porch.

Not the woman, the wranglers who'd just started working for him. Noah Beal and Cole Wyman were former marines, disabled vets whose abilities were often underestimated, guys who needed the work and took pride in doing a good job. Josh felt lucky to have them.

He grabbed his battered straw hat, opened the front door, and stepped out on the porch. "Morning. You guys want a cup of coffee before you head out?"

"I'm good," Cole said.

"Me, too," said Noah.

Both men were in their late twenties, two or three years younger than Josh's thirty-one. Cole, who had lost both legs just below the knee to an IED, had dark blond hair and a face women loved. He wore metal lower limb prostheses, and he could do damn near anything any other man could do.

Noah had brown hair and more rugged features. He'd lost an arm in Kabul, but it didn't slow him down. Determined to live their lives to the fullest, both men managed to get in a workout at the gym most days and had the hard bodies to prove it.

Noah was married to a smart and pretty young woman who suited him perfectly. Cole, whose girl had broken up with him when she discovered he had lost his legs, was resentful and unsure of himself when it came to women, still finding his way with the opposite sex.

They all headed off to the vehicle shed where he kept a

pair of four-wheel ATVs, a UTV side-by-side, and his white Ford F-150.

"How much longer till you finish the east pasture, you think?" he asked.

"We've got at least four more days," Cole said.

"You're actually ahead of schedule," Josh told them. "When you're finished, you can start on the pasture to the north. Whole ranch needs new fencing. Ought to keep you busy for a while."

The men climbed onto the ATVs, one of which towed a trailer loaded with fencing materials, and they took off down the two-track lane into the fields.

Josh glanced around. Still no sign of the woman. He'd thought she would at least show up on time the first day. But then he'd never been a good judge of women.

Heading into the barn, he caught movement out of the corner of his eye as he stepped into the shadowy interior. The smell of hay and horses drifted on the slight morning breeze, and dust motes hung in the air.

He strode forward, heard the scrape of a shovel against hard-packed earth, paused in front of one of the empty stalls, stopped dead in his tracks at the sight of his new hire shoveling horse manure into a wheelbarrow.

He blinked, felt like rubbing his eyes to make sure he was really seeing what he was seeing. She was a pretty little thing—he'd noticed that yesterday. About five-four, small-boned but curvy, probably in her late twenties. She hadn't heard him approach, which gave him a moment to watch her.

As she bent over to shovel another load, formfitting stretch jeans with jewels on the pockets outlined a fine little ass he did his best to ignore. When she straightened, her T-shirt stretched over a pair of full breasts that sent a slice of heat straight into his groin. She must have heard his softly muttered curse because she stopped working and turned.

"Good morning," she said brightly. "I thought I'd get an early start. I hope I'm doing it right. I figured any way that worked was probably okay."

He hooked a thumb in the pocket of his jeans. "Shoveling is shoveling. Looks like you're doing just fine."

She had big green eyes in a heart-shaped face, freckles across the bridge of a small, very nice nose. Shiny copper curls fell softly around her face almost to her shoulders. He felt an unwelcome urge to run his fingers through them, see if they were as silky as they looked.

"Where's your daughter?" he asked.

"She's coloring in the yard. I just have to walk to the barn door to see her."

He hadn't thought to look. Was it okay to leave a kid outside all day? Hell, he had no idea. He'd pretty much raised himself, so he figured she'd probably be fine as long as the weather was good. And he'd keep an eye on her himself. It was only three days.

"When you finish, come find me. I'll give you something else to do."

Since he didn't want her there and wasn't thrilled that she was actually doing the work, he put her out of his mind as best he could. That he found her attractive only made him more certain she should leave.

An hour later, he was working a little bay filly on a lunge line in the training ring when he saw her walking toward him, a smile on her face. He didn't like the little kick he felt, not one bit.

"I'm done with the stalls," she said. "I dumped the wheelbarrow into the pile out in back. I hope that was okay." She wiped her hands on the front of her stretch jeans, not exactly work clothes, but she was obviously new to this. Most likely she couldn't afford to buy the kind of clothes that would be more appropriate.

If she kept working, at least she'd collect some pay before she left.

"Follow me." He led her back into the barn, over to the tack room. Half a dozen saddles sat on sawhorses and twice that many bridles hung on the walls.

"There's a stack of rags next to the door, saddle soap and brushes in the cupboard, whatever else you need. None of this stuff's been cleaned since I bought the ranch, probably not for years."

"When did you buy it?"

"End of February."

She walked over and opened the cupboard. He wished he hadn't noticed the blisters on her hands. Dammit, he'd known she wasn't cut out for hard labor the minute he'd laid eyes on her. The woman had City Girl stamped all over her.

Still, a deal was a deal. She could stay there three days.

He wondered what her story was. Clearly, she'd run into trouble. He hoped that trouble didn't follow her here. He'd had enough of it already.

"Is it okay if I take this stuff outside where I can see Ivy?"

"Fine with me. Let me know when you're done." He left her there and went back to the two-year-old filly he was training. He'd get a good price for the horse when he was finished, a good price for all of them with any luck.

He thought of Satan. The horse had been on the ranch when he'd bought the place. He was a gorgeous animal, pure black with a white star on his forehead, a sixteen-hand papered quarter horse with great confirmation. He'd be the perfect stud for the broodmares he'd bought.

Too bad the stallion was as wild as a peach orchard boar, completely unmanageable and more than a little dangerous. He'd give it a little more time, but if Satan didn't start making some progress soon, he would have to put the animal down.

No way could he sell him. Sooner or later a horse that crazy wound up badly hurting or killing someone.

He wondered what had turned the stallion into such a demon, or if the animal had been born that way. Whatever the case, he didn't have time to worry about it now. Josh untied the rope, tugged the filly into the middle of the arena, and went back to work.

Chapter Four

Tory had never been more exhausted in her life. As she stood at the kitchen sink, every bone in her body ached. She had blisters on her hands, and the back of her neck was sunburned from raking up straw outside the barn.

Tomorrow she'd wear a hat and sunscreen, and the gloves Josh had loaned her. In what she called her past life in Phoenix, her job as an advertising executive had put her in charge of a whole team of marketers, men and women who came up with commercials, jingles, and slogans that could make or break a company.

She'd been a dedicated career woman who had worked long hours, had jogged and done yoga to stay in shape, or exercised at the gym. She'd worked hard, but it was nothing like the backbreaking labor she had done today.

The last job Josh had given her had been a little easier—putting the tool shed into some kind of order. He'd let Ivy sit by the door while she worked. Since she was detail-oriented by nature, organizing people and projects was one of the things she did best. She thought he'd been pleased with the job she had done.

And her hands hadn't suffered any more damage.

An image of her new employer popped into her head.

He'd looked good the first time she had seen him, with his amazing body, dark blue eyes, and square-jawed, handsome face. Slap a worn-out cowboy hat on his head to go with those snug jeans and big boots, and he could stop hearts in half the women in Texas.

Fortunately for both of them, he didn't seem attracted to her. This was good, she told herself. The last thing she needed was another man. Any man, and especially not one who would draw every feminine eye within fifty miles.

Something tugged on the hem of her T-shirt. Tory looked down to see Ivy staring up at her. "When are we eating, Mama?"

Inwardly she groaned. The thought of standing on her feet another hour while she fixed supper was enough to make her weep. "I have to look in the pantry, sweetie, see what I can find." And pray there was actually something she could make edible. This morning, she had made do with cereal, then fixed sandwiches for lunch from a can of Spam she had found.

She trudged across a kitchen painted butter yellow with walnut cabinets and Formica countertops. Like the rest of the trailer, it was neat and clean, a simply furnished two-bedroom, two-bath unit. A brown plush sofa sat in front of an older TV against the wall in the living room, and there was a queen-size bed in the master bedroom covered with a handmade blue-and-peach-colored quilt.

She winced as she opened the door to the pantry, breaking one of the blisters on her hands. She had Band-Aids in the medicine kit she carried with her. She just needed the energy to get them.

She glanced into the pantry. A big can of Hormel chili sat beside a jar of Newman's Own spaghetti sauce and a couple of packages of pasta. Assorted canned vegetables and fruits, and the box of Honey Nut Cheerios she had discovered that morning rounded out the inventory.

Josh had been right. There was enough in the house to last at least three days.

Ivy walked up beside her. "SpaghettiOs!" Spotting one of her favorite meals, she grabbed the can off the shelf and started jumping up and down. "I want SpaghettiOs!"

There is a God, Tory thought as she stretched her back and tried to work a kink out of her neck, and He had her sincere thanks. Along with the can of biscuits she had seen in the fridge, supper was a done deal.

She wondered why the food was still in the trailer, had a hunch Josh had lived there until recently. Some of his shirts still hung in the back bedroom closet. She could tell from the outside that he'd done extensive work on the barn. The house looked like something built in the forties, so it had probably needed plenty of work, as well.

She figured he was moving his things into the main house a little at a time. She'd be happy to help him if he'd just let her stay.

She turned on the oven and opened the can of biscuits while Ivy set the table. A knock at the door had her head coming up. A little shiver of apprehension chased down her spine.

Surely Damon couldn't have found her again. Perspiration dampened the palms of her sore hands. She carefully wiped them on the front of her jeans.

"Stay here."

Making her way to the door, she checked the peephole, then breathed a sigh of relief to see Josh standing on the porch. An instant later, her relief disappeared. What was he doing there? What did he want? She thought of the fat little bald owner of City Cleaners in Albuquerque who had expected fringe benefits, and prayed Joshua Cain didn't expect more from her than the grueling hours she had already put in today.

She took a deep breath and opened the door. "Hi. Did you . . . umm . . . need something?"

He must have read the worry in her face for he took a step back, giving her plenty of room. "I don't need anything, but I thought you might." He held up a jar with something thick, dark, and gooey inside. "For your blisters. My mother used to make it for me. I did ranch work in the summers when I was a kid."

The feeling of relief returned. Tory took the jar from his big, calloused hand. "Thank you."

"I should have brought some Band-Aids. I wasn't thinking. If you need some—"

"I have some. Thank you." She wondered if she should ask him to come inside, but she didn't really know him, and when she looked up, he had already taken a few more steps back from the door.

"I'll see you in the morning."

She nodded. "Good night."

She tried not to watch him walk away, but with that tight behind, a clean white T-shirt stretched over the muscles in his back and biceps, she couldn't resist. Thank God Damon hadn't completely destroyed her feminine instincts.

"I don't like that man, Mama. He looks mean."

Ivy's words snapped Tory back to sanity. Closing the door, she walked over to her daughter. "He's my boss, sweetheart. He was just being nice." She held up the jar of salve. "His mother used to make this for his blisters. Wasn't it nice of him to bring it over?"

Ivy ignored her. "I'm hungry. When are we having our SpaghettiOs?"

"I'm going to fix them right now."

Supper didn't take long and she had Ivy in bed soon after they had finished their meager meal. Tory took a couple of Advil, curled up on the sofa, opened a book, and read for a while. But it didn't take long before fatigue settled in and her eyelids began to droop.

Closing the book, she headed for bed, grateful to be sleeping on a mattress instead of the seat of the car.

Morning came way too early. Rolling out of bed with a groan, Tory showered and dressed, then got Ivy up and ready for the day. She was determined to keep this job. Iron Springs, the nearest town, wasn't a place Damon would ever look for her.

She wondered what had happened to him after she'd left him tied up that night. He'd always been resourceful. She was sure he'd found some way to escape before too long.

She had driven for hours that night, finally pulling into a cheap motel. After that, they had moved from one town to another, always searching for someplace safe, never satisfied they had found it.

Now she was back in Texas, figuring Damon wouldn't think she'd return to a place he had found her before, and this time she was way off the grid. She paid everything with cash, not credit cards. The cell phones she used were disposable. The only person she ever called was her best friend, Lisa Shane, whom she phoned about once a week.

At first she had missed the techno world of texting, email, Facebook, and Twitter, but little by little, she had accepted the loss as a necessity. Going one step further, when she finished talking to Lisa, she tossed the cheap plastic phone so even if Damon somehow got hold of Lisa's cell, he wouldn't be able to find her.

It was costly, but Lisa was her last connection to the life she had left behind. They were best friends and Tory was desperately in need of a friend. Her greatest hope was that sooner or later Damon would get tired of looking for her.

He'd give up and go back to his life in Phoenix. Sooner or later she and Ivy would be safe.

Which reminded her how much she needed to keep this job.

The morning was still early, but she needed to get going. She glanced up at a knock on the door. Tory walked over and looked through the peephole, saw Josh on the porch. She pulled open the door.

"You got a minute?" he asked.

She glanced over to where Ivy sat at the kitchen table. "I'll be right back, sweetheart." Walking out on the porch, she closed the door. "What is it?"

"I have a neighbor friend, an older lady named Clara Thompson. She loves kids. I was thinking maybe she could stay with Ivy while you were working . . . you know, just for the next couple of days."

"I don't know her. I can't leave Ivy with someone I don't know."

"I figured you'd say that." He stepped back. "Mrs. T., come say hello to Tory."

A silver-haired woman walked toward her, smiling as she climbed the steps with plenty of vigor for a lady Tory guessed to be in her late sixties.

"I'm Clara Thompson. Josh phoned last night and asked me to stop by this morning. He said you had a sweet little girl. He thought you might need a sitter for a couple of days."

Clara Thompson had kindly blue eyes and a warm, sincere smile. She looked like the grandmother Ivy had never had. She'd been a baby when Tory's mom had died in the same car accident that had killed her husband. Unfortunately for Ivy, Jamie's mother had no interest in kids.

"I'm sorry," she said. "I'd love to have you sit with Ivy, but the truth is, until I get paid, I can't afford—"

"Oh, no, dear, I don't expect you to pay me. I love children and now that my three are grown and moved away, that big house gets mighty lonely."

A sitter would be the answer to her prayers, and Mrs. Thompson seemed really nice. With the exception of Damon, Tory had always had good instincts about people, and Josh seemed to trust the lady.

She glanced up at the sky. Yesterday had been perfect weather, but clouds were drifting in, hinting at rain.

Just then Ivy opened the door. "Aren't you going to work, Mama?"

"Ivy, honey, this is Mrs. Thompson. She's a neighbor."

Mrs. Thompson smiled down at the little girl. "Hello, Ivy. It's nice to meet you. I have two great-granddaughters about your age, but they live in Houston so I don't get to see them very often."

"You're a grandma?"

"That's right."

"Mrs. Thompson is going to sit with you, sweetie. I saw some cookie mix in the pantry. Maybe you two could make a batch of chocolate chips. They're your favorite." She flicked a glance at the older woman.

Mrs. Thompson smiled at Ivy. "That sounds like fun. You like to bake, Ivy?"

"I do!" Ivy grinned and jumped up and down. "We get to bake cookies!"

Mrs. Thompson turned back to Tory. "I brought some toys and games, things my great-granddaughters like to play with when they visit. We'll have all sorts of fun things to do."

Tory was torn. She really needed the woman's help, but she didn't want to take advantage. "Are you sure, Mrs. Thompson?"

"Of course I'm sure. I'm just glad Josh called me."

Tory looked at Josh. It had been so long since anyone had helped her. She blinked back the unexpected sting of tears and hoped he wouldn't notice. "Thank you."

Josh gave a faint nod, tugged his hat down on his forehead, turned, and strode off down the steps.

Tory led the woman into the house, showed her around, and got her and Ivy settled. "There are books and crayons on the table and Ivy's always been good at entertaining herself."

"We'll have fun," Mrs. Thompson said. "Don't you worry."

Kissing the top of her daughter's head, Tory left the house and headed for the barn, her mind turning to the job she'd been hired to do.

The way the stable was laid out, each stall had a short fenced-in run that allowed the horses to move inside and out. Their stalls had to be cleaned every day, but it wasn't too big a problem since they were outside a lot of the time.

She was halfway there when she spotted Josh, but he was no longer alone. It took a moment to realize the two men he was talking to were both disabled, one a double amputee fitted with metal prostheses, the other a man with only one arm.

Both men were good-looking, not as tall as Josh, but lean and wide-shouldered, with biceps bulging from the sleeves of their T-shirts. She wondered if they might be soldiers wounded in the war, wondered if maybe Josh was former military, too.

She had noticed a scar on his right side that first day when he'd had his shirt off. He certainly looked tough enough to have been a soldier, though his several days' growth of beard was gone today.

Tory kept walking, hoping to avoid him. The less she talked to him, the less chance he'd find an excuse to fire her.

He strode into the barn a few minutes later, while she was shoveling out her first stall. She could sense his presence even before she saw him, a shift in the air like an electrical pulse. It made her heart speed up a little.

"You don't need to do that today," he said as he approached. "I'll find something else for you to do."

She set the shovel down and leaned on the handle. "If I don't do it, who will? You?"

He shrugged those wide shoulders. "It's no big deal. I was

shoveling manure before you got here. I can do it again. Like I said, I'll find you something else to do."

No way, Tory thought. Stable hand was the job she had applied for. It was the job he needed done. "I'm fine right here. Three days. That was our deal. I'll find you when I'm finished. Okay?"

He looked like he wanted to argue. Instead he clenched his jaw and shook his head. "You're a stubborn little thing, aren't you?"

"I'll do a good job for you, just like I promised."

Those cool blue eyes ran over her, making the inside of her stomach lift.

"Fine. Suit yourself." Turning, he walked out of the barn, and Tory breathed a sigh of relief. If she proved herself, maybe he would let her stay. She already found herself liking the ranch, the wide-open spaces and fresh air, horses and cattle roaming the pastures. Maybe she could pay Mrs. Thompson enough to get her to sit on the workdays.

She walked over and picked up the shovel. Her hands were sore, but the salve Josh had brought over had helped, and gloves made the job a lot easier. Of course, they didn't keep her back from hurting.

She'd get used to it, she told herself. She was tough and she was determined. She had Damon Bridger to thank for that.

Chapter Five

"Sir, you can't go in there. Mr. Phillips is on the phone."

"Yeah, well, if he wants his paycheck, he'll get off the fucking phone." Damon clamped down on his temper and softened his tone, along with his expression. He flashed the receptionist one of his most disarming smiles. "Sorry, I'm a little frustrated. You're just doing your job. I didn't mean to take it out on you."

She smiled back a little shyly. "It's okay." She stood up. "I'll just tell him you're here."

He kept his smile in place, softened it even more, kept his eyes on her face, making her blush. He had skills when it came to women. He was good-looking and he knew how to be charming. Add to that, he had money and plenty of it. Women fell all over him. As long as he stayed in control, he knew exactly how to handle them.

He checked her name on the sign on her desk. "I appreciate that, Amy. But I'll just tell him myself." Before she could stop him, he'd pulled open the frosted half-glass door and walked into private investigator Marvin Phillips's office.

Phillips swung his feet down from the top of the desk. He was about the same height as Damon, a little over six feet, but older, in his midforties. He was balding, while Damon had a thick head of wavy black hair. He preferred hiring people who were physically inferior. It gave him a little edge.

"Get off the phone," Damon demanded.

The detective's features tightened. "I'll have to call you back." Phillips hung up, but didn't rise from behind his desk. "I thought you were coming in this afternoon."

"I'm tired of waiting. I want results. Where is she?"

"I don't know where she is. Not yet. I told you that when you called. I've found her for you twice already. I can do it again—if you're sure that's what you want."

"What's that supposed to mean?"

"It means chasing this woman all over the country is not a good idea. Surely by now, you realize she isn't coming back to you."

"What the hell do you know? She'll come back. It's just a matter of time." He didn't tell the detective he didn't plan to give her any choice. Victoria belonged to him. He'd bring her back whether she wanted to go with him or not.

"She was in Carlsbad a little over three weeks ago," Damon said. "You must have found something since then." He didn't mention what had happened to him in New Mexico. Every time he thought about how Tory had tricked him, humiliated him, made a fool of him, he wanted to wrap his hands around her pretty neck and squeeze.

It had taken him hours to drag himself into the kitchen, get his bound hands on a butcher knife, and cut himself free. When he found her, she'd pay for that, along with everything else she had done.

"Did you talk to Lisa Shane?" he asked. "They were best friends. She must know where Tory is."

"I talked to her. She hasn't heard from Victoria since she left Phoenix. I'm working a couple of other angles. Sooner or later she'll turn up again."

"I'm paying you a small fortune. The longer it takes, the

more money you make. That better not be what's going on here."

Phillips rose from his chair. "I said I'd come up with something and I will. Sooner or later everyone makes mistakes. She'll turn up somewhere and I'll find her."

"I'm tired of waiting." Damon strode to the door and pulled it open. "You've got a week. Then I'm done with you." Turning, he stormed out of the office.

A week. Then he'd do it his way.

The thought sent a rush of adrenaline through him. He wouldn't waste time. He'd do what had to be done to get the answers he needed.

He almost hoped the detective failed.

Josh worked the rest of the afternoon. One of the mares was ready to foal. He had brought her in from the pasture and put her in the barn, then gone back to work on the cow barn, which, as the oldest structure on the ranch, was practically falling down.

He was gutting the interior, knocking out the old rotted boards that made up the stalls. As he slammed the hammer against the wood, splintering it and sending pieces flying, he thought of his encounter with the redhead working in the other barn.

She was a handful, that was for sure. Stubborn to a fault, and prickly even when he was trying to help her. Since she was only going to be there one more day, he'd wanted to make things a little easier, give her a less difficult job, something that wouldn't make her hands bleed and her back ache.

He shook his head. *Bullheaded woman.* If she weren't such a pain in his ass, he might admire her. At least her word was good. She'd said she'd give him three days' work as a stable hand and she was determined to do it.

The hell of it was, it wasn't going to matter. The last thing he needed was a sexy little redhead distracting him from the goals he'd set for himself. And Tory Ford was a definite distraction. Soft curves in all the right places, high full breasts, lips the color of strawberries.

Every time he thought of her, he remembered the way she looked in those blue denim stretch jeans, bending over to shovel out the stall. The rhinestones on her back pockets flashed like beacons, pointing to her perfect little ass.

He'd wanted to move up behind her, drag those fancy jeans down over her hips, wrap his hands around that narrow waist, and—

Josh clamped down on the thought. Tory was a nice young woman, the mother of a sweet little girl. She deserved to be treated with respect.

But the fact was, he was a man, and though he hadn't been celibate since his return to Texas, he'd been too busy to make up for all the months he'd been deployed in the Middle East. He needed her gone before he took advantage, and he intended to make that happen tomorrow.

He sighed as he picked up the hammer. At least with Mrs. Thompson here, he didn't have to worry about the little girl and neither did Tory. In the meantime, he had plenty to do.

Working off a little of his frustration, Josh slammed the hammer against the rotted wood.

The hours slid past. When Tory checked on Ivy, she found Mrs. Thompson teaching her to play Candy Land. They both seemed to be having fun.

Earlier Josh had suggested Tory bring Ivy out to the barn after lunch to visit the litter of kittens one of the feral cats had recently birthed. Ivy was excited to see them. The little girl ran all the way there.

"Where are they, Mama?"

"In that last stall, sweetheart. They're curled up in the straw."

Ivy whirled around, blond ponytail flying, and raced ahead, then slowed to walk quietly into the stall. "Oh, Mama, aren't they cute?"

Tory smiled. "They're having their lunch, same as you just did."

A few feet away, Ivy sank down in the straw to watch them nurse. The mother was gray with white fur on her chest. There were two gray kittens, two orange. Tory had noticed a big orange tom prowling around the barn.

"There's four of them, Mama."

"They're too little to handle yet," a deep voice said. "But they grow up fast." Josh stood outside the stall, his arms folded on the top board as he looked down at them.

The grin slid off Ivy's face. She reached for Tory's hand. "I wanna go back in," she said, sinking into herself the way she had begun to do whenever there was a man around. Especially a big man like Josh.

He looked from the little girl to Tory, must have read the concern on her face. "It's all right," he said softly. "I was just getting ready to saddle Sunshine and give her a ride. Enjoy the kittens."

He turned and walked off and Tory could hear him talking in that soft way of his to the palomino mare in the second stall. Leading the horse out of the stall, he began to groom her, his brushstrokes swishing through the air. It didn't take long before the mare was saddled and ready.

Josh slid a boot into the stirrup and swung aboard, settling himself with impressive ease. As he reined the horse out of the barn, the man looked like every woman's cowboy fantasy. Every woman but her, she told herself.

Tory glanced over at Ivy, who seemed to be fascinated by

the kittens. "We need go back to the house, sweetheart. I have to get to work again."

The day passed swiftly with so much to do. That night, Tory fell into another exhausted slumber, but she wasn't as sore as she had been the night before.

She awoke anxious and unsettled the morning of the third day. She knew she'd been doing a decent job, but it might not be enough. A man doing the same work wouldn't have a child to worry about. A man could have helped Josh stack the heavy straw bales that had arrived from town, or helped him dig postholes where he was putting in new fencing around one of the training rings.

The good news was Clara Thompson showed up again that morning just as she'd promised.

"You're a lifesaver, Mrs. Thompson. I'll never be able to repay your kindness."

"Everyone needs a little help once in a while, dear."

Not wanting to be late, Tory kissed Ivy good-bye and headed out to the barn. She had almost reached the wide double doors when a dark red Dodge pickup rolled to a stop in front, throwing up a cloud of dust. The two men she had noticed yesterday climbed out of the truck and Josh strode toward them.

When the men spotted her, they stopped and turned, forcing Josh to introduce them, though clearly, he didn't want to.

"Guys, this is Tory Ford. She's been working here the last couple of days. Tory, meet Cole Wyman and Noah Beal."

Tory silently prayed she would still be working there tomorrow and the day after that. "Hello," she said.

"I'm Noah." The dark-haired man extended his right hand, the only one he had, which she shook. "That's Cole," he said. "He's not nearly as friendly, but he's harmless."

"Thanks," Cole said darkly. He tipped his blue-and-white

Dallas Cowboys' baseball cap in greeting, then settled it back over his gleaming blond hair. "Nice meeting you, Tory."

"It's nice to meet you both. If you'll excuse me, I need to get to work." As she walked away, she could hear Josh handing out orders and prayed one of the men wouldn't wind up getting her job.

Instead the hours slipped past. She broke for lunch at noon, went inside to find Mrs. Thompson had used the rest of the Spam to make sandwiches, ate, and headed back to work.

When she finished with the morning chores, she went in search of Josh, but he was nowhere to be found. Wandering out to one of the pastures where she had seen him working, she walked along the fence in search of him, stopping at the sight of the most beautiful jet-black stallion she had ever seen.

He was breathtaking, tall and powerfully built, with a long black mane and tail and a white spot in the middle of his forehead. He snorted when he saw her, stopped stock-still to watch her. He snorted again and lifted his magnificent head.

"Hello, pretty boy. Aren't you just a beautiful thing? I wonder what your name is." She loved horses, though she had only ridden a couple of times, short, paid-for trail rides among the saguaro cactus north of Scottsdale on a very tame horse. She hadn't seen the stallion in the barn, but then, keeping such a free-spirited creature confined would have definitely been a crime.

"I wonder if you would let me pet you." He seemed to be drawn to the sound of her voice. He nickered and started walking toward the fence, stopped a few feet away, looking at her with big, watchful brown eyes. She ducked through the fence and walked a little closer. Blowing out a breath, he lowered his head and plodded up to her, stopped right in front of her.

"What a good horse. I wish I knew your name." Stroking her hand over his powerful neck, she ran her fingers through his coarse black mane. The animal closed its eyes and rested his head on her shoulder.

"Oh, you are so sweet. I bet you'd like your ears rubbed." She patted his neck and straightened his topknot, gently rubbed his ears. He made a sound that was almost a sigh.

"Tory . . ." Josh's deep voice drifted softly toward her. "I need you to listen to me. I need you to do exactly what I tell you."

The horse's head shot up and he snorted.

"I want you to slowly back up, one step at a time, until you're out of the pasture. Okay?"

There was something in his voice that put her on alert. She looked back at the stallion, whose ears now lay flat against his head. He stomped his front hoof and bared his teeth.

Tory took a step backward, first one and then another. She wasn't far from the fence, and yet the fear she saw in Josh's face made it seem a mile away. The stallion didn't follow. His eyes were fixed on Josh, who ducked between the strands of fencing and slowly walked toward her.

Josh moved in front of her, putting himself between her and the stallion, when the animal charged. "Run!" he commanded and she did, racing the last few feet to the fence, ducking between the strands of wire to safety on the opposite side.

Josh was right behind her, the stallion on his heels, its head down, teeth bared, the whites of its eyes showing. Josh turned, jerked off his hat, and waved it in the stallion's face. The animal whirled away as Josh ducked to safety on the other side of the fence right beside her.

The stallion whirled back and raced toward them, slamming into the fence, neighing wildly, baring his teeth, screaming as if he were in pain.

"You okay?" Josh asked.

Tory's gaze shot back to the stallion, her heart pounding like a wild thing. "I guess he doesn't like you."

Josh slapped his hat against his thigh and jammed it back on his head. "What the hell were you doing in there?"

Her chin went up. "I was looking for you. If you didn't want me going into the pasture, you should have told me."

He sighed and glanced away, tugged the brim of his hat a little lower. "You're right. I should have said something. Cole and Noah know better than to go into Satan's pasture. I should have warned you, too."

"Satan? That's his name?"

"Satan's Star, and believe me it fits him. He's a real man-eater. I should have warned you. I could have gotten you seriously injured, even killed. Ranch life isn't easy—one of the reasons the job you're doing isn't for you."

Her heart sank. "Wait a minute. I've been doing good work, haven't I? I've done everything you've asked me to."

"I'm not complaining about the work you've done. It's just not a good idea. I need someone with some muscle, someone who can help with the heavy lifting. Cole and Noah have enough to do. I need another man." Those blue eyes zeroed in on her face. "And I'd appreciate you not suing me for being honest."

Tory sighed. "I won't sue you," she said glumly. "I never really would have." Because he was right. She just wasn't big enough or strong enough to do the kind of manual labor he needed to help him run the ranch, even with two other men.

She would have to go back on the road, find another town, look for another job. The thought made her eyes sting.

Josh pushed his hat back with the tip of his finger and started to say something, but instead of finishing his sentence, he looked over her shoulder back at the beautiful black horse, pawing the ground and snorting, running back and forth along the fence.

"When you were out there with Satan . . . I've never seen him that calm. What did you do to him?"

Her gaze followed his to the magnificent stallion. "I don't know exactly. He seemed to like the sound of my voice. Or maybe he liked the way I smell. I always wear perfume. Mostly Chanel."

The corner of his mouth twitched. "You're saying my horse has expensive tastes?"

She smiled. "I don't know. He was really sweet until you walked up. I think you scared him."

"Are you kidding me? *I* scared *him*?"

"Yes. He was just reacting in order to protect himself."

Josh started to argue, then turned and looked back at the horse. The stallion was still watching their every move. "You game to try something?"

"If it doesn't require my getting trampled to death, sure."

Amusement curved his lips. She was beginning to think he actually had a sense of humor.

"I'm going to walk away," he said. "As soon as I'm back far enough, I want you to walk toward the fence. Don't get so close he can get to you, just walk toward him. Talk to him the way you were doing before. Let's see what happens."

He moved backward until the horse started to ignore him and started watching her instead. Tory began walking slowly toward the fence, talking softly, repeating the same meaningless phrases she'd said before.

"Hey, pretty boy. Star, that's what I'm going to call you. You have that gorgeous white star right in the middle of your forehead. I bet you're not nearly as mean as people say you are. I bet you're really a very nice horse."

As if in answer, the stallion lowered his head and trotted

up to the fence just a few feet away from where she stood. He nickered softly.

Tory moved closer to the fence. Too close, apparently, as she heard Josh's softly muttered curse. Fortunately, he didn't come up behind her. Star blew out a deep breath and pushed his head toward her. Tory rubbed his topknot and ears just as she had before.

"Maybe I'll come see you again, bring you an apple or something. Would you like that, big boy?"

His deep sigh tugged at her heart. He seemed so lonely. She could almost feel it. "Bye, Star." Turning, she walked away.

"I can't believe I just saw that," Josh said when she reached him. "It was stupid, but it was amazing."

"It wasn't stupid. I could tell he wasn't going to hurt me."

"Oh, so now you're an expert on horses? Somehow I didn't get that impression before."

"Okay, so I've never worked on a ranch and I don't know squat about horses. It was a feeling, you know? Like we were communicating in some way." She shrugged. "But maybe I'm wrong. Like you said, I don't have any experience with horses."

Josh glanced back at the stallion. "Look, why don't you take the rest of the day off and we'll talk about everything later?"

"I need to keep working even if it's my last day. I need the money."

"Fine, you can work out the day. Can you cook?"

"I'm a pretty fair cook. Why?"

"There's a chicken thawing in my kitchen. Why don't you let Mrs. T. go home early, take Ivy over to my place, and cook the chicken for supper."

"Except for Clara Thompson, I haven't seen a woman around. I take it you aren't married."

"Nope. Never have been. Cook me some supper and at the end of the day, we'll talk, see if we can figure something out."

Her eyes flashed to his. "Are you saying you might let me stay?"

"I said we'd talk about it, okay?"

Hope reared its beautiful head. She was cooking him supper. If she fixed him a good enough meal, maybe he would keep her on. She felt safe here in a way she hadn't in weeks. Months, really.

Tory thought of Damon and hoped she wasn't deluding herself.

Chapter Six

He must have lost his mind. Josh couldn't believe he was actually considering letting the woman and her little girl stay.

But he'd always had a weakness for people in trouble, and he knew in his bones this woman was.

Taking out some of his frustration, he slammed the hammer against another rotting board in the cow barn, sending splinters and bits of wood flying. That same weakness had sent him to Cole Wyman's front door when his friend Noah Beal had told him Cole was out of the marines, back in Texas, and nearly suicidal. That Cole needed something to do to help him get his life straightened out before it was too late. Noah believed a job on the ranch would be the perfect solution.

Both men worked there now and were doing a terrific job. Noah was happy to be outdoors and Cole's confidence was returning, his attitude getting better every day. They took pride in the work they were doing, something hard to find these days. Josh had money and because he did, he could afford to help other people, though he preferred helping those who were trying to help themselves.

As he slammed the hammer against another piece of rotten wood, he thought of Tory. Every time he caught a whiff of her perfume his groin tightened. Hell, he was as bad as the horse.

He blew out a long, slow breath. She needed a job, no doubt about it, but how many nights would he lie in bed thinking about her, lusting after her?

If she stayed, he'd have to find a way to take care of his needs somewhere else. Maybe he'd call Billie Joe Hardie, one of the waitresses over at Jubal's Roadhouse. She was always up for a good time.

One thing he couldn't do was sleep with Tory. Hell, he had no idea if she would even be interested, but the fact remained, he couldn't have a physical relationship with one of his employees. It was bad business all around. Those kinds of situations never ended well, and he had a feeling Tory Ford would agree.

So he'd talk to her, work out some ground rules. If she still wanted a job, he'd find her something to do.

He found himself looking forward to the chicken dinner she was fixing. He wasn't much of a cook himself; truth was he barely got by. Plus he was exhausted at the end of the day. Finding the energy to cook a meal was sometimes just too much trouble. It would be nice not to have to worry about it.

And there was the horse. The big black stallion would make the perfect stud for his mares if there was a way to tame him. Josh wasn't willing to put the Ford woman in jeopardy, but the connection she and the horse seemed to share was definitely worth exploring.

That alone was reason enough to keep her on, at least for a while.

Knocking the last board in the stall aside, he walked over to the lumber pile and picked up one of the boards he'd already measured and cut to the right length. When he finished hammering the new board in place, he checked his watch.

The afternoon had slipped toward evening. Noah and

Cole had already gone home. Another half hour and he'd be done for the day. Josh retrieved a second board and started pounding in nails.

Tory finished the salad she had prepared, adding a can of mandarin oranges from the pantry to the lettuce she'd found in the fridge. Walking over to the oak table in the big open kitchen, she straightened the pretty blue-checked place mat in front of one of the high-backed oak chairs, and tugged a matching blue-checked napkin through a blue glass ring. There was a nice set of white plates she planned to use.

She wondered where the dishes and linens had come from. Even the blue-flowered dish towels looked feminine. The living room, on the other hand, was masculine: brown leather sofas and chairs, a black-and-white cowhide rug in front of the fireplace, oak tables and bookshelves, a big flat-screen TV.

A photo book of horses rested on the coffee table, where Ivy sat on the floor coloring. Tory had noticed books on cattle and ranching in the bookshelves.

Maybe Josh had a girlfriend who had helped him pick things out for his new home. He'd told her he wasn't married, but that didn't mean he didn't have a woman. A man who looked like Josh could have his pick.

Tory didn't like the little tug of regret that thought stirred. She sighed. It really didn't matter if Josh was involved with someone or not. She wasn't interested in Joshua Cain, and he wasn't interested in her.

She just needed a way to make a living and a place to stay where she and Ivy would be safe. While they were there, she could formulate a plan, do some research, find a city where she could disappear and Damon Bridger would never find her.

A little voice warned she might be kidding herself. There

was a chance Damon would never give up his search, that there was nowhere she could hide where he wouldn't find her.

But surely even a person as close to crazy as Damon had turned out to be wouldn't waste his entire life trying to exact revenge.

Her mind went back to the weeks after he'd attacked her in Phoenix. Damon had been arrested, but with the fancy attorney his father hired, he was out of jail in hours. She had stupidly believed beating someone nearly to death would result in at least several months in jail. Instead, he'd been sentenced to rage management, counseling, and community service.

She had never been safe from him again.

She thought of their last encounter and a faint shiver slid down her spine. How long had he stayed tied up? Had someone called the police? If so, was she wanted for a crime of some sort? Surely protecting yourself wasn't illegal.

She sniffed as an odd smell reached her, frowned when she caught a whiff of smoke. With a shriek, she rushed toward the oven. As she opened the door, thick black smoke poured into the kitchen.

"Ohmygod, ohmygod!"

"The house is on fire, Mama!" Ivy raced in from the living room.

"It's okay. Everything's okay. It's just the chicken." *Just the chicken? Ohmygod*! Grabbing a set of pot holders, she pulled the carefully prepared bird out of the oven and set it down on top of the stove. She slammed the oven door but it was too late. The smoke was so thick she could barely see across the room, and the outside of the bird was burnt to a black, ugly crisp.

"Eww, Mama, it looks awful."

"This can't be happening," Tory said.

"Tell me that isn't my supper." Boots thumped on the floor as Josh walked into the kitchen.

Tory's eyes slid closed. She should have known. The man had an uncanny sense of timing. She felt like bursting into tears.

Instead she forced herself to turn and face him. "I don't know what happened. It's been in there way less than an hour."

She looked up at him, read his disappointment, and the tears she'd been fighting welled in her eyes. He was going to let her go. She'd be back on the road looking for work, looking for a safe haven for her and Ivy.

It was just too much. Her last hope had gone up in smoke, just like the chicken. A sob escaped. Then another.

"Hey, it's okay," Josh said. "It's not the end of the world. It's just a chicken."

She wanted to say *it's the end of my world*. Or at least it felt that way. Another sob escaped. She tried to salvage her dignity. "It wasn't my fault. It was your damnable—darnable oven."

She brushed a tear from her cheek. "I set it at three twenty-five. It should have been perfect!" Then she covered her face and started crying. And she couldn't seem to stop.

Dammit, dammit, dammit. She couldn't do this. She just couldn't!

A hard body stepped into her space and she felt the heat, felt Josh's powerful arms go around her, ease her against his chest.

"Hey, it's going to be okay. You don't have to leave. We'll figure something out."

The softly spoken words finally penetrated her anguish, his voice as soothing as a summer rain. She relaxed into his strength, for several seconds just held on to him. It was stupid. It was embarrassing. She felt like a fool.

With a shaky breath, she stepped away. "I'm sorry." She wiped the tears from her cheeks. "I don't cry. I mean, I'm not a crier. Not usually."

"Only after you set a chicken on fire?"

She felt the faintest tug of a smile. "Yeah, only after that." She was still looking at Josh when she glanced over at Ivy. The little girl crouched on the floor against the wall, completely drawn into herself, her eyes huge, her face as white as a sheet.

Tory ran to her, swept her up in her arms. "Oh, honey, it's okay. Everything's okay. Everybody's fine."

"He . . . he hurt you. He . . . he made you cry."

"No. Josh didn't make me cry. It was the chicken. I was crying because I ruined his supper, but he wasn't mad, sweetheart. He was being nice."

The little girl looked over at Josh. Two pairs of blue eyes assessed each other.

"I wouldn't hurt you or your mother," Josh said softly. "I'd never do that. I promise you, Ivy."

Ivy hid her face in Tory's neck. She gave her little girl a fierce hug, then set her back down on her feet. "I'm going to finish making dinner for Josh, and then we'll go home, okay? In the meantime, you can finish your coloring, all right?"

Ivy nodded. Turning, she took off for the living room, settled back down on the floor. Picking up a crayon, she went back to work as if nothing had happened.

Kids, God love 'em.

"We need to have that talk," Josh said, regaining Tory's attention. "Somewhere private. It's warm outside. Now would be a good time."

"What . . . what about supper? I can salvage the chicken. I'll take off the skin and make some gravy. I've got a nice salad to go with it, some potatoes. You'll like it, I swear."

"After," he said, then turned and walked outside.

Tory sighed. Damon had tried to beat her into submission,

but Josh could make her jump through hoops with only a single word.

Tory didn't like the notion.

But she walked out onto the porch.

He shouldn't have held her. Now he'd never get the imprint of her soft breasts and feminine curves out of his head. Add to that, it was completely out of line. He was her boss. She was his employee.

Aside from satisfying his physical needs once in a while, he didn't have time for a woman. He had plans for the ranch, goals, ambitions. And he was still coming to grips with the changes in his life, the transition from being a soldier to a civilian.

On the surface, he had everything under control, but every once in a while, he had a disturbing flashback or a nightmare. It wasn't uncommon for soldiers who'd been in combat.

Eventually it would fade away, but until that time, he needed his space, his privacy. The last thing he wanted was a woman living right there on the ranch.

But damn he felt sorry for her. She'd been sure he was going to fire her, and he could see her desperation. He'd told her she could stay. Unless there were unknown factors, he wouldn't break his word. But as he had said, they needed to talk.

Tory shoved the screen door open and stepped out into the cool evening.

"I need a beer," Josh said. "You want one?"

She looked up at him. "Sure. I'd love a beer."

"I'll get them." A woman who liked beer. That was a plus.

He returned a few minutes later, twisted off the top to a Lone Star, and handed it over. Twisted off the cap to the other one and took a long swallow.

Tory took several sips. "Thanks. After a long day, that really tastes good."

They sat down on the porch, she in the swing while he took a seat in a wire mesh chair a few feet away. He tipped up his beer and took another long swallow, felt the relaxing burn of the bubbles going down his throat.

"Here's the thing," he started. "I know you're in some kind of trouble."

She opened her mouth but he held up his hand. "I know you're on the run. I don't need to know what happened to you in the past or why you're here. The way your little girl reacts to a man pretty much gives me the story. What I need to know is if the sheriff or the cops are going to come pounding on my door. I need to know if you're running because you've done something illegal."

Tory sat up straighter in the swing. "No. I haven't done anything wrong. I've never even had a speeding ticket."

"Be easy enough for me to find out. Howler's a small county. Police Chief Logan over in Pleasant Hill owes me a favor. I could have him check you out."

"Seriously? Do I look like a criminal to you?"

Amusement slipped through him. With her petite frame and fine features, Tory Ford looked as far from a crook as he could imagine. "No, but looks can be deceiving."

"I'm not wanted by the police. At least I don't think so, since I didn't really do anything wrong."

He didn't even want to know what that meant.

"I admit there are people I'd rather not know I'm here," she finished.

"Your husband?"

She swallowed, shook her head. "Jamie died in a car accident right after Ivy was born."

Maybe that was the sadness that crept into her face every once in a while. "So an ex-boyfriend." He knew by her expression it was true. "He hurt your little girl?"

"No."

"Just you then."

Her chin came up.

"You must have family somewhere. You can't go to them for help?"

"No family. My mother died in the crash that killed Jamie." She glanced away, an instant of pain in her eyes. "My dad ran out on us and I haven't seen him in years." Her fingers tightened around the bottle of beer. "I thought you didn't care about my past."

"I don't. Long as you're straight with me, I won't say anything to anyone. But you'll need groceries, other necessities, which means you'll be in and out of town. There's no way for you to stay completely off the grid. The good news is the folks around here won't bother you. As for me, all I want is a day's work for a day's pay. You've done that so far."

"I won't disappoint you. Just tell me what you need and I'll do it."

Josh clamped down on where that thought led. What he needed from Tory Ford was something he wasn't going to get. He took a drink of his beer, set it down on the wire mesh table in front of the swing.

"You might have noticed I'm still not finished unpacking. I could use some help with that, and keeping the house clean. I need breakfast in the morning, a lunch packed so I can keep working through the middle of the day, and supper ready at dark. You think you can handle that?"

"Absolutely."

"You can bring your daughter when you come over. That way you won't have to worry about a sitter."

Tory relaxed back on the swing. "That'd be great. Thank you."

"I don't know how long this is going to last, but we can try it for a while. At least you'll have a little money in your pocket when you leave."

She just nodded. He still didn't know much about her, but he didn't really want to. With any luck, whoever she was running from wouldn't find out she was here. Or better yet, the guy would quit looking.

Josh took another long draw on his beer and rose from the chair. "How about that supper you promised? I'm still holding high hopes you can make something halfway decent out of that burned-up bird."

Tory grabbed her beer off the table and stood up from the swing. "I'm on it. It shouldn't take that long." She crossed the porch and opened the screen door. "Just one thing."

"Yeah, what's that?"

"I need you to get that oven fixed. I don't want to burn up any more chickens." As she stepped into the house and the screen door slammed closed, Josh smiled.

He wondered if the stove really had malfunctioned, and hope resurfaced. He almost never used it. Hell, maybe it actually had failed.

Another thought occurred. If he could keep his mind off sex, it ought to be an interesting next few weeks.

Chapter Seven

The late afternoon air was cool this high in the Arizona mountains, the sky bluer than it was down in Phoenix. Damon unloaded the twin bed mattress from the pickup he had borrowed from his best bud, Anson Burke. He and Burke went way back. They'd partied together, done drugs together, shared women, and once during a booze-and-cocaine bender, wound up in bed together, though neither of them wanted to revisit that particular episode.

Nor had he mentioned to Anson the peculiar tastes that had begun to consume him. That was his business and his alone, his pleasure to enjoy.

The mattress was cumbersome as he carried it into the cabin. The dilapidated wood-framed structure had a screened-in porch, a living room with an old iron stove for heat, a kitchen along one wall, a tiny bedroom, and an ancient bathroom.

The cabin had belonged to his mother's father. His grandfather had loved to come up to the mountains and hunt. The old man had brought Damon with him a number of times, said he had a knack for stalking, moving in for the kill.

His mother had died when Damon was twelve. His grandfather had Alzheimer's now and was living in an old folks' home. With both of them out of the way, Damon had taken over use of the cabin, which was remote and completely secluded.

Perfect.

He had taken the day off from work to make the two-hour drive up and finish the project he had started with Tory in mind. He'd had to modify his plans a little but he found himself looking forward to the change in direction, and he was almost ready.

Dragging the mattress across the wood plank floor, he opened the door leading down to the basement. He had hired a couple of teenagers camping in the area to empty and clean the space out, had them scrub down the cement walls and floor with ammonia.

He dragged the mattress down the wooden stairs he'd reinforced and let it fall to the floor, went down and shoved it against the wall. He glanced over at the small refrigerator he had brought down, at the Porta-Potty behind the curtain he'd hung in the corner.

A satisfied smile lifted the corners of his mouth. Just a few more days and he could execute the first part of his plan. He'd have to be flexible, make adjustments as he went along, but he was used to that. In a way it was just like hunting.

Except this time his quarry was human.

Tory couldn't put the trip to town off any longer. She was cooking for Josh now, as well as for her and Ivy. She needed canned goods, meat, milk, bread, fresh fruit and vegetables. She needed staples like flour and sugar. Josh's pantry was emptier than the one in the trailer.

She got her daughter up and dressed—Ivy was in the mood for a little pink-striped pinafore since they were going into Iron Springs. She was the most girlie little girl Tory had ever seen.

"How do I look?" Ivy twirled around so Tory could see, her full skirt flaring out as she turned.

"I think the white patent shoes might be a bit impractical for a ranch, but you look very pretty."

Ivy smiled. "You look pretty, too, Mama."

"In jeans and a white cotton blouse? I don't think so."

"Yes, you do. Your hair always looks like fire. I bet Josh likes it."

Tory felt her face heating up. "Where did that come from? Josh is my boss. I work for him. There's nothing more to it than that."

Ivy seemed to relax. Her daughter was thinking of Damon, how nice he had seemed in the beginning and how rotten he had turned out to be.

"You ready to go?" she asked.

"I'm ready."

A soft knock sounded at the door. Tory checked the peephole, saw Josh on the porch.

She pulled open the door. "Good morning. I was just getting ready to leave." She had already cooked his breakfast and made him a sack lunch. "Is there something you need?"

"I was thinking maybe you'd be smart to leave Ivy with Mrs. Thompson and go into town by yourself. If someone's looking for you, they'll be looking for a woman and a kid, not a woman on her own."

It was a good idea. At least for a while.

"Mrs. T. lives just off the highway at the end of the road from the ranch," he said. "A big two-story white house that sits back in the trees. It'd be right on your way."

"She told me she lived there, but I'd have to call her, find out if it's okay."

"I talked to her earlier. She'd love to have Ivy come over for a couple of hours."

Josh was right about one thing. The fewer people who knew she had a child, the safer they would be.

"Okay. I'll drop Ivy off and pick her up on the way back."

She looked up at Josh. She needed money for his groceries. She hated to ask him for an advance, but she had to pay for her own food, as well.

She opened her mouth, but he was already pulling an envelope out of the back pocket of his jeans.

"Money for groceries and whatever else is on your list. Just bring me the change and receipts. Also, there's three days' pay for the work you've done."

She relaxed as she accepted the envelope. "Thank you for that."

"It's your money. You earned it. From now on you'll get paid every week, just like Noah and Cole."

She nodded. When he looked at her with those amazing blue eyes, she had a hard time looking away. "I'll be back in a couple of hours."

She went inside and got Ivy, went out to the Chevy and settled the little girl in her booster seat, then went around to the driver's side and slid in behind the wheel.

Half an hour later, with Ivy safe in Mrs. Thompson's well-kept older home, Tory arrived in Iron Springs. She gassed the car, topping off the tank as she hadn't been able to do in days, all the while keeping an eye on her surroundings, a habit she'd developed after she'd left Phoenix.

Parking in the lot in front of Iron Springs Food and Pharmacy, she took a moment to pull her red hair into a ponytail, then stuff it beneath the Texas Rangers' baseball cap she had bought at a truck stop on I-20 in Abilene.

She should probably dye her hair instead of trying to hide it, but it was her best feature and she was vain about it. Her long red curls had nearly reached her waist when she was with Damon. On the run, she had decided to cut it very short, but it had simply been too painful. So, like giving up her name, she had cut it shorter but not changed it completely, refusing to let Damon win.

She checked her image in the rearview mirror. The bright color wasn't completely hidden, but it wasn't that noticeable, either.

She did the grocery shopping, buying enough to last a week, then ran an errand for Josh, stopping at Miller's Mercantile to pick up a bottle of horse liniment he had called ahead to order. Mrs. Miller, the owner's wife, was a little too chatty, but nice.

"So you're working for one of those good-looking Cain boys, the one who just bought the Iron River Ranch." Cathy Miller was a buxom, broad-hipped woman with silver-streaked brown hair. Tory had a hunch she knew everything that went on in Iron Springs.

"He was a war hero, you know," Cathy said. "Famous hereabouts. He was a sniper in the marines. Killed a hundred enemy soldiers while he was protecting our troops. There's a story about him in a book about the war."

She hadn't known, but she'd love to read it. "I didn't know about the book, but now that you mention it, I remember hearing something on the news about a war hero returning to Texas."

"That's him," Mrs. Miller said. "That's our Josh."

Tory wondered why he'd left the military, if he'd been wounded as she suspected, wondered if he'd bought the out-of-the-way property in the hope of finding a little peace.

Before she headed back to the ranch, she was going to stop at the bookstore, see if they had a copy of the book.

Tory took the brown paper bag with the liniment. "Thanks, Mrs. Miller."

"Oh, it's just Cathy. We don't stand on formality around here. What was your name?"

Tory pretended not to hear her as she shoved open the door, ringing the bell above.

"Say hello to Josh for me," Cathy called after her.

Tory turned and waved. She had hoped to get in and out unnoticed. At least the woman didn't know her name. Not even the name she was using.

Two hours after she'd left, she headed back to the ranch with a brief stop at Mrs. Thompson's to pick up Ivy. Wearing a borrowed blue-flowered smock made for one of the granddaughters over her pink-striped dress, Ivy grinned from ear to ear. "We had so much fun, Mama!"

Tory felt a tug at her heart. It wasn't fair to continually uproot the little girl. She needed stability in her life, a place she could feel safe and loved.

Tory needed to start working on a plan, researching different cities, other states. Surely there was somewhere Damon couldn't find them.

Surely.

But the bitter truth was there was no way to know.

By the time she got back to the ranch, the book tucked into her purse, the urge to read it, to know more about Josh was nearly overwhelming.

As soon as she finished putting the groceries away, she took Ivy back to the trailer, unpacked her own food, and curled up on the sofa in the living room. While Ivy played with one of her dolls, Tory opened the book and immediately became immersed.

A trade-size paperback with photos, the title was *Military Snipers*. It was a collection of true stories about men who had served as snipers in the army, SEALs, and marines.

Thumbing through the pages looking for Josh's name, she found it in a story called "Ultimate Hunter." It told of a group of marines on a mission gone wrong, twelve men trapped in an abandoned building, little more than a mud hut, in the desert sixty kilometers outside Kandahar. The men had come upon an unexpected force of Taliban fighters and been pinned down with no way to escape. They had been trapped for hours, three men killed as they held off the assault through the night.

In the darkness, Josh had managed to find a way out. He'd been able to skirt their attackers, a group of well-armed insurgents bent on killing every last American soldier, and set up a sniper's nest behind a mound on a ridge a quarter of a mile away.

The enemy, armed with AK-47s and shoulder-fired rocket propelled grenades called RPGs, were little by little destroying the structure providing cover for the troops, exposing the men and making them easy targets. It was only a matter of time until all of them were killed, and there was no help on the way.

From Josh's position on the distant hill, he eventually managed to take out every Al-Qaeda soldier, all twenty of them, allowing his remaining men, some of them severely wounded, to cross the desert to the extraction point, where they were picked up by helicopter and returned to base.

According to the article, it was only one of a number of successful missions Josh had completed before he was severely wounded and eventually left the special operations branch of the marines.

Tory closed the book and sat there stunned. She had rightly guessed he was a soldier. What had happened to him was part of his past, part of what made him the man he was today. She had a feeling he had bought the ranch as a way to heal, to leave the past behind and look toward the future.

Before she left Texas, she would do everything in her power to help him.

* * *

The days on the ranch had been progressing smoothly. With the warm, sunny weather, the pastures grew lush and green. And yet Josh had been feeling restless and edgy, as if lightning might strike out of a clear blue sky or a tornado might appear on the horizon.

Though the clock seemed to be ticking down to something he couldn't quite grasp, there were chores to be done, things he needed to accomplish.

Along with his regular chores, he had started Tory working with Satan. Nothing dangerous, just feeding the stallion, petting him, talking to him. Mostly, just getting acquainted, winning the stallion's trust.

Josh never let her go into the pasture, the training pen, or anywhere near Satan—whom Tory called Star—when he wasn't close by. He had to be careful. He didn't want her getting hurt.

The stallion liked her—that was for sure. The minute he spotted her, he came running. Josh made a mental note to call the former owner of the ranch, dig deeper, find out more of the stallion's history.

It was late when he headed for bed that night. At first he had trouble falling asleep, his uneasiness returning, like standing on the edge of a precipice waiting for the ground beneath him to crumble.

When he finally sank into a fitful slumber, he was back in Afghanistan, the rat-a-tat-tat of machine gun fire echoing in his ears, along with the rattle of battle armor as his men ran for cover into a dilapidated mud hut in the middle of the desert. Two were dead, one of them bleeding and dying, nothing anyone could do.

It took a moment to realize the loud banging on his front door wasn't part of the dream.

"Josh! Wake up, Josh!" More banging. "The barn's on fire! Josh, wake up!"

Fear gripped him. Terrified for the horses, he shot out of bed, dragged on his jeans, and raced barefoot and shirtless through the living room. The sky was unnaturally bright outside the window as he jerked open the front door and ran flat-out toward the barn.

Orange-and-red flames licked out of the hayloft, clawing their way into the sky. The windows were ringed with tendrils of red, exploding as the fire grew hotter inside.

Tory ran ahead of him, racing toward the fire. His heart nearly burst when she disappeared into the smoke-filled interior.

"Tory! Tory, wait!" Josh raced after her, running full speed across the yard into the burning building. He spotted her opening one of the stall doors, trying to shoo a bay gelding out of the stall. When the wild-eyed animal just stood there trembling, she grabbed a rope, looped it around the animal's neck, and started tugging, but the horse still refused to budge.

"Cover his eyes!" Josh yelled over the roar of the fire as he grabbed a couple of towels off the stack next to the tack room door. "He's afraid of the flames!"

He tossed one of the towels to Tory, who put it over the horse's eyes and started running with him out of the barn. Josh was leading two of the animals out to safety when she ran back in, heading for another stall. She looped her rope over the head of the little gray mare who was about to foal, covered her eyes, and tugged the mare toward safety.

He led another gelding outside, his worry building. The flames were burning through the rafters, chewing through the roof. Any minute the whole ceiling could come crashing down. "Get out of here, Tory! I'll get the other horses. You've got to get out now!"

There were only two horses left, Sunshine, his palomino mare, and Thor, a big buckskin gelding that was his favorite to ride. Sunshine was in the far back corner, impossible to reach, and time was almost gone. He opened the buckskin's stall.

Josh took a last glance around, didn't see Tory, and prayed she'd done what he'd told her. Looping the rope over the buckskin's head, he covered the horse's eyes with the towel and ran out of the stall. As he raced for the door, he heard Sunshine's pitiful neigh, but there wasn't time to save her. If he went back inside, he'd die.

He looked around for Tory as he burst through the smoke into the cool night air, but he didn't see her. "Tory!" When she didn't answer, everything inside him went cold. "Tory!"

If she was inside, the smoke was so thick he'd never find her. A huge chunk of the roof came down, right over Sunshine's stall. He glanced around, frantic now. Tory was in there. He knew it.

Josh pressed the towel over his mouth and started running back to the barn, raced through the door just as Sunshine came thundering toward him, Tory hanging on to the rope around the mare's neck.

The mare jerked free and kept running. Josh grabbed Tory, swung her up in his arms, and ran out of the barn—just as the roof came crashing down.

Chapter Eight

Tory sat on the damp grass a safe distance from the burning barn. Two red fire trucks sat next to each other out front, one of them a tanker. Half a dozen firemen in full turnout gear handled the heavy hoses, shooting massive streams of water out of the tanker onto the flames, sending up thick white columns of smoke.

She managed to tear her gaze away from the fire as Josh walked up, his face and torso black with smoke. He was barefoot, wearing only a worn pair of jeans, his chest bare. Even covered in greasy black soot, all those muscles were ridiculously distracting.

When she'd run out of the trailer, she hadn't had time to put a bra on under her T-shirt. She could still feel the imprint of those hard muscles as he'd carried her at breakneck speed out of the burning building.

Tory shivered. She'd come within seconds of dying. Adrenaline still pumped like a drug through her veins.

"You all right?" Josh asked.

"I'm okay." Considering she had almost died. "What about the horses?"

"I opened the gate to one of the pastures and they ran right in. They're fine."

"What took the fire department so long to get here?"

"Department's all volunteer." Too restless to sit down, he paced back and forth as he watched the fire crew at work. With his property going up in flames, she didn't blame him.

"Plus we're ten miles from town." He looked back at the burning structure, most of it collapsed in on itself, occasional red-and-orange tendrils still licking through holes in the blackened wood. Volunteer firemen worked skillfully to knock down the last of the blaze. "Barn's a total loss, anyway."

"What do you think happened?"

"No idea."

"I'm glad none of the horses were hurt."

He stopped pacing and turned to face her, clamped his hands on his hips. "What the hell were you thinking? I told you to get out of the barn. Dammit, you could have been killed!"

She shrugged. At the time she didn't feel as if she had any choice. "Sunshine was in there. I couldn't just leave her."

"Sunshine is a horse! You're the mother of a little girl!" He glanced around. "Where is she, anyway? Where's Ivy?" A thread of worry colored his words.

"I just checked on her again. She was asleep when I spotted the fire. She still is. Once she crashes, she doesn't wake up till morning."

Josh ran a hand over his short brown hair. "Next time I tell you to do something, you do it. You understand?"

A memory of Damon slipped into her head and she drew back from him a little. "Or you'll what?"

Josh gave her a long, assessing look. "Christ, I'd never hit you, if that's what you're thinking. I've never hit a woman in my life. I don't plan to start with you."

He sighed and crouched down next to her on the grass. "What you did in there. It was incredibly brave. You helped me save the horses. Saving Sunshine was stupid, but it was brave."

Tory's gaze swung to his. "I'm not stupid, Josh. Don't

ever underestimate me. I saw a chance to save the mare and I took it. You would have done the same thing."

Some of the tension seeped out of his shoulders. He sighed as he sprawled on the grass beside her. "You're right, I would have. I'm sorry." He glanced off, staring at the fire for the longest time, as if watching the flames had sent him someplace into the past.

Those blue eyes finally returned to her, deep and intense. For a second it was hard to breathe.

"I know what it's like to lose someone," he said a little gruffly. "I've had friends die in battle, soldiers who had wives and kids. Death comes swift and hard, sometimes out of nowhere. You scared me. I'm sorry I yelled at you."

She was surprised at his apology. Damon wouldn't have done it. A hundred times, she wondered how she could have been duped so badly by a man like him.

Tory sighed. "I probably should have listened to you. I took a dangerous chance. It probably *was* stupid."

He stared at her as if he were trying to figure her out. "It was brave," he said.

The fire chief walked toward them. She couldn't see him clearly but beneath his helmet, he appeared to be a man in his fifties with a bushy salt-and-pepper mustache.

"Sorry, Josh," he said. "Not much to save."

"Barn went up like tinder. All that straw . . ." Josh shook his head. "It's a miracle we were able to get the horses out."

The chief's gaze swung to Tory. "I'm Chief Leland."

"Tory Ford." In the cool night air, without a bra, her nipples were standing out against her T-shirt. She'd always had full breasts, which the chief didn't miss. She crossed her arms over her chest.

"Why don't you go on home?" Josh suggested softly. "Get a little sleep? Nothing more you can do here."

"There'll be an investigation," the chief said. "As soon as the fire cools down enough, the arson boys will be out to take a look. Depending on what they find, they may need a statement."

"She'll be here tomorrow if they need to talk to her," Josh said.

Tory's gaze returned to the fire chief, who was clearly speculating on their relationship. Josh was giving her a chance to escape.

"I think I'll go in." She needed to keep an eye on her daughter, but she didn't want to mention Ivy unless she had to. "I'll see you in the morning." She was a few feet away when she heard the fire chief's voice.

"I don't think I've seen her around," he said to Josh as she continued toward the trailer.

"She's my housekeeper," she heard Josh say. She was fairly sure what the chief was thinking when Josh added, "Not *that* kind of housekeeper."

As she neared the porch, Tory glanced back at the dying fire. She wondered what had caused the blaze and felt sorry for Josh. He would have to rebuild, but at least the horses were safe.

She started up the front porch steps. The adrenaline had bled from her system. Her legs were shaking, her stomach unsteady. Climbing the stairs was suddenly a Herculean task.

She thought again of the fire. It was a terrible accident. A terrible loss for Josh.

But what if it wasn't an accident? a little voice asked. *What if the fire was set on purpose*?

Was it possible Damon had found her? In the last weeks they were together, he had changed so much. At the end, he'd become insanely jealous. The man who had beaten her nearly to death wouldn't think twice about burning down another man's barn, even if it killed a stable full of the man's valuable horses.

Tory's skin prickled as she stepped inside the house. Heading down the hall, she stopped to check on Ivy, but as before, the little girl was deeply asleep. Quietly entering her daughter's bedroom, she paused to press a kiss on the top of Ivy's head.

Coming close to death made her appreciate the amazing gift she had been given even more than she had before. It made her even more determined to keep her little girl safe.

It was an accident, she told herself as she walked into her bedroom. There was cleaning solvent in the barn, other flammable liquids, several tons of straw to fuel the flames.

But as she lay in bed trying to fall asleep, Damon's image appeared, the look of fury on his face when she had left him tied up on the floor.

She was still awake at dawn, more exhausted than when she had gone to bed. Until she knew what had caused the fire, she didn't expect to get much sleep.

Josh didn't bother going to bed. Wanting to make sure the hot spots were all out, the fire crew didn't leave until after dawn.

When Tory showed up to make breakfast, she brewed a big pot of coffee and carried it and a stack of Styrofoam cups out to the exhausted men. They were more than grateful.

Normally, when she arrived in the mornings, Josh did his best to be outside working. He came in to eat, then went back to work, figuring the less time he spent with her the better.

Tory had been a distraction before last night, but after carrying her out of the barn, he knew the exact fullness of her breasts, the way her nipples tightened into tiny buds in the cool night air. He knew the feel of her delicate curves, the silky texture of her fiery curls against his skin.

He wanted her. He tried to tell himself he'd just been too long without a woman. He tried to convince himself that any woman would do. Then he remembered the way she had run into the burning barn, risking her life to help him save his horses, save the beautiful palomino mare, and he knew it wasn't the truth.

He wanted Tory Ford, wanted her in his bed until he'd had his fill. He had no idea how long that would be; he just knew he hungered for her sweet little body every time she was near.

It wasn't going to happen. Tory worked for him. She was raising a child. It hadn't taken long to figure out she wasn't the kind of woman who was interested in a one-night stand. Not the kind who would be willing to trade her favors for a raise in salary or an easier job.

Since he wasn't interested in a relationship beyond the physical, Tory was off-limits. If he wanted sex, he had to find someone else.

Unfortunately, he couldn't work up the enthusiasm to look.

He sighed as he left the house and crossed the yard toward the dead embers of the burned-out barn. The occasional wisp of smoke was all that remained of the blaze that had destroyed the big wooden structure he had spent weeks rebuilding.

He looked up as Noah's pickup pulled into the yard, slid to a halt, and Cole and Noah jumped out.

"Holy shit!" Noah stalked toward him. Cole remained frozen, staring at the destruction. "What the hell happened?"

"Won't know till the arson squad comes out," Josh said.

"You don't think it could have been set on purpose?" Cole asked.

"We'll have to see what they find out."

"Could have been an electrical fire." Cole tipped up his baseball cap. "Wiring's pretty old in there."

"Maybe," Josh said. "Cleaning supplies, other flammables in the tack room, plenty of straw once the blaze got going."

"Those arson guys are good," Noah said. "They'll figure out what caused it."

Josh's gaze went back to the pile of blackened, soggy

lumber. "They'll probably be here this afternoon. Fire is dead out. Ashes should be cool enough by then."

"Maybe we can round up some help to rebuild," Noah suggested.

"Maybe." Linc had a good crew working at Blackland Ranch. Maybe his brother would loan him some of the hands. "We can't do anything till the arson investigation is complete. In the meantime, we've still got fences to mend, and the cow barn isn't finished. We're going to need it now. We'd better get going."

They set off as they usually did, Noah and Cole heading off on the ATVs to work on the fence line. Josh had planned to saddle one of the horses and ride out this morning. A gelding named Irish Whiskey was showing potential as a cutting horse. Good ones were valuable and hard to find. He wanted to do a little more work with the cattle, see if his hunch was right.

Not gonna happen now, not with all the saddles and riding tack destroyed.

This afternoon, he'd drive into town, pick up some replacement gear at the mercantile. All new saddles, bridles, blankets, halters, brushes, lead ropes, and dozens of other necessities weren't going to come cheap.

It was after lunch when a red van pulled up in front of the burned-out barn, the words ARSON INVESTIGATION printed on the side. Two men got out, walked over and introduced themselves: Bill Wheeler, a big older guy with a shaved head and thick neck, and a good-looking Asian around Josh's age named Tim Chin.

"We'll be a while," Bill said. "We'll let you know what we find out."

"Appreciate it."

"You got insurance?" Wheeler asked.

"Some. Not enough. Worse, I just rebuilt the damn thing."

A look passed between them. Josh had a hunch they had just crossed off a possible motive.

He didn't want to leave for town till he knew what had happened so he went to work on the cow barn while the men examined the still-smoldering remains.

It was a couple of hours later that the investigators showed up in the doorway.

"Got a minute?" Tim Chin asked. They were wearing heat-protective gear and heavy firemen's boots. Tim pulled off his fireproof gloves as he and Josh walked outside to join Bill Wheeler.

"Electrical or flammable liquids?" Josh asked. "I figure it has to be one or the other or a combination of both."

Chin glanced at Wheeler, then back. "It was arson, Josh. Multiple ignition points. Traces of accelerants. Combined with the straw, that's the reason it went up so fast."

Anger and disgust washed through him, making his jaw feel tight.

"You got any idea who might want to burn you out?" Wheeler asked.

"Not a clue." But he meant to find out.

"No enemies you can think of?" Chin added.

"If I was still in Afghanistan, I'd say I had a whole army of enemies. Here, no. Right off, I can't think of anyone who'd go to this kind of extreme."

"Give it some thought," Wheeler said. "The sheriff's going to be out here asking the same questions."

Josh bit back a curse. Sheriff Emmett Howler was a real dickwad. How he had kept the job for twenty-plus years, Josh had no clue. On top of that, he had a major hard-on for anybody with the last name Cain.

Back in his brother's wild high school days, Linc's best friend, Beau Reese, and the sheriff's son, Kyle Howler, had tried to rob a convenience store. Howler had been the arresting officer.

Beau and Kyle, underage at the time, had their records sealed and received light sentences. Linc, at eighteen, had been tried as an adult and sentenced to two years in prison.

With the help of the grandfather of the girl Linc had married, he was able to turn his life around. Linc and Beau had both become incredibly successful, while the sheriff's son had ended up addicted to drugs and alcohol.

Howler blamed Linc. The fact that Josh's last name was Cain wouldn't be helpful.

Josh waited while the men loaded their equipment back into the van, then watched the van pull away. He was heading for his truck to make the trip into town when he saw Tory hurrying toward him, her fiery curls bobbing up and down.

An unwanted surge of heat settled deep in his groin. "What's wrong?" he asked, clamping down on his hunger and forcing himself to focus.

"Nothing, I just . . . I wanted to know if the investigators found the cause of the fire."

He hated to tell her. He didn't want to scare her, and the notion of a firebug on the loose wasn't good news. On the other hand, he needed her to be wary, watchful for anything out of the ordinary.

"Turns out the fire was arson. Someone used flammable accelerants in multiple locations. The blaze was started on purpose."

Her face paled. "Are they . . . are they sure?"

"There wasn't any doubt."

"Oh, God."

"Until they catch whoever did it, you need to be vigilant. I don't know if it was personal or just some nut who likes to watch things burn, but we need to be on the lookout."

She nodded. "Yes, yes, of course." He could tell she was upset. She could have died last night. He wasn't happy, either.

"I-I need to get back to work. I've got something on the

stove." She tried for a smile but it didn't quite surface. "I'll keep my eyes open."

Josh watched her hurry toward his house, his mind going over possible suspects. He and Ramirez hadn't parted on particularly good terms, but Diego had another job even before he'd quit and he didn't seem too upset. Josh had fired the teenager who had stolen from him but surely burning down the barn would have been overkill.

Still he'd give the kid's name to the arson guys, and the sheriff if he asked. Aside from that, he couldn't think of anyone.

A more sinister thought arose. What about the guy Tory was running from? Was there a chance he had found her? And if he had, was he the kind of man who would go as far as arson to punish her in some way? She was obviously afraid of him. He'd left the little girl terrified of men in general.

Tory seemed a sensible woman. He couldn't help wondering why she would let a guy like that into her life, especially with a child to consider.

He'd told her he didn't need to know about her past and he'd meant it. But the situation had changed last night when his barn had gone up in flames.

He needed to talk to Tory and he needed to talk to her now. Josh headed back to his house.

Chapter Nine

Josh followed Tory to the house, but when he walked through the front door, Tory and Ivy weren't there. There was nothing in the oven. Hell, the oven wasn't on.

Suspicion rolled through him. Heading for the trailer, he climbed the porch steps and started to knock on the door. His hand froze as the door swung silently open and he heard voices coming from the hall leading to the bedrooms.

Remembering the look on Tory's face when he had told her the fire was arson, he pushed the front door open and stepped inside. Heading down the hall, he stopped when he reached her open bedroom door, saw her madly throwing clothes into a suitcase, taking hangers out of the closet and tossing them onto the bed.

Suspicion gave way to irritation. No way had she set the fire then risked her life to save the horses, but something was definitely going on.

Propping his shoulders against the doorjamb, he crossed his arms over his chest. "Going somewhere, Tory?"

She jumped as if he'd shot off a cannon. She saw him and her body sagged in relief. "Josh . . . I thought . . . What are you doing here?"

His irritation crept up another notch. "If you're quitting, I'd appreciate at least a couple of days' notice."

She looked at the jeans and blouses strewn all over the bed, looked back at him, and her eyes filled. "I have to go. I didn't mean to cause you any trouble. I'm so sorry, Josh."

It wasn't what he'd expected her to say. He pushed away from the wall and walked toward her. "You think it was him? Is that what's going on here?"

"I-I don't know." She blinked and wiped a tear from her cheek. "It could be. I'm afraid it's him."

"He's that bad? He'd burn down a barnful of horses just to get back at you?"

She released a shuddering breath. "He's that bad, Josh. The night I tried to leave him, he beat me nearly to death." She looked past him out the window, toward the lush Texas grasslands and the mottled gray sky overhead.

"I don't know how he fooled me so completely," she said. "When I met him, I thought he was this really great guy. We'd only been dating a couple of months when he asked me to marry him. I said yes. I thought he would make a great dad for Ivy. As soon as we moved in together, things went rapidly downhill."

"Was it booze? Drugs?"

"Not at first. Later it was both, but I don't think that was his problem. We'd only been living together a month before I realized I was in trouble. We started fighting and he got more and more violent until I wound up in the hospital. His family is rich and powerful. Instead of jail, Damon got rage counseling and community service."

"What happened after that?"

"Damon started harassing me right away. I was able to get a restraining order, but it didn't really do any good."

"Yeah. Piece of paper making something illegal doesn't keep people from breaking the law."

"No, it doesn't. I finally gave up and left Phoenix."

"How long ago was that?"

"Five months. I took a job in Houston but Damon followed me, started harassing me again. After he strangled the neighbor's kitten and tossed it on my doorstep, I knew we had to leave. I found a job in Carlsbad, one I really liked. Things were good. I thought maybe he'd given up, but three weeks before I came to the ranch, Damon found me again. After that I was on the road until I got here."

"What happened in Carlsbad?"

She took a shaky breath. "Damon and I had a little . . . umm . . . altercation."

"You got into a fight? How bad was it?"

"Not nearly as bad as it could have been. I was prepared this time. When Damon broke into my apartment in the middle of the night, I used a stun gun to incapacitate him, tied him up, and left him on the floor. Damon was really pissed."

Imagining the scene, Josh felt the pull of a smile. "Yeah, I bet he was."

"I've been extremely careful since then, disposable phones, paying cash for everything, but maybe somehow he found out I was here."

She returned to her packing, threw in another dress. Josh walked over and caught her shoulder, turning her to face him.

"Look, we don't know for sure it was him. It could just be some firebug passing through who gets his kicks out of burning things down. Until we find out, there's no reason for you to leave."

She swallowed, looked up at him. "Thank you for saying that, but—" Fresh tears welled, making her eyes look bigger and greener. "I can't let you take that kind of risk."

Maybe if she had said something else. Maybe if her concern hadn't grabbed him like a fist, he could have just let her leave. He had returned to Texas for peace and quiet. The last thing he needed was more trouble.

But there was no way he could just abandon her. "What about you, Tory? What about Ivy? If this guy's as bad as you say, how are you going to protect your little girl?"

A soft sob caught in her throat. Josh looked into those troubled green eyes and the next thing he knew he was pulling her into his arms. "You're not going anywhere. You're staying right here where you'll be safe."

He could feel her trembling, feel the way her body relaxed into the strength of his. For a moment, she rested her head on his chest. It felt good—way too good. He reminded himself this was a woman who needed his help, nothing more.

She took a shaky breath and looked up at him. "Are you . . . are you sure?"

He wasn't sure of anything except there was no way he could send this woman and her little girl away, not with some lunatic tracking them.

He eased her back a little before she discovered holding her was making him hard. "Like I said, we have no idea who burned the barn. If it's him, we'll find a way to deal with it. Until then, we go on the way we have been, but we keep our eyes open. I'll talk to Noah and Cole, let them know what's going on."

"Oh, God, they might be in danger, too."

He almost smiled. "They're marines, honey. They can take care of themselves. They've faced a lot worse than some creep who beats up women."

Those strawberry lips curved. He wanted to lean down and kiss her.

"You were a marine, too, right?"

"That's right."

"Why did you leave the service? I noticed the scar on your side. Were you wounded?"

"Yeah." He didn't say he'd been shot three times and blown up with an IED. Somehow it seemed overkill.

She reached out and lifted his T-shirt, stared at the twisted flesh on his side that had healed far better than he had any right to expect. The brush of her fingers felt like a white-hot brand.

"It looks bad," she said.

"It was." He moved farther away before he did something stupid. "The point is I'm not going to let this guy hurt you. If he comes, we'll take care of him."

"He's rich, Josh. He might not come alone. The truth is I have no idea what Damon will do, how far he'll go to get revenge."

"Damon. What's his last name?"

"Bridger. Damon Bridger. But it isn't fair to you—"

"Let me worry about that." He reached out and touched her cheek. "You just keep cooking those great meals and I'll take care of the rest, okay?"

She stared at him for the longest time before she finally nodded. "Okay."

"Good. Now unpack and get back to work. By the way, what's for supper?"

"It was going to be meatloaf and mashed potatoes."

He almost groaned. "Sounds great." He was heading for the door when Ivy came running into the bedroom, her little brown velvet horse clutched tightly against her chest.

"I'm ready, Mama. Let's go!"

"We're staying, honey. Josh says we can stay."

Ivy's attention shifted warily in his direction, then returned to her mother. "We can't stay. What about Damon? We have to go." Her big blue eyes filled with tears. "We have to leave, Mama!"

Careful to keep his distance, Josh crouched in front of the little girl. "Listen to me, Ivy. I'm not going to let Damon hurt you. I promise you that. You don't have to leave. You'll be safe here."

Ivy ignored him. "We have to go, Mama! We have to run away!"

"You can stay on the ranch, Ivy," Josh said. "I'll keep you safe."

Solemn blue eyes, wet with tears, locked on his face. "Damon's really mean."

"If I have to, I can be really mean, too. Only I don't hurt women and little girls."

Ivy stared at him, trying to decide if she should trust him. She ran to Tory and hung on to her waist. "Josh says we can stay."

The little girl was taking a risk, counting on him. The knowledge made his chest feel tight.

Tory managed to smile at Ivy. "Let's go cook Josh some supper, okay?"

"'Kay." Still clutching her stuffed pony, Ivy raced out into the hall.

Tory looked up at him. Her lashes were damp. "No one's offered to help us in a very long time. Thank you."

The tightness returned to his chest. "Nothing to thank me for yet. I'll see you at supper."

Glad to get away from his unfamiliar emotions, Josh walked out of the bedroom. He didn't know how it had happened, but he had a woman and a kid in his life—the last thing he needed. A woman and a child with a threat hanging over their heads.

A woman he wanted and couldn't have.

He wondered if things could get any worse.

And knew damn well they could.

Tory returned to Josh's kitchen, mixing hamburger with bread, eggs, and spices to make the meatloaf recipe her mother had taught her. Her job on the ranch was simple:

cooking, laundry, keeping house, running an occasional errand. She should have been bored to death.

In Phoenix, she'd been an advertising exec at a prestigious marketing and advertising company with all the perks a position like that entailed. She had worked long hours and traveled more than she wanted, but she was a vice president in upper-level management. The job was challenging, and she made a very good salary.

Now she was in the middle of Nowhere, Texas, doing simple tasks like fixing sandwiches and folding laundry. But she was also breathing fresh air instead of smog, relaxing in the evenings instead of picking Ivy up late from the sitter, having to hurry straight home and put her to bed.

She was able to spend time with her little girl as she hadn't been able to do since Ivy was born. Tory was teaching her the alphabet and numbers, working on basic reading skills, playing cards, and just having fun.

The time spent with her child was more precious than Tory ever could have imagined. Living and working in her dog-eat-dog, super-hectic world, she hadn't known how much she was missing.

She wished she could call her best friend and talk to her about it. She had a feeling Lisa would be one of the few people who would understand. They hadn't talked in ages. Tory had run short of money after her last phone call and hadn't thought to pick up a new disposable when she was in town.

Next time, she told herself as she formed the meat and spices into a loaf, put it into a baking pan, and shoved it into the oven, which now worked perfectly thanks to Josh.

After that first night, he'd suggested she cook enough extra for her and Ivy's supper instead of having to fix two separate meals. Of course, that meant Josh was paying for some of the food she was eating. It was good of him to offer and so far the arrangement was working great.

Late afternoon slipped away, the sun sinking low on the horizon. In the evenings she liked to sit out on the porch in front of the trailer and listen to the night sounds: the wind luffing through the trees, the cattle and horses moving around in the pasture, the hoot of an owl.

In the early mornings, birds sang and squirrels played tag in the yard. She had spotted the cutest rabbit, hurried to show Ivy, who had squealed with delight. It was a different life out here. She'd never realized how much she liked the country until she'd left the city.

Supper was almost finished when she heard a knock at Josh's front door. An anxious, uneasy tremor moved down her spine as she walked past where Ivy sat watching TV in the living room, checked the peephole, and pulled the door open.

A heavyset man in a tan sheriff's uniform stood beneath the covered porch. He took off his beige cowboy hat and tucked it under his arm. Not wanting him to see Ivy, Tory stepped outside onto the bricks that ran the length of the house and closed the door.

"May I help you?"

"Sheriff Emmett Howler. I'm lookin' for Joshua Cain. I need to talk to him about the fire last night." Along with the cowboy hat, he had a belly that hung over his belt and a thick Texas accent.

"I'm sorry, Josh is in town. I'm not sure what time he'll be back."

"You're Tory Ford?"

"That's right."

"Got your name from Bill Wheeler. You're Cain's house-keeper, I guess."

The way he was looking at her, as if he knew some dirty little secret, she felt the need to set him straight. "I do his cleaning, his laundry, prepare his meals. I live in that double-wide over there." She pointed to the trailer. "What can I do for you, Sheriff?"

"How long you been workin' for Cain?"

"Going on two weeks."

"You seen any sign of anyone suspicious hangin' around, someone who oughtn't to be here?"

"No, I haven't seen anyone."

"Where you from, Miss Ford?"

"It's Mrs. I was married. My husband was killed in a car accident several years ago."

"I see. The way you talk, don't sound like you're from around these parts. So where y'all from?"

The question made her stomach burn. She heard the sound of a truck pulling in, said a silent *thank you* when Josh climbed out and started striding toward them.

"There's Josh now." She stepped back as he walked up on the porch. "The sheriff's here about the fire. He wants to talk to you." Josh must have read her worry. His gaze zeroed in on Emmett Howler.

"What can I do for you, Sheriff?"

"If you two will excuse me," Tory said, "I need to get back to my cooking." Before the sheriff could object, she slipped into the house and closed the door, then took a place next to the window so she could watch the men and hear their conversation without being seen.

She had a hunch Josh knew she was there. He seemed to have a sixth sense about whatever was happening around him. She thought maybe it was his military training.

"Too bad about the fire," the sheriff said. "Prob'ly got the barn insured, right?"

"I've got a little insurance, enough to cover about eighty percent of the building and what was inside."

"Lucky you didn't lose any horses."

"I'm grateful for that."

Howler tipped his head toward the door. "Woman's only been workin' here a while. Any chance she set the fire? You know what they say about a woman scorned."

A muscle in Josh's cheek subtly tightened. The beard shadow was back. He only seemed to shave every few days. Tory wished it didn't make him look even sexier.

"She's my employee," Josh said. "Other than that, I don't have a relationship with the lady. As far as the barn goes, if it hadn't been for Tory's help, I wouldn't have gotten all the horses out."

The sheriff pondered that. "Any idea who mighta' done it?"

"You might check out a kid named Randy Stevens. Worked for me a few days. Stole a five-gallon can of gas and I fired him for it. He wasn't happy about it."

"Randy Stevens? Jim Stevens's boy? Good kid. I doubt he'd do anything like that."

"Probably not," Josh said. "I just thought I should mention it."

"Good way to ruin a kid's reputation, accusing him falsely of somethin' like that."

Josh's jaw went tight. "I didn't accuse him. I thought you'd want to know. If there isn't anything else, I need to get back to work."

It was beginning to get dark, a wall of clouds rolling over the flat green lands in the distance. Fading sunlight glinted on the surface of a distant pond.

The sheriff sauntered away, walked out from under the covered porch. "I'll let you know what we come up with," Howler said. "You might want to keep an eye out, though. Sounds like you could have an enemy somewheres about."

Josh made no reply, just stood watching as the sheriff walked to his white, blue-trimmed, extended cab patrol pickup, hefted himself inside, started the engine, and drove away.

Tory opened the door and walked out on the porch.

"You okay?" Josh asked.

"You showed up at just the right time. I'd rather the sheriff didn't start digging around, stirring things up."

"Howler's a real dumbass. The chance of him finding the arsonist is none to minus zero."

She chuckled. "You think it might have been this kid, Randy?"

"I don't know. Wheeler called while I was in town. The accelerant was gasoline. Randy Stevens stole a five-gallon can of gas and I fired him for it. Maybe he figured using it to burn down the barn was payback. Howler's not going to check it out, which leaves it to me. Randy may be young, but if he committed arson, he's dangerous. He needs to be in jail."

"I don't want to wish him bad luck, but I hope they catch whoever's responsible."

"Yeah. Speaking of which, I talked to Cole and Noah, brought them up to speed. You got a photo of your ex?"

"I had pictures of him on my cell phone. I threw it away when I left Phoenix. I couldn't stand to look at him. Plus I didn't want him to be able to track me. Of course he managed to find me anyway. Since then, I've been using a disposable."

"Smart girl."

"No photos, but we could use your computer, search the Internet for a picture. I just . . . I don't want to leave any traces he might be able to follow."

"We'll make sure that doesn't happen. In the meantime, how about a general description? What's he look like? Short? Tall? Fat? Thin? Any tattoos, identifying marks?"

"Damon's good-looking. About six-one, thick black hair, olive complexion, nice build. Not like you, but nice."

Josh's mouth edged up.

"He's smart and he's charming. That's how he sucks you in. He finds out what interests you and makes it seem like the two of you have a lot in common."

"All right, that helps. Anything else?"

"He's diabolical. He isn't just bad, he's evil. He killed a stray dog I was feeding when we lived in Phoenix because I said something he didn't like. That's when I started making plans to leave. In Houston, he murdered my neighbor's kitten. He's a psychopath and he's terrifying."

"Hey, take it easy. The guy's not coming near you, okay?"

She realized her hands were balled into fists and forced herself to relax. "Sorry. I don't like to think about him."

"You don't have to. So far there's no reason to believe he did it. But just to be safe, Cole and Noah will be checking the perimeter several times a day. I'll be keeping an eye out around here. He shows up, we'll be ready." He flashed a wide, reassuring smile. "All you need to think about is making the perfect meatloaf, okay?"

Josh didn't smile that often, but when he did, it was devastating. Tory felt hot all the way to her toes. "Okay."

Josh left to unload the supplies he'd brought back from town and Tory went in to check on Ivy and finish supper. If Damon had burned down the barn, if he had followed her to Iron Springs, Josh would deal with him. His promise made Tory feel safer.

And it scared her to death.

Chapter Ten

Damon slowed the rental car as he drove past the house. It was dark, a layer of clouds hiding the moon. There were no lights on, nothing to disturb the blackness. At this late hour, Lisa would be sleeping. He hadn't planned to take things this far, but the little redheaded bitch who belonged to him had eluded him long enough.

He'd found her in Houston without much trouble, but it had taken him months to find her in Carlsbad—even with the help of his overpaid detective. After the way she'd hurt him that night, left him bound and humiliated on the floor of her apartment, she could run to the ends of the earth and he would still find her. He wouldn't give up until he did.

More than a month had passed since then. It infuriated him that she'd been able to hide from him so long. Worse yet, this time she had completely disappeared and even his pricey investigator had no idea where to look for her.

A problem Damon planned to remedy tonight.

He parked the car in the alley behind the simple three-bedroom tract house in the Desert Hills subdivision on the east side of Phoenix. Pulling on a pair of snug black leather gloves, he headed for the rear gate, opened it, and slipped into the backyard.

Lisa Shane was Tory's best friend, the only close friend she had. Her father had left her mother when Tory was just a kid. She'd told him once that her old man had remarried and was living in Florida with a whole new family. He had severed his ties with her and she had severed hers with him. Her mother had died a few years before Damon had met her.

He took his time, made a cursory examination of the house but saw no sign of an alarm system. *People were such fools*.

Of course, it didn't really matter. He'd been able to get past most digital alarms since he was in high school.

He took a set of lock picks out of his pocket. He'd been what the teachers had called a troubled teen. His parents were divorced. His dad had raised him and his dad was filthy rich.

As a teenager, Damon had more spending money than any other kid in school, but the adrenal rush he got from breaking into a house while the owner was in there sleeping, or beating up some itinerant on the sidewalk was a thrill he'd craved like a drug.

Over the years, it had taken more and more to get that kind of rush, but the high was a fire in his blood.

By the time he'd graduated college, his need had become so powerful he realized it was something beyond the realm of normal, something he would have to control.

It took some effort, but he had learned to do just that.

As an executive in his father's real estate development company, he made a fat salary for doing a minimum of work, lived in a beautiful condo, and fucked pretty much any woman he wanted. He was good-looking and he could be charming, a talent he used to get what he wanted.

Until Tory, he'd kept his personal life separate from the secret life he led, but the little whore he had stupidly fallen for and planned to marry had managed to destroy his hard-earned control.

He could still remember how furious he'd been when he'd

seen her getting out of another man's car. That night he'd managed to tamp down his anger, letting only a little of it show. She was a cheating whore, he'd discovered, and sooner or later, he intended to make her pay.

Still, he enjoyed her in bed and he didn't mind keeping her around. They'd only had one real argument—something about her wanting to go out with her girlfriends, which he had strictly forbidden.

Then came the night he'd caught her moving out of his house. As if he'd allow her to make that decision. His temper had finally snapped. He could still remember the rush he'd gotten when he'd dealt with the conniving little bitch. Hitting her, punishing her, watching her bleed made him feel like a king.

After accepting his ring, then cheating on him, she deserved everything he'd done to her that night. Everything he planned to do once he got his hands on her again. All he had to do was find her.

Damon put the lock picks to work, quickly opened the back door, and slipped silently into the house. Making his way quietly down the hall, he reached the master bedroom.

His dick throbbed at the sight of the pretty young woman in bed, the sheet pushed down to expose the top half of her body in a sheer lavender nightgown. Moonlight silvered her long, pale blond hair, and her lips were slightly parted.

He imagined what he could do with that pretty mouth and felt a fresh rush of heat. Moving farther into the room, he eased all the way up to the side of the bed. For a moment he just watched her, enjoying the rise and fall of her breasts, the shadow of her nipples beneath the lavender silk.

Taking a deep breath, he steadied himself, reached out, and clamped a hand over her mouth. Lisa jolted wide awake and shot up in the bed, fighting and thrashing and trying to scream. His gloved hand muffled the sound.

Shoving her back down in the mattress, he used his body

to pin her to the bed. He could feel her heart thumping, feel her soft breasts against his chest, feel her mound. It was really turning him on.

"Take it easy and I won't hurt you." She was trembling. It aroused him even more, and he started getting hard. "Keep quiet and I'll move my hand. Okay?"

By now Lisa had seen his face. She recognized him and managed to nod. Her eyes were big and blue and wide with fear. Knowing he was the cause made his heart race almost as fast as hers. He eased his hand away.

"What . . . what do you want?"

He gave her one of his charming smiles. "Now is that any way to greet an old friend? It's been months since we've seen each other."

Some of her courage came back. "Get off me, Damon." She struggled. He didn't move.

"I want to know where Victoria is."

Lisa shook her head. "I don't . . . I don't know."

He wrapped a hand around her throat and tightened his hold just a little. Lisa gasped in a breath.

"You know. She's your best friend. Tell me where she is."

She swallowed. He could feel the up-and-down movement beneath his hand and sexual heat slid through him.

"She . . . she calls me, but she never says where she is. That's . . . that's the truth. I really don't know where to find her."

"Where's your phone?"

Barely able to move her head with his hand around her neck, she slid her eyes toward the nightstand. "Over there."

He picked up the phone with his free hand, went to recent calls, and ran back through the list of dozens of phone calls, but there was no way to know which number belonged to Tory.

His fingers tightened around her throat and he jerked her

into a sitting position. "Look through the numbers. Find the one that belongs to her."

"You're hurting . . . hurting me." She tried to pry his fingers loose but he squeezed until she stopped.

"Behave yourself and I won't hurt you. Find the number that belongs to Tory."

"It's . . . it's always a disposable phone. She gets rid of it after she calls and buys . . . buys a new one."

Fury made his hand shake. He tightened his grip until she gagged and started thrashing. Damon loosened his hold.

"How often does she call?"

"Every . . . every week or so."

He couldn't track Victoria's phone the way he'd planned. But she would call her friend again. He would have to go to plan B. It was a lot more dangerous, but the rush was already working its way through his blood. He yanked Lisa to her feet. "Put on some clothes."

"What? Why?"

He backhanded her across the face. "You don't ask questions, you just do it."

Tears sprang into her big blue eyes. She rubbed her cheek and glanced past him toward the door, but he blocked any chance of escape. She moved to the dresser, pulled out a bra, panties, jeans, and a yellow T-shirt, turned and started for the bathroom.

"Put them on in here."

She shook her head. "No way. I'm not letting you watch me."

He needed to be on his way. He'd humor her—this time. He tipped his head toward the bathroom door. "Go ahead."

As soon as she went into the room and started to close the door, he caught up with her and shoved it open. No window inside, just glass blocks to let in light. "Hurry up." Stepping back he allowed her to close the door.

Minutes passed. When she didn't come out soon enough,

his temper started to rise. He'd give her a little longer, then kick the door open and drag her out.

The knob turned and Lisa walked into the bedroom. In the moonlight, her face was nearly as pale as her silver-blond hair.

"Put on some shoes," he said.

Eyeing the bedroom door, which he stood in front of, she sat on the edge of the mattress and put on her sneakers, then got up and faced him.

"I'm dressed, Damon. Now finish whatever you have planned and get out of my house."

"Oh, I'm getting out." A cold smile curved his lips. "The thing is, you're coming with me."

She cried out as the stun gun hit her in the chest. Another hit and she collapsed bonelessly to the floor. The lesson Victoria had taught him worked perfectly. Lisa's body jerked a few times, her eyes and mouth open, but she didn't move.

Damon stunned her again, then hauled her up and tossed her over his shoulder, using a fireman's carry to get her out of the house.

Once he reached the alley, he opened the trunk of the rental car and dumped her inside, used the plastic ties he'd brought with him to bind her hands and feet, stuffed a gag in her mouth and tied it in place with a scarf. Then he got into the plain white, four-door rented Toyota and started the engine.

As he drove away, the thrill was nearly overwhelming. He'd had no idea how good it would feel to have someone completely at his mercy.

The possibilities were endless.

And he finally had a way to reach Tory. She would call sooner or later. He didn't like waiting, but he could be a patient man. Especially when he had a pretty blonde to keep him entertained. Damon turned the corner and drove off down the street.

* * *

Days passed. The gray mare had her foal, a beautiful little black filly, the cutest thing Tory had ever seen. Ivy could sit in front of the stall for hours just watching her.

Instead of watching the foal, Tory had started the annoying habit of watching Josh through the window above the kitchen sink. Lately everything about him seemed to intrigue her—the way he moved, his almost soundless footsteps, the way he appeared in one place then seemed to disappear without ever actually walking away.

Sometimes when he rode one of the horses out of the barn, he looked so good she could barely tear her eyes away. On a warm day, he worked with his shirt off, putting all those glorious muscles on display. She wanted to touch him, run her fingers over all that hard male flesh.

It was insane. She didn't understand it.

In the beginning, before Damon had turned into a monster, the sex had been good. She had enjoyed the closeness, the intimacy, but she hadn't lusted after him. She hadn't thought about what it would be like to kiss him, how his hands would feel on her body. What he might do to her in bed.

Until Josh, she had never lusted after a man before. Jamie had been her high school sweetheart, neither of them sexually experienced. After the beating Damon had inflicted, she'd been afraid she might never want to go out with a man again, certainly would never feel the kind of hungry need she felt for Joshua Cain.

Maybe it was his protective nature, the way he was putting himself out there to help her. Maybe it was the way Ivy had put her trust in him when the little girl had been so afraid of men before.

Whatever it was, Tory did everything in her power not to let him know how strongly he affected her. She didn't want to be the woman the sheriff and the fire chief thought she was, a kept woman Josh paid for the use of her body.

She didn't want him to sleep with her and have him think of her that way, too.

Instead, she stayed away from him as much as she could and he seemed to do his best to stay away from her. If it weren't for Star, she would barely have to see him at all, except at supper.

But Josh refused to let her anywhere near the stallion unless he was close by. He didn't want her going into the pasture, always made sure she remained on the other side of the fence.

Josh stayed far enough away not to upset the horse, but near enough to guide her or step in if something went wrong. So far that hadn't happened.

They'd set up a schedule. Josh had officially hired Mrs. Thompson to come over and stay with Ivy for a couple of hours in the afternoon so he and Tory could work with Star. She had bought carrots and apples at the store and the stallion loved them.

Now she also grained him. At first he hadn't liked the feed bag she eased over his head, snorting and dancing and backing away. But little by little, his curiosity got the better of him and he returned to the fence to explore the object in her hand.

"It's all right, Star. This silly bag won't hurt you. And wait till you taste what's inside."

The molasses-covered grain was a special treat, which the animal quickly discovered when she held the bag up to give him a taste.

Eventually, he allowed her to ease the strap over his head. Tory rubbed his ears and played with his topknot while he ate. When the grain was gone, she walked back over to where Josh stood by the fence.

"I want to go into the pasture. He's never tried to hurt me. I don't think he will."

"Not yet," Josh said. "I've got a call in to the man who owned the ranch before I bought it. I know he wasn't the stallion's original owner. I'm hoping he can tell me who was. I want to know as much as I can about Satan—"

"Star," she corrected.

"Fine. I want to know as much about Star as I can before you get close enough for him to hurt you."

She sighed. Star tossed his head and nickered. She thought of his sleek black coat and long-lashed dark brown eyes. "I wonder if he'd ever let me ride him."

Josh's eyebrows shot up. "Are you kidding me? You don't know how to ride and this sure as hell isn't the horse for you to learn on."

She told herself not to say it, but the words spilled out of her mouth before she could stop them. "Maybe you could teach me."

Something hot and glittering flashed in his eyes, then it was gone. "You want me to teach you to ride," he said darkly.

"Why not? This is a ranch, isn't it? You have a whole bunch of horses. Surely one of them is tame enough for me to handle."

He shoved his hat back with the tip of his finger, then tugged it into place again. "I don't have time. I've got to rebuild the barn."

It was true, but she didn't think that was the reason. "You're right. You've got a lot to do. It's no big deal."

Those incredible blue eyes slid over her body in a way that made her nipples peak beneath her cotton blouse. For a moment he closed his eyes as if he were in pain.

"Fine, I'll teach you to ride. I'll pick a horse and starting tomorrow, we'll ask Mrs. T. to stay an extra hour in the afternoon. That suit you?"

Excited, she nodded. "I'm a quick learner. With any luck it won't take too long."

"Yeah, with any luck," he grumbled. He turned toward the pile of black rubble that once was a barn. "I'm heading into town. So far the sheriff hasn't done squat. I want to talk to Randy Stevens."

Since the night of the fire, there hadn't been any more trouble. Tory thought that if Damon had burned down the barn, he would have done something else by now. But the sheriff hadn't made an arrest yet, so everyone on the ranch stayed wary.

"You don't have to worry about supper," Josh said, surprising her. "I won't be home."

She wanted to ask him why, but she had a hunch she didn't want to know. "All right."

"In the meantime, stay away from Satan."

"His name is Star."

He made no reply, just shook his head, turned and strode away. She watched the movement of his muscular behind and tried to ignore the hot tug low in her belly.

She wished she had a disposable phone so she could call Lisa. Her best friend was an expert on men. Surely she could suggest a way to deal with the situation Tory found herself in.

She thought about catching up to Josh, asking him to buy her a cheap disposable phone, but she didn't want to inconvenience him.

She thought about tomorrow and the riding lesson he had promised to give her. Images arose of a different sort of riding, and heat scorched her face. Tory shoved away her embarrassing thoughts and headed for the house.

Chapter Eleven

Josh pulled his white Ford F-150 up in front of Jim Stevens's house, a nice brick ranch-style not too far from town. Randy was out of high school but as far as Josh knew, the kid still lived at home.

Josh hadn't lived in Iron Springs that long, but the town was small enough he already knew a lot of people. The story written about his career as a marine sniper had made him a local celebrity.

The help he'd given Beau Reese and the Pleasant Hill Police Department during a hostage rescue two months ago had made him even more recognizable—unfortunately.

Josh climbed out of the truck and walked up the cement path, climbed the steps, and knocked on the front door. It took a while, but when the door finally swung wide, Randy Stevens stood on the other side of the opening.

"You got a minute?" Josh asked.

The lanky black-haired teen glanced over his shoulder as if checking to be sure no one was around. "I guess so." He stepped outside and closed the door.

"You hear about the fire over at my place?"

Randy shrugged his slim shoulders. "Everybody in town heard about it."

"Sheriff Howler talk to you?" Josh asked.

"About what?" Randy stuck his hands into his jeans pockets and rocked back on his heels.

"About the possibility you stole five gallons of gas from me, I fired you, and as payback you used the gas to burn down my barn."

Randy's dark eyes flared, then went hard. "You got nothing on me, soldier man. You think I burned down your barn, prove it."

"I didn't say you did it. I asked you if the sheriff talked to you about it."

"He and my dad are friends."

"Fine, then I'm the one asking you. Did you burn down my barn?"

Randy smirked. "You shouldn't have fired me."

Josh clamped down on his temper. "You aren't even going to deny it?"

The kid just shrugged. "I didn't say I did it. I know my rights. I'm not sayin' nothin'." But the look on his face made it clear he was the one who'd set the fire and he was proud of what he'd done.

Fury sent a jolt of adrenaline into Josh's veins. "What about the horses, Randy? Killing helpless animals didn't bother you?"

Randy's spine stiffened. "I knew you'd get 'em out. They weren't in any real danger."

"You little shit." Josh grabbed the kid by the front of his T-shirt and shoved him up against the wall. "You damn near got a woman killed! You really want to spend the rest of your life in prison for murder?"

"Let me go!" Randy squirmed.

Josh slammed him up against the wall again. "You come near my place, I swear I'll shoot you on sight. And one thing you've probably heard about me—I don't miss."

The door swung open and Randy's father appeared. "What's going on out here?"

Josh let Randy go, but stood between him and escape. "I'll tell you what's going on. That spoiled kid of yours burned down my barn and nearly killed my horses."

"That's ridiculous." Jim Stevens was black-haired like his boy, but filled out in the chest and shoulders from years of hard work. "Randy would never do a thing like that."

"You don't think so? Why don't you ask him?"

Stevens's gaze swung to his son. "Tell the man you had nothing to do with that fire."

Randy glanced away.

"Randy, tell Josh you weren't involved in the fire."

Randy looked at Josh. "Okay, I didn't do it. He's just making it up." He turned back to his dad. "Happy now?"

Stevens caught his son's chin and held it immobile. "Look me in the eye and tell me you didn't set that barn on fire."

Hot color rushed into Randy's face. At nineteen, he was plenty old enough to know right from wrong.

"Did you set that barn on fire?" his father pressed.

Randy's mouth thinned and his narrow face went iron hard. He jerked away. "He had it coming! He had no call to fire me!"

"Good God!" Jim Stevens looked appalled. "This is what comes from your mother's refusal to discipline you. I let her raise you and look how you turned out! I should have paddled your ass years ago instead of letting your mother spoil you rotten. Now get in the house!" He shoved the kid inside and slammed the door behind him.

Stevens shook his head. "I don't know what to say. I can't wrap my head around it."

"You're not going to be able to ignore this, Jim. If you do and it happens again, someone might get killed."

Stevens blew out a shaky breath. "I won't ignore it. I promise you. I'll figure a way to make it right."

"You can't make this right for your son. That won't solve anything. Randy has to make it right for himself."

Stevens ran the back of his hand over his mouth. "You're right. I'll call Emmett Howler, turn the boy in myself. My wife will go ballistic, but maybe if I'd stepped in sooner, this wouldn't have happened."

Josh just nodded. "I'm sorry."

"So am I," Stevens said.

Turning, Josh walked back to his truck, got in, and fired the engine. Making a U-turn, he headed back the way he had come. It was five o'clock somewhere and he really needed a drink.

He checked his watch. Hell, it was five-thirty right now in Iron Springs. Pulling onto the highway, he headed for Jubal's Roadhouse. After his run-in with the kid, it was way worse than a Lone Star night. He needed a shot of Jack Daniel's.

The good news was, Damon Bridger hadn't set the fire. At least for now, Tory and Ivy were safe.

He hit the hands-free button and pushed the number for the landline he used for business. He'd been putting off hiring someone to design an Iron River Ranch webpage and set up the ranch's bookkeeping and tax records, but he'd need to do it soon.

The phone rang a couple of times before Tory picked up, which reminded him to buy her one of those throwaway phones to use when she was in the trailer. He didn't like her being over there with no way to communicate.

"Tory, it's Josh," he said.

"Hey, Josh."

Just hearing her voice made his groin tighten. He couldn't believe it. "You don't have to worry about Bridger. Randy Stevens set the fire."

"Oh, God, that's the teenage boy you hired?"

"Randy's nineteen. Grown up enough to know the difference between right and wrong."

"Did the sheriff arrest him?"

"Not yet, but odds are he will. His father's taking care of it. I trust him to handle it."

"At least it wasn't Damon. I can't tell you what a relief that is."

"Yeah. Listen, I've got to go. You and Ivy have a good night."

"You too," she said softly.

He was hard by the time he hung up. It made no sense. She wasn't even his type. He liked big, buxom women, the kind who could handle what a man his size had to give. Not some petite little female half afraid of men. For him sex was a stress reliever. He didn't want to have to hold back, worry about hurting the lady in his bed.

He stopped by the grocery store to pick up a couple of items and buy that phone, then headed for Jubal's, even more in need of a drink after talking to Tory. When his phone rang, he hit the hands-free. "Josh Cain."

"Josh, it's Noble Blanchard." The guy he'd bought the ranch from. "I got your call about the stallion."

"What can you tell me about him?"

"I bought that horse as part of a package deal, just the way I sold him to you. The previous owner was a fella named Porter Sturgis. Sturgis is kind of an a-hole, if you don't mind my saying. Treats his stock really poorly."

"Makes him worse than an a-hole in my book."

"Sturgis had the stallion for a while, but the horse was raised from a colt by a woman named Amanda Bonner. When she was killed in a boating accident, the horse was sold to Porter."

"You think Porter's mistreatment was what made the stallion so crazy?"

"I hate to spread gossip, but yes, that's what I think."

"I appreciate the help, Noble." And it might just be the answer to the question he'd wanted answered.

Why did the stallion respond to Tory and no one else?

After talking to Noble, Josh believed the obvious might be correct. The horse trusted her because she was a woman.

He ended the call as he pulled into the parking lot of Jubal's, a false-fronted wood-framed building at the edge of town that looked like something out of the Wild West. Even had a board walkway out front.

Jubal's was a locals' joint that served good food and cheap pitchers of beer. The place catered to both cowboys and bikers, mostly without trouble. *Mostly*.

As he shoved through the swinging doors, peanut shells crunched beneath his boots. Pool balls clacked on green felt tables in the back, and Garth Brooks sang "Friends in Low Places" from the digital jukebox in the corner.

He hadn't expected to see Cole and Noah sitting at the bar or Linc's blond wife, Carly, seated at a battered wooden table next to her high school girlfriend, Brittany Haworth, a blue-eyed brunette.

At the moment, Britt's gaze was locked on Cole, though he didn't seem to notice. When she realized Josh had caught her staring, her cheeks turned apple red.

He bit back a smile as he approached, leaned down, and kissed his sister-in-law on the cheek. "Hey, Carly."

She turned. "Josh! It's so good to see you. It seems like ages. You remember my friend Brittany, don't you?"

"Sure." He smiled. "Hey, Britt."

"Hello, Josh. Why don't you join us?"

He pulled out a chair and sat down, then turned back to Carly, who was picking at the last of an order of French fries. "So you and Linc are back at the ranch?"

"I'm staying out there. I had some stuff to do at work." Carly was the owner of Drake Trucking. She and Linc had met when a drug lord had threatened Carly's business. "Linc's in New Mexico. Work's been really crazy for him lately."

At the bar, Noah spotted Josh and waved, and Josh waved back. "Have you met Noah Beal and Cole Wyman?" he asked, thinking of the pretty brunette who seemed so interested in Cole.

"Cole went to community college with Britt," Carly said. "Linc introduced us to Noah in here one night. They're friends of yours?"

"They work for me. Great guys." Josh waved them over and both men slid off their stools and walked over to the table.

"Ladies." Noah, always friendly, flashed a warm smile. Cole gave a curt nod of his head.

"Why don't you two join us?" Carly suggested.

"Why not?" Noah agreed. The men pulled chairs up to the table. Josh ordered a shot of Jack Daniel's to settle him down and a Lone Star to quench his thirst. He bought Noah and Cole each a fresh beer. The women hadn't finished the ones they were drinking.

They talked for a while, mostly about the fire. "I heard it was arson," Carly said. "Have they caught the guy who did it?"

"It was a kid who worked for me. I left it to his dad to handle things. I don't think we'll have to worry about it happening somewhere else."

"That's a relief," Carly said.

They chatted a little while longer. Finally Noah rose from his chair. "I hate to have to leave such sterling company, but I've got a sexy wife waiting for me at home and a job that starts early in the morning. 'Night, y'all."

Cole had barely said three words and Brittany hadn't

talked much, either. Didn't look like that relationship had much chance of getting off the ground.

"I better be going, too," Cole said.

"Me too," said Brittany.

"Why don't you walk Britt out to her car?" Josh suggested, figuring maybe he could give his friend a little push. "You never know who might be lurking out in the dark." Though there was rarely any sort of problem at Jubal's.

Cole nodded. "Sure."

Brittany flushed. "You don't have to do that if you don't want to."

Cole's head snapped up. "Why not? You think if trouble comes, I won't be able to handle it?"

Britt's dark eyes widened. "No, of course not. You're in amazing shape. I don't think any guy in here would be stupid enough to go against you."

Cole blinked as if he were coming out of a fog. He cleared his throat. "Sorry. I'll walk you out. Make sure you get to your car okay."

Brittany beamed. "Thank you." She was a beautiful woman, which Cole had just seemed to notice. Or maybe he'd noticed a long time ago, but after losing his legs, no longer had the self-confidence to do anything about it.

As soon as they were gone, Carly stood up from her chair. "I have to go, too."

"I'll walk you out." Before he had the chance, Billie Joe Hardie stepped in his way, a tall, leggy woman in a short, tight skirt, with lots of blond hair, big cleavage, and plenty of it on display.

She flashed a sexy smile. "You aren't leaving yet, are you, honey? I was hoping you'd buy me a drink."

"My car's parked right in front," Carly said. "I'll be fine. Have fun."

Waving her fingers in farewell, she was gone before he

could stop her, and aside from the shot of Jack, the reason he had come to Jubal's tonight was standing right in front of him.

He hadn't known for sure she'd be there, but he had definitely hoped so.

"What are you drinking?" he asked as she sat down in the chair across from him.

"Same as you, hun."

The waitress walked up just then, a willowy blonde named Rita who went with one of the bartenders. "What'll y'all have?" she asked.

"The lady wants a shot of Jack, Rita."

"You got it." Rita returned a few minutes later, set a shot glass down on the table, and wandered away. Billie Joe picked up the whiskey and tossed it back, set the glass sharply back down.

"I've got a bottle of this stuff at home," she said. "You ready to blow this joint and have a little fun?" Billie Joe smiled and he caught a whiff of her strong perfume. She moved, giving him a look down the front of her low-cut blouse.

His gaze went over the blowsy woman in front of him. When had his tastes shifted from too much of a good thing to smaller was just enough? When had the notion of taking this woman to bed become more a chore than a pleasure?

It was crazy, but suddenly leaving the bar with Billie Joe was the last thing he wanted. He took a long draw on his beer, set it back down.

"I'm afraid I'll have to take a rain check, Billie. I've got a couple of things I need to do out at the ranch."

She gave him a seductive glance from beneath the heavy mascara on her lashes. "Well, now, that's a real shame, cowboy."

"Maybe next time." But he didn't think so.

He'd find someone else, he told himself. There had to be a woman somewhere in Iron Springs who appealed to him, someone besides a tempting little redhead who was nothing but a handful of trouble.

Finishing off his beer, he crossed the room, shoved through the swinging doors, and walked out into the humid Texas night. Along with the hard truth that Billie Joe wasn't the woman he wanted, he didn't like leaving Tory out at the ranch alone. Not until things settled down and he could be sure she and Ivy were safe.

He didn't want to think about the restless night he'd be facing. For two cents, he'd turn around and walk back inside, at least get a little sexual relief.

Instead he climbed into his truck, fired up the engine, and drove back to the ranch. With any luck, by now Randy Stevens was in jail. At least he wouldn't have to worry about an arsonist.

Only a brutal stalker and the woman and her little girl he had sworn to protect.

Chapter Twelve

Lisa curled up naked beneath a scratchy wool blanket on the mattress in the corner. Her wrists were bound in front of her with nylon ties, her ankles also bound. She had been locked in the basement since Damon had broken into her Phoenix home, tased her, and taken her to a log cabin somewhere in the Arizona mountains.

At least the gag was gone. There was no reason to scream for help when there was no one around to hear her. She had tried, yelled until her throat was raw, but it hadn't done any good. As Damon had known it wouldn't.

Just thinking of him brought a rush of tears and sent a shiver of revulsion over her skin. He was an animal. A monster. The night he had brought her to the cabin, he had tied her up, beaten her, and raped her. Her ribs ached and her lip was split and swollen.

She had tried to fight him, twisted her ankle trying to get away from him, but he was strong and he was brutal, and he clearly got pleasure out of her resistance.

How had he fooled her and Tory so completely?

She thought of killers like Ted Bundy and John Wayne

Gacy, guys people had thought were really nice. Just like Damon.

She shivered. Would he go as far as murder? Maybe he already had. She knew his identity. How could he let her go?

The thought made her stomach roll with nausea.

Forcing the grim thought away, she glanced at her surroundings as she had done a thousand times, looking for something she'd missed, some way to escape.

All she saw were rough cement walls, the cold cement floor, and a set of wooden stairs leading to a door into the main part of the cabin.

From the more than two hours it had taken to drive there, she figured the place was somewhere on the way to Flagstaff or Williams. She had skied Snowbowl. She knew there were dozens of remote cabins all through the mountains north of Phoenix.

She shifted on the mattress, her wrists pulling against the thin band of white nylon biting into her flesh. She sucked in a breath at the pain and eased into a more comfortable position.

Though she was securely bound, she was free to move around the basement, to access the small refrigerator Damon had stocked with food, the bottles of water stacked beside it, to reach the portable toilet behind the curtain in the corner.

Before and after he'd raped her, he had forced her to shower in the tiny bathroom upstairs. As she thought back, Damon had always been overly fastidious, his shoes polished to a glossy sheen, his black hair perfectly groomed, his expensive suits impeccably tailored.

Both she and Tory had been impressed with his good looks and charm when they had first met him. Lisa had even been a little envious that Damon had been attracted to Tory instead of her.

What a joke that was. A joke definitely on her.

She surveyed her surroundings. It was late. Moonlight

streamed into the basement through narrow windows on two sides at the top of the cement walls. The windows tilted out, opening enough for ventilation but too small for her to fit through. It was agony to be so close to freedom and not be able to escape.

She lay back on the mattress, which appeared to be brand-new. She thought that Damon had recently outfitted the basement with her kidnapping in mind. Or more likely he had prepared the basement for Tory. She wondered where her friend was now, prayed she was okay, desperately needed her to call.

Sooner or later, Tory would phone. The two of them had been friends since they had met in junior college, the kind of friends who stood by each other through an ugly divorce, a difficult pregnancy, the death of a husband. The kind of friends who could count on each other no matter what.

Now Damon had Lisa's phone and there was no way to know what would happen when Tory called. It had been Friday night when Damon had abducted her. Two sunny days had passed outside the narrow windows. She could see stars again. It had to be late Sunday or sometime after midnight early Monday morning.

When she didn't show up at work, someone would call the house. Would they start looking for her? Probably not the first day, but if she didn't show up on Tuesday and didn't answer her cell phone, one of the girls would go to her house to check on her.

If she didn't answer the door, whoever it was might call the police, but if the cops went inside, they wouldn't find much: the bed mussed but no real sign of a struggle. The stun gun had been efficient and Damon had been wearing gloves.

How long before they started really searching for her? And how would they have any idea where to look?

Her stomach twisted into a cold, hard knot. Unless Tory called on Lisa's phone and Damon answered.

If Damon picked up, Tory would know something bad had happened. As soon as she found out Lisa hadn't shown up for work, she would know Damon had done something terrible to her. She would call the police and they would arrest him, force him to tell them where he had taken her.

But what if he convinced them he knew nothing about her disappearance? The man was an amazingly good actor. She and Tory could both attest to that. She prayed the police would figure out the truth before Damon came back to the cabin.

Before he forced her to submit to him the way he had before. If he did, she would do it. She wanted to live. She would do whatever it took to survive until she could escape.

She fisted the hands bound in front of her. She would find a way out of the cabin and once she was free, she would make Damon Bridger pay.

Today was Tory's riding lesson. The morning slipped past going over alphabet cards at the kitchen table at Josh's house with Ivy. When Mrs. Thompson showed up and the time for her lesson drew near, she realized what a bad idea it was.

Every minute she spent with Josh was turning into an agony of sexual frustration. She wanted him. And though she kept trying to convince herself having sex with Joshua Cain would be a stupid thing to do, she couldn't deny the urge.

She kept thinking about last night, how she'd wondered where he was, whether he was with another woman. She knew he was attracted to her. At least she was fairly certain. When he looked at her, the hot gleam in those deep blue eyes spoke volumes.

Last night, she'd found herself waiting up, watching for

his pickup headlights to come rolling down the dirt road back to the ranch. She'd felt a ridiculous wave of relief when he'd pulled up in front of his house well before nine P.M.

She didn't think he had been with a woman last night, but Josh was a virile man and a man like that had needs. Sooner or later, he would find himself a woman, and the straight truth was, Tory wanted to be that woman.

She glanced up at a knock on Josh's front door. She always kept the door locked just in case. Seeing Josh, she waved good-bye to Mrs. Thompson and Ivy and pulled the door open.

"You ready for your riding lesson?"

Riding lesson. Dear God in heaven. Her eyes ran over the hot male in front of her. Tory swallowed, trying to block the image that rose in her head.

She managed to smile. "Ready as I'll ever be."

In his usual faded jeans and a dark blue T-shirt that hugged his chest and biceps, he pushed up the brim of his beat-up cowboy hat, waited for her to walk past him across the porch, then fell in behind her.

Her heart was racing and it had nothing to do with the sudden realization she was actually going to have to learn to ride a horse.

"You ever been on a horse before?" Josh asked when they reached the cow barn, which he and Cole had reinforced after the horse barn burned down.

It wasn't much, but at least it provided a shady place out of the weather for the animals and a room off to one side for the new saddles, bridles, and other miscellaneous tack Josh had purchased.

"I went on a couple of desert trail rides before I had Ivy. The horses were pretty old."

Josh walked over to where a little sorrel with two white stocking feet stood saddled and ready. "This is Rosebud.

She's twelve. Nice and calm, but she's not like those rental horses. Rose has plenty of spunk." He scratched the mare's forehead. "Don't you, girl?" The horse nickered softly.

Josh ran a hand along the animal's sleek neck. The confident glide of his fingers made Tory's skin feel hot. Rosebud rubbed her head against his shoulder.

Josh had a way with animals. She had noticed that before. Except for Star.

"We'll need to adjust your stirrups."

She took a deep breath. "Okay."

"Put you knee here and I'll give you a boost." He clasped his fingers together and bent down. Tory put her knee in his cupped hands and he boosted her so easily she nearly went over the other side of the saddle.

Josh chuckled. "Sorry. I forgot how little you are." The minute he said the words, the smile slid off his face. Why the thought upset him, she had no idea.

"You didn't hurt me. I'm fine."

He was all business again, adjusting the stirrups, showing her the correct position, how to hold the reins, keep them loose and low, with just enough pressure. The problem was that in order to show her, he had to touch her, and every time he touched her, she wanted to slide off the horse into his arms.

Oh, this was so bad. How had she ever come up with such a stupid idea?

Josh must have agreed because he got quieter and quieter, as if forcing each word out was a challenge.

"Let's . . . umm . . . go into the arena." He led Rosebud into the fenced-in ring and directed Tory to ride in a circle, first walking, then trotting. Josh taught her to post, which kept her from bouncing around like a fool.

She rode for an hour, found herself enjoying the feel of the animal responding to her subtle commands.

"You're doing great but we'd better stop for the day. You'll be sore tomorrow if we don't."

A hot mental picture arose. She'd be pleasure-sore if Josh did what she wanted him to do.

As he tied the mare to a ring in the wall, she glanced down at him, into eyes as blue and hot as the tip of a flame. Josh reached up and wrapped his hands around her waist. Tory set her palms on those wide shoulders and felt his amazing muscles bunch. It was too much. She couldn't take it anymore.

When he swung her to the ground, she didn't let go, just went up on her tiptoes, slid her arms around his neck, and kissed him for all she was worth.

Josh growled low in his throat. A moment's hesitation, then he was kissing her back, his tongue in her mouth, hers in his, walking her backward till she came up against the rough board wall.

Tory slid her hands beneath his T-shirt, ran her fingers over the hot, smooth skin underneath, traced the jagged line of his scar. His muscles flexed and tightened and she moaned.

Josh tugged his T-shirt off over his head, tossed it away, and kissed her again, long, slow, and deep. Tory traced his six-pack abs, his pecs, wrapped her fingers around a thick bicep. She was hot all over, barely able to breathe. All those beautiful muscles felt better than she could have imagined, and Josh really knew how to kiss.

His fingers worked the buttons on the front of her blouse, fumbling, trying to unfasten them. Tory did it for him, tugging so hard on the last button it went flying across the barn. When he popped the clasp on the front of her bra and filled his hands with her breasts, she thought she might actually faint.

But when she started to peel the blouse off her shoulders,

Josh went still. He caught her hands, pushed them aside, and began to pull the fabric back in place.

"Noah and Cole are coming in for fresh supplies."

Tory whimpered. *No*. She was shaking. *God, this can't be happening*.

Leaving her to refasten the rest of the buttons—all but the missing one—he grabbed his T-shirt and pulled it on over his head.

"Go back to the house. I'll take care of Cole and Noah."

She just nodded, her face the color of a tomato. She was beginning to realize what she had done. She'd almost had sex with Joshua Cain, had physically attacked him out in the cow barn. *Oh. My. God*.

She didn't know whether to apologize or pack her bags and head off down the road. She wanted to tell him she had never done anything like that before but if she did, she would probably sound like an idiot.

Moving quickly as the men roared up on their ATVs, she headed back to the house, pausing for a moment outside the front door to compose herself, praying Mrs. Thompson wouldn't notice the pulse fluttering at the base of her throat or the slight flush remaining in her cheeks.

She prayed she would still have a job in the morning.

Oh, dear God.

"We came back for a fresh load of fence posts," Noah said. "Got farther along than we thought we would."

He nodded. "That's good. You get a chance to check on those cows up by the pond?"

Determined to keep his gaze from straying to the house, Josh forced himself to concentrate on the work that needed to be done and not the feel of Tory's full breasts in his hands.

The memory sent a fresh rush of heat into his groin, making his already snug jeans even tighter.

"They were fine," Cole said. "Got plenty to eat, that's for sure."

"There's a crew coming in tomorrow," Josh said. "Heavy equipment to tear down what's left of the barn and haul it away, get the pad ready for building the new one. I'll need you here to help."

"No problem," Cole said.

"Be smart to get a new barn up as soon as possible." Noah glanced over at the pile of charred, blackened wood. "Weather can be crazy around here."

"That's for sure," Josh said, thinking at the moment, he was the one who'd gone crazy.

The men headed over to the stack of fence posts and spools of twisted wire and began reloading the supply trailer.

Josh went back to work on the cow barn. He tried to concentrate on tearing out the big, termite-riddled frame around the wide double doors, replacing it with new lumber, but his mind kept returning to Tory.

What could he say to her? How could he explain what he had very nearly done? He still didn't understand how an innocent little kiss had exploded into something so hot it had very nearly cost him his highly prized control.

If Noah and Cole hadn't shown up, he was pretty damn sure he would have taken Tory right there in the dirty old cow barn.

What the fuck was he thinking?

He wasn't using his head, that was for sure. Or at least not his big head. He couldn't remember ever feeling so close to the edge, and he sure as hell didn't like it.

Not one bit.

He didn't know what he was going to say to her. If she didn't need his protection so badly, he would give her a fat chunk of severance pay and send her down the road. He would be doing her a favor, doing the best thing for both of them.

But he couldn't do it. Not with her predator ex-boyfriend still on the hunt.

He'd talk to her, he decided. They were both adults. They could discuss what had happened, come to an understanding of why it couldn't happen again.

Tory was a smart girl. She understood it wasn't right for a boss and his employee to share a physical relationship. He'd talk to her tonight after she put Ivy to bed. Make sure they were both on the same page.

He just needed to work up the nerve.

Chapter Thirteen

Tory worried the rest of the afternoon. What could she possibly say to Josh? It was entirely her fault. The man was simply teaching her how to ride a horse and she had attacked him. She was so far beyond embarrassed she couldn't believe it.

And yet there was a tiny secret part of her that wished he hadn't stopped when he had. A tiny feminine part that wanted to take that wild, amazing ride all the way to the finish.

She wanted him now more than ever. Would he see the hunger stamped in her face the moment he looked at her? She prayed to God he wouldn't. If he did, he would probably fire her on the spot.

Or maybe not. The way he'd touched her, kissed her, there was a chance he had wanted her as much as she'd wanted him.

Either way, it wasn't going to happen. She would tell him that as soon as she saw him, explain that something she didn't completely understand had happened but she wouldn't allow it to happen again.

She thought about it the rest of the afternoon and the entire time she was making him supper, mentally preparing herself to face him. By the time she had the ham baked and the green beans with bacon cooked, she was ready.

Unfortunately, Josh didn't come in to eat. After an hour of waiting, she fixed him a plate and shoved it into the oven, bagged up her portion, and put the rest of the food in the refrigerator. She took Ivy's hand, and they walked back to the trailer.

By the time they had finished their supper and she had put Ivy to bed, she was sure Josh had decided to fire her. She would have to leave the ranch, find a place in another town, another state. She felt sick just thinking about it. She tried to mentally prepare herself, but kept clinging to the fragile hope he would let her stay.

She wasn't willing to barter herself—offer sex in exchange for keeping her job. That was never going to happen, though the notion had an embarrassing amount of appeal. Still, there was a chance they could come to some kind of understanding. She should at least give it a try.

It was getting late. She'd give anything to talk to Lisa, tell her what was happening, get some best-friend advice. Lisa was her rock, the one person she could always count on.

Tory toed off her sneakers and was starting to get undressed when she heard Josh's familiar three quick raps on the door. Her pulse kicked up. Hurrying across the living room, she stopped to check the peephole just to be sure, then pulled open the door.

Josh stood on the porch, his features grim. Her heart squeezed.

"You got a minute to talk?" he asked.

She swallowed, nodded, stepped out on the porch and quietly closed the door. The night was warm, a light breeze rustling through the thick green grasses. She could hear birds lifting off a pond close to the house.

Josh pulled something out of his back pocket and set it on the wooden table next to the door. Moonlight slanted down, illuminating the cleft in his chin and the planes of his handsome face. "I bought you a phone when I was in town."

Thank God. Now she could call her friend. "You can deduct it from my—"

He held up a hand, silencing her.

"Thank you," she said.

Josh looked down at her. They both started to speak at the same time. "I'm sorry about what happened," they said in unison.

"It wasn't your fault," they both said.

"I'm sorry," she said softly.

"Not your fault," Josh said, but of course it was.

His hand came up to her cheek. He was staring at her mouth. She looked into those blue, blue eyes and everything inside her clenched.

She told herself not to do it, that it was too big a risk. But her heart wasn't listening. Rising up on her toes, she very softly kissed him. Josh went utterly still.

"We can't, Tory." He pushed a copper curl away from her face.

"I know. It shouldn't have happened the first time."

Josh just nodded. Bending his head, he brushed a featherlight kiss over her lips, just the briefest of touches. Her breath hitched, came out on a sigh.

His eyes darkened, the blue turning nearly black. "I want you," he said. "So damned much."

"I want you, too."

Josh's big hand slid into her hair. He pulled her into his arms, his mouth crushed down over hers, and Tory melted. When her lips parted in invitation, his tongue swept in. Instead of stopping, it was as if something broke free. Josh took, demanded, didn't back away, made her want everything she had missed out on that afternoon.

His kiss was hot, wet, and deep, his hands in her hair, holding her in place as he ravaged her lips. Tory shoved up his T-shirt. Josh dragged it off over his head and tossed it away. Her hands ran over his chest, tracing the hard planes and valleys, the twisted flesh on his side, a mark of honor from the war. In the moonlight he looked like a warrior fashioned in bronze.

Josh unbuttoned her blouse, his fingers steadier this time but not much. He shoved the fabric off her shoulders, let it fall to the porch. Tory unhooked her bra and shrugged it off, rose up and kissed him, felt the heat of his hands on her breasts, big hands, strong and calloused, hands that seemed to know exactly how to touch her, caress her, make her burn.

She moaned, everything inside her aching with need and on fire. Trembling, she bent and pressed her mouth against a flat copper nipple. Josh's fingers slid back into her hair, holding her in place as she circled the hard tip with her tongue.

He groaned, dragged her mouth back to his and kissed her, first one way and then another, kissed her and kissed her and kissed her. Both of them were breathing hard, gasping for air when he pulled away.

"Tory, baby, if we don't stop now, I won't be able to."

"I don't want you to stop." She leaned up and pressed a kiss against his jaw, felt the rough stubble she found so appealing.

"I don't want to hurt you, honey."

"You won't hurt me. Please, Josh. I need you."

"Jesus, God, you have no idea how bad I want you." He kissed the side of her neck, nipped the place below her ear just hard enough for her to feel it. "I'm not a gentle lover. If I take you, you'll know it. Are you sure?"

Heat and need rolled through her, followed by an instant of uncertainty as she thought of Damon. But this was Josh. He had helped her when no one else would. He had been kind to Ivy. This was Josh and she trusted him.

And she wanted him like she had never wanted another

man. Just once, she wanted to experience this wild desire, wanted to claim this moment of passion for herself. "Yes . . ."

The single word was all the encouragement he needed. In minutes her jeans were gone and she stood on the porch in nothing but a pair of white cotton bikini panties. The next thing she knew, those were gone, too, and he was kissing her again, lifting her, wrapping her legs around his waist.

His belt buckle jangled. His zipper buzzed down. She was hungry for him, dizzy, and on fire.

"I don't want to hurt you."

"I want you inside me. Please, Josh."

His big hands gripped her bottom as he moved backward, propping her shoulders against the wall. Kissing her hard, he surged upward, taking her deep, filling her completely. When she gasped, Josh cursed.

"I'm sorry. I—"

"Don't stop. Oh, God, Josh, don't stop." She moved on him, taking him deeper, feeling his heavy arousal, the heat, moaning, destroying the last of his control.

Josh drove into her again and again. He was big and he was hard and he felt incredible. Tory clung to him as the first wave struck, sent pleasure burning through her. She moaned and clung to his neck.

The second climax shocked her, left her limp and barely able to hang on. He rode her into another amazing climax— impossible, she thought as he finally let himself go, reaching his own powerful release.

Time spun out, seemed to stand utterly still. Eventually they began to spiral down, Tory limp against Josh's chest. Kissing her one last time, he slowly lowered her to her feet.

Her legs were shaking. She felt exhausted yet alive with energy. Tory stared up at him. "Oh. My. God."

He frowned. "Did I hurt you?"

She couldn't stop a smile. "You were amazing."

His wide shoulders relaxed. "That's good. Better than

good. I'll be right back." He was wearing a condom, she realized, and couldn't believe this was the first time she had thought of protection. *Oh. My. God.*

The good news was, thanks to Damon, she was on a tiny birth control implant called Nexplanon that lasted for up to three years.

Josh returned a few minutes later, grabbed her panties and jeans off the porch, and handed them over. "I came here to talk. I guess it's too late for that now."

Her face colored. She couldn't believe she had actually had sex with Josh Cain against the wall in front of her house.

She didn't know whether to apologize again or just leave before he fired her. Instead, she put her panties back on and pulled on her jeans, put on her blouse without the bra.

"I can see your mind working," Josh said as he dragged his T-shirt over his head. "What's going on in that female brain of yours?"

"I don't know. I can hardly think."

His mouth edged up for the first time that night. "In this particular case, that's not a bad thing."

"I don't understand how it happened. I couldn't seem to help myself. It was like I went a little crazy."

"I know the feeling. How long since you've had sex?"

"If that was sex, I've never had it before."

Josh laughed and the sound turned her inside out.

"This is not how I saw this going down," he said.

"How did you see it going down?"

"If you want the truth, I didn't see it happening."

"Ever?"

"No, but now that it has, I'm not sorry."

"We can't do it again."

His jaw locked and he glanced away. "I know."

"You're my boss and it wouldn't be right."

He just nodded. "That's what I came here to tell you."

He sighed. "If you still want to stay, I give you my word it won't happen again."

She believed him. If a man like Josh Cain gave you his word, he kept it. Sex with him would never happen again.

That was what she wanted, wasn't it? She didn't want to be the kind of woman the sheriff and the fire chief thought she was. Add to that she didn't believe in strictly physical relationships—friends with benefits—and she knew that was all this was.

On the other hand, she was a grown woman raising a child. She was a woman with needs like any other woman. She could do whatever she wanted. And she wanted more of Joshua Cain.

So why the hell not?

She heard the words tumbling out of her mouth even before they completely registered in her brain. "On second thought, we're both adults. Why not enjoy ourselves for as long as the attraction lasts? Eventually I'll be leaving, moving somewhere Ivy and I can make a new life. In the meantime, as long as I'm what you want and you're what I want . . ."

She let the words trail off. The next instant, she was pressed against the wall, with Josh's mouth crushing down over hers. The kiss went on until her head spun and her knees went weak.

Finally he let her go. "You sure about this?"

"If you're sure I'm what you want."

"Oh, you're what I want. I think we've established we're both currently in lust."

She nodded. "Yes, I suppose that explains it. But it won't be easy, not with a child in the house."

The corner of his mouth kicked up. "Don't worry, honey, we'll figure it out."

Tory looked into his hard, handsome face and felt a rush of longing that should have been a warning.

Instead she just said, "Okay."

Tory checked on Ivy. The little girl was curled on her side clutching Pansy, deeply asleep. Leaning over, Tory kissed her forehead, then headed down the hall to her bedroom. Until tonight, the bed had never looked empty and uninviting.

She thought about what had happened between her and Josh. She had known by the look in those amazing blue eyes that he'd wanted her again, but he had just kissed her and said good night.

Part of her was grateful. He was giving her time, giving them both a chance to rethink the situation. She wondered if, in the cold light of day, she would regret what she had done, wondered how Josh would feel.

But Tory's decision was made. Just this once, she was taking something for herself. No matter how brief the affair, she wanted this time with Josh.

She looked at the cheap plastic phone he had bought her. She desperately needed to talk to Lisa. She had never needed her friend's advice more. But it was late and tomorrow was a workday.

Pulling on an oversize T-shirt, she set the disposable on the nightstand in her bedroom and slid beneath the covers. First thing in the morning, she would call her best friend.

Chapter Fourteen

Another endless day had passed. It was late, the moon spearing light between the branches of the pine trees in the dense forest around the cabin. But Lisa couldn't sleep. It was cold and musty in the basement, the scratchy wool blanket tossed over the mattress not nearly warm enough.

She huddled, shaking, her teeth chattering, cursing the monster who had brought her here. She'd thought that by now he would have returned. He would be back, she was sure—it was only a matter of time.

Time, usually something she'd never had enough of, dragged endlessly here. But during those endless hours, she'd had time to think, time to come up with a plan.

Instead of dreading their next encounter, Lisa found herself praying for Damon's return, praying for the chance to put her plan into motion. She was ready, more than ready.

She glanced at the spot on the rough cement wall, the circle she had scratched into the cement with her fingernails. They were broken now, two of them bloody, but the sharp edge she had marked was easy to find.

Where are you? she thought. *I'm waiting for you, Damon.*

She had accepted the fact that sooner or later Damon was

going to kill her. After what he had done, he couldn't let her live. He would kill her if she let him.

She wasn't going to give him the chance.

A distant sound reached her, drawing her attention to the window. As if her prayers had been answered, she heard the whine of an engine coming up the dirt road, the crunch of gravel as a car pulled up in front of the cabin.

Her pulse began racing as the engine went off and the car door opened. She clamped down on the urge to scream for help. The windows were too high for her to see out, but she knew in every cell of her body it was Damon.

She listened to the thump of heavy footfalls crossing the screened-in porch, then the lock turning, the door opening and closing. He was here. He had come to satisfy his sick desires. She couldn't let herself think what he planned to do, couldn't let herself remember the last time.

It wasn't going to happen again.

She was going to escape.

Overhead she could hear him walking around the cabin. He'd be coming down any minute now. Moving awkwardly, as fast as her bound ankles would allow, she made her way over to the wall. Taking a breath, she pressed her forearm on the jagged piece of cement and jerked her arm down, slicing long and deep enough to make sure there'd be plenty of blood.

Hissing against the pain, she made her way clumsily back to the mattress and lay down, smearing the blood running down her forearm over the mattress beneath where she sat and between her legs.

The basement door opened. In the moonlight, she could barely make out Damon's evil, handsome face as he descended the stairs.

"Hello, sweetheart," he said. "Did you miss me?"

She swallowed the bile that rose in her throat. "I didn't miss you, Damon. I loathe the sight of you."

"You loathe me? I would think after the last time, you would know better than to speak to me that way. I doubt you've forgotten the punishment I meted out."

Her ribs still ached; one of her eyes was swollen shut. She fought not to whimper.

"Loathe me all you want," he said as he descended the stairs, "I'm still going to fuck you." He paused to flip the light switch, illuminating the single stark bulb in the ceiling overhead. "We'll enjoy ourselves; then in the morning, you're going to call your office. You're going to tell them you have the flu and you'll be out the rest of the week."

Oh, God. She should have known he would have it all figured out.

He took another step and paused. "What is that on the mattress?"

She gave him a disgusted smile. "It's blood, Damon. I started my period."

He recoiled as if she had slapped him, just as she had known he would.

"Well, your timing is just perfect, isn't it? I'm not about to touch you in your filthy condition. You need a shower. There are supplies in the bathroom under the sink. Once you're clean, you can use your mouth on me."

Her lip curled, making her hatred clear. "I guess you thought of everything."

"Get up." Careful not to get too close, he waited for her to stand and make her way toward him. Since it was impossible for her to climb the stairs with her ankles bound, he pulled out a vicious-looking folding knife and cut through the plastic tie.

It was all she could do not to attack him, try to pry the knife from his hands and stab it into his malevolent heart. Instead, she waited, stuck to her plan.

Careful to keep her injured arm out of sight, she climbed

the wooden stairs in front of him. Damon stayed a few feet behind.

When they reached the tiny bathroom, he shoved her down on the toilet seat, pulled back the plastic shower curtain, and turned on the water. She was sure he'd drag her into the freezing spray, but instead, he turned and sliced through the plastic tie on her wrists.

"Get yourself cleaned up. If you're thinking of doing something stupid, I still have the stun gun." Damon stepped out of the bathroom and closed the door, and Lisa nearly wept with relief.

So far her plan was working. She had gone over every detail she remembered of the tiny bathroom, believing this was her best chance to get away. She hadn't expected him to free her hands, but she was naked and injured from the last beating he had given her. And as he had said, he had the stun gun.

She shivered at the thought. Clenching and unclenching her fists, she rubbed her bruised and injured wrists. She could do this.

She had to.

As silently as possible, praying Damon wouldn't hear, she slid the old-fashioned lock on the bathroom door into place.

"Hurry up in that shower or I'll come in and drag you out."

This was it. Moving quickly, she grabbed a towel and wrapped it around her hand, dragged in a harsh, steadying breath and punched her fist through the glass in the window over the toilet.

"What the hell?" The doorknob rattled as she cleared as many of the broken shards out of the way as she could, then stepped up on the toilet, pulled herself up over the sill, and dropped down on the other side.

The second she started to run, she heard the door crash

open and Damon rush into the bathroom. "You bitch!" he screamed.

Lisa kept running. She had reached the trees by the time the front door slammed open, then the screen door, and Damon rushed outside. Foul words spewed like venom off his tongue as he raced after her, heading for the trees where she had disappeared. Lisa just kept running.

The dirt road leading up to the cabin had turned off a paved road at the bottom of the hill. She remembered that from the time she had spent in the trunk of Damon's car. If she could make it to the road, maybe she could flag down a vehicle.

Stones and twigs cut into her bare feet. Rough bark scraped her skin as she ducked under branches and tripped over rocks, but she kept running. Nothing was going to stop her. Not as long as her heart beat and she had breath in her lungs.

Careening down the mountain, her pulse pounding wildly, she heard him behind her. *Keep going. Keep going.* Downhill, downhill, following a dry streambed, slowing now, picking her way more carefully. Spotting an indentation in the bank, she crouched and ducked inside, hiding, listening for his footsteps, her heartbeat roaring in her ears.

She could hear him, battering his way through the forest, not worried about making noise, knowing there was no one around to hear.

She had to keep going. No other choice. Bursting out of her hiding place she ran and ran and ran. Then she saw it, a ribbon of pavement winding its way through the woods below. A little ways off, twin beams of light rolled along at a leisurely clip moving in her direction.

Hope soared and a fresh burst of adrenaline burned through her, giving her shaking legs the strength to move. Stomach churning with fear, she raced down the hill, trying to time her arrival for the moment the car rounded the curve.

She reached the road, saw the car coming, a compact SUV with two people inside. Glancing over her shoulder, she caught a glimpse of Damon behind her and the knot in her stomach tightened.

You can do it. Don't give up! She burst into the road just as the car rounded the bend. Lisa started waving madly, forcing the car to slow, screaming, forcing the words out of her dry throat.

"Help! Help me!" The SUV rolled to a stop. "Please help me!"

The driver's door opened, a slender young man stepped out of the car. She heard the echo of a gunshot, saw the horrified look on the young man's face, felt a burning, tearing pain in her back. Then her body went numb and her vision blurred as her head hit the pavement and she was hurled into darkness.

The demolition crew arrived early the following morning, a big yellow Caterpillar backhoe, an old red Mack dump truck, and an extra hired hand to help Josh, Noah, and Cole with the cleanup. Josh had a skip loader parked next to the tool shed.

Not quite ready to face Tory after the hot sex they'd had last night, he left a note for her on the kitchen table, brewed coffee, fixed himself an egg sandwich, and went to work.

Until last night, he had done his best to behave as her employer and keep his distance. But he'd been attracted to Tory Ford since the day she'd driven up in front of the barn, since she had bulled her way into his life, she and her irresistible little girl.

He had tried to keep his distance, but he was a man, not a saint, and he wanted Tory more than he had wanted any woman he could recall. Apparently, she wanted him, too, and that was all the justification he needed, even if his conscience nagged him.

Since thinking about having her again was making him hard, he bent and dug his shovel into a load of heavy black ash, hoisted it up, and dumped it into the wheelbarrow. Noah was busy knocking apart half-burned boards that had once been part of a stall, while Cole walked over to fire up the skip loader.

The sun beat down, shining directly overhead. Josh took off his hat and mopped his forehead with his arm, settled his hat back on.

When he looked up, Tory was walking out of the house carrying a tray piled with sandwiches, a pitcher of lemonade, and a stack of red plastic cups. She smiled and the kick he felt went straight to his groin.

She was so damned pretty. His mind began to imagine ways he would take her the next time they were together, but he shut the thought down. Maybe by now Tory had come to her senses and changed her mind.

"I figured you guys would be hungry by now," she said. "Where should I put the tray?"

He walked over to the back of his pickup and lowered the tailgate, took the tray from her hands, and set it down.

"Sandwiches look great. Thanks." The roar of the powerful diesel engines stopped. The guys clustered around the tailgate and the sandwiches began to disappear.

"So how was your morning?" he asked, just to hear the sound of her voice.

"Not as good as I'd hoped. I used the phone you bought me to call my friend in Phoenix. It's been a while since we talked. I was really looking forward to catching up but the call went straight to voicemail. I called her office but they said she wasn't there. She didn't call in this morning and she didn't show up yesterday, either."

"Is that unusual for her?"

"Yes," Tory said. "Lisa's extremely responsible. I'm worried about her. I phoned a friend of hers and asked her to go by Lisa's house and check on her. Shelly said she'd stop by on her way home from work. I figured it was okay to give her the number of the disposable since I can always get rid of it."

He didn't like that she had to be so careful. No one should have to hide themselves the way Tory did.

"Something probably came up," he said. "No use worrying till you know what's going on."

"You're right, but still . . ." She glanced toward the house. "I need to get back."

"I'll walk you." They left the men to finish their lunch, and he walked Tory up on the porch. "I've been thinking about last night," he said.

Her head came up and her gaze found his. "I'm not sorry. I hope you aren't, either."

Relief slipped through him. "I'm not sorry."

"So . . . umm . . . maybe you'd like to come over later. After I put Ivy to bed."

His blood heated, began to hammer through his veins. "Yeah. Okay. Great."

"I'd better go. I'm fixing spaghetti for supper."

"Spaghetti sounds good." His mouth edged up. "I'll have my dessert later."

Tory blushed crimson. Turning, she opened the door and disappeared inside the house.

Josh took a couple of deep breaths, imagined himself in an ice-cold shower, and went back to work.

Tory's day continued downhill. First, she couldn't find Lisa, then the five o'clock news on KTEF 6 was bad. A terror attack at Houston's Hobby Airport had killed six people. The entire city was in lockdown, though the police had shot and killed the two men responsible for setting off a bomb in front of the ticket counter.

Commentators were speculating the attack might be linked to the terror cell that had plotted to blow up the state capitol a few months back. They thought the recent lone wolf knife attack in Austin might have been another member of the cell.

News like that was always upsetting, but at least it kept her mind off Josh and what was going to happen when he came over later that night. A prospect that both thrilled and terrified her.

Then things got worse. Shelly called. Lisa wasn't at home and it didn't look like she'd been there for the past few days. Her plants were dying and the curtains throughout the house were closed. The weird part was her car was in the garage, her purse sat on the kitchen table but her phone was nowhere to be found.

Shelly had tried calling Lisa over and over, just as Tory had been doing, but the calls just kept going to voicemail.

"I'm calling the police," Shelly said.

"Yes, I think you should. I'm really worried about her."

"Me too. I'll keep you posted. I know how close you two are." Shelly ended the call. As worried as Tory was, she had no choice but to go ahead and finish making supper.

Since Josh would be working late, she made a plate for him and put it in the oven, then took Ivy and their portion back to the trailer. After supper, Tory put Ivy to bed and read *The Little Red Hen* for what seemed the hundredth time, until her little girl finally fell asleep.

As she returned to the living room, Tory thought of Josh and the evening they had planned, but her mind kept straying to Lisa and what might have happened to her. Nothing she came up with made any sense. She was pacing the floor of the living room when Josh rapped softly on the door.

"Hi," he said as he walked inside, leaned down, and kissed her. He must have read the worry in her face because he gently caught her shoulders. "Something's wrong. What is it?"

Her eyes burned. "My friend Lisa. She's missing. I'm really scared for her, Josh."

He started to say something but the phone rang just then. Tory hurried to answer it. "Yes?"

"It's Shelly. I've got bad news, Tory."

Her stomach clenched. "Wh-what is it?"

"Lisa's in the hospital in Flagstaff. She's in critical condition."

Tory felt the blood draining out of her face and she started to tremble. Josh guided her over to the sofa and gently eased her down.

"She's in a coma," Shelly was saying. "As soon as she's stable, they're airlifting her to Scottsdale Memorial."

"What . . . what happened?"

"The police aren't sure, but . . . Tory, Lisa was shot."

She made a little sound in her throat and Josh took the phone from her hand.

"My name is Josh Cain. I'm a friend of Tory's. Tell me what's going on."

His jaw hardened as Shelly retold the story. Then he handed back the phone and stood in front of her with his hands on his hips and his legs braced apart.

"I'm . . . I'm on my way back to Phoenix," Tory said. "When you see Lisa, tell her I'm on my way." She could pay for the trip on her credit cards. She hadn't used them because she didn't want Damon to find her. Now she had no choice.

"I'll tell her." Shelly started crying. "The police think she was abducted from her house, Tory. She's in really bad shape. The doctors don't know if she's going to make it."

Tory bit back a sob and blinked against tears. "Tell her I'm coming. I'll be there as soon as I can."

"When she wakes up I'll tell her. I promise."

The call ended and Tory started crying. Josh sat down beside her and drew her into his arms. "Easy, honey. I'm right here, okay?"

She looked up at him and the tears in her eyes rolled down her cheeks. "The police think Lisa was abducted, Josh. Whoever did it, shot her. Who would . . . who would do something like—"

Her heart jerked and her head shot up. "Oh, my God. Oh, my God, Josh, what if it was Damon?"

"Hey, wait a minute. You don't know he had anything to do with this. You can't jump to conclusions."

"Damon knows she's my closest friend. Maybe he thought she knew where I was. Maybe he took her so he could force her to tell him." Fresh tears welled. "If it was him, what happened to Lisa is my fault."

Josh gripped her shoulders. "Whatever happened, it wasn't your fault. None of this is your fault. If you're right— and we have no reason to think that yet—the only person to blame is Damon Bridger."

"We have to tell the police. We have to call them."

"You can't do that, Tory. You don't have any proof."

He was right. Damon was cunning and he was extremely smart. If he had abducted Lisa, he would have taken every precaution, done everything in his power to hide his identity.

"I have to get to Phoenix. I've got room on my credit cards. I was afraid to use them, but now—"

"I'll take you to Phoenix. I've got money. There's no need to use your cards."

"I can't do that, Josh. This isn't your problem. It never has been."

His features turned hard. "I'm making it my problem—as of right now."

Tory made no reply. She needed his help. Desperately. Aside from that, you didn't argue with a man like Joshua Cain once his mind was made up.

Chapter Fifteen

They decided to leave Ivy with Mrs. Thompson. It was a difficult decision, but the thought of dragging her little girl through long hospital corridors, or keeping her for hours in waiting rooms that smelled like antiseptic, seemed a far worse option.

"She'll be fine," Mrs. Thompson said when Tory explained what had happened. "We'll play games and bake cookies. We'll have a pajama party. You just take care of your friend."

Tory managed to smile. She was grateful that Ivy was so caught up in playing with Mrs. Thompson's antique dollhouse, she barely noticed when Tory and Josh left the house.

"I know it's stupid," she said, fighting the urge to cry as the pickup headed for town. "But we haven't been apart since I got out of the hospital."

"She'll be fine," Josh said.

"I know." She turned in the seat to look at him. "What about the ranch? Do you think Cole and Noah can handle it? The cows seem pretty self-sufficient. What about the horses?"

"They'll be fine. Cole's staying in the house at night. He

knows a kid who'll take the job as a stable hand, boy about nineteen who loves to ride. He'll get paid but he'll also be able to ride on the weekends whenever he wants. Cole thinks he'll be a great fit."

"That's one problem solved, but—"

"Noah and Cole will both be there in the daytime to look after the livestock. If there's a problem, one of them will call and we'll figure a way to handle it."

Tory leaned back in her seat. She thought of the man sitting next to her, a slightly different Josh than she had seen before. This man was completely in charge, more assertive, totally in command of the situation. Odds were this was Josh the marine.

Her thoughts returned to Lisa as the pickup rolled toward town. Shelly had called early that morning. Lisa had been medevaced to the hospital in Scottsdale. Mr. and Mrs. Shane were flying in from New York but they couldn't get there until tomorrow.

Lisa had never been close to her family, who had wanted her to marry one of her dad's wealthy friends instead of having a career. But Lisa was still their daughter, and they had to be sick with worry.

Tory really needed to get there.

"Airport security's going to be a nightmare after the terror attack in Houston," she said.

Josh flicked her a sideways glance. "Won't be as bad as you think."

"Why not?"

He smiled. "Because we aren't flying out of Dallas-Fort Worth. I called my brother. I don't like asking him for favors, but I figured this was important. According to Linc, the Iron Springs Municipal Airport has a five-thousand-foot runway. He's sending a jet to pick us up and take us to Arizona."

"You're kidding, right? Your brother has a private jet?"

"Company jet. Citation SII. Linc owns half of Texas American Enterprises."

Her eyebrows shot up. She had seen Tex/Am trucks on the highway. Everyone knew the Dallas corporation was mega-successful, but she hadn't connected the business in any way to Josh or his family.

As an advertising exec, she had flown on a chartered jet a couple of times, but those days seemed an eternity ago.

"I can't believe your brother is loaning us his plane."

"Yup. We can be in Scottsdale in about two hours."

She said a silent prayer of thanks. She needed to get to Lisa as quickly as possible and now she would be there in very short order. "It costs a fortune to fly one of those things."

Josh just smiled. "Linc's always asking me if there's anything I need. This time I said yes."

It wasn't long before the pickup was parked at the airport and they were settled aboard Lincoln Cain's fancy Citation jet.

"From sleeping in the backseat of my car in the Walmart parking lot to this—" She gestured toward the plush cream leather interior and polished mahogany tables. "I feel like I've stepped into an alternative universe."

"Yeah, I know what you mean. It's not the life for me, but it suits my brother. Linc's as comfortable on a jet as he is on the seat of his Harley."

"Your brother rides a Harley?"

"He says it relaxes him."

"Sounds like an interesting man."

He flicked her a hooded glance. "He's happily married."

Tory just smiled. "Believe me, one Cain brother is more than I can handle."

Which was pretty much true, though at the moment, with her friend's life hanging by a thread, sex wasn't a high priority.

She glanced over at Josh, who had relaxed back in his

seat, and guilt slipped through her. "There's something I need to tell you."

Those blue eyes swung in her direction. "Yeah? What is it?"

"My name isn't Ford. My real name is Victoria Bradford."

His features tightened. "You're kidding me. You lied about your name?"

"I had to. I went by Terry Rutherford for a while, but I hated being someone else. When I got to the ranch I felt a little safer so I used Tory Ford, which was closer to my actual name."

"I don't like being lied to, Tory."

"I'm sorry. I should have told you sooner. I wanted to, I just . . . I don't know . . . it's hard for me to trust people anymore."

"What else haven't you told me?"

"Nothing. I swear. You're the only one who's ever helped me. You deserve the truth. I meant to tell you the other night, but we . . . umm . . . got distracted."

His expression changed. His eyes heated as he remembered their encounter; then the corners crinkled with amusement. Finally, he relaxed. "Okay. But from now on, no secrets, all right?"

"No secrets. I promise." Except how attracted she was to him. But every woman deserved to keep a few thoughts to herself.

Josh settled back in the deep leather seat. Tory took a deep breath as the wheels started rolling down the runway. A few minutes later they were airborne. The flight smoothed out. While Josh fetched a couple of sodas from the galley, Tory pulled out a deck of cards.

"Any chance you like to play poker? Or I can just play solitaire."

His interest sharpened. "You play poker?"

"My dad taught me when I was a kid. Three Card Stud or Texas Hold 'Em?"

Josh eyed her with suspicion. "Texas Hold 'Em. What are the stakes?"

Clothes sounded good, but getting naked on Lincoln Cain's fancy jet was probably not a good idea. "How about toothpicks? I saw a box of them in the galley."

Josh unfastened his seat belt and got up from his chair. "Good a way as any to pass the time."

They played till the plane started its descent. Unfortunately, the game ended with the two of them nearly even, which impressed Josh and insulted her. She didn't tell him she was way out of practice and he was in for trouble the next time they played.

The landing at the Scottsdale Airport was smooth, just the brush of wheels before the plane settled and taxied down the runway. At the executive terminal, they picked up the vehicle Josh had rented from Avis, a black Jeep Cherokee, and headed for the hospital.

Scottsdale Memorial, a beige, four-story stucco building constructed in a flat-roofed, high desert style, loomed ahead. Josh parked the Jeep in the lot and they went inside. Tory felt his hand at her waist as they walked up to a woman with short-bobbed, faded gray hair sitting behind a computer screen at the front desk.

"We're here to see Lisa Shane," Josh said. "Where can we find her?"

The woman typed in the name. "Ms. Shane is in intensive care. Take the elevator up to the second floor, turn right, and head down the hall. You'll see a nurses' station. They can give you more information there."

"Thank you." They started in that direction, Josh walking beside her, his features unusually stiff.

"How long were you in the hospital after you were wounded?" Tory asked, sensing the problem.

"Two months. I was lucky."

"You consider spending two months in the hospital lucky?"

His eyes found hers. "I was lucky to be alive. Some of my friends didn't make it."

"I'm so sorry, Josh."

"When I got back to Texas, I got involved with a program that helps wounded vets. That's how I met Noah and Cole and a lot of other good men."

She fell silent. No wonder he looked so grim. She remembered the story she had read about him. He'd lost good friends, spent months in the hospital. This place had to be bringing back bad memories. She wished she could have spared him, but she was glad to have him along, though clearly he would rather be home.

Home. When had she started to think of Texas as home? It was dangerous. She couldn't afford to get attached when she might have to leave.

She thought of Ivy, how much it would hurt to tear her away from the first place she felt safe. She missed her daughter already, wondered what she and Mrs. Thompson were doing. She would call as soon as she could.

The elevator dinged and the door slid open. Josh walked her up to the nurses' station and she spoke to a nurse in green scrubs.

"My name is Victoria Bradford. I'm here to see Lisa Shane." She was glad she had told Josh her real name. What had happened to Lisa was a police matter. There was no way she could lie to the authorities.

"Family only," the nurse said, a woman in her forties, heavyset with pretty gray eyes that matched her hair. "Are you family?"

"Lisa's sister," Josh said, before she could blurt out the truth. Apparently, she would be lying after all.

"Ms. Shane is just out of surgery. There's a waiting room

down the hall. The doctor will speak to you as soon as he gets a chance."

"Thank you," Tory said.

They made their way into the waiting room and sat down on a pale blue vinyl sofa. There were a couple of other people in the room, a Hispanic woman with a little boy three or four years old who sat on the floor, coloring. A pale old man with long gray hair sitting at the far end of the room, a cane propped against his knee.

Tory picked up a *People* magazine off the stack on the table and started thumbing through the pages. She wished she had her iPad, which she'd hocked along with her laptop after she'd fled Carlsbad.

Finally, the door opened and a tall, slim man with curly brown hair walked into the room and approached with determined strides.

"You're here for Lisa Shane?" he asked.

"That's right."

"I'm Detective Jeremy Larson. Lisa Shane doesn't have a sister, so who the hell are you?"

Her nerves kicked up. Beside her, Josh stiffened.

"I'm her best friend, Victoria Bradford. This is Joshua Cain. We just flew in from Texas."

The detective's dark eyes swung to Josh. "You're also a friend of Ms. Shane's?"

"Never met her. I'm here for Ms. Bradford."

The detective's expression said he wasn't happy about the deception. He pointed toward the door. "Both of you. We need to talk. There's a room down the hall where we can speak privately."

They made their way out of the waiting room and along the corridor to a private room with a bleached wood table and four matching chairs. There were desert scenes on the walls. The detective closed the door and joined them at the table.

"How did you hear about Ms. Shane?" he asked, taking the seat across from her.

"Lisa's friend, Shelly Burman, has been keeping me informed," Tory said.

Larson nodded, apparently fitting the pieces together. Taking a notepad out of his pocket, he flipped it open and pulled out a pen. "You're the woman who first figured out Lisa was missing. That correct?"

"That's right. I called Lisa Tuesday morning, but she didn't pick up so I called her office. They said she hadn't phoned in that day and hadn't shown up the day before, either. That isn't like her. I called Shelly and asked her to stop by Lisa's house. Lisa's car and purse were there but Lisa wasn't. Shelly and I both thought it was time to call the police."

"How much do you know about what happened?"

"Not much," Tory said. "Shelly said the police believe Lisa was abducted from her home. I know she was shot."

The detective released a slow breath. "It appears Ms. Shane was held prisoner for several days before she escaped. There's no proof she was raped since there's no DNA evidence. But she was badly beaten and from what the doctors are reporting of her injuries, my guess is the guy tied her up and sexually assaulted her. Probably wore a condom. I need to know if you have any idea who might be responsible for the attack."

Her mind started screaming. Lisa had been abducted, beaten, and probably raped. All she could think was *Damon, Damon, Damon*. But there was no evidence, no proof it had anything to do with him.

"I don't . . . I'm not sure."

"You're her best friend. You must have talked to her often.

Did she mention anyone? A guy at work she was having trouble with? Someone following her? A guy she met in a bar? Anyone like that?"

Damon, Damon, Damon.

"Tell him, Tory," Josh softly urged.

She swallowed. "There is someone . . . a person who might do something that terrible. But I don't have any proof."

Larson clicked the top of his pen. "What's his name?"

"Damon Bridger. He's . . . he's my ex-fiancé."

The detective stopped writing. "Your ex was involved with Lisa Shane?"

"No, but . . ." She took a fortifying breath. "Damon knows she's my closest friend. He's been stalking me for months. If you check your police records, you'll see he was arrested for assaulting me last year."

"He beat her, put her in the hospital," Josh said darkly. "The bastard ought to be in prison."

The detective eyed him a moment, then turned back to Tory. "Tell me about Bridger."

"After the assault, I moved away from Phoenix, but Damon followed me. I moved again, and he showed up there. I'm living in Texas now. So far he hasn't been able to find me."

"What's Bridger's connection to Lisa Shane?"

"Lisa and I stay in touch. Damon knows that. Maybe he kidnapped her to find out where I am." Her eyes welled with tears. "But Lisa couldn't have told him because she doesn't know."

Larson's dark eyebrows drew together. "You think this guy Bridger would go that far?"

She wiped away a tear. "I don't know. I think there's a chance he would."

"All right, we'll check it out. Okay if I call you Victoria?"

"Tory," she said.

"One thing I can tell you, Tory. If Damon Bridger did this, he'll pay for what he's done."

She only nodded. Her throat felt too tight to speak.

"Do the police have any leads?" Josh asked.

"The sheriff's office has deputies scouring the location where Ms. Shane was picked up. There are dozens of cabins in the area and miles of dirt roads. Most of the residences are owned by seasonal users so they're empty much of the time. So far the deputies haven't been able to locate the place she was being held prisoner."

"Are they sure that's where he was holding her?" Josh asked.

"Not for certain. She was naked when she was shot. One theory is she was being transported from one location to another, possibly in the trunk, somehow managed to get out of the vehicle and get away."

Josh's big hand reached for Tory's beneath the table. His warmth and strength seeped into her and she was finally able to breathe.

Detective Larson rose from his chair. "That's all for now. I need contact information for both of you. Where are you staying?"

"Marriott Courtyard," Josh answered. "It's just down the street." It was good he had found a place because Tory hadn't been able to think that far ahead.

Larson shoved the notepad across the table and Josh wrote down his contact numbers. "Thanks to Bridger, Tory doesn't have a smartphone."

"I'm using a disposable," she said, and rattled off the number.

"All right, thanks." The detective picked up his notepad, shoved it and his pen back into his pocket. He was halfway to the door when it swung open and the doctor, a small, silver-haired man with wire-rimmed glasses, walked into the room.

"Dr. Barnard?" Larson asked.

"That's right."

"I'm Detective Jeremy Larson. I'll need to talk to your patient as soon as possible."

"I understand, Detective, but it's going to be a while. And there's a chance it may not do you any good." He turned his attention to Tory, who had risen from her chair. "You're her sister?"

Tory hesitated.

"Close enough," the detective said.

"Aside from the gunshot wound to her lower back and the injuries resulting from the assault, Ms. Shane suffered a severe cranial trauma when she fell and hit her head. A blow that hard can cause retrograde amnesia. There's a chance of memory loss. In this case it could be extremely pronounced. At the moment we're more concerned with the possibility of brain swelling."

A sound slipped from Tory's throat.

"We're hoping we won't have to operate, but there's always a chance. For now, that's all I can tell you."

"How long before you know more?" Josh asked.

"It's a waiting game now. I'll let you know where we are as time goes along."

"Thank you," Tory said, a lump constricting her throat.

"You need to stay strong," the doctor said. "Lisa is going to need you."

Tory bit her lip. She shook the hand the doctor extended; then he turned and walked out of the waiting room.

"I appreciate your cooperation," Detective Larson said to her and Josh. "I'll be in touch." The tall, lanky policeman followed the doctor out the door.

Despair sat like a heavy weight on her chest. Tory turned to Josh, who pulled her into his arms and held her as she wept for her friend.

Chapter Sixteen

Sitting behind the wide mahogany desk in his office on the top floor of the Bridger building, Damon pressed the phone against his ear.

"You're a sweetheart, Melanie. I really appreciate your keeping me updated on her condition—Lisa being a friend and all. I'm sorry to hear she isn't doing better."

Yes! He wanted to shoot his fist into the air. The hands of fate had granted him a reprieve.

"I'm happy to help," Melanie said.

"Why don't you let me thank you properly? How about dinner at that new French restaurant they just opened out on Camelback Road?"

"Oh, that sounds wonderful. What night, Damon?"

"Saturday work for you?"

"I'd love that. I heard it was expensive but really, really worth it."

"Okay, it's a date. I'll call you later in the week just to confirm. Unless something comes up, we'll plan on Saturday night."

"I'll look forward to it. Talk to you soon."

Damon hung up the phone. *Unless something comes up—* and he would make sure it did. He didn't have time to date, even if nailing Melanie was a sure thing.

He thought about the information the pretty, dark-eyed nurse had given him. Besides the gunshot wound, Lisa had suffered brain trauma from hitting her head on the pavement. The result was severe retrograde amnesia.

From what Melanie could find out, when Lisa had finally awoken after surgery, she had no memory of what had happened to her. Nothing at all for weeks before she was found running naked down the road.

Melanie Romano, the nurse he had hooked up with last month at the Peacock, had just brought news that saved his bacon.

Damon leaned back in his black leather chair and looked out the windows of his corner office at the vast grid of Phoenix streets and freeways stretching out in all directions.

He'd been frantic after Lisa's escape. He hadn't expected it, hadn't been finished with the little blond whore, not by a long shot. He hadn't realized how much he was going to enjoy having her under his control, the feeling of almost godly power. He hadn't even begun to have his fill of Lisa Shane.

But once she'd run, he'd had to stop her. He couldn't let her go to the police. Shooting her had been his only option. He was a better than average marksman, so the gunshot should have been fatal, but it wasn't. He'd been sure she would die on the way to the hospital but that hadn't happened, either.

Certain she wouldn't live long enough to give the cops his name, he'd gone back to the cabin that night, boarded up the broken window, and used Clorox to clean up the blood.

The place was way out of the way, just one of dozens of other seasonal residences, nothing suspicious about it. The odds of the police finding it were slim to none. Even if they looked inside, unless they searched hard, they wouldn't see the basement door.

It pissed him off that he'd had to toss Lisa's cell phone. Sooner or later, Tory would have called and he would have had her. But he couldn't risk the cops' finding it in his possession.

He was in the clear for now, but he could still be in very deep trouble.

Lisa hadn't died, and ever since he'd read the story of her rescue in the newspapers, he'd been frantically trying to come up with an idea, a way to silence her for good.

Eventually, he had calmed down and gotten himself under control, begun to formulate a plan. He'd thought of Melanie right away, remembering she had mentioned she worked at Scottsdale Memorial.

She'd been a tiger in bed the night they'd hooked up, had clearly hoped to see him again. He'd called her as soon as he had read in the papers that Lisa was being transported to the hospital.

He'd met Melanie for drinks and happened to mention that the poor girl who'd been abducted was a friend of his ex-girlfriend's. He'd said he was worried about her. Melanie had volunteered to find out her condition. Hell, by the time the evening was over, she'd believed it was her idea to call him daily with updates.

Women were so fucking easy. Just compliment them, tell them how smart they were, pretend to pay attention to whatever they were saying, and you were in.

He'd had to work harder for Tory. She was smart, a little shy around men, still mourning her dead husband but ready to move on.

He'd been fiercely attracted to her, determined to have her.

He had studied her likes and dislikes, spent time with her and her kid, only to discover she was a bitch like all the rest.

It burned him to admit he had fallen for Tory. Fallen hard enough to buy her an expensive engagement ring. She belonged to him now and that wasn't going to change.

He almost smiled. The way things were shaping up, this might actually work out better. From what he'd learned, he didn't have to worry about Lisa, at least not for a while. He could deal with her at his convenience.

And he was almost certain that sooner or later Tory would hear about Lisa's abduction and resulting hospital stay. When she did, she wouldn't let her shirttail hit her sweet little ass before she came running back to Phoenix.

Today he'd asked Melanie to let him know the names of Lisa's visitors. "Just in case I want to say hello."

Melanie had promised to look into it.

Damon thought of Tory and the punishment he intended to mete out once he had her in his basement prison, and his dick went thick and hard.

It wouldn't be long now. She'd be under his complete control. He could do anything to her he wanted.

Damon could feel the hungry need in every cell of his body.

It was after midnight. They'd been at the hospital all day again today. Josh used the hotel room key to open the door to room 221 and walked Tory inside. Unsure where their relationship stood, he had rented two adjoining rooms. So far they hadn't spent more than a few hours in the rooms, mostly to shower and change into fresh clothes before returning to the hospital.

Tory had called Ivy as often as possible. Though the little girl kept asking when her mother was coming home, according to Mrs. Thompson she had been well behaved so far. She was really a good kid.

Lisa's friend, Shelly Burman, a short, slightly pudgy young woman with short blond hair, also spent a great deal of time at the hospital. Friends and coworkers had stopped by. And Lisa's parents were there.

The Shanes, an older couple, were with Lisa now, giving Tory and Shelly a break from the routine. From what Josh could tell, if any good came out of this, it would be the renewed connection between Lisa and her parents, who had been devastated by the vicious attack on their only child.

Lisa was recovering as well as could be expected. The surgery to remove the .45 caliber slug that had damaged her right kidney had been successful. The swelling in her brain had begun to subside, saving her from emergency cranial surgery, and she had been upgraded from critical to serious condition.

The bad news was she didn't remember anything about the abduction—not who had done it, not where she had been taken, not how she had escaped. Nothing that would help the police. Nothing that connected Damon Bridger to the attack.

For now at least, Josh was relieved.

He knew all about Bridger. After the fire, he'd gone on the Internet to find out as much as he could. Careful not to leave a trail, he had looked the guy up on social media, found he had a Twitter account and a Facebook page. He was a good-looking guy who, at least on the surface, seemed completely normal.

Which made Josh even more wary.

Normal men didn't savagely beat up women.

Josh had asked a friend of Linc's, a detective in Dallas named Ross Townsend, to go deeper, find out everything he could. Townsend had e-mailed him a file that included the basics: Damon Montgomery Bridger, thirty-one years old, same as Josh, graduated from the University of Arizona with a degree in business, made a fat salary as a vice president of the Bridger Real Estate Company, his father's company, but word was he mostly lived off Daddy's generosity.

The file also included Damon's arrest for assault against Victoria Bradford, the only smudge on his pristine record. It mentioned the mild sentence he had received and the restraining order Tory had been granted.

There was nothing in the file that was particularly helpful, but if trouble arose while they were in Phoenix, Josh wanted to be prepared.

In the meantime, the investigation was moving forward with little success. Detective Larson had spoken to them several times, asking questions or giving them information, including the news Damon Bridger had a solid alibi for the night of the abduction and the days that followed.

According to the police, he had spent that Friday night at a friend's house, a stockbroker named Anson Burke, drinking beer and watching an ice hockey game on ESPN. Damon had worked that weekend in his office, where he'd had several meetings with employees. The alibi had been verified by the employees as well as by his father.

The night Lisa had escaped, Damon had been at another friend's house, a part-time real estate salesman, part-time computer guy named Isaac "Izzy" Watkins. According to Izzy, he and Damon had played video games till the early hours of the morning.

Josh held on to the hope Bridger wasn't involved in the abduction. Which made him think of Tory. He glanced over to where she perched on the edge of the mattress, her eyes closed, half asleep.

"Tory, honey, you need to get in bed and get some rest. You can't do anyone any good if you make yourself sick."

Her big green eyes fluttered open. "I know."

"You need me to help you get undressed?" Just saying it made him start to get hard, made him feel like a letch for even thinking about sex. Truth was he hadn't stopped wanting Tory since the night he'd taken her on the porch.

"I can do it," she said, and Josh gave an inward sigh of relief.

Leaving her to change into the long, white cotton nightgown she had brought with her, he went into his own room, stripped, and hit the shower. When he finished, he turned the water from hot to cold, hoping it would help cool the lust in his blood.

Back in his room, he dragged on his jeans and went next door to check on Tory. She was lying in bed, the covers pulled up.

"You okay?"

She released a tired sigh. "I guess. I keep thinking about Lisa, how terrible it must be for her, not being able to remember what happened. But Lisa's really strong. That gives me hope she'll be okay."

Josh sat down on the edge of the bed. "You're strong, too, honey. You'll get through this. With any luck, so will your friend."

"The police don't think Damon did it."

"So far there's no proof he had anything to do with it. There are lots of crazies out there. Could have been any one of them."

"I wish I could convince myself. In my head, I just keep seeing the look on his face when he was hitting me, kicking me. It was like he turned into some kind of monster. I can't get the notion out of my head that he's the guy responsible."

He thought of what Bridger had done to her and his hand unconsciously fisted. He forced himself to relax.

"You can't keep thinking about it, Tory. You need to leave it to the police." Josh leaned over and kissed her forehead. "Get some sleep, okay?"

"I know you have to get back to Texas. I can't expect you to stay here much longer."

She was right. He couldn't stay away from the ranch forever. "Let's not worry about that now." He stood up from the bed and started for the door.

"Why did you get two rooms?" Tory asked softly.

Josh turned, his gaze sweeping over her, taking in the fiery curls tousled around her face, the lips that tasted as good as the strawberries they reminded him of. Her eyes were sleepy but there was something else in them now.

"I wasn't sure exactly where we stood. I thought I would leave it up to you."

And he needed his own space. There was always the chance he'd have one of his occasional nightmares. He'd had a bad dream last night just before dawn, reliving a bloody battle to the death. He'd awoken covered in perspiration, his heart pounding like a hammer. He didn't want to burden Tori with that.

On the other hand, having sex with her was an entirely different matter.

"So . . . does that mean if I asked you to stay, you'd be okay with it?"

His whole body tightened. "Baby, you have no idea how okay I'd be. But if I stayed, I wouldn't want to sleep, and you really need to rest."

"I won't get any rest if I can't fall asleep. I have a feeling you could help me with that."

Hot need surged through him. His blood thickened, began to pulse through his veins, pool low in his groin. He wasn't an idiot. The lady was issuing an invitation he wanted to accept more than he wanted to see his next sunrise.

He pulled a foil-wrapped condom out of his wallet and tossed it on the nightstand. Buzzing down his zipper, he stepped out of his jeans, turned to see Tory pulling her nightgown off over her head, letting him admire her luscious little body.

Josh took the gown and tossed it away, then slid naked

into bed beside her. Her eyes found his. A slender finger ran over the muscles across his chest, trailed down over his abs, and he went harder than he was already.

"It seems like it's always me making the first move," she said. "I don't know why that is. I was never this way before."

He nipped her lush bottom lip. "I've never waited this long for an invitation before." He kissed her, sinking into her soft, sweet fullness, feeling a wash of heat that burned through every muscle and sinew in his body.

He cupped a pale round breast, massaged gently. "From now on, I'm not waiting."

Bending, he took the hardened peak into his mouth and suckled greedily. He'd warned her. Tory had had her chance to back away. Now that he'd had a taste of her, she was a fire in his blood. He wanted her and he meant to have his fill.

Hot, deep, lusty kisses followed, pushing the limits of his control. Determined to make it good for her, he forced himself to slow down, to coax instead of ravage, to stroke and tease until he had her squirming beneath him.

He was painfully hard, hanging on by a thread. "I want you," he said. "I need you, baby."

Her fingers dug into his shoulders. "Please, Josh."

Kneeing her legs apart, he settled betweem them, then eased himself inside. Hot blood pulsed through him. When Tory arched up, taking him deeper, a low growl slipped from his throat.

Clamping down hard on his control, he tried to go slow, but his body wanted none of it. He tried not to hurt her, tried not to be greedy and take her too hard, but Tory wouldn't let him back away.

She was an equal partner in this, and when he turned over on the mattress, taking her with him, lifted her on top of him and gave up control, she proved it.

She rode him until she reached her peak, her soft cries, and the sweet contractions of her body urging him to take what he'd wanted since the day she had driven her old blue Chevy up in front of his barn.

Holding on by a thread, Josh rolled her beneath him and surged deep, took her hard, took her and took her, driving her up all over again, and this time when she came, he joined her, spinning out the pleasure, the rapture, letting the need slide away.

They lay quiet for a time, lazily spiraling down. It felt good just having her beside him. With a last, soft kiss, he eased out of bed, took care of the condom and returned, drew her close and tucked her against his side.

Drowsiness settled over him. He should get up, sleep in his own room just in case, but she felt so good snuggled against him, he let himself drift for a while. He wasn't sure how long what they had would last, but he planned to enjoy it until it ended.

One thing he knew, as long as Tory was with him, she was under his protection. She and her little girl.

It was a job Josh took seriously.

If Damon Bridger knew what was good for him, he would stay the hell away.

Chapter Seventeen

Another day passed. Lisa's condition was upgraded to stable. Her parents were at the hospital with her, other friends, and family.

Lisa was in good hands, and Tory missed her little girl. Ivy was restless for her mother, and Josh had a ranch to run. It was time to go home.

"You're going to be okay," Tory said to Lisa as she sat in the chair next to the hospital bed, holding on to her best friend's hand.

Lisa was swathed in bandages, still hooked up to a heart monitor. An IV dripped fluids into a tube taped in her arm. A bandage around her head covered a patch of shaved blond hair, but she still looked beautiful.

"You're the strongest person I know," Tory said. "You'll make it through this."

"I know . . . I will." Lisa moistened her lips. "I just . . . wish I could remember. It's like a big black . . . hole with . . . nothing in it."

Tory poured some water into a paper cup and held it up for her friend to sip. "Maybe it's better you don't remember."

Lisa swallowed, then lay back on the pillow. "I've thought

about that. The doctors say it's possible I might . . . never remember any of it. They don't really . . . know."

Tory squeezed her hand.

Lisa managed to smile. "I like your Josh. He's really . . . hot."

Tory smiled back. "Yeah, he is."

Lisa's expression changed. "Be careful, Tory. Make sure he's . . . everything he seems."

Tory glanced away. "I'll be careful." Lisa was thinking of the vicious, brutal abuser Damon had turned out to be. They hadn't talked about him. Lisa didn't remember who was responsible for her abduction, and the police had confirmed Damon's alibi.

"I pray they catch whoever did this to you," Tory said.

"So do I."

"I'll call, see how you're doing. I'll stay in touch this time." Even if it would be taking a risk. Bending over, she pressed a kiss on Lisa's forehead, turned, slung the strap of her purse over her shoulder, and walked out of the hospital room.

In the hall outside, Josh waited beside the door. Was he everything he seemed? She had no reason to doubt him, and yet, after Damon, it was hard to trust her instincts the way she had before.

"You ready to go?" Josh asked.

"I'm ready to go home."

"Home? You mean Texas?"

"Yes."

Josh actually grinned, making him look so handsome her stomach fluttered.

"Home sounds good to me," he said. "I'll start making arrangements as soon as we get back to the room."

The afternoon was gone by the time they left the hospital, the sun sitting low on the vast desert horizon. The hot orange ball silhouetted the tall, spiny cactus thrusting up from the landscape, and the temperature hovered in the nineties. The air was dry and hot as they crossed the parking lot and climbed into the shiny black rented Jeep. Josh buckled his seat belt, waited for Tory to buckle hers, then cranked the engine.

"How about a burger or something before we call it a night?"

Tory hadn't been hungry since she had left Texas, but Josh was a big, strapping man. He needed to eat. "Burger King or Carl's?"

"There's a Sonic Drive-In a few blocks down the road. It's on the way."

"Good enough," she said.

Josh turned the Jeep in that direction. The vehicle rolled along with the traffic, the radio playing country music, Josh's favorite and fast becoming hers, too. As the SUV continued down the street, Tory noticed him glancing in the rearview mirror.

"What is it?"

"I'm not sure. There's a brown Buick behind us. I saw that car in the hospital parking lot this morning. The guy sitting inside never got out. As warm as it was, it seemed kind of odd, but I didn't think much about it at the time. When we walked out just now, the Buick was in a different location, but the guy was still sitting behind the wheel."

"Maybe he's waiting for someone."

"Yeah, maybe." But Josh kept an eye on the mirror as they continued down the road. The Jeep turned into the drive-in and pulled into a space next to an automated menu. As they placed their order, the Buick drove on past, rolling leisurely down the road.

"He kept going," Tory said. "Must be just a coincidence."

"Could be." But Josh still seemed wary.

The burgers, fries, and chocolate shakes they ordered

arrived, and Tory discovered she was ravenously hungry. Maybe it was relief that nothing had happened while they were in Phoenix. Maybe it was knowing they were on their way home. Whatever it was, she dug into her burger.

"Linc said he'd send the jet back whenever we're ready." Josh munched a handful of golden brown fries. "I need to call him."

"I'll really be glad to get back. Do you think we'll be leaving tonight?"

"Probably need to give him a little notice." Josh's amazing blue eyes swung toward her and she didn't miss the hot gleam there. "Might as well get a good night's sleep and leave first thing in the morning."

Her breath hitched. Just thinking about another night in bed with Josh Cain was enough to send her temperature into the danger zone. "That's sounds . . . sensible."

Even if they left tonight, by the time they got back, Ivy would be in bed. Better to let the little girl get a good night's sleep and pick her up in the morning.

They finished their burgers. Josh started the engine, and the Jeep pulled out of the lot, heading down the street toward the hotel. She noticed him checking the rearview mirror.

"The Buick's back. It just pulled in behind a Toyota pickup. Looks like we're being followed."

Alarm shot through her. "You don't think it's Damon? Did you get a look at the driver?"

"Guy had thinning brown hair and wore glasses. It wasn't Damon."

"No, that isn't him. Besides, Damon drives a BMW." She turned to look behind her. "I don't see him."

"Five cars back. I'll turn the corner up here, see if he follows. Don't let him catch you looking."

She flipped down the sun visor and used the mirror to

watch the traffic as Josh turned the corner. "There he is! The Buick just turned the corner behind us."

"It's not Damon but there's a good chance it's someone working for him."

"I think that's how he found me in Carlsbad. I think he hired a private investigator."

Josh's features hardened. "Guy wants to know where we're going? Let's let him find out."

Tory sat back in the seat, her nerves strung taut. Josh slowed as they approached the Marriott, slowed even more as they pulled into the parking lot, letting the Buick get even closer.

"Plate number's AKJ1302," he said.

Tory memorized the number. "Maybe we can find out who the car belongs to."

"Oh, we can find out." Josh pulled the Jeep into a space, turned off the engine, and both of them climbed out. "Might be able to speed things up."

They walked into the lobby of the hotel. "Go on up to the room. I'll be along in a minute."

Tory stopped. "Wait a minute—what are you going to do?"

"If Bridger hired this guy to keep track of you, his job isn't finished yet."

As if Josh had a crystal ball, Tory looked through the glass front doors to see the Buick pulling into the parking lot. They both stepped back so the driver wouldn't see them, watched him park in a space where he could watch the entrance to the hotel.

Something appeared in the window of the car. "What's he doing?" Tory asked.

"Taking pictures. Stay here. I'll be back in a minute."

Josh headed down the hall and disappeared out one of the side doors. Tory stayed out of sight next to the big glass window in the lobby. Across the room, the desk clerk stood behind the counter, checking in another couple.

Tory looked back out the window, catching a glimpse of Josh at the rear of the parking lot before he disappeared between a pair of parked cars. Except for the lights illuminating the parking lot, it was too dark to keep track of him.

She almost smiled. If Josh didn't want to be seen, she probably couldn't spot him even in the daylight.

She spotted him a couple of times as he cut a path toward the Buick, moving in that silent way he had that seemed almost ghostly.

The next thing she knew, the door of the Buick shot open and the driver flew out of the car. One of Josh's big hands clamped around his neck and the camera went flying, landing on the pavement, rolling a couple of feet before it came to a stop. Josh backed the guy up against the car.

Tory gripped the purse slung over her shoulder and flew out the hotel's front door.

With his hand wrapped around the guy's throat, Josh shook him like the rat he was. "Who the hell are you? I want your name and I want it now."

"Hey, buddy, take it easy, okay?" The guy tried to pry Josh's fingers away but there was no chance of that.

"No, it's not okay. You've been watching us all day. Who are you?"

When he didn't answer, Josh shook him again. "This is going to get a whole lot worse before it gets better."

"All right, okay. My name is Floyd Wickham. I'm a private investigator." From the looks of the faded old Buick, Wickham's wrinkled khakis, and sweat-stained yellow polo shirt, not the high-dollar variety. "I was hired to keep an eye on a woman named Victoria Bradford. I take it she's your girlfriend."

Josh didn't answer. His relationship with Tory was none of the guy's business. Besides, he wasn't sure about it himself.

He let Wickham go but stayed right in his face. From the corner of his eye, he saw Tory running toward them. She stopped a few feet away.

"Who hired you?" Josh asked.

"I'm not at liberty to say."

Josh grabbed a fistful of Wickham's shirt and hauled him up on his toes. The detective was at least three inches shorter and twenty pounds lighter, not much of a challenge. "I asked you a question."

"He'll fire me. I need the work. This was supposed to be an easy job."

Josh let him go, grabbed his wrist, and bent it backward until Wickham crouched to avoid the pain. "How bad do you need the use of your right arm?"

The detective made a hissing sound between his teeth. "Okay, okay, I'll tell you. His name's Damon Bridger. Got the hots for your girlfriend, I guess."

Josh eased his hold. "How'd he know we were here?"

"Some nurse at the hospital gave him your names, said you were visiting one of the patients. Bridger hired me to follow you, take pictures, figure out where you were staying. He asked me to find out as much about you as I could."

"Did you?"

"I dug around. You're kind of a celebrity in Texas, so yeah, it was easy to find out what I needed to know. I talked to Bridger this morning, emailed him the photos I took. I told you were a special ops soldier. Marine sniper. A war hero."

Josh swore foully.

Behind his horn-rimmed glasses, Wickham's eyes darted around as if he were hoping someone might come to his rescue. No one did.

"Keep talking," Josh said, bending the wrist a little for emphasis.

Wickham moistened his dry lips. "Not much else to say.

Bridger wanted more photos." He glanced down at the camera. "Looks like that isn't going to happen now."

"You tell him where we were staying?"

"I just found out when you pulled in."

"So not yet."

"No."

Josh let him go. He glanced at Tory. Wickham might not have told Bridger the name of their hotel, but he'd told the guy enough to find her in Texas. When she looked up at him, he read the resignation in her face.

"You aren't going to run," he said. "This is ending. Now."

"Josh . . ."

He turned back to the PI. "Get out of here, Wickham. Keep your mouth shut or I'll shut it for you. Got it?"

The detective blanched. "Yeah, I got it. What about my camera?"

Josh leaned down and picked it up. He pulled out the memory card and handed the camera to Wickham. "I don't want to see you back here again."

The investigator rubbed his wrist. "Don't worry, I won't be back."

Josh walked Tory up to the room. As soon as the door closed, he pulled out his cell phone and brought up his contacts list.

"Who are you calling?"

"A friend. Guy named Hamilton Brown. I've got something I need to do, and I don't want to leave you here alone. Not with Bridger trying to track you."

"Josh, we need to talk about this. Now that Damon knows about us, he knows where to find me. I need to get back to Texas, get Ivy, and leave."

On the other end of the line, the phone was ringing. "You

aren't running this time, Tory. You're staying in Texas. We're going to end this."

Ham picked up the phone. "Hey, Superman, that you?"

"It's me, Ham." He was glad she hadn't heard the name he'd been tagged with in the military. No way was he letting her know. "Listen, I'm in Phoenix and I need a favor."

"Name it, man. I owe you my life. Ain't nothin' you can ask I won't do."

"I was just doing my job, same as you."

"My wife thanks you anyway. Tell me what you need."

Josh glanced over at Tory, turned his attention to the man on the other end of the phone. "I need you to look out for a friend of mine while I run an errand. She's got a stalker, guy named Damon Bridger. Bridger's bad news, Ham."

"Guys like that are my meat and potatoes. What can I do?"

"I don't think Bridger knows where Tory is at the moment, but he hired a PI, guy named Floyd Wickham, to follow us. He tracked us to our hotel. If Wickham's stupid enough to call him, Bridger might come after Tory. I don't want to leave her alone."

"Where are you?"

"Marriott Courtyard in Scottsdale near the hospital. Room 221."

"If the traffic gods are with me, I'm twenty minutes away."

"I'll see you soon." Josh ended the call and went into the other room.

He pulled his duffel out of the closet and collected the gear he would need. Opening the room safe, he took out the Beretta nine mil he had brought with him from Texas, not a problem since they were flying private and his concealed carry permit was reciprocal in Arizona.

As he clipped the holster onto his belt and pulled his T-shirt over it, Tory walked into the room.

"What's going on, Josh? I've got a right to know."

"I told you. I've got an errand to run. The friend I called is Hamilton Jackson Brown. We served together in Afghanistan a couple of years back. He was wounded in action, left the marines. We stayed in touch through that wounded vets group I support. Ham works for a company called Maximum Security. They've got a branch in Dallas. I trust Ham to keep you safe."

"He's a bodyguard?"

"That's right. I'll just be gone for a couple of hours. With Ham here, I know you'll be okay."

"Where are you going, Josh?"

"Probably better if you don't know in case something goes wrong."

"Tell me you aren't going after Damon. Please tell me that."

"All right, I'm not going after Damon."

She propped a hand on her hip. "Why don't I believe you?"

He leaned down and kissed her. "Because you're a very smart lady."

"Josh, you can't—"

A sharp knock at the door interrupted them. Josh walked over and pulled open the door and a big, beefy African-American walked into the hotel room, making it suddenly seem too small.

Dressed in jeans and a black T-shirt with an old-fashioned iron manacle on the front, the Maximum Security logo, Ham was about the same height as Josh, around six-three, but heavier, with a barrel chest and bulging biceps. He was handsome until he turned sideways, revealing the terrible burn scars that covered half his face.

Josh clasped his hand, leaned in, and gripped his shoulder, bumping the holster Ham was wearing. "Ham, meet Victoria Bradford. Tory, my good friend, Hamilton Brown."

Tory stuck out her hand and Ham's big palm engulfed it.

If she noticed the scars on his face, she didn't react. "Nice to meet you, Ham."

"You, too, Tory."

Josh walked over and pulled open the door to the adjoining room. "This'll give you a little more space. There's snacks and water in the fridge in there. You can watch TV or something. I shouldn't be gone too long."

"Not a problem. Take all the time you need."

Josh walked back to Tory. "Don't worry, okay?"

"Are you kidding?"

He bent his head and kissed her, turned around, and strode out of the hotel room.

Resigned to the situation, Tory went over to her suitcase and unzipped the outside pocket, reached in, and pulled out a deck of cards. She turned to the big man standing in the doorway between the two rooms and held up the deck.

"Sports on TV in there or a game of poker in here?"

One of Ham's thick black eyebrows went up. "Poker? You play poker?"

She wiggled the deck. "Three Card Stud or Texas Hold 'Em?"

Ham shoved away from the door and flashed a wide white grin. "Texas Hold 'Em." Rubbing his big hands together, he sat down at the round table in front of the window.

Tory grabbed the baggie of toothpicks she had taken off the plane and joined him. They cut the cards, Ham drawing the king of hearts, winning the deal. Tory did her best to keep her mind on the game and not think of Josh and what might be happening.

But it wasn't that easy to do.

Chapter Eighteen

Plugging Bridger's address into the GPS that came with the rented Jeep, Josh headed for North Scottsdale. Driving out Thompson Peak Parkway toward McDowell Mountain, he turned into an area of expensive Spanish-style townhomes.

Bringing up Google Maps on his cell, he'd looked at the satellite map location of Bridger's condo, could tell the residence wasn't in a gated community.

The luxury development sat at the base of a ridge of mountains covered with cactus and mesquite; the spectacular desert views drove up the prices of the homes, Josh figured, toward the million-dollar mark.

He wondered if Tory missed the luxury lifestyle she had left behind with Bridger, had the odd thought that maybe he should go ahead and remodel his kitchen and bathrooms the way he had planned, then viciously shoved the notion away.

He wasn't looking for a future with Tory. He was far from ready for anything that resembled settling down.

He drove past the address, a ranch-style rose-beige structure with a red tile roof on a sandy lot landscaped with barrel cactus and wispy mesquite trees. A waning moon lent a shadowy purple glow to the distant rugged mountains.

A light burned inside the house, he saw as he drove past,

continuing along the winding streets, then circling back around and stopping down the block.

He turned off the engine and sat there watching, assessing his surroundings, looking for any sign of trouble, best ingress and egress, multiple avenues of escape. After his years in the military, these things came as naturally as breathing.

A lady walked her tiny white poodle along the path beside the road, up the walkway to her front door. She unlocked the door and disappeared inside. A teenager on a bicycle zoomed past, the neon soles of his sneakers lit by some internal light as he pumped furiously, propelling himself around the corner out of sight.

Since he didn't need a gun to deal with a worm like Damon, Josh left his pistol in the glove box, popped the bulb out of the overhead light, and cracked open the door. Stepping out of the Jeep, he quietly closed and locked the vehicle.

The street was quiet, just the sound of the wind through the drooping mesquite branches. Josh skirted the residence, looking for cameras and alarms. Through the window of the garage, he spotted a high-end ADT system, but it wasn't that late so it hadn't yet been turned on. No security cameras in sight.

He crossed the sand to the patio and reached the back door. Pulling a set of lock picks out of his pocket, he inserted, twisted, and opened the lock, used the hem of his T-shirt to turn the knob so he wouldn't leave prints.

Checking to be sure no one was around, he stepped inside the house. Voices came from the family room. The big flat-screen TV was on, no other light in the room.

Moving in that direction, Josh recognized Damon Bridger from his Facebook profile—black hair neatly cut and styled, wide, muscular shoulders. Lounging in a brown leather chair that matched the sofa, he was watching *Game of Thrones* while he talked on his cell phone.

From the overworked lines he was tossing out, Josh figured it was a woman and felt a sweep of pity for any female who ended up in Bridger's path.

"Thanks, Melanie. You're a doll. We'll make it next Saturday for sure." The call ended and Josh moved closer, coming quietly up behind the chair. He looped an arm around Damon's neck and started to squeeze, holding him immobile.

Bridger thrashed and tried to escape but it wasn't going to happen. "Calm down before I hurt you. We're just going to have a little chat."

Damon made a sound of outrage, tried to move again, and finally nodded. Josh eased his hold.

"You want . . . want money? My wallet's in the bedroom. There's five hundred bucks in there. You want more, I can get it for you."

"Shut up, Damon. I don't want your money." Josh turned him loose, rounded the chair, and stood in front of him. Damon shot to his feet, but Josh shoved him back down.

"You know who I am?" Josh asked, certain the PI had sent him a picture.

Bridger looked him over, clearly recognized him. "You're Cain. Hot shit ex-marine sniper."

"There's no such thing as an ex-marine, Damon. Be smart if you remembered that."

"Fine. What do you want?"

"I think you know what I want. I want you to leave Victoria Bradford alone."

Bridger's mouth thinned. He was a good-looking guy, dark-eyed, well-built from what Josh could tell by the fit of his T-shirt and jeans, and in good physical condition.

"Tory's under my protection," Josh continued. "You know what that means?"

"That means you're the guy who's banging her. She tell

you we're engaged? Tory's mine. No one is going to change that."

"Bullshit. Tory stopped being yours the day you started abusing her. You put her in the hospital, Damon. She's done with you. It's way past time you figured that out."

Damon made no reply.

"I'm giving you a warning. I won't do it again. You come near Tory and you'll be dealing with me. You know I was a sniper. I killed more men than I want to recall. But killing a dickhead like you wouldn't bother my conscience a lick."

As he turned and started for the door, Damon shot out of the chair, grabbed Josh's shoulder, and spun him around. He swung a left Josh ducked, swung a solid right that clipped his jaw and sent a jolt right through him. The guy could throw a punch, no question about that.

Josh dodged another left jab and swung back, his fist connecting, slamming into Damon's face, sending him flying backward till he crashed against the wall.

"Get up," Josh said. "There's nothing I'd like better than to beat the fuck out of you."

Damon stayed where he was. He might be strong and in shape, but he wanted no part of taking a punch.

"Get out of my house. Get out before I call the police."

"Just remember what I said. Stay away from Tory. This is the last warning you're going to get." Turning, he strode out of the family room. Behind him, he heard something shatter against the wall.

Josh turned and walked back. "Did you do it? The girl? Lisa Shane? Was it you?"

"Get the fuck out now!"

Summoning his self-control, Josh strode out of the house, slamming the front door behind him. His blood was running hot. He wanted to go back inside and give Bridger the beating he deserved. He wanted to tear the dirtbag apart limb by limb.

Trouble was he could actually do it. He had the training, the skills. Since he was done with killing, that wasn't going to happen.

Not unless Bridger came after Tory again.

If he did, Josh intended to keep his word.

Tory finally managed to fall asleep. She and Ham had been playing cards for what seemed hours but actually wasn't that long when Josh finally called Ham and told him everything was okay. Apparently, he wasn't ready to come back to the room because he asked if Ham could stay a little longer.

Tory kept worrying.

It was late, the end of another exhausting day at the hospital. When Ham suggested she get some sleep while he went into the adjoining room and watched sports on ESPN, she agreed.

It took a while, but eventually she fell into a bottomless slumber. She wasn't sure how much time passed before she felt the mattress dip, recognized Josh's familiar weight as he settled in the bed beside her.

"Everything's okay," he said, curving his naked frame around hers spoon-fashion. "I'll tell you all about it in the morning."

She started to protest, to press him for more, but the feel of his warm mouth against the nape of her neck and the hard ridge cradled against her convinced her to wait.

"I need you," Josh said, nibbling an earlobe as he cupped and massaged a breast. "I need to be inside you."

There was something in the way he said it, something that pulled at her, told her this was important. She gave herself up to him, let him work his magic. Her nightgown slid up to her waist. His hand smoothed over her bottom as he reached around to touch her, tease and torture and drive her insane.

Her body began to move of its own volition, silently begging for more. Still nestled against her, her back to his front, Josh slid deep inside, then came up off the bed, taking her with him so she was on her hands and knees and he was behind her. God, he felt so good, fit her so perfectly.

His hard body cocooned her, his hands smoothed over her hot damp skin. Gripping her hips to hold her in place, he began to move, slowly at first, then faster, deeper, harder. Pleasure rolled through her, hot and intense. Need coiled low in her belly. Her mouth went dry while her body flushed with heat.

Deep thrusts carried her higher. She moaned and started coming, gave in to the hot, thick ripples of sensation that blotted everything but the hunger burning through her.

Josh didn't let up, just kept driving into her until she came again, so fiercely she cried out his name. Seconds later, he followed, his muscles taut as he reached his own release.

Little by little, the pleasure slowly spun out. Josh eased her back down on the bed and snuggled her against him. No condom tonight. They had talked about it. She was on birth control. She hadn't been with a man since she'd left the hospital after the beating, and Josh had been checked. Being so natural with him felt incredible.

She had always wanted another baby, imagined a little boy who looked just like Josh. Ivy would love a little brother. Tory pushed the image away. They were nowhere near that kind of thinking. There was no reason to believe they ever would be.

Josh moved her curls aside and pressed a last soft kiss on the side of her neck. He snuggled her a few minutes, then gave in with a sigh, eased out of bed, and left her alone in the bed.

She was in deep trouble with this man. She should have

learned her lesson with Damon, should be holding back, keeping her emotions in check until she could be certain he was the man he seemed.

But there was something about Josh Cain, a combination of incredible strength tempered with a hint of vulnerability that drew her as no man ever had.

She wished he had told her what had happened with Damon, but he was already asleep in the other room. She could hear his deep breathing through the open door; clearly, he was as tired as she. Tomorrow would be soon enough to find out what had happened, she told herself.

But tomorrow came sooner than she expected when her sleep was disturbed by a determined pounding on the hotel room door. Tory had a feeling it wasn't going to be good news.

While Tory slept in the other room, Josh rose and showered. He'd just dried off when he heard knocking outside the door to the other room. He had a bad feeling he knew who it was.

Cursing, he pulled on just his jeans and hurried into Tory's room, saw her grab her robe off the chair and pull it on.

"Scottsdale Police! Open the door!"

Sonofabitch. He'd known this could happen. He wasn't a fool. He'd hoped Damon would have the balls to keep his mouth shut, keep the conversation between the two of them. He should have known it was too much to expect from a slimeball woman-beater like Bridger.

He checked the peephole, saw uniformed officers, took a deep breath, stepped back, and pulled open the door.

"We're looking for Joshua Cain. That you?"

"That's me."

"We've got a warrant for your arrest, Mr. Cain. You'll need to come with us."

Josh held up his hands, showing them he wasn't a danger, which wasn't actually true, but still . . . "I won't give you any trouble, but I need to make a call first. The guy who's pressing charges? The lady had a restraining order against him. There's a chance he'll come after her. I need to phone a friend of mine, a bodyguard. He'll make sure she's safe while I'm gone."

Officers McElroy and Rodriguez shared a glance between them. They assessed Tory, who clutched her robe together, her face pale and frightened. She looked sleep-rumpled, her fiery hair tousled around her face, and sexy as hell.

"What's the bodyguard's name?" McElroy asked.

"Hamilton Brown. Works for Maximum Security."

"I know him," Rodriguez said. "Good guy."

"Make the call," McElroy said.

Josh pulled out his phone and called Ham, who answered groggily, still sleepy from being up so late last night. "Not you again."

"Sorry, buddy. I'm headed for jail. I need you to look out for Tory."

"Jesus, man. I thought you said nothing happened last night."

"I said nothing much."

Ham sighed. "I should have figured. Whatever you need to do, don't worry about Tory. I'm on my way." Ham hung up the phone and Josh turned to the cops. "Mind if I finish getting dressed?"

"Make it fast," McElroy said.

Josh started for the adjoining room and the older cop followed. Josh noticed he'd unsnapped his holster, letting his hand rest on the butt of his pistol. If Josh had wanted to disarm him, the gun wouldn't have mattered. With any luck, those days were past.

Tory hurried after them. "What happened last night?" she asked as Josh grabbed a bright blue, Dallas Cowboys T-shirt and pulled it on over his head.

"Damon and I had a chat. I told him not to bother you

again. That didn't sit well. He swung at me. I swung back. Then I left."

"That's it?"

He sat down to pull on his socks and boots. "Pretty much."

He didn't tell her that afterward he'd been too wound up to come straight back to the room. That his confrontation with Damon, thinking about him with Tory, thinking about the beating Bridger had given her, had pushed him right to the edge.

He'd left the Jeep in the hotel parking lot and walked down the block to the Silver Spur Saloon, drank three beers and a shot of Jack.

Afterward, he'd been calm enough to come up to his own room, thank Ham, and send him home. But the edginess hadn't completely left him, the powerful need for Tory he hadn't expected to feel and didn't really like.

It wasn't until he had taken her, claimed her in some primal way, that the restless feeling had left him and he had been able to sleep.

He looked over at her now. She was biting her lower lip, worry stamped into every line of her face. He felt bad about that, but Damon had to be dealt with. He didn't regret what he had done.

"I know an attorney here in town," she said. "But he specializes in family law. I'm not sure—"

Josh tossed her his cell phone. "Call Linc. Explain things, tell him what's going on. He'll know what to do."

He had phoned his brother last night before he'd gone to see Damon, had asked him to send the jet back to pick them up. It was scheduled to arrive at noon. Way it was looking, that might have to change.

"Time's up, Cain. Turn around and put your hands behind you."

Josh did as he was told and McElroy locked the cuffs in

place. "Stay here till Ham shows up," he said to Tory as McElroy nudged him forward.

Tory caught his arm. "I'm sorry I got you involved in this."

His pulse shot up. "I told you, dammit, this isn't your fault. No one's to blame but Bridger."

"Let's go." Rodriguez pushed him out of the room.

Chapter Nineteen

Tory had never met Lincoln Cain. She wasn't prepared for the big, handsome, powerful man who strode across the tarmac in her direction.

"Looks like you're in good hands," Ham said from beside her. He had helped her pack up both hotel rooms, taking Josh's holstered pistol from the nightstand and stuffing it into the satchel that held his clothes. Tory had checked out of the hotel and Ham had driven her in the rented Jeep out to the airport. He was going to catch a cab back to get his car, still parked in the hotel lot.

"Call me if you need me," he said.

"Thanks for everything, Ham."

"Just stay safe." Ham turned and walked away as Linc closed the distance between them, his strides long and purposeful.

During their brief but intense phone conversation, Linc had told her the plane would be arriving at the airport an hour later than scheduled, but that he would be on it.

Dressed in a short-sleeve button-down yellow shirt and a pair of expensive beige slacks, he moved with the authority of a man used to being in charge. He was worth millions, she knew, having Googled him that morning before Ham arrived. And every inch of his six-foot-five-inch frame oozed success.

She'd known Cain was going to be on the plane, but she hadn't expected to see the smartly dressed blond woman in the white linen skirt suit walking beside him, his wife, Carly Drake Cain.

Tory looked down at the stretch jeans she was wearing with a sleeveless peach print blouse and a pair of open-toed sandals and thought of the tailored skirt suits and expensive heels she had once worn to work.

Each time she had run from Damon, she had left some of her things behind. When Damon had found her in Carlsbad, she'd been forced to abandon the last decent clothes she still owned.

"Victoria?" Even Linc's voice sounded powerful.

"I'm Tory." She held out her hand, which Linc wrapped in both of his.

"It's nice to meet you," he said.

"You too."

"We're neighbors. We're still working on rebuilding the big house so we're out at the ranch quite a bit. If work hadn't been so hectic, we would have met sooner." He turned. "This is my wife, Carly."

"Hello," Tory said.

Carly leaned over and gave her an unexpected hug. "I'm so glad we got to finally meet you."

Tory's russet eyebrows went up. "I didn't realize Josh had mentioned me."

Carly smiled. "He told us you were staying at the ranch. You wouldn't be there if he didn't care about you."

Tory returned the smile. She supposed that was true. Josh was definitely the kind of guy who took in strays.

She glanced up as a man in a navy blue pin-striped suit came off the plane and crossed the tarmac to join them. He was fortyish, with silver threaded through his light brown hair, stylishly dressed.

"Tory, this is Nathan Temple," Linc said. "He's a criminal attorney. He's going to handle things for Josh."

Criminal. The word made her stomach burn. Josh was no criminal. And yet as she looked at Nathan Temple, relief washed through her. The attorney had competence and professionalism written all over him.

Plus, a man as successful as Lincoln Cain would only hire the best.

"It's really good to meet you, Mr. Temple. How soon can you get Josh out of jail?"

Carly and Linc exchanged amused glances. Maybe she was being a little too pushy, but she couldn't stand to think of a vital man like Josh being locked behind bars.

"Please call me Nate," Temple said, "and it shouldn't take long. I need to get down to the jail and talk to him, find out what's going on."

"The Jeep that Josh rented is parked in the lot." She dug the keys out of the small leather purse slung over her shoulder.

"I'll drive," Linc said, holding out one of his big hands.

Since he didn't look like the kind of guy who ever lost an argument, she simply handed them over.

They all piled into the Jeep, Tory in back with Carly, who had insisted Nathan Temple ride up front with her husband. Linc punched the address for the Scottsdale Police Department into the GPS and drove the Jeep out of the lot.

"You said Josh mentioned I was staying at the ranch," Tory said to Carly as Temple cranked the air conditioner up another notch. It was a little after one in the afternoon and the Arizona heat was climbing.

"I heard about it first in town," Carly said. "Iron Springs is a small community. Everyone knows Josh has a pretty new housekeeper living out at the ranch."

Tory glanced away. "Yeah, I can imagine what they're saying."

Carly reached over and caught her hand. "What they're saying doesn't matter. Linc and I had to deal with the town gossips, too. One thing I learned—all that matters is what makes you and Josh happy."

Tory smiled, liking Carly right away. "Thank you for saying that."

"Josh and Linc talk fairly often. Josh explained about your friend, Lisa, and the terrible things that happened to her. Of course you had to come back to Phoenix."

"I'm just so glad she's going to be okay."

Carly squeezed her hand. "Josh told Linc about Damon Bridger and how you ended up in Texas."

"Josh told Linc about Damon?"

"Both of us know about him. We know you have a little girl. Josh says she's adorable."

She wasn't sure how she felt about Josh discussing her personal business with his family, but knowing how he felt about her daughter took away some of the sting.

"Her name is Ivy." She thought of her little girl as she gazed at the sandy desert landscape passing outside the window. "I need to get back to her, but I can't leave Josh. It's my fault he's in jail."

"Why is that?" Linc asked from the driver's seat.

"If Josh hadn't been trying to protect me, he wouldn't have gone after Damon and he wouldn't have been arrested. I don't know exactly what happened last night but I should have found a way to stop him."

A rumble of disbelief came from Cain's broad chest. "I don't think that was going to happen, no matter what you did."

Maybe not, she silently conceded. Josh could definitely be strong willed.

"In some ways, my brother's a lot like me," Linc said.

"He's protective of the people he cares about. If he feels one of them is in danger, he isn't going to stand by and do nothing. I doubt there was any way you could have stopped him from doing something he believed was necessary."

Maybe Linc was right, but whatever had happened last night, she wasn't going to abandon him now.

"We're going to get Josh out," Linc said. "We're going to fix this, Tory. You can count on that."

She relaxed back in her seat, her worry easing a little. Everything about Lincoln Cain said he would keep his word.

Her worry resurfaced as the Jeep turned off Indian School Road into the parking lot of the Scottsdale Police Department, a flat-roofed structure painted a bright sunflower yellow. In front, big glass windows looked over the parking lot.

For the next half hour, Tory and Carly sat in the waiting area while Nathan Temple and Linc were in the back talking to Josh. Making use of the time, they both made phone calls, Carly calling her Drake Trucking office in Iron Springs while Tory phoned Mrs. Thompson.

"I'm really hoping we can come back today," she told the older woman. "I'll call you as soon as I know for sure."

"Ivy's really been good, but she misses you. She keeps asking when you're coming to get her."

Tory's heart pinched. "Could you put her on the phone?"

"She's right here." There was a pause while Mrs. Thompson handed Ivy the phone.

"Mama?"

"I'm here, sweetheart. Are you and Mrs. Thompson having fun?"

"When are you coming home, Mama?"

"There's a chance Josh and I will be back this afternoon, honey, but I'm not sure yet. I'll be there as soon as I can, I promise."

"I really miss you, Mama."

Her throat went tight. "I miss you, too, sweetheart. I'll call you as soon as I know for sure. Be good for Mrs. Thompson until I get there." Tory ended the call and wiped a tear from her cheek. She looked up to see Carly watching her.

"You'll be home soon."

She shrugged, a little embarrassed. "We haven't been apart overnight since we left Phoenix months ago." She sighed. "Before that I was always working. I was an ad exec for the Elwin Davis Group, one of the big firms in the city. My job meant everything to me. I never realized how much I was missing."

"Linc and I want kids. But I want to make sure my company's running smoothly first. Then I can take as much time off as I need."

"Kids are great," Tory said. "You won't be sorry."

Carly smiled. "I know Linc will make a fantastic father."

Tory hadn't missed the warm, occasionally heated glances between husband and wife. The two of them seemed perfectly suited. She hoped they understood how lucky they were.

She turned at the sound of footfalls, looked up to see Josh walking down the hall next to Linc and Nathan Temple. All three men were impressive: Cain exuding power and authority, Temple intellect and competence, Josh courage and strength.

He hadn't had time to shave. The scruff was back, darkening his jaw, adding to his masculinity and amazing sex appeal. She felt a little tug, hoped she wouldn't blush.

Tory stood up and waited, letting Josh set the tone of their reunion. She could feel those intense blue eyes on her, warm, but there was something more in them. Regret? Uncertainty?

Suddenly she understood. He thought he had somehow failed her. No way could she let him think that.

Tory walked over to him, reached up and slid her arms around his neck. "Are you okay?"

Hard arms came around her, pulling her close. "I'm okay. Damned glad to be out of there. I didn't mean to turn this into a circus."

"You did what you thought was right."

He looked into her eyes and his jaw hardened. "Bridger comes near you, I'll do a lot worse than punch him in the face."

"Take it easy," Temple warned. "This is not the place. Let's get out of here."

Color rose beneath Josh's cheekbones. He reached for Tory's hand, laced her fingers with his, and pulled her toward the door. Once they were all in the Jeep, a tight fit with three big men and two women, Linc drove out of the lot toward the airport.

Along the way, Temple explained that Josh had been released on a five-thousand-dollar bond, which he'd posted. Not all that high because the mild assault was a misdemeanor, not a felony.

"Bridger wanted to add breaking and entering to the charges but there wasn't any sign of forced entry," Temple said. "At least we don't have that to worry about."

"What happens if Josh is convicted?" Tory asked.

"The maximum penalty is six months in jail. But that isn't going to happen."

The lawyer explained that he had contacted an associate here in Phoenix, an attorney named Aaron Guinness. Guinness had alleged mutual combat—Bridger had also thrown a punch and Josh had a bruise on his jaw to prove it. The attorney had threatened to file countercharges against Bridger if he continued to pursue his allegations.

"I don't think this is going to take long," Temple said. "Aaron is one of the best attorneys in Phoenix. In the meantime, Josh can wait for word back in Texas."

Tory felt a rush of relief. As soon as they reached the airport, she called Mrs. Thompson and told her they were on their way home. She also talked to Ivy, who was clearly eager to see her.

But as they boarded Linc's jet, her worry returned. Damon knew about Josh, knew he had brought her to Phoenix. The private investigator Damon had hired had no doubt told him Josh owned the Iron River Ranch in Iron Springs, Texas.

There was a very good chance Damon would come after her. And after the fight Josh had had with him, Josh was now in the crosshairs, too.

She should pack her things, take her daughter, and leave the state. Get as far from Iron Springs as she possibly could. It was the right thing to do and the only solution.

She closed her eyes as the jet roared down the runway and lifted into the air. When she opened them, Josh was watching her.

"I know what you're thinking," he said.

Tory sighed. "Maybe you do. I don't know how, but you always seem to."

"You aren't running. I told you before, if he comes after you, we'll deal with him."

"He's already filed charges against you. If you try to protect me, you might end up in prison."

"He'll be on our turf this time. This is Texas. Here we have the right to protect ourselves from scum like Damon Bridger."

"Staying wouldn't be fair to you. You didn't sign on for this when I drove up in front of your barn."

"I knew you were in trouble that first day. I let you stay then. I want you to stay now."

He wanted her to stay. The words soothed her troubled

heart. She looked into those beautiful blue eyes. "Are you sure?"

"Never more certain, baby."

She leaned across the seat and very softly kissed him. "Thank you." She was staying. At least for now.

She still wasn't sure what she was going to do if Damon showed up at the ranch.

She'd keep a bag packed for her and Ivy just in case.

Chapter Twenty

Halfway through the flight, Josh and Linc came out of their seats and sat down together at the back of the plane so they could talk.

"You know you have a problem," Linc said. "And it isn't the charges Bridger filed against you."

Josh ran a hand over his unshaved jaw, feeling the familiar roughness. "I know."

"You think he'll come after the girl?" Linc asked.

"I don't know. I warned him what would happen if he did. He knows my background, knows I'm former military. Maybe he'll be smart enough to leave her alone and move on."

"What's your gut say?"

Unconsciously, his hand fisted. "I think he'll come. His ego won't let him back away."

"You figure that's what's driving him. Ego?"

Josh thought about the wild look in Bridger's dark eyes when Josh had asked him about Lisa Shane. "Maybe. Could be something a lot worse than that. Tory thinks Bridger might be the guy who abducted her friend. Takes a special kind of pervert to torture a woman that way."

"You think Bridger did it?"

"Police don't think so and his alibi holds up."

"But Tory's friend can't remember."

"No, and that might be the only thing keeping her safe. She told Tory she was going back home with her parents for a couple of months. They live somewhere in upstate New York."

"Kidnapping's a federal offense. The guy who took her is in very deep trouble. Good chance he'll want to take care of loose ends."

"And Lisa is definitely that. At least she'll be leaving the area as soon as she's released. That ought to buy the cops some time to find this guy."

"Unless he was just passing through. Women all over the country disappear without a trace. Lisa was lucky to escape."

"Yeah."

"What about Bridger?" Linc asked.

"I've asked Ham to keep an eye on him for the next few days, make sure he doesn't head for the airport."

"You can't watch him forever."

"No. With luck, Bridger will decide Tory isn't worth the trouble."

"Security is expensive. If you need money to pay—"

"I don't need your money." He looked up at his older brother and smiled. "I've never told you this, big brother, but thanks to you, money isn't a problem. I bought stock in Texas American the day it went public and every chance I got after that. I've made a bundle, plus a nice little income." He grinned. "I'll be fine—as long as you keep up the good work."

Linc chuckled. "We're definitely brothers."

And Josh was damned glad. Growing up, he had never had much family, just his mom, who had died when he was a teen. Linc had no other family, either. It felt good to be able to count on each other.

"What about you and Tory?" Linc asked. "I like her. So does Carly."

"I like her, too. Probably too much. The thing is, I'm not

really ready for a family. I've got some personal issues I need to deal with. I've got to get the ranch up and running, and I have no idea how long that's going to take."

"I don't think we're ever really ready for the things life throws in our path. Sometimes we have to make adjustments." He glanced up the aisle toward where Tory sat. "She might be worth it."

Josh made no reply. He loved having Tory in his bed—no doubt about it. He liked her and her sweet little girl way more than just a little. But he wasn't ready to go beyond that, and he didn't think Tory was either. She was still reeling from her disastrous relationship with Bridger. Josh could give her a little stability, give her time to get grounded, centered.

But more than that . . .

He wasn't ready to go there.

"I want you to keep me updated on this," Linc said. "Okay if I ask Temple to keep me in the loop?"

"Absolutely. Ask Ross Townsend to email you anything new that comes up on Bridger. No way to know where this is going. I might need your help again."

Linc just nodded. Done with their conversation, he unbuckled his seat belt and returned to his seat beside Carly while Josh sat back down next to Tory.

When she looked up at him, those bright green eyes held so much trust his chest clamped down. Josh found himself reaching for her hand. It occurred to him that he wasn't just protecting Tory because she needed his help.

He was doing it because he didn't want to lose her. It wasn't a feeling he'd ever had before.

It was a dangerous feeling.

They were back on the Iron River Ranch. Tory had returned to her daily routine, housekeeping, home-schooling Ivy; plus she had a new project she found interesting and challenging—building a website for the ranch.

When the horses Josh was training were ready to be put up for sale, the website would be a terrific way to advertise them.

She planned to set up social media: Facebook and Twitter, LinkedIn, Instagram, Pinterest, anything that would help. Designing the site appealed to her creativity. Plus, using her years of experience and expertise seemed the perfect way to repay Josh's kindness.

In the afternoons sometimes, she brought Ivy out to the pasture to watch the horses—from a safe distance, of course. Of all the animals, Star was Ivy's favorite. He was just such a magnificent creature.

And the stallion was definitely making progress. Tory and Josh had been going into the pen with him, though Josh insisted they stayed close to the gate.

Everyone was working long hours, gearing up for the barn raising. Lots of folks from the community would be there to help, as well as Carly and Linc.

That morning, Tory refilled Josh's coffee cup while he sat at the kitchen table eating his breakfast. He was almost finished when his cell phone rang. Digging the phone out of his jeans, he checked the screen and his face lit up.

"Hey, Coy. Man, it's good to hear from you. It's been way too long."

Tory smiled at how excited he was. Then his smile slipped away.

"What?" He set his fork back down on his plate. "You're kidding. When did it happen?"

She couldn't hear the reply but her pulse started thrumming. The look on Josh's face said something was terribly wrong.

"Jesus, I can't believe it. Do the cops have any leads?" Josh leaned back in his chair. "That's rough, man. How's

Dolores holding up?" He blew out a heavy breath. "When's the funeral? Okay, just let me know and I'll be there. I'll see you then." He hung up the phone and just sat there.

"What happened, Josh? What's wrong?"

His face looked pale, his expression grim. "That was Coy Whitmore, a vet friend of mine. He called to tell me one of the guys I served with in Afghanistan was killed, guy named Pete Saldana. Pete was murdered, shot dead in some back alley outside a place called Buzz's, a local beer joint where Pete hung out. Cops haven't got a clue who did it."

"Oh, Josh, I'm so sorry."

"Funeral's this week. Coy's going to let me know what day."

"You want me to come with you?"

He shook his head. "Ivy needs you. Pete lives—lived—with his wife in Fairfield. It's only a couple of hours away. I'll be down and back the same day."

"Are you sure? I could ask Mrs. Thompson to babysit again."

"I'll be with friends. Noah and Cole will be here to keep an eye on things, so you don't need to worry."

"I'm worried about you, not me."

His gaze went to hers. "I'll be fine." Shoving up from his chair, he left his breakfast unfinished and walked out of the house.

Tory's heart went with him. She thought of the story she had read, "Ultimate Hunter," thought of the men who had fought and died beside him in the war. He was out of the military now, but he was still losing friends.

It didn't seem fair. But then life was never easy. It was a lesson Damon had taught her.

Damon was feeling the itch. The clawing need that burned deep in his belly. He needed a woman. Badly. But not just in his bed. Ever since he'd abducted Lisa and held her prisoner, nothing less than having a woman completely at his mercy would do.

As far back as high school he had sensed this unnatural need in him. Back then it had frightened him. By the end of his senior year, he'd accepted that he was different. He'd begun to explore that difference, allow himself to enjoy it.

Hurting things, both animals and people, having them in his power was a soaring high and fiercely sexually arousing. He'd read about people like him, how they'd been abused as kids, how their perverted parents had messed up their heads.

That wasn't his story. Aside from losing his mom, he'd had it good as a kid. Nothing to complain about. Nothing that would explain his behavior. He was just unique. In a way he was proud of it, though by necessity it had to remain his secret.

Over the years, he had learned to control his needs, keep himself in check. On the surface he lived a normal life. People accepted him, even liked him. Women loved him.

Tory had been the flash point. He had fallen in love with her, had believed he might actually become the normal man he seemed on the surface. But the urges never really left him. The night he had beaten her into submission, he had felt such an unbelievable thrill, he'd been forced to accept completely who he really was.

Lisa had added fuel to the fire burning inside him. Taking her, using her, had made him feel like a king. He understood now what he had to do, the only thing that would satisfy this craving that never went away.

He needed a woman. It was Victoria he wanted, but she was in Texas with Cain. He had plans for Cain, but he didn't have time for that now, and the hunger refused to let him wait any longer.

He'd considered going to a prostitute, but a woman soiled by so many men disgusted him. He would find a redhead, someone who looked like Tory. A substitute for his fantasies.

He would lock her in his basement prison and force her to submit to his will.

Anticipation poured through him, so sweet he could taste it on his tongue. Images appeared in his head, and beneath the fly of his trousers, he went hard. He needed to start searching, find the right candidate.

Looking forward to the challenge, Damon leaned back in the chair behind his desk. And he smiled.

Chapter Twenty-One

Tory rose early the day of the funeral. Clearly upset, Josh hadn't come over last night. Even if he had, he wouldn't have stayed. It bothered her, but spending the night had to be his decision, and it didn't look like that was going to happen anytime soon.

Dressing hurriedly, she got Ivy ready for the day, fed her a bowl of Cocoa Puffs, her favorite; then they went over to the main house to make breakfast for Josh before he left for Fairfield.

She heard the screen door slam behind him as he came in from outside and set his plate of bacon, eggs, and toast on the table. He sat down to eat, but mostly just toyed with his food, swallowing without much interest.

Tory thought she could have burned the entire meal and he wouldn't have noticed.

Eventually, he gave up any pretense, shoved his plate aside, and rose from the table. "I've got to get dressed and get out of here." He headed for his bedroom while she cleaned up the table and put the dishes in the dishwasher.

He was gone longer than usual. When he walked back into the kitchen, she understood why. He was wearing his full marine dress blues, a white, billed cap tucked under one arm.

For several seconds she just stared. He was clean-shaven and perfectly groomed, wearing pressed blue trousers with a red stripe down the side, navy jacket covered with medals and ribbons. She didn't know what most of them stood for but she recognized bronze and silver stars.

The uniform fit him perfectly and it said everything about him: that he had served his country with honor and courage; that he had been a decorated hero; that he had suffered and survived.

She looked at him standing there and thought he was the most handsome man she had ever seen.

"You look . . . ." She wanted to say incredible. "Like a soldier."

He glanced away. "Pete was a special guy, one of the best. His family wanted a full military funeral. Pete deserves it."

"Is there . . . umm . . . anything you want me to do while you're gone?"

He thought for a moment. "You're still working on the website, right?"

"Yes." It seemed insane to be talking about mundane subjects when Josh was leaving to pay his respects to a friend who'd been senselessly murdered.

"I've hired a webmaster," she said, "a woman I worked with in Phoenix. She's really good. We're designing the pages together. I need to get some photos, pictures of the ranch and one of each of the horses."

He just nodded, his mind clearly on the loss of his friend. "I appreciate your help with this." A faint smile touched his lips. "I didn't realize I was hiring an expert in marketing when you drove up to the barn that day. I got way more than I bargained for."

She smiled and shrugged. "At least all those years I spent in advertising weren't a total waste."

His slight smile faded. She felt a pang in her heart at the misery in his face.

"I need to go." He started for the door, but Tory caught his arm.

She went up on her toes and very softly kissed him. "Drive safely. If you decide to stay overnight, just let me know."

"I'm not going to stay. I'll be back tonight at the latest."

She took a step backward, but Josh hauled her into his arms, bent his head, and kissed her far more thoroughly. Then he turned and walked away, pausing only long enough to settle his cap on his head before pushing through the door.

Tory stood on the porch and watched him drive away, watched till his pickup disappeared down the dirt road leading out of the ranch.

It was early afternoon when she heard the roar of an engine rolling back down the dirt road toward the house, too early for Josh to be home. For an instant, her nerves kicked in.

But the last time Josh had heard from Ham, Damon was still in Phoenix, continuing his usual routine: work, play, and picking up women at his favorite upscale bars. Tory prayed he had finally accepted that she was out of his life for good.

Knowing Cole and Noah were working near the house— she suspected because Josh wanted them to stay close—she walked out on the front porch. Josh's newest hire, a black-haired teen named Tyler Murphy, had already finished cleaning the makeshift stalls in the cow barn and left for the day.

She watched the car approach, a beautiful bright red Stingray convertible. It hadn't rained the past few days. The sun was out, the afternoon warm, but the forecast warned of a coming storm.

Two women sat in the car. She recognized Carly Cain in the driver's seat, blond hair pulled back and clipped at the nape of her neck, sitting next to a beautiful brunette with long, mahogany-brown hair. Tory walked toward them as they climbed out of the car.

"Hi, Carly. Wow, what a fabulous car."

"It is, isn't it? Linc bought it for me for Christmas. I have to say I love it. Carly, this is my friend Brittany Haworth. Britt's a teacher at Iron Springs Elementary. We've been BFFs since high school."

"It's great to meet you, Brittany."

"You too, Tory."

"I'm afraid you missed Josh. A close friend of his died. The funeral's today in Fairfield."

"I'm sorry to hear that. Josh has already lost enough friends. But the truth is we came to see you. I've been dying to meet your little girl."

A warm feeling spread through her. She hadn't really made any friends since she had left Phoenix.

She smiled. "Come on in. Ivy's watching TV, and I've got a pitcher of lemonade in the fridge."

As the women walked up on the porch, she noticed Brittany looking over at the cow barn. Cole and Noah were hard at work. Cole had his shirt off, and to say the man was ripped would be an understatement. Tory didn't blame the brunette for staring.

As she led the women inside, Ivy ran up, shiny blond ponytail bouncing against her back. A little pink gathered smock with a unicorn on the front covered a pair of pink leggings.

"Ivy, these are friends of Josh's. His brother's wife, Carly, and her friend Brittany."

Carly crouched down to Ivy's height. "It's nice to meet you, Ivy. Josh told us all about you."

"He did?"

"Well, he told Linc about you and Linc told me so I feel like I know you already."

"You're pretty," Ivy said.

Carly reached out and touched her cheek. "So are you, sweetheart."

"Brittany's a teacher," Tory said.

Ivy looked up at her. "I can't go to regular kinnygarten because we move around too much. But Josh says we can stay, so maybe I can go to your school when I'm old enough."

Brittany kept the smile on her face. Tory wondered how much Carly had told her about Damon and what had led to the roundabout journey that had ended in Iron Springs.

"We have some very nice schools around here," Brittany said. "And the bus could pick you up right out at the gate."

Ivy swung her gaze to Tory, clearly excited. "Can I, Mama? Can I go to regular school?"

She swallowed. "We'll see, honey. School doesn't start till September. We've got a long time before then."

"But maybe?"

"Maybe."

Apparently satisfied, Ivy hurried back to the living room, plopped back down in front of the TV.

Tory busied herself getting down glasses, filling them with ice, pouring the lemonade, and handing the glasses around.

"I hope I didn't speak out of line," Brittany said, taking a sip.

Tory shook her head. "Not at all. It would be wonderful if Ivy could go to kindergarten in the fall. But the truth is a lot could happen between now and then."

She wasn't just thinking of Damon; she was thinking of her relationship with Josh. There was no way to know where it was going, if they would still be together in the fall. The thought stirred an ache in her chest.

She looked up at Brittany, saw that her gaze had wandered

out the window. From where she stood, she could watch Cole working.

"I've got an idea," Tory said. "It's hot outside, and the guys have been working hard all day. Why don't we take them some lemonade, too?"

Brittany beamed. "That's a great idea."

Tory glanced at Carly, who gave her a grateful smile. Clearly there was some matching going on here.

"Come on, Ivy, honey. We're taking a quick walk outside."

"'Kay." She jumped up and ran to join them. "I'm ready to go."

Tory got down a tray for the lemonade and some red plastic cups, poured a cup for Ivy, and they all took their drinks outside. The men spotted them and tossed aside their tools.

When Cole reached for his shirt and began to shrug it on, Tory bit back a smile at Brittany's disappointment.

"We thought you might be thirsty," Tory said, setting the tray down on a piece of plywood on top of a pair of sawhorses.

She poured two glasses and handed one to Noah. Brittany handed the other to Cole, whose eyes turned hot and dark, the attraction between them clear.

They headed for the shade of the cow barn. While Noah chatted with Tory, and Carly and Ivy played with the big yellow cat, Cole and Brittany wandered deeper into the shadows of the barn.

Noah chuckled. "Maybe Cole has finally met a woman who won't let him give her the brush-off."

Tory followed his gaze to the couple talking softly, Cole laughing at something Brittany said. "Why would he want to do that?"

"He's a man with no legs—or at least that's the way Cole sees himself. In his mind, that makes him less than a man."

"It's obvious Brittany doesn't see him that way," Tory said.

"Britt's been crushing on Cole since junior college," Carly said. "And if you tell him that, Noah, you're a dead man."

Noah chuckled. "I won't tell him. I just hope he's smart enough to appreciate a beautiful woman like Britt. She's pretty both inside and out."

"Yes, she is," Carly agreed.

They stood in the shade and finished their lemonade. Cole and Brittany joined them, and the men went back to work. Tory walked the women over to Carly's flashy red convertible.

"I'm really glad we came," Carly said through the window as they settled inside.

Tory smiled. "Me too. I hope you'll come again soon."

"We'll be here for the barn raising," Brittany said with a last glance at Cole.

"It's going to be fun." Carly cranked the powerful engine and the sports car rumbled to life. "I still can't believe Linc bought me this. I usually drive one of the company pickups."

"It's gorgeous."

"I thought he was crazy when I saw this parked out front Christmas morning, but I totally fell in love with it. I don't get to drive it that often, but I figured today was the perfect day."

Now that she was a mother, the car Tory would most love to have was a compact SUV. "It was great having you," she said. "Come back anytime."

"Thanks for the lemonade," Brittany said. "And . . . umm . . . everything else." A conspiratorial look passed between them and both of them grinned.

Tory waved as Ivy ran up beside her and the Stingray roared back down the dirt road toward the highway. She thought of the friends she had made.

It had been a very good day for her.

She just wished it had been a better day for Josh.

The service was almost over. Josh stood in a line of soldiers off to one side of the open grave next to Coy, a big, blond, hard-boiled former marine who lived up in Gainesville. A dozen other marines in DBs stood on the grass close by, some of them wounded vets Josh already knew, others soldiers and vets he'd met today.

Pete's big extended Hispanic family filled rows of white plastic chairs set up beneath a canopy on the lawn, many of them openly crying, not afraid to show emotion. The vets were more stoic. They had learned to deal with loss a long time ago.

The area around the casket was filled with flowers, their sweet scent wafting through the air. The service overflowed with mourners. Pete was a popular guy in the community. An American flag draped over Pete's coffin.

At the back of the crowd, a couple of men stood out from the rest, guys in dark suits with short-cropped hair. Like a lot of men who had served, Josh could smell law enforcement a mile away. Off-duty police? Detectives, maybe? Feds? He had a hunch it was some of each, couldn't help wondering why the feds would be there.

So far Pete's killer hadn't been apprehended. Maybe they hoped he would show up today to revel in his accomplishment. Sadly, it wasn't uncommon.

Josh steeled himself as a line of marines raised their rifles and fired three volleys, a final salute to a man who well deserved the honor. The sound recalled the nightmare he had suffered last night, waking covered in sweat to the imagined sound of explosions. He was glad he hadn't spent the night with Tory.

The chaplain said a final prayer and in the distance, a lone bugle played taps. The flag was folded and presented to Pete's wife, and the service was over.

As the mourners began to depart, Josh fell in among them. He was only a little surprised when one of the suits singled him out, this guy's sport coat less expensive, a little rumpled. A local cop, he guessed.

"You're Cain, right? Joshua Cain?" The man was midthirties, average height, nothing much different about him except his interest.

"That's right."

"You were a friend of Pete Saldana's?" It sounded like a question but it wasn't.

"Right again. Who are you?"

"Detective Craig Milburn, Fairfield PD. You got a minute?"

"If it'll help you find the prick who murdered Pete, I've got all the time you need."

They walked a little ways away, out of earshot of the dispersing crowd. Josh lifted his white cap to catch a little of the breeze, then settled it back on his head.

"Any reason you can think of that someone might want to murder your friend?" the detective asked.

Josh shook his head. "Everybody loved Pete. He was just one of those guys, you know? His nickname in the Corp was Amigo. He was a friend to everyone."

"Yeah, that's the picture we've been getting. You know he was killed execution-style? Forty-five-caliber slug to the back of the head. Looks like he walked out of the bar for a smoke and the guy came up behind him. A hit like that . . . it makes us think he was involved in some kind of criminal activity. Drugs, maybe. Could be a lot of different things."

Josh started shaking his head. "Not Pete. He was a hero, straight shooter all the way. He had kids. He wanted them to look up to him, be proud of him. He was determined to be a good role model."

"Good role models don't usually end up getting their brains blown out."

Josh's jaw tightened. He didn't like this guy or the direction this conversation was taking. And it certainly wasn't the time or place. "You're wrong. Do your job and prove it." Turning, he walked away.

What the hell had happened to Pete? Had he pissed someone off badly enough to get himself killed? Everything inside Josh urged him to find out.

But he wasn't in the marines anymore and Pete was no longer one of the men who fought beside him. The Josh he was now had responsibilities, a ranch to run, a young woman and her daughter to look after. He needed to let the police handle Pete's murder.

From the cemetery, he and Coy and the other guys stopped by Pete's house to pay their respects to Dolores and the rest of Pete's family. From there they went to one of the local saloons to toast their friend and drown their grief.

Josh had a couple of beers and headed home. As a kid he had never really had a home, just a place to eat and sleep. He and his mom had lived in a fleabag apartment where his drunken dad dropped by once in a while to beat up on his wife and son.

Josh thought of the ranch he was building, thought of Tory and Ivy, and was surprised to discover how eager he was to get back.

Chapter Twenty-Two

Ham called the next morning, disturbing the big workday Josh had planned, work that needed to be done for the barn raising on Saturday.

According to his last conversation with Ham, there hadn't been any new leads in the investigation. Lisa had left for New York, but had never recovered her memory.

Josh pressed the phone against his ear. "Hey, Ham, what's up?"

"Could be nothing. Saw something on the news last night. Probably doesn't have anything to do with what happened to Lisa Shane, but I figured you'd want to know."

Unease crawled through him. "Tell me."

"A girl went missing. Early twenties, waitress at a dive bar out in Carefree. She left around two A.M. after her shift was over and just disappeared. Apparently, it wasn't unusual for her to go home with some guy from the bar so no one worried when her car was still in the lot the next day. When she didn't show up for her next shift, I guess one of her friends got worried. No sign of her since the night she disappeared."

"Carefree's not far off I-17. Easy access to the mountains up north. Could be the same guy who took Lisa."

"Could be. Bridger's still in Phoenix. I've been checking on him off and on. He's still going to the office, hasn't changed his routine. I wouldn't have called except . . ."

"What is it?"

"The thing is, Josh, this girl . . . she was a pretty little red-head about Tory's size."

The news felt like a kick in the stomach. "Jesus."

"Could be a coincidence. Hell, maybe she just took off with some dude and the two of them are shacked up somewhere."

He relaxed a little. As Ham said, it could be nothing. Even if it turned out to be something, didn't mean it had anything to do with Tory. Lots of crime in Phoenix. "You're right. We need more information. Stay on it, will you?"

"I've got friends in the Phoenix PD. They promised to give me a heads-up if anything breaks."

"Really appreciate it. Thanks, Ham."

"I heard about Pete. Life really sucks sometimes."

"Yeah, it does." Josh ended the call and stuck the phone back in the pocket of his jeans. He had work to do, way too much to be worrying about a so-far nonexistent threat.

He wasn't about to say anything to Tory.

He hoped he'd never have to.

Josh pushed the phone call out of his mind and went back to work. All week, Cole and Noah had been working with a mason, laying the cement-block foundation for the barn he intended to build. A local architect had drawn the plans. The main barn would be serviceable but not overly large, configured so he could add on as his horse-breeding operation developed over the years.

Tory had been amazing, doing all of the organization,

making the work look easy while he found the job frustrating and confusing.

Things were moving in the right direction, but there was still the problem of the charges against him in Phoenix, leaving a cloud of worry hanging over his head.

Thursday afternoon was humid, the damp air hot and sticky as Tory walked next to Josh to the cow barn. She adjusted the white straw cowboy hat he had bought her to protect her fair skin from the sun. The boots she was wearing she had purchased for herself.

They were riding in the pasture now instead of the ring. She had come to love it and she was getting better every day—or at least thought she was. It was pretty much a daily routine, though a couple of times they had gotten distracted and ended up making love in the tack room.

The riding lesson went perfectly. Afterward, they headed for the grassy pasture where Star placidly grazed. In order for the stallion to earn his keep, he needed to be tame enough to work with the people who handled him and not hurt the mares he would be breeding.

If the horse would accept Josh, then maybe he could learn to accept other people, too. Maybe at last Star could fulfill his tremendous potential.

Tory cupped her hand around her mouth to call out to him, but the stallion caught her scent, his head shot up, and his ears flashed forward. With a soft whinny, he galloped toward the fence, slowed to a trot, and walked right up to her. With his gleaming black coat and perfect conformation, he was so beautiful a soft pang throbbed in her heart.

The horse eyed Josh a moment, apparently decided he wasn't a threat, very carefully picked up the apple Tory had placed in the flat of her hand, and crunched it down.

Josh moved forward, joining Tory at the fence. "Hey, buddy. You like that, don't you?" His voice was soft and deep, but also firm. She knew from personal experience how hard that voice was to resist.

Josh fed the stallion the other half of the apple and continued rubbing and stroking.

"I'd say we're making real progress," he commented as they headed back to the house. "Tomorrow I'm going to try to halter him while you keep him occupied."

"I think he's beginning to trust you."

"Yeah. It's a good feeling."

Preparations for the barn raising were coming together the way they'd planned. Better yet, the following morning Nate Temple called—the charges against Josh had been dropped.

Aaron Guinness's threat to file countercharges, along with Damon's prior arrest for assault against Tory and the restraining order once granted against him, had apparently been enough for his attorney to convince him. He had a reputation as a businessman to consider, as well as the reputation of his father's company.

Damon—probably at his father's insistence—had grudgingly agreed to a dismissal.

According to Guinness, there was a good chance Damon had never intended for the arrest to go any further. He'd just wanted to see Josh handcuffed in front of Tory and hauled off to jail.

Saturday finally arrived and it seemed as if half the town showed up to help build Josh a new barn. To the accompaniment of pounding hammers and buzzing saws, the men scrambled up and down ladders and carried lumber, all of them working together like a perfectly choreographed dance.

By midafternoon, the sides of the barn were in place and

half a dozen men slid metal panels into position on the roof, securing them with metal screws.

Tory had everything well-organized, from where to stack the building supplies for easy access, to which crews would work where. She had even assigned young Ty Murphy to handle parking cars in the field in front of the barn.

A group of local women joined Tory, Carly, and Brittany, either working with the men or helping keep everyone fed and hydrated during the hot early June day.

By the time the sun had slipped below the horizon, the barn had been completed exactly as planned. Exhausted men and women gathered around makeshift sawhorse tables where a potluck supper waited. Plastic plates were loaded with slices of beef from the big haunch Josh provided, plus homemade casseroles, salads, and desserts.

Strings of sparkling white lights hung above rented tables and chairs. Everyone grabbed beers or poured glasses of wine from ice-filled tubs, then wandered over and sat down to eat.

Tory and the other moms fed their kids first, then Ivy went to play with friends she had made that afternoon. Tory hadn't seen her daughter so happy since before she had moved in with Damon.

She sighed. Even if it didn't work out with Josh, maybe they could stay in Iron Springs. She could rent a place, find a job, make it work.

Tory refused to think how seeing Josh with other women would make her feel. She would handle it, she told herself. *Somehow*.

She was smiling when she felt Josh's beautiful blue eyes on her.

"You made this work today," he said softly. "I don't think the barn raising would have been half as successful if you hadn't pulled it all together."

"I had help. It wasn't just me." Still, she couldn't resist feeling pleased.

"You organized everything. The day ran like clockwork because of you." He leaned over and kissed her, and something she was afraid to feel stirred deep inside her.

"I'll be over tonight," Josh said in that soft, deep voice that sent a warm flush over her skin. "If that's okay."

Oh, yeah. It was more than okay. Her body was already thrumming just thinking about it. "Umm . . . sure."

People stayed awhile longer, but after such a tough day, everyone was exhausted. Families packed up their leftovers, loaded their cold boxes into their cars, and headed home.

Since there was a ton of cleanup, Mrs. Thompson took Ivy home with her. Tory had a hunch Mrs. T. wasn't just being helpful but doing a little matchmaking, as well.

Cole offered to drive Brittany home, and she was thrilled to accept. Noah and his wife, Natalie, a svelte, black-haired beauty whom Tory had liked immediately, also remained.

As Josh and Cole finished folding and stacking tables, Noah walked up. "Looks like we may have a problem."

"Yeah, what is it?" Josh asked.

"We got company and it doesn't look friendly." Noah turned toward the road leading into the ranch, a scowl on his face.

Tory heard the roar of engines growing louder as they approached. In the distance, a group of bikers rolled down the dirt road toward the house, their headlights drilling shafts of white through the darkness.

Her pulse kicked into gear, began to race as fast as the engines. There were eight of them, guys in black leather on low-slung, customized motorcycles with extended front wheels.

"What the hell?" Josh and Noah walked up next to Cole,

the three men forming a protective wall against the uninvited visitors.

Tory hurried up on the porch out of the way and Britt and Natalie joined her. Instead of stopping, the bikers revved their engines and began circling the yard, doing wheelies in the dirt, knocking over stacks of chairs, jerking down strings of lights, destroying everything in their path.

One of the bikers deliberately rammed a cold box, smashing it to pieces. Several headed for the supplies left from building the barn. One leaned down to grab a bucket of nails, then tossed the contents all over the ground. Another grabbed a power saw and slammed it against the barn wall, sending pieces of metal flying.

Josh suddenly moved. One of the bikers shouted a curse as Josh grabbed him by the back of his black leather vest and yanked him off the motorcycle, which raced off and slipped over into the dirt. Josh spun him around, drew back and slammed a fist in his face, then swept his legs out from under him as he went down. The biker hit the ground hard, shouting a string of obscenities.

Josh dragged a guy with a handlebar mustache off a metallic red Harley and knocked him down, while Noah hooked his good arm around the neck of a guy with greasy black hair and tattoos, jerking him backward off the bike into the dirt.

Cole took over, grabbing the guy by the front of his black T-shirt, hauling him up, and punching him in the face. When the man swung back, Cole ducked and drove a fist into the guy's stomach, doubling him over. He followed with a blow that sent the biker sprawling in the dirt.

The rest of the bikers slid to a halt, jammed down their kickstands, and rushed to join the fray. Josh and his friends were outnumbered more than two to one, but they were marines trained to fight.

Josh threw solid punches, drove an elbow into a biker's stomach, brought a knee up hard beneath his chin. Whirling, he lashed out with a boot, kicking one of the men squarely in the groin. The biker grabbed his privates, doubled over, and rolled on the ground in pain.

Tory stood frozen but Josh kept moving. Hitting, kicking, throwing left jabs and right punches. When he pitched a red-bearded biker over his shoulder, sending him flying up on the porch, Tory's trance was broken. She grabbed an empty lemonade pitcher and crashed it over the biker's head.

Glass went flying and the man went down. He groaned, but managed to crawl away. She didn't miss Josh's quick grin before he turned and swung at a gigantic biker with a gray goatee and a sleeve of tattoos on each arm. The big biker's nose exploded in a geyser of blood.

The tide seemed to be turning. Along with the others, the big guy ran for his motorcycle, silver with a red skull on the tank. The men cranked their engines and roared out of the yard, throwing dirt up behind their back wheels.

One of the riders pulled a gun and shot out two of the new barn windows as the group blasted back down the dirt road.

Tory's heart was still pounding as the sound of their engines faded, their taillights turned onto the highway and shrank to red dots in the distance.

Josh strode toward her, moving like a big-screen superhero. Tough and strong, he was all smooth motion and no wasted energy. He pulled her into his arms and just hung on. Tory was trembling. She could feel his heart beating hard inside the wall of muscle across his chest, feel her own heart thundering.

"You okay?" he asked.

She nodded. "How about you?"

He reached up and touched a cut that slashed across his cheek. Then he grinned.

Tory huffed out a breath. *Men.* "So I guess that means you're fine."

"I can't believe that just happened," Natalie said.

"Weren't the guys amazing?" said Britt, her eyes riveted on Cole. A cut ran diagonally through one blond eyebrow and one of his pant legs was torn above the top of his prosthesis.

"You were wonderful," Britt said to him as he walked up on the porch.

Cole caught her face between his hands, leaned over and kissed her, hot and deep. "It's been a long night," he said gruffly. "Let's go home." There was no mistaking the husky note in his voice or what it meant.

Britt just nodded, a look of adoration on her face. Tory had a hunch Cole was no longer worried about proving his masculinity, though the way the two were staring at each other, odds were he'd be proving it again a little later that night.

Noah grabbed a dirty dish towel from the pile on the porch and handed it to Natalie, who wiped the blood off his knuckles and dabbed at his split lip. He wrapped his arm around her.

"You gonna call the cops?" he asked Josh.

"Not tonight. I'll call the sheriff's office in the morning."

"We can give descriptions of some of them. They weren't wearing MC jackets or helmets so we don't know if they belong to a club."

"We can tell the sheriff what happened, but don't be surprised if it doesn't do any good. Howler wouldn't walk across the street to help a Cain."

Noah and Cole knew about the animosity between Emmett Howler and the two Cain brothers.

"Asphalt Demons are local," Noah said. "You think it was them?"

"No way. The Demons are friends of my brother's. They might even be able to help us. What I can't figure out is why anyone would come here just to cause trouble."

Noah snorted a laugh. "Guys like that . . . they don't always need a reason."

Josh didn't disagree. "Why don't you and Natalie go on home? I'll finish cleaning up in the morning."

"You gonna need some help?"

"It's your day off. Enjoy it. I'll see you Monday."

With a weary nod, Noah took his wife's hand and led her off to his shiny Dodge pickup.

Josh turned to Tory. "I'll walk you home."

He stayed close beside her as they crossed the yard and climbed the steps to the front door of the trailer, examining his bloody knuckles along the way.

"I need to get cleaned up before I come over. I'll see you in a little while." Those amazing blue eyes slid down her body, as hot as the tip of a flame. He grinned. "We won't have to be quiet tonight."

Her stomach contracted and she smiled. "No . . ." she whispered softly.

Josh bent and kissed her, lingered and deepened the kiss before he turned and strode back toward his house.

He was still jacked up from the fight. In a different way, so was she. Seeing him in action was an amazing turn-on, the way he handled himself, the confidence, the beauty of his movements, the way his muscles flexed and tightened.

Josh would come over and she would be waiting. Knowing what would happen when he got there shot a curl of heat low into her belly.

It wasn't until she started undressing that her thoughts

returned to the bikers and what they had done. Why had the ranch been singled out? What was the cause of the men's animosity?

But as Tory lay in the darkness waiting for Josh, no answer came.

Chapter Twenty-Three

Standing on the front porch of her little white-shuttered gray house, Brittany unlocked the front door and led Cole inside. They hadn't talked much on the ride over, but Britt could feel his eyes on her, sense his hungry need.

She knew he wanted her. She wondered if he understood how much she wanted him. She'd been attracted to Cole Wyman since the day she had first seen him at City College, a blond god the girls all fantasized about. He'd had a serious girlfriend back then, gotten engaged before he'd joined the marines and gone off to war.

He'd been wounded in action, lost both his legs, and finally come home. He was single now and her attraction to him hadn't lessened.

Britt flipped on the light switch as he closed the door behind them and a lamp went on next to the sofa. She felt his hands settle at her waist, big, strong hands turning her around to face him. Lowering his head, he kissed her, softly at first, then deeper, pulling her close, letting her feel his desire.

Hot need moved through her. She hadn't been with a man since her fiancé had dumped her for her neighbor's wife. She hadn't realized how much she had missed being touched, held, kissed, until tonight.

Sliding her arms around Cole's neck, she leaned into him and he deepened the kiss, taking it to a whole new level. She swayed, trembled, moaned into his mouth. Warm kisses traveled along her neck down to her shoulders.

"I want you," he said. "I haven't been able to stop thinking about you since the night I saw you at Jubal's."

"I want you, too," she said, but didn't admit she had lusted after him for years.

He unbuttoned the front of her blouse and stripped it away, unhooked her bra and eased it off her shoulders. One of his big hands cupped her breast and she felt almost dizzy. As he bent toward her, she laced her fingers in his thick blond hair and arched her back, giving him better access, letting him work his magic. He kissed her again, then lifted her up and carried her down the hall to the bedroom.

She could feel the uneven hitch in his steps as he moved, thought for the first time of the prostheses strapped to what remained of his legs. The thought slid away as desire burned through her, the desperate need that seemed to expand with each passing moment.

Cole kissed her as she unbuttoned his short-sleeved western shirt, pulled it free, and stripped it away. A dusting of golden blond hair fanned over his hard-muscled chest, arrowed out of sight below the waistband of his jeans.

She pressed her mouth against his skin and felt his muscles bunch, but when she reached to unfasten his belt, Cole drew away.

"I haven't been with a woman since I came back from the war. I don't want to repulse you."

Her heart twisted. "I want you, Cole. I don't care about your legs. It's not your legs that make you a man. It's your heart and your soul."

Cole looked down at her and something glistened in his

eyes. He blinked and it was gone. He took a shaky breath. "I'm not ready," he said with a shake of his head. "Maybe another night."

Britt caught his arm before he could turn away. "Cole, please. Nothing about you could ever repulse me. We don't have to make love. We can just sleep together. Please . . . stay with me tonight."

Uncertainty moved over his features. He wanted to stay; she could see it. He reached out and gently touched her cheek. "Next time." Bending down, he very softly kissed her. Grabbing his shirt off the floor, he turned and walked out of the bedroom.

At the sound of the front door closing, tears spilled onto Brittany's cheeks. And the ache she felt for Cole would not go away.

The echo of rifle shots rang in the distance, the rat-a-tat-tat of machine gun fire kicking up dirt in the streets of the village. A group of marines had been caught out in the open. They hunkered down in a depression in the sand, pinned by sniper fire from a makeshift bunker at the top of a distant hill. With no way for the men to reach cover in the vacant mud structures that had once been a town, the sniper was picking them off one by one.

On the rooftop of an empty building eight hundred meters away, Josh lay flat on his belly, the crosshairs of the M40A5 on the tripod in front of him sited on the distant hill. He was settled in, waiting. Waiting.

When the sniper popped up to take out his next target, Josh pulled the trigger. The suppressed rifle shot made a faint thumping sound and seconds later, the top of the man's head disappeared.

Josh breathed a sigh of relief. His men were safe, at least for the moment.

He had just risen from his position when he heard a scream and a man armed with a heavy steel knife rushed out of nowhere, slashing with his long, gleaming blade. Josh snagged the man's wrist, gripped hard, spun, and sent the knife sailing off the roof.

Wrapping his fingers around the assailant's throat, he—

"Josh! Josh, wake up! You're dreaming! Wake up!"

Small fingers pried his hand away and his eyes popped open. He looked down to see Tory staring up at him, her pretty green eyes filled with worry.

Josh leaped out of bed. "Jesus! Jesus, Tory, I'm sorry."

He scrubbed a hand over his face, wiping away the perspiration. "I shouldn't have stayed. I should have gone home like I always do. I'm sorry."

She didn't back away, just grabbed her robe and followed him out of bed. "You didn't hurt me. You just scared me."

"I didn't hurt you, but I could have. Jesus, I could have . . ." He bit off the words, didn't say, *I could have killed you.*

"I know you're upset. Was the dream something that actually happened?"

He glanced away, swallowed. "I was on a rooftop in Afghanistan hunting an enemy sniper. Guy with a knife came out of nowhere. We fought. I ended up breaking his neck."

She fell silent. "You were touching me but you weren't hurting me. I don't think you would have."

He shook his head. "I don't know. . . ."

"Is it PTSD?"

He sighed. "Not like my buddies have. Just an occasional bad dream."

"Does it bother you to think of the men you killed?"

His jaw hardened. "I did what I was trained to do—protect our troops. I feel bad about the men I couldn't save."

There was no condemnation in her eyes. He shouldn't have felt so relieved.

"Do you think you should talk to someone?"

"I talk to Cole and Noah and they talk to me. It helps a lot. The nightmares aren't so bad anymore."

She slid her arms around his waist and smiled up at him. "Maybe I can make you forget them completely. Why don't we go back to bed?"

He was tempted. He loved her sexy little body, loved the way she could make him feel. But he was in too deep with Tory already. And the nightmares worried him.

Josh eased her away. "I think I'm going to head on home. I need to get to work anyway." He leaned down and kissed her. "Get some sleep, baby."

When he walked out the front door, dawn grayed the horizon. Was he a danger to Tory or someone else? Or was what had happened nothing more than a very vivid dream? What would have happened if he hadn't awoken when he did?

Until he knew for sure, it was a risk he wasn't willing to take.

First thing Sunday morning, Josh phoned Sheriff Howler. An hour later, a white extended cab pickup with bright blue SHERIFF lettering on the side drove up in front of the house and the heavyset sheriff got out.

Josh pushed open the screen door as Howler swaggered up on the porch.

"Daisy said you called, said you had some trouble last night." Daisy was the older woman who ran the local sheriff's department.

"That's right. Bunch of bikers showed up and tore hell out of the place." He tipped his head toward the strings of broken lights scattered around, the general mayhem he hadn't yet cleaned up.

"Cole Wyman and Noah Beal were here. Ended up in a brawl. The bikers shot off a few rounds, broke some windows in the barn, took off and haven't been back."

"What brought them after you?" Howler asked. "You have a beef with one of them?"

Josh ignored a trickle of irritation. "I've never seen any of them before. You had complaints from anyone else?"

"No, just you." The sheriff lifted his tan cowboy hat and scratched his head, settled the hat back in place, and tugged down the brim. "Seems like trouble has a habit of following you around, don't it?"

Josh said nothing. From the corner of his eye, he saw Tory at the kitchen window, listening to the conversation.

"You'll need to come down to the office and file a complaint," the sheriff said. "Give us some kinda description."

"All right."

Howler stared off toward the dark red, newly constructed barn. "You know, Randy Stevens confessed to burnin' down your barn. Jim brought the boy in hisself. Randy's doin' community service."

Should have been a whole lot more as far as Josh was concerned, but it was better than letting the kid skate completely.

"His dad's a good man," Josh said.

"That he is." Howler turned toward the smashed cold box, the pieces of red plastic scattered all over the ground. "I'll keep an eye out. If I hear anything about these hombres, I'll let you know."

"Thanks. I'll be in town tomorrow. I'll stop by your office and file that complaint."

The sheriff nodded. Tugging on the brim of his hat, he stepped off the porch and walked back to his pickup. Tory came out of the house as the truck drove away.

"I heard what he said. Looks like we're the only ones they've bothered. I wonder why that is."

She was standing just a few feet away. Josh couldn't help thinking how pretty she looked in the morning, with her fiery curls and peaches-and-cream complexion. He ignored an itch to have her that was becoming way too strong.

"Linc and Carly stayed the night at Blackland Ranch. I talked to Linc earlier, asked him to see if he could set up a meet with Tag Joyner. Tag's president of the Asphalt Demons. Linc called back. Tag's meeting my brother and me at Jubal's Roadhouse tonight."

He smiled down at her. "You feel like a night on the town?"

Her big green eyes widened, but he saw none of the apprehension that had been there after she'd roused him from the dream.

"That sounds like fun," she said. "I'll talk to Mrs. Thompson when I pick up Ivy, see if she'll babysit tonight."

"Roadhouse isn't much, but you've been cooped up on the ranch awhile. I figure any place is bound to look good."

"There is that. I hope Tag Joyner can help us."

Josh looked at the destruction around him. "Yeah, so do I."

Chapter Twenty-Four

Jubal's Roadhouse turned out to be a wood-frame building outside the Iron Springs city limits. With its false front, wooden boardwalk, and double swinging doors, Tory thought it looked like something out of the eighteen sixties.

Spotting a row of motorcycles parked in a line out front, she caught Josh's arm.

"It's okay," he said. "Those belong to the Demons. The black Harley with the silver conchos on the seat is Linc's."

Tory glanced up. "Seriously?"

Josh grinned. "Yeah. He and Carly rode over from the ranch."

She had to admit she was impressed. It occurred to her that if Carly could ride a hot-looking Harley, she was ready to do more than walk and trot Rosebud around the pasture.

For years, she'd run a top-notch advertising team for one of the largest, most successful firms in Phoenix, earning a fat salary in the process. But something as simple as riding still remained a challenge.

A challenge she was enjoying and mastering a little more every day. Expanding her abilities felt good.

They pushed through the swinging doors together and stopped just inside. A jukebox played Willie Nelson, and peanut shells littered the floor. A long wooden bar stretched in front of them and the clack of pool balls resonated from the back.

Several female heads swiveled in Josh's direction, openly admiring the tall, broad-shouldered cowboy in dark blue jeans, boots, and a pressed denim shirt. He was wearing his good straw cowboy hat tonight, and Tory had to admit he looked delicious.

Dressed in a short jeans skirt and a white ruffled tank that dipped low enough to show a little cleavage, she fit right in with the women, cowboys, and bikers who sat at scarred wooden tables scattered around the plank floors.

She was glad she was wearing her cowboy boots, even if they were plain brown and already a little worn. Her hair was getting longer, falling in loose copper curls that just brushed her shoulders.

She felt Josh's hand at her waist and looked up to see a possessive gleam in his eyes. She could still recall the stunned look on his face when she had walked out of the double-wide onto the porch where he was waiting.

Clearly, she needed to exchange her T-shirts and jeans for a sexy skirt and blouse more often.

"Stay close," he said softly. "Half the guys in here are undressing you with their eyes and the other half are trying to figure a way to get you in bed."

She flushed. Surely he was kidding. But when she looked around, she caught several openly admiring glances.

"This way." Josh urged her toward a table off to one side. She almost didn't recognize Carly and Linc, who wore black leather as easily as expensive business suits.

They rose as she and Josh approached. Carly gave her a hug and Linc kissed her cheek. "So he finally let you out of the house," Linc said, his massive biceps straining the sleeves of the snug black T-shirt beneath his black leather vest. "I thought maybe he had you chained to the bed."

The heat returned to her cheeks. Carly elbowed him, and he grinned, digging sexy indentations into his cheeks.

"Ignore him," she said, but she grinned back. Lincoln Cain was impressive, no doubt about it. But no more so than his wicked-hot, blue-eyed brother.

"Tag's over there with Baldy, Wolf, and Lenny." Linc pointed to a group of bikers sitting a few tables away. She could read the name ASPHALT DEMONS on the back of a vest worn by a blond biker with his hair pulled into a ponytail.

A guy with shoulder-length shaggy brown hair got up and strode toward them, pulled out a chair, spun it around, and sat down facing them.

He turned to Josh. "Hey, bro, good to see you."

"You too, Tag." Josh introduced Tory. Linc ordered another pitcher of beer and more glasses.

The drinks were served by a busty, big-haired blonde who was eyeing Josh like a juicy piece of meat. If he noticed, he didn't encourage her. Tory ignored a bubble of jealousy she pretended not to feel.

Linc poured glasses of beer for her and Josh, and filled a glass for Tag.

"Linc says you've had some trouble," Tag said to Josh, taking a drink of his beer.

"That's right. Group of bikers vandalized the ranch after the barn raising. Tore things up, got into a slugfest with me and a couple of marine buddies who work for me, fired off some shots. Any guess who it might have been?"

"I don't have to guess. I know who it was. Part of a bunch that call themselves the Street Marauders. Operate out of South Dallas. Deal drugs, run prostitutes, stuff like that. I heard they were in town."

Josh shook his head. "I don't get it. I've never even heard of these guys. What the hell beef did they have with me?"

"The Marauders work for hire. Advertise on the Internet

in some of those soldier-of-fortune magazines. If the job pays enough, they're up for just about anything."

Tory's pulse kicked up as the first stirrings of alarm moved through her. *Someone paid them?*

Josh leaned forward in his chair. "You're saying someone hired those guys to tear up my place?"

"Most likely. If they stopped at vandalizing your property, that's probably all they were paid to do. Could have been a whole lot worse."

Josh slanted Tory a look and she knew he was thinking the same thing she was. Her heart was thrumming. She didn't want to believe it was Damon, but she did.

"They still in town?" Josh asked.

"I heard they left late last night. After Linc called this morning, I asked around. Looks like they're back in Dallas."

"So their job here is done," Josh said darkly.

"At least for now." Tag stood up from his chair. "That's all I got. But I've put the word out. If the Marauders show up in the area, you'll be the first to know—and you won't have to deal with them alone."

Some of the stiffness eased in Josh's shoulders. He was making friends here, Tory thought. Good friends, it seemed.

"Thanks, Tag."

The biker tipped up his chin in farewell, then sauntered back to his table of friends.

Tory's chest felt as if it were being squeezed in a vise. "It had to be him."

Linc's gaze sharpened. He glanced from Tory to Josh, whose jaw looked tight. "You think Damon Bridger hired those guys to give you trouble?"

"That's the only explanation that makes any sense," Josh said.

"It was him," Tory said flatly.

"You don't have any proof," Linc argued. "No way to connect him to what happened."

Josh surged up from his chair. "I'm going to Phoenix. I'm putting an end to this once and for all."

Tory shot to her feet and gripped his arm. "You can't confront him, Josh! He'll have you thrown in jail again and this time you won't get out!"

Linc and Carly both stood up. "Tory's right," Linc said. "You can't just charge in there and beat the guy to a pulp. You have to think this through, come up with a plan."

"I don't want to go in there and beat him to a pulp. I want to end him."

"Josh!"

"Take it easy, all right?" Linc said. "I'll send Townsend to Phoenix, put him in touch with your PI friend, Hamilton Brown. Maybe they can find out whether or not Bridger is responsible."

Josh looked like he was going to explode. He took a deep breath, finally managed to bring himself under control. "All right—for now. Maybe Ham and Townsend can find out what's going on. But this is ending—soon. If Bridger is willing to go as far as hiring outlaw bikers to tear up the ranch, he isn't going to stop until he gets to Tory. I'm not letting that happen."

"There's still a chance what happened had nothing to do with Bridger," Linc said.

Josh's features remained tight. "You're right. We need to be sure." His arm went around Tory, keeping her close. "I'm kind of out of the mood for this. What do you say we go home?"

Her insides were shaking. It had never occurred to her that Damon might be behind the bikers' attack. "I'm more than ready."

"Maybe we can pick up something to eat on the way," Josh suggested.

Tory just nodded. She let Josh guide her out of the bar, her mind going over what Tag Joyner had said. All the way to the truck, she kept thinking of Damon. Linc might not be sure Damon was responsible, but Tory was. Though she'd prayed it wouldn't happen, she'd been worried about something like this.

Her chest clamped down. She couldn't avoid it any longer. She knew what she had to do.

Josh ended up pulling into the Iron Springs Café for something to eat and a piece of homemade apple pie, but Tory's appetite was gone. By the time they stopped at Mrs. Thompson's to pick up Ivy, she was mentally packing, getting ready to leave.

"Ivy's already dressed for bed," Mrs. Thompson said when they arrived. "We baked cupcakes." She handed Tory a flat plastic container with dark circles visible through the lid. "Chocolate with chocolate frosting."

"They look great. Thank you."

Ivy was half asleep when Josh carried her out to the pickup for the short ride home, then into the double-wide trailer.

"I'll sit with her till she falls back to sleep," Tory said to Josh, sitting down in the chair next to the little girl's bed. But it only took a few minutes before she was breathing deeply, fast asleep.

Easing her tired feet, Tory pulled off her boots and socks and tossed them into her bedroom on her way back down the hall. She was sifting through one plan after another when she walked into the living room and found Josh sitting on the sofa.

"I'm staying here tonight," he said, casting a dark look her way.

She'd been afraid of that. She had things to do to get ready. She needed to get out of there—the sooner, the better.

"What about your nightmares?" She crossed her fingers, hoping the reminder would be enough to send him home.

"I'll sleep on the sofa."

Urgency clawed at her. "Why do you want to stay?"

"You know why. Because I'm not letting you run. Tell me that's not what you're planning. Give me your solemn word you won't pack up and leave the minute I'm out the door."

She couldn't do that. She wouldn't lie to him, and she would never break her word to Josh. Surely if she told him the truth, he would realize she was right.

"I need to go, Josh," she said softly. "We both know it. As long as I stay here, bad things are going to happen. Once I'm gone, Damon will figure that out and leave you alone."

Josh shot to his feet, his features dark and intense. He gripped her shoulders. "You aren't leaving because of some maniac who plans to do God-only-knows-what once he gets his hands on you. I'm not letting that happen."

Tory gasped as his mouth crushed down over hers. Heat blasted through her the way it always did when he touched her. She moaned and clung to his shoulders. Josh kissed her as if his life depended on it, as if he couldn't get enough.

He walked her backward till her knees hit the sofa. She went down and Josh followed. His mouth found the side of her neck and his teeth nipped an earlobe. Shivers crawled over her skin and need burned through her, making her hot and wet.

Josh popped the snaps on his denim shirt and peeled it off, pulled off her tank, popped the front of her bra and stripped it away. When his mouth fastened on her breast, a little whimper came from her throat and moisture settled deep between her legs.

"I need you," he said. "I won't let him hurt you." He shoved her jean skirt up around her waist, pulled her panties off, and tossed them away. His kiss was rough and hungry, burning and endless. She was so hot, so needy.

Josh freed himself and then he was inside her. Tory moaned. Josh took her deep, driving hard. She wrapped herself around him, dug her fingers into his powerful shoulders. His heavy weight pressed her into the cushions and she loved it, loved his fierce masculinity. Her body began moving in sync with his, arching upward, taking him deeper, demanding more.

Josh rode her hard, taking what he wanted, giving her what she needed, driving her up to the peak, making her whole body burn. Pleasure, pure and raw, poured through her, and a shattering climax struck. Tory clung to him, felt his hard muscles go rigid. An instant later, Josh followed her to release.

Afterward they lay together, drifting in a sensual haze, slowly spiraling down.

"Don't leave," Josh said, kissing her softly one last time, curling her against him on the sofa. "Promise me."

There was something in his voice. . . . She remembered the nightmares he suffered and the story she had read about him. She thought of what he had done to protect his men, thought of the friends he had lost.

It occurred to her that though she needed his protection, perhaps Josh needed her, too.

"I'll stay," she said softly. "I promise."

His hard body relaxed. He tucked her closer against him, and in minutes they were asleep.

When she awoke late in the night, a light blanket was draped over her, but Josh was gone.

Chapter Twenty-Five

The day was overcast and grim, with a dense layer of heavy black clouds, the wind whipping through the branches of the trees, hurling dead leaves across the ground. The horses were skittish, the cattle uneasy, sensing the coming storm.

Josh headed over to the cow barn where young Ty Murphy, the black-haired teen who was now his part-time stable hand, had been working.

"Looks like you're done with the stalls," Josh said.

"Yes, sir."

"I've been working a three-year-old gelding that shows real promise. I want to see how he responds with someone else on his back. Cole says you're a good rider. Can you handle him?"

The kid grinned ear to ear. "You bet. Which horse?" He was a handsome kid, features so perfect he was almost pretty. But unlike his two predecessors, Ty Murphy had a core of integrity.

"The sorrel out in the field behind the ring. That's Red. Bring me the buckskin, Thor. He can be a little cranky, and he needs work on his neck rein." He glanced toward the open grasslands. "We won't be able to stay out too long. Not with the storm coming in."

"I'm on it, boss."

Josh turned to Noah and Cole. "I thought you two could work in the new barn today, maybe get a few stalls put up, stay out of the weather."

"Sounds good," Noah said.

Cole just nodded. He'd been in a dark mood all morning. Josh had a feeling it had something to do with Brittany, but he didn't ask. Cole wasn't the type to share his feelings, at least not often. Hell, neither was he.

Which made him think of Tory and what had happened between them last night. As soon as she'd figured out the bikers could have been hired by Damon, he'd known she was going to run.

What he hadn't known was how much it would upset him. He tried to tell himself it was just his protective instincts kicking in, but it was way more than that.

He cared for Tory and little Ivy. The thought of Damon Bridger hurting either one of them made him physically sick. That she would put herself and Ivy in danger to protect him made him a little crazy.

Fortunately, she was staying. She had given him her word and Josh knew she would keep it. He trusted her in the same soul-deep way he trusted the men who'd fought beside him in the war. He didn't know how it had happened, only that it had.

Ty brought the horses in and he and Josh saddled them. Josh retrieved the hunting rifle he kept in the gun safe in the bedroom he'd set up as an office, a .308 Winchester with a Sightron long range scope. You never knew what you might run into out there. Snakes and wild boars could be a problem.

And there was Damon Bridger.

He slid the rifle into the scabbard at the front of his saddle and swung aboard. Ty swung up on Red. As they rode away from the barn, the kid sat straight in the saddle yet relaxed, holding the reins loosely but clearly in control.

Josh gigged the buckskin, heading for the trail that wound through the grasslands. There was an old cabin out there that overlooked the river, a place he liked to go when he wanted to think. He'd check the stock ponds on the way, make sure they were accessible.

They had just reached the first gate when the phone in his pocket began to vibrate. "Hold a minute," he called out, pulling rein.

The buckskin danced, eager to get moving, a little uneasy with the uncertain weather. The sorrel snorted and side-stepped, but the kid held him easily.

Josh looked at the screen but didn't recognize the caller number. He pressed the phone against his ear. "Josh Cain."

"Josh, it's Iceman. I've got bad news."

His stomach contracted. Iceman was Kirby Waldruth, a marine vet and friend. They'd talked at Pete's funeral. "What is it, Ice?"

"Coy Whitmore is dead. Rifle shot through the driver's-side window of his pickup. Bullet struck him in the temple."

His mouth went dry. "*Jesus*. Jesus, Ice, what the hell happened?"

"Not real sure. Cops haven't figured out who did it."

"Sonofabitch." He scrubbed a hand over his face. "First Pete, now Coy. What the hell's going on?"

"I don't know. Neither do the cops. They think the killings are unrelated. Just coincidence. They're calling it a possible hunting accident. The police in Gainesville are all over it, but so far no leads."

"Two of our guys murdered in just a few weeks? Doesn't sound like coincidence to me."

"Two different towns, hundreds of miles apart. Two different weapons used in the murders. It could be."

Josh made no reply. His instincts were screaming. He had learned to listen to them a long time ago.

"Can you make it to the funeral?" Kirby asked.

"A hundred armored tanks couldn't keep me away."

"I'll call as soon as I get word when it is."

"Thanks, Ice." Josh ended the call. Coy wasn't married, didn't have any kids. But his parents were great people and they would be devastated.

Josh softly cursed.

"Bad news?" Ty asked.

"Real bad. Friend of mine was murdered."

"Jeez, that's fucked up."

Josh cast him a glance.

"Sorry."

"That's all right. It really is fucked up."

The kid looked out over the rippling grasses in the pasture, obviously disappointed the ride would be canceled. "So I guess we won't be going."

"Oh, we're going. The last place I want to be is cooped up in the house. I need some air and this is the best way I can think of to get it." He nudged the big buckskin through the gate, into the open field. "I need a few minutes. I'll meet you at the stock pond. Wind's picking up. Red may get a little nervous so stay alert."

"I will," Ty said, clearly eager.

Josh urged Thor into a trot, then a canter. Soon he was bending over the animal's neck, the buckskin running flat out, black mane and tail flying, the ground rushing beneath them.

Thor was a damned fine horse. He would fetch a good price when it was time to sell him. Or maybe Josh would keep him.

The buckskin's hooves pounded the earth. It gave him something to think about besides the murder of one of his best friends.

* * *

Damon paced the floor of the wood-paneled office where Izzy Watkins clattered away on his keyboard, working his seemingly limitless Internet magic tricks.

Izzy was a real kiss-ass. The guy would do just about anything to be included in Damon's pussy posse. He loved the women Damon's money and good looks scooped up, loved the booze and the drugs.

Damon liked him well enough, and his skills as a computer geek, combined with his unshakable loyalty, made him a real asset.

"How's it coming?" Damon asked, stopping to peer over Izzy's bony shoulders. Already losing his blond hair at the age of twenty-nine, Izzy wore round-rimmed glasses and was slim, not much to look at, but he knew the deep dark secrets of the computer world inside and out.

Izzy rubbed his hands together. "Got some good stuff going on here. Guy won't know what hit him."

Damon found himself smiling. Izzy knew about his engagement to Victoria, knew about her betrayal and who she was currently fucking, Joshua Cain.

Izzy had been the one to come up with the mercenary-for-hire website called The Dark Side. An ad on the site had led Damon to the Street Marauders. The cell phone pictures he'd received from the raid showed the vandalism, including the shot-out windows in Cain's barn. It wasn't enough to stir the cops into a frenzy, just enough to tweak Cain's nose and let him know who was in charge.

The hassle of identity theft was going to be even better. Given the distance between him and Cain, given the fact he couldn't get to Tory—not yet—it would have to be enough.

It was the same way he'd felt about the trashy little redhead. His dick stirred to life as he thought about the things he had done to her, the way he'd had her on her knees, the way she had begged him to stop.

He hadn't been sure he was ready to see it completely through, but in the end, the pleasure he'd found had dissolved any misgivings he had.

"All finished," Izzy said, leaning back in his chair. He chuckled. "That ought to keep the bastard busy for a while."

Damon nodded, though he had no idea what Izzy had actually done. It didn't matter as long as it caused Cain trouble. "Good work."

Izzy shot him a look. "We still heading for the Peacock?"

Damon's favorite hangout. He wasn't really in the mood but he had to keep his minions happy. He still owed Izzy for the alibi.

"Sure, why not? It's still early. Night hasn't really gotten started yet."

Izzy grinned and got up from his chair. Damon headed down the hall of the cheap, nineteen-fifties, flat-roofed house where Izzy lived.

He thought of the redhead and how she'd made him feel, and his mouth watered. He hadn't expected the itch to start again so soon. He needed to get to Tory, end his obsession with her. Once he'd dealt with her, he could bring himself back under control.

Perhaps it was time to start planning.

For the second time in a few short weeks, Tory watched Josh walk into the kitchen wearing his marine dress blues. Her heart ached for him.

He paused next to the round oak table. Red-striped blue trousers, stiff-collared navy jacket, clean-shaven, every inch of him perfectly groomed.

This morning, he hadn't even made the pretense of being

able to eat. He had lost a very good friend. He was focused on that loss and on paying his final respects.

But one thing was different this morning. Tory was going with him.

"I'm ready whenever you are," she said. She'd been glad he'd asked her to go, though it hadn't taken long to realize she had nothing appropriate to wear.

When she'd mentioned going shopping, Josh had insisted on going with her. She didn't like being dependent on him for protection or anything else, but until they knew for sure what was going on, she didn't have much choice.

It had taken more persuasion than she would have liked, but he'd finally agreed to let her and Ivy wander the shops along Main Street while he ran some errands—as long as she let him pay.

At a boutique called Sassy's, she purchased a pretty little blue sundress with tulips on the front for Ivy, and a modest black skirt-suit and a peach silk blouse for herself, the kind of clothes she had worn to work back in Phoenix.

A decent pair of mid-heeled black patent pumps and a matching over-the-shoulder bag had managed to survive the arduous cross-country journey that had landed her in Texas.

"It's a little over two hours to Gainesville," Josh said, breaking into her thoughts as she stood in the kitchen. "We'd better get going."

Since the guys had planned a get-together after the funeral, they'd decided to spend the night. Mrs. Thompson had agreed to watch Ivy, who loved to stay with her. Tory thought the older woman would babysit for free if Josh didn't insist on paying her.

Gardening was their latest project. Ivy was tending her own vegetable patch, which seemed like such a good idea Tory had decided to plant a garden at the ranch.

Tory grabbed her overnight bag and Josh grabbed his.

They gathered up Ivy and her things and headed out to the pickup.

"You look pretty," Ivy said to Josh as he lifted her into her booster seat.

His mouth edged into the faintest of smiles, the first in days. "Men don't look pretty, sweetheart. They look handsome."

Ivy giggled. "I like your suit."

He laughed. "Thanks. I like yours, too." She was wearing her new blue sundress, though she would have to change before working in the garden.

It didn't take long to get Ivy settled at Clara Thompson's; then they were heading out of town. The storm had moved on by the middle of the week, leaving the weather hot and damp.

As the miles slipped past, they talked about their families. Tory told him about Jamie and the terrible wreck that had killed both him and her mother.

"It was the worst day of my life. If I hadn't had Ivy, I'm not sure I would have survived it."

"You're strong, Tory. You'd have made it."

Josh had opened up as he rarely did and talked about his mom, how hard it had been growing up back then, losing his mother to lung cancer, how lucky he was to have found his older brother.

"Linc's the best. I always know I can count on him, and he knows he can count on me."

Eventually, the ride came to an end. Tory walked next to Josh across the manicured green lawns of the cemetery, with Josh's white gloved hand holding on to hers. His jaw was set, his expression hard beneath the brim of his round white, billed cap.

But when he looked at her, his hard look softened and she caught a glimpse of pain. Everything inside her ached for him. Tory was glad she had come.

Chapter Twenty-Six

The ceremony was over. Josh led Tory across the grass to meet a few more of his friends. The guys couldn't wait to tell her they called him Superman—a name they'd hung on him because of his shooting skills. He was no Superman, but it was true he rarely missed.

He stepped up to make introductions. "Tory, this is Kirby Waldruth." The guy was a blond, blue-eyed, unrepentant rogue. "He's the friend who called about Coy."

He clapped another friend on the back. "This is Mac Mc-Donough." Red hair and freckles. "And this joker is Lavon Harvey. We call him Night." He was African-American, every bit as dark as his name, and at night he was deadly.

Lavon tipped his cap. "Ma'am." He was tall, lean, tough, and loyal. Josh felt lucky to know him.

"It's nice to meet all of you," Tory said. "I'm sorry for the loss of your friend."

The mood darkened at the reminder.

"You two going over to Coy's parents' house?" Kirby asked.

"We'll be there."

They talked a little longer, and then Kirby and the men began to disperse. The rest of the crowd started wandering away. As they walked back toward Josh's truck, a group of marines from out of town were being stopped on the way to their vehicles by a couple of men in dark suits—police detectives, Josh figured. There were now two murders to solve.

"What's going on?" Tory asked.

"I'm guessing they're cops or feds. They're talking to the guys from out of town."

Just then a black-haired, olive-skinned man in a navy blue suit walked up to him. "You Joshua Cain?"

"That's right."

"I'm Detective Rafe Dominguez, Gainesville PD. I'd like to talk to you about your friend."

Josh nodded. "All right." He stepped over to the side, out of the way, eased Tory along with him. "What do you want to know?" He didn't introduce her. She had enough trouble without adding more.

But the detective was determined to do his job, which in a way was a plus.

Dominguez arched a black eyebrow. "And you are?"

"Victoria Bradford. I didn't know Coy Whitmore. I'm just here with Josh."

Dominguez nodded. "When's the last time you spoke to Coy?" he asked Josh.

"We talked at Pete Saldana's funeral. You know about Pete?"

"We know."

"But the police just think both of them being shot in the head is a coincidence."

"Be easier to think that. Starting to look like it might be something else."

"Yeah, like what?" Josh asked.

"Both men knew each other, both came out of Marine Corp Special Operations. Different teams, I gather, but both in Afghanistan at the same time. Pete's been back in the States longer than Coy. But they stayed in touch."

Maybe this guy had a brain. "So where's that information take you?"

"Killer could have been a friend, someone they both knew. Someone they both pissed off. Could be woman trouble. Looks like Whitmore was quite the stud here in Gainesville. Big on one-night stands. Saldana was a family man but there's always a chance he was playing around. They were friends. Maybe they shared a woman and someone didn't like it."

"Not Pete."

"Whitmore liked to gamble. Played poker. Lost too much on occasion. Saldana liked to play the horses. We're working that angle."

"Could be a lot of things," Josh said. "Whatever's going on, I don't think it's coincidence."

"Maybe not. We're just getting started. You got anything to add that might point us in the right direction?"

He couldn't think of a thing. Coy had always been a rounder, a little too wild for his own good. He'd been wounded, had to leave the marines, but he'd never really settled down. Pete wasn't like that. When his wife found out she had breast cancer, Pete had left the military to help with his kids.

"I wish I had something," Josh said.

The detective handed him a card. "You think of anything, call me."

He just nodded. The whole mess had his stomach tied in knots. He set a hand at Tory's waist, urging her back toward the pickup parked along the curb.

From the cemetery, they stopped at Coy's parents' to express their condolences. They ate a little of the massive spread of food and drinks people had brought over; then the guys changed clothes in Coy's old childhood bedroom and they headed for a spot called the Bird's Nest, where Kirby had reserved the back room.

A lot of guys Josh knew were there, some with women, vets Coy had known, friends of his in the Corp, friends of Coy's who lived in Gainesville. Some of them were drinking beer, some tossing back tequila shooters.

Josh ordered a Jack straight up, wished he could just upend the bottle and drink till he couldn't feel the pain of losing another friend, but he was driving and Tory was with him.

He caught her around the waist and lifted her up on a bar stool. She peeled off her black suit coat, leaving her in a little peach silk blouse that draped over her pretty breasts and made her look way too sexy, as far as Josh was concerned.

She ordered a Coors Light, sipped the beer, and was a good sport as the guys reminisced about Coy. Josh found himself laughing at the crazy things his friend had done and it really felt good.

"I remember a night at Camp Lejeune before he went spec ops," Mac said. "We were in this bar called the Queen of Hearts. Coy was drunk when we got there. He spent an hour trying to get this gal to leave with him. Then he goes to the head and when he comes out, one of his best buddies has left with her."

"Coy was really pissed," Kirby said. "The other guys were laughing so hard, Coy finally gave up and started laughing, too. Coy was always cool."

The guys chuckled and even Tory smiled, if a little sadly. The stories went on, began to turn bawdy as the men got drunker.

"Time to leave," Josh said. "I need to pay the bill; then we're out of here."

Unfortunately, on the way out of the bar, a drunken cowboy found Tory a little too appealing.

"What's your name, sweet thing?" He was big, good-looking if he hadn't been so wasted.

"She's with me," Josh warned, urging her forward, but the cowboy blocked her way.

"He don't own you, sweetheart." He leered, stuck out his hand. "Name's Cody. You wanna dance? What do you say?"

Josh clamped down on his temper.

Tory politely refused. "Thanks, Cody, but at the moment, I'm not available."

"Aw, come on." The cowboy shouldn't have grabbed her, shouldn't have pushed his luck, not when Josh was wound tighter than a calf roper's pigging string. Not when he was just itching to work off some of his frustrations.

Grabbing the cowboy by the front of his western shirt, Josh drew back to punch him, but Mac caught his arm.

"Take it easy, Superman. Guy's just drunk and your girl's real pretty. Give the dude a break."

He sighed. Mac was right. He wasn't usually like this. He was usually fairly even tempered, and he'd never been this possessive of a woman.

Pulling his arm free, he shoved the guy a couple of feet away. The cowboy swore foully, but didn't come back for more.

"Sorry," Josh said to Mac.

"Wouldn't take much to have all of us in a fight. We'd probably feel better if we did."

Josh knew he would. He felt Tory's hand in his. "Come on, soldier. Time to go."

He didn't argue. Even better than a fistfight would be taking Victoria Bradford to bed.

Knowing it was past time to leave, Tory led Josh out to his truck. She stuck out her hand, palm up. "Give me the keys."

"I'm all right. I didn't drink that much."

"Kirby bought you another shot of Jack and you had a couple of beers. Just to be safe, give me the keys."

One of his eyebrows went up. "You sure you can drive this thing?"

"Sure. I worked on an ad for Ford trucks. I had an idea to appeal to female drivers, but I wanted to test it out. I drove a big dually, didn't have a lick of trouble."

He grunted. "You're just full of surprises." He dropped the keys into her hand. "She's all yours."

Tory climbed in behind the wheel and adjusted the seat while Josh climbed in on the passenger side, and they strapped themselves in.

From the Bird's Nest, Tory drove to a nearby Holiday Inn where Josh had made a reservation, getting the directions from Siri on his iPhone. As the truck cruised along the street, she shot him a sideways glance. He was leaning back in the seat watching her, amusement touching his lips.

"What?"

"I never thought a woman could look cute driving a truck."

She laughed. "I don't look cute. I look competent. Behave yourself."

His smile broadened into a grin. "You know you don't mean that." He was flirting. He didn't do it often. She really liked it.

She parked the pickup. They grabbed their overnight bags and went into the motel lobby, walked up to a young man in a white shirt and skinny black tie.

"May I help you?"

"Reservation for Joshua Cain."

The clerk pulled it up on his computer. "Here it is. I'll need a credit card."

Josh fished his Visa out of his wallet and tossed it on the counter.

The clerk ran it and frowned. "I'm sorry, sir, the card was denied. Would you like to try another one?"

"There's nothing wrong with the card. Try it again."

The clerk tried it, looked embarrassed this time. "I'm sorry."

Josh grumbled, took out his American Express. "No limit on this one."

The clerk smiled and ran the card. The hand that held on to the credit card trembled. "Apparently, there's a . . . umm . . . problem with this one, too. They're instructing me to hold on to the card. I'm very sorry, sir. I don't have any choice."

"They're telling you to keep my credit card? That's crazy. It must be your machine."

"I don't think so."

Tory opened her wallet and took out her Mastercard. "Let's see if this one works." She had paid it off months ago, been afraid to use it since. The billing address was a mailbox in Carlsbad and she'd kept it that way.

Josh snatched the card out of her hand. "No way." He handed it back to her. "You're not paying for the goddamn motel room."

He returned his attention to the clerk, opened his wallet to take out a handful of bills. "It's only for tonight. How much is it?"

"I'm afraid for security reasons, we don't take cash."

Tory could see Josh's rising temper in the lines digging into his forehead. "Get your manager out here," he said.

As if someone had pulled his string, the manager, a heavy-set man with a mustache and double chins, appeared behind the counter. "Is there a problem?"

"Something's wrong with your credit card machine. How much for a room?"

The manager turned to the computer screen. "A king-size, non-smoking is one hundred thirty-five dollars, plus taxes and fees. Comes to one fifty-seven and thirty-seven cents. We have a strict rule against taking cash, but—"

He looked Josh over, took in his clean-shaven face and

short dark hair, the prime physical condition he was in and the way he carried himself. "Military?" the manager asked.

"Marines."

"In your case, we can make an exception, and I thank you for your service."

Josh relaxed. "It's a mistake. There's nothing wrong with my credit cards, but thank you, anyway." He paid the amount due. They grabbed their bags and headed up to the room.

Tory figured tomorrow Josh could get things straightened out.

It wasn't until they got back to Iron Springs that Josh discovered it wasn't just his credit cards that were a problem. His bank accounts had been cleaned out and his loan on the ranch was now in foreclosure.

And Tory knew exactly who to blame.

Chapter Twenty-Seven

Tory knew what to do to straighten out Josh's accounts—Damon had done the same thing to her.

After she had left Phoenix and moved to Houston, Damon had immediately begun to harass her. He must have had a friend who knew how to hack into computer systems because he managed to destroy her credit, run up her cards, and empty her bank accounts.

He had even been brazen enough to admit he'd done it, though she never had any proof. He just wanted her to come home, he'd said. He'd make everything right if she just came back to him.

In those early days, she hadn't yet accepted reality, hadn't realized her life, as she knew it, was over. Back then, she'd been determined not to let him win.

She had managed to undo the identity theft and clean up her bank accounts and credit cards, but Damon's harassment had only gotten worse, until she'd finally been forced to leave Houston.

At least she knew what to do for Josh.

Working in his converted bedroom-office, Tory leaned back in the chair in front of his computer and rubbed the ache in her neck. She'd been sitting there for hours, either on the Internet or the phone, determined to fix the mess she had brought down on Josh's head.

She heard his footfalls as he walked into the office, turned to see him standing there in a pair of worn jeans and a snug-fitting dark blue T-shirt. A zing of sexual awareness slipped through her, sending a flush into her cheeks that made her freckles stand out. She hoped he wouldn't notice.

"How's it going?" he asked, coming up to look over her shoulder.

"I made a list of everything you gave me, your bank accounts, IRAs, stocks, and bonds. Location, numbers, amounts, anything pertinent. The ranch is your only mortgage. I'm not quite sure what to do about stopping the foreclosure, but I'll figure it out."

He smiled. "I know you will. I wouldn't have had a clue how to fix this. You're a handy lady to know."

Guilt swept through her. "If I hadn't driven up in front of your barn, you wouldn't be having this problem."

Josh drew her up from the chair. "I don't even want to think about what might have happened if you hadn't driven up in front of my barn. Bridger could have found you. He could have—" He broke off at the look on her face.

"Sorry. I'm glad you're here, that's all." He kissed her softly and eased her back down in the chair.

As soon as they'd figured out his accounts had been hacked, Tory had called the credit card companies and had Josh give them notice of the theft. Acting that quickly, there was a fifty dollar limit per card, no matter how high the fraudulent charges.

Josh would be okay there, except for the hassle of getting new cards and giving the new numbers to accounts that billed directly to the card, like Amazon and the feed store and the mercantile in town.

As Josh's representative, she had phoned the bank. There was something called the Electronic Fund Transfer Act, which protected consumers, again with a fifty dollar liability charge. The money stolen out of Josh's bank accounts would be replaced.

Next she phoned in a fraud alert to the credit reporting companies so no one could make purchases using his name and Social Security number. A report would come back showing any problems, and there would be a freeze on opening new accounts.

"You'll need to change all of your passwords," she said. Josh groaned, but Tory just smiled. "Sorry, but you're going to have to come up with something a little more sophisticated than 'river ranch one.'"

Instead of laughing, his features hardened. "I can't believe that guy. I'd like to stomp his balls into a grease spot on the pavement."

Tory's eyes went wide. Josh rarely said things like that. Then she grinned. "Yeah, me too."

Josh laughed. She noticed him doing that more often.

"We still need to call the Social Security hotline," she said. "And the utility companies, just to make sure he hasn't screwed things up there. And you'll have to get a new driver's license." She sighed. "At least it only cost you a couple of hundred bucks."

"Yeah, thanks to you."

"Are you sure you don't want to call the police?"

"It'd be the sheriff out here, and we both know how much good that would do."

Tory made no reply. She didn't like the sheriff any more than Josh did.

After all the time Tory had spent on the computer, Josh figured she deserved a break. They had stopped to pick up Ivy that morning on the way back from Gainesville, but the little girl had begged to stay and work in her garden. Mrs. Thompson seemed delighted to have her.

Now that the credit repair was done, they had the afternoon to themselves, and though it was hot, it was also cloudy and a little breezy, and being from Phoenix, Tory didn't seem to mind the heat.

She wanted to see the ranch, she'd said, and being proud of the home he was building, Josh was excited to show her more than just the closest pasture.

They headed for the barn. Josh saddled Rose for Tory and Thor for himself. The big gelding had become his favorite, one of the most reliable horses on the ranch.

They rode through the first gate, Tory handling the mare with an ease that pleased him, something he hadn't really expected from a city girl like her. They started across the pasture toward the trail that wound along the creek to the river at the back of the ranch, the buckskin alert, the mare following his lead.

"Josh, wait!" Tory suddenly called out. "Someone's coming!"

He pulled rein and turned in the saddle, his gaze going past the house to a plain black SUV rumbling down the dirt road.

"Looks like our ride is going to have to wait," Josh said, worried something else had gone wrong.

Whirling the buckskin, he gigged Thor into a trot, then a gallop, glanced over to see Tory galloping up beside him, a grin on her face, her fiery curls flying out behind her. She was handling the mare like a pro.

An odd pressure expanded in his chest. He wasn't sure what it was, but it did feel good having her riding beside him.

They slowed to pass through the gate, then rode past the trailer toward the house. Cole walked out of the barn just as the black Chevy Suburban pulled up and the engine turned off. Josh swung his leg over the back of the saddle, stepped to the ground, and handed Cole the reins. Noah took the mare's reins and Josh swung Tory to the ground.

"Who is he?" Cole asked.

"No idea." But the colored light bar in the front grille said it was an unmarked police car and his nerves kicked up another notch.

"Don't unsaddle the horses till we see what's going on," Josh said, still hopeful.

The men led the horses into the shade of the barn and disappeared out of sight while a big man in a brown suit with a short blond buzz cut unwound himself from inside the SUV.

Josh flicked a glance at Tory, who stood close beside him, clearly as worried as he.

The blond man pulled off a pair of wraparound sunglasses. "You Joshua Cain?"

"That's right."

"FBI Special Agent Quinn Taggart. I'm a friend of your brother's."

Josh remembered hearing about him. He'd helped Linc and Carly out of a jam. He'd also helped his brother's partner, Beau Reese.

"Taggart. I know who you are. This is Victoria Bradford. Why don't we go inside out of the sun?"

Taggart nodded. Josh held the door open for Tory, and Taggart walked in behind her. Josh followed them inside and closed the door.

"How about a glass of lemonade?" Tory suggested.

"Sounds good," Taggart said.

They pulled out chairs and sat down around the kitchen table. Tory brought over the pitcher and glasses and took a seat.

Josh poured for all of them. "So what can I do for you, Agent Taggart?"

Taggart glanced pointedly at Tory.

"It's okay," Josh said. "You can speak freely."

"All right." Taggart took a drink of lemonade. "You were in

Gainesville for a funeral yesterday. Your friend Coy Whitmore was murdered."

"That's right."

"A couple weeks back another friend of yours was killed."

"Murdered," Josh corrected.

"I stand corrected. The first man who was murdered was Pete Saldana. According to our information, both these men were special operations marines."

Josh's gaze sharpened on Taggart. "The police have been looking for a connection. You think that's what it is? Someone killed them because they were soldiers?"

"It's beginning to look that way. For more than a year, Homeland Security has been dealing with a group of terrorists working in Texas. Your brother ran into trouble with a guy named Bharat al-Razi. In February, there was an attack on the Texas State Capitol."

"Beau Reese helped find the terrorists."

"That's right. A billionaire named Jamal Nawabi is now in prison for financing the cell that planned that attack."

He nodded. "My brother and I talked about it. Some of it I read in the papers."

Taggart took a long swallow of his drink. "During the sweep of the capitol and in the days that followed, members of the cell were either arrested or killed. We believed we had everyone involved."

"*Believed*," Josh repeated. "Past tense? Are you saying there are more of those guys out there?"

"Unfortunately, we now know several members of the cell escaped. Recently, one of them was killed when he attacked a retired police officer in Austin. We believe another man, the leader of the group, organized the recent bombing at the Houston Airport."

"I thought the men who set off the bombs were killed," Tory said.

"They were, but we don't think they planned the attack.

We think the bombing was funded by their billionaire sponsor, Nawabi, who's somehow still managing to pull the strings from behind bars."

"Wait a minute. Are you saying someone in the cell killed Saldana and Whitmore?" Josh asked.

"We won't be sure till we have him in custody. We've spread a wide net, but so far it hasn't caught anything. It was the death of your friends that alerted us to the situation."

"That being two marines dead in a little over two weeks," Josh said. "Both shot in the head. The cops trying to figure out who wanted them dead and why."

"That's right. When the most compelling link they found was the men's shared military service, they called in the FBI. Turns out Saldana and Whitmore were both in Afghanistan at the same time."

Josh nodded. "Deployed at the same time, both fought against the Taliban."

"And so did you."

Silence fell. Josh flashed on a memory, the echo of explosions and the rattle of heavy gunfire. He had relived it in his nightmares more than once.

Tory's worried gaze locked with his. She was no fool. She understood exactly where this was going.

"My team was one of several that were there," Josh said. "A lot of marines fought in Afghanistan."

"You think Josh is also in danger?" Tory asked.

"Unofficially, yes. That's the reason I'm here. Officially, we're still investigating. But if there's a member of a terrorist cell still at large in Texas and he's already killed two other men, Josh could very well be a target."

Josh softly cursed. It wasn't as if he didn't have enough trouble already. He was trying to protect Tory from Bridger. Now he had a new threat to worry about. Even if she wasn't the target, there was always a chance of getting caught in the crossfire.

"What about the other marines who fought over there?" Josh asked.

"We're contacting any soldier who fought there during the same time period Saldana and Whitmore were there. Anyone currently out of the service and back in Texas. We don't know why the shooter specifically targeted your friends, but we're working on it."

They talked a while longer, exploring other possibilities. Taggart asked if there was any chance Saldana and Whitmore could have had a mutual enemy, someone in the marines.

"I don't think so," Josh said. "Both of them were well liked, in and out of the military."

Taggart downed the last of his lemonade. "If you think of anything, I'd appreciate a call."

Taggart rose from his chair and handed Josh a business card. "Keep your eyes open, Josh. You've got the training and the experience. Word in town is you have two other marines working on the ranch who could be of help. Be watchful. With any luck, we'll figure this out and have the guy in custody before much longer."

"I appreciate your coming, Agent Taggart," Josh said, also rising.

"Unless we're somewhere official, it's just Quinn."

Josh extended a hand. "Thanks."

He walked Taggart out on the porch. As soon as the SUV disappeared down the road, Tory came out on the porch and Cole and Noah walked out of the barn.

"Looked like a cop," Noah said.

"FBI Agent Quinn Taggart," Josh said. "He's a friend of Linc's."

He set a hand on Tory's waist, keeping her close even as he scanned their surroundings for anything out of place:

colors, movement, shapes, sizes. Watching for trouble still came as naturally to him as breathing. Now he was glad.

"Was Taggart here about the murders?" Cole asked.

He nodded. "Looks like Pete and Coy were killed by the same guy. Could be he's a terrorist."

"Whoa. Say that again." Noah wiped the sweat off his forehead with an elbow.

"Remember the airport bombing?" Josh said. "FBI thinks the guy who planned it got away. There's a chance he's responsible for killing Pete and Coy. Might have something to do with us fighting the Taliban in Afghanistan."

"*Us?*" Cole stepped forward. "I don't think I like the sound of that."

"Not if two parts of that *us* are dead," Noah added.

"They're still investigating," Josh said. "Could be something else altogether, but it'd be a good idea if all of us kept an eye out. Taggart thinks it shouldn't be long before they'll have the guy in custody."

Cole's jaw hardened. "We're already on the lookout for Bridger. What's one more asswipe?"

On that note, the men walked back into the barn. The sound of hammers and the buzz of a saw replaced the unpleasant conversation.

"So I guess we don't get to go for our ride," Tory said glumly.

"Darlin', I'd really like to take you, but it's probably not a good idea. Maybe the FBI will get lucky and catch this guy right away."

"Sure, then all we'll have to worry about is Damon." She sighed. "When do our lives get back to normal?"

Since it didn't look like it was going to happen anytime soon, Josh made no reply.

Chapter Twenty-Eight

"I'm not staying in the house," Tory said. "I have things I need to do. I'm not going to hide out for God knows how long until they catch the killer—if they ever do."

She propped a hand on her hip. "Who's to say he won't just disappear somewhere in the country or head back to Afghanistan or whatever hellhole he came from?"

The corner of Josh's mouth kicked up. "He won't be able to get through the airports."

"Yeah? Well, he got in somehow. Which means he knows how to get back out. Are you going to stay in the house? Because if you recall, *you* could be a target—not me."

His blue eyes pinned her, but they held a trace of humor. "I'm supposed to be your boss, remember?"

"I'm supposed to be your cook, remember? That means I need fresh vegetables for supper. That is the reason I'm planting a garden."

She started to stomp away, stopped, and turned back. "And dammit, be careful. If something happened to you—" A sharp pang cut off her words and her eyes burned. Turning, she hurried away.

Was this ever going to end? Not only did they have Damon to worry about, now there could be a terrorist in the mix.

Josh caught up with her at the tool shed. She'd picked out a spot for the garden behind the main house that was flat and accessible to water. She set out a rake, shovel, and hoe, but by the time she picked up the trowel, her eyes were brimming with tears.

She felt Josh's big hands on her shoulders, turning her around. He took the trowel from her hand, set it down with the other tools, and pulled her into his arms.

"Hey. Everything's going to be okay."

She slid her arms around his waist and pressed her face into his chest. "Two of your friends are dead. I'm afraid for you. I can't stand to think of you getting killed."

Josh kissed the top of her head. "I'm not going to get killed, all right? I was a soldier. A good one. I know how to take care of myself. I just need to be sure you're not in danger."

When she looked up at him, Josh lowered his head and very softly kissed her. He eased back and touched her cheek. "I'll be watching for this guy every minute, okay?"

"What about a gun? I know you have weapons."

"Fine, I'll start carrying, but if I do, I'm teaching you how to shoot."

"I know how to shoot. I bought a .38 revolver when I got to Houston and took gun safety classes. Unfortunately, in Carlsbad I started thinking I was safe—big mistake—and hocked it when I got low on money."

"Wow. You know how to shoot. You manage to keep on surprising me."

Tory wiped the wetness from her cheeks. "Good for me."

Josh laughed. "I'll carry the tools for you."

She let him. But with every step he took toward the back of the house, she scanned the area behind him. She thought of the funeral in Gainesville. Those men were soldiers, too, and someone had killed them.

For the first time she realized she wasn't just enamored of Josh, she was in love with him.

Since she was pretty sure he was only in lust with her, loving him was a stupid thing to do.

He set the tools down on the ground where she showed him and took a look around. "Good spot," he said. "I'll get some chicken wire in town and put it up around the perimeter so you won't have to worry about deer and rabbits. I'll pick up some soaker hose, too. That should work to keep it watered."

"That'd be great."

He looked down at her, hands on his hips, looked back at the patch that would soon be a garden. Something shifted in his features, flickered in his eyes. He glanced back at the garden. A muscle flicked in his jaw the instant before he turned and walked away.

Tory's heart started pounding. She knew that look on a man's face, knew exactly what he was thinking. She ran to catch up with him and grabbed his arm, snaring his attention.

"What?" he asked.

"The garden. It's not what you think. I'm not . . . it doesn't mean anything. I'm not trying to trap you. We said as long as it was what we both wanted. I didn't mean to overstep."

The muscles loosened across his shoulders, but didn't completely relax. "Hey, it's just a garden. A ranch needs a garden, right? Let me know if you need anything else." He started walking, didn't look back.

She should have realized how permanent it would seem, a garden that she would take care of. As if she assumed she would continue to be part of his life. As if they were more than just friends with benefits.

Her throat felt tight. She thought of Damon. She had believed he cared about her, even loved her. Nothing could have been further from the truth.

She needed to start planning for the future, find a place where she could make a home for her and Ivy. She couldn't continue to rely on Josh. She'd been a fool to let her guard down.

She looked over at the patch of ground where she'd imagined the perfect little garden and swallowed past the lump in her throat.

All she saw now was a barren patch of dirt.

Josh called Linc later that afternoon. "It's Friday. I was wondering if you and Carly are coming out to the ranch this weekend."

There was a pause on the other end of the phone. "Haven't decided. Why?"

"I need to fill you in on a couple of things. Rather do it in person, but if—"

"We'll be there. Why don't you come over to the house for supper? We'll pick something up and bring it with us. Say about eight?"

"That'd be great."

"You bringing Tory?"

He wanted to. And that was what bothered him. He wanted to be with her all the time. When he wasn't with her, he was thinking about her. He wasn't ready for a family. He had goals, things he needed to do. And what about his nightmares? He needed to deal with the past before he could think about the future.

He told himself he had no choice but to bring her and little Ivy with him. The thought of leaving them alone with all the trouble swirling around made his chest feel tight.

"Tory and Ivy, if that's okay."

"Sure. I'm just about to convince Carly to go off the pill. Might as well get used to the patter of little feet around the house."

Josh chuckled. He was getting way too used to the sound himself. "I'll see you at eight."

He disconnected and went in to tell Tory not to worry about making supper. He found her out in the garden, turning over soil with a shovel. He didn't like the feeling that moved through him as he watched her: desire, and a surge of protectiveness so strong his back teeth clenched together.

"Hey, babe, we're invited to supper at Blackland Ranch. We can pick Ivy up on the way."

She leaned on the shovel, her forehead glistening with perspiration. "I didn't know this was going to be so much work."

"Maybe you aren't cut out for ranch life, after all," he said, but as the words spilled out, his stomach knotted.

"Maybe not," she said. She carried the shovel over and leaned it against the side of the house, walked back to where he stood.

"I don't want to get in the middle of a family dinner. Ivy and I can just stay here."

He shook his head. "Too much going on. I don't want to leave you by yourself."

"I'll be fine."

No way was he leaving her. "Linc and Carly want you to come."

She hesitated, seemed surprised. "Are you sure?"

"Yeah." *And I want you to come*. But he didn't say that. He needed to take some time, figure things out. "I won't worry if you're with me."

"Okay, if you're sure."

He wished he didn't feel such a wave of relief.

He wished he knew what the hell to do.

Supper was over. Chinese food from some fancy restaurant in Dallas that cooked specialty items just for Linc. Carly, Tory, and Ivy were sitting in the living room. Josh could hear them laughing as Linc led the way down the hall to his home office so they could talk.

His brother walked behind his wide, dark oak desk and sat down, pulled open the bottom drawer and took out a bottle of Stagg Kentucky Bourbon, the expensive whiskey he favored. He poured two fingers neat into each of two crystal glasses and handed one to Josh.

Sitting in one of the dark oak chairs on the other side of the desk, Josh accepted the drink and took a sip.

Linc sipped his own drink and leaned back in his chair. "What's going on?"

"FBI came to see me. Your friend Quinn Taggart. Turns out my buddies may have been killed because they fought in Afghanistan."

Linc straightened. "How's that?"

"Taggart seems to think the guy who shot them might be involved in the same terror cell that's been plaguing half of Texas. Same group you and Beau each dealt with at one time or another."

"I thought those guys were all either dead or locked up."

"Apparently, one of them's still on the loose."

"What's it got to do with you?"

"Pete Saldana and Coy Whitmore were both special ops, both deployed in the Middle East at the same time."

"The same time as you?" Linc asked, already a step ahead.

"I was there then, too."

Linc leaned forward, shirtsleeves rolled up to his elbows. "So Quinn thinks this guy could be coming after soldiers who fought in Afghanistan?"

"It's possible."

Linc leaned back. "Well, after that story they wrote about you, half of Texas knows you were there, that you're back home now, and where to find you."

"Unfortunately." The story hadn't been his idea. One of

the military higher-ups thought the book would be good military PR.

"You've talked to Cole and Noah? Told them to watch for this guy?" Linc asked.

He nodded. "They're on alert. I'll talk to Ty Murphy in the morning. The thing is, the guy could have already left the state. Even if he's still in Texas, there are other guys he could target."

"Don't forget the book," Linc said darkly.

"Hard to forget the damned book." Josh took a drink, let the burn roll through him. "The good news is Taggart thinks they'll have the guy in custody fairly soon."

"Let's damn well hope so. You need some extra men?"

"I called a couple of vets I know who work security in Pleasant Hill." The next town over. "They're going to keep an eye on the house and grounds at night."

Linc leaned back in his chair, took a long drink of whiskey. Josh figured he was doing his best not to interfere.

"You hear from Taggart, you'll let me know," Linc said.

Josh nodded, took a drink, savored the taste of the expensive liquor. "There's one more thing."

Linc cocked an eyebrow. "What's that?"

"Tory's ex-boyfriend hacked my identity. Created total havoc."

Linc's mouth tightened. "Send me a list of all your account numbers and I'll have Glen Barker, our CPA, get with Beau's computer whiz, Rob Michaels, see if they can pull things back together."

"Thanks, but it's already handled. I would have been up a creek without a paddle if it hadn't been for Tory. She was amazing. She cleaned up the mess, but—"

"But you need to figure a way to stop this guy."

"Yeah. Tory shouldn't have to live this way."

"And neither should you."

Josh just grunted. "Let me know if you come up with

something. Aside from heading for Phoenix and pounding him into the sand, I'm drawing a blank."

A calculating look came into Linc's dark eyes. "He's a businessman, right? Real estate? I know people in Phoenix. Maybe it's time for Damon's company to feel the pinch."

"It's his dad's company, unfortunately."

"Might be even better." Linc swirled the whiskey in his glass, shot the last of it back. "Let me give it some thought."

Both men rose from their chairs. It was time to rejoin the women. The anticipation that moved through him wasn't a welcome feeling. He was in real trouble with Tory.

And he didn't see an end to it anytime soon.

Chapter Twenty-Nine

Aside from everyone being on alert, life on the ranch went on as usual. The June weather was growing hotter, more humid, the sky overcast one day, the sun broiling down the next.

Worried about Ivy, they decided to leave her with Mrs. Thompson during the day, at least till things settled down. The older woman loved having her and it gave Tory time for her riding lessons and working with Star.

They still needed photos to finish the webpage, but Josh's old camera wasn't really up to the task, and now was not the best time to be out on the ranch. Since she'd done plenty of photography in the advertising business, Tory figured taking the photos herself would save money, and it would be fun.

Josh planned to buy whatever gear they needed, but for now, they were staying close to the house, concentrating their efforts on the stallion.

Star seemed to be growing more and more docile every day. As long as Josh was with Tory, the horse remained placid, even seemed affectionate. The stallion was in a separate pasture from the rest of the horses, but the animals stood together at the fence and they didn't seem to bother him.

Josh wasn't planning to use Star for breeding until he was sure it was safe, but Tory had every hope the stallion would be able to live a normal, productive life.

The afternoon slipped away. "I'll see you at supper," Josh said, striding off to the barn. Cole and Noah had gone off on the ATVs, out checking on the rest of the horses and the few head of Black Angus cattle Josh was raising. Tory knew they were also keeping an eye out for any sign of trouble.

She had just walked into the kitchen to start supper when she looked through the window above the sink and spotted a dark brown four-door Chevy Impala heading down the road toward the house.

The car pulled up, a rental with an Enterprise license plate on the front. The driver opened the door and stepped out and she recognized Detective Jeremy Larson, Phoenix PD.

Nerves sent her pulse up a notch. Removing her apron, she hurried through the living room and opened the front door to see the tall, lanky detective walking up on Josh's porch.

"Detective Larson. What a surprise. Please . . . come on in."

The detective ran a hand through his curly brown hair and stepped into the living room. Behind him, she saw Josh coming out of the barn, striding in their direction.

"I just got off a flight from Phoenix," Detective Larson said. "Drove from DFW straight out here. I'm hoping you can help me."

"Of course."

The door opened again and Josh walked into the house. "Detective Larson. What's going on?"

"I was just telling Ms. Bradford—"

"Tory, please," she said.

"I was saying that I just arrived from Phoenix, drove straight out from the airport. I'm hoping Tory can help me."

"That's a long way to travel," she said. "Why don't we sit down at the table and I'll get us something cold to drink."

"Sounds good." Larson and Josh both followed Tory into the kitchen.

"I'll get it," Josh said.

Walking over to the fridge, he brought out the pitcher of lemonade Tory always kept there, filled three glasses with ice, and poured them full. He carried the glasses over and set them down on the table. Larson sat down and Josh took a seat next to Tory.

"What can I do for you, Detective?" Tory asked.

He took a sip of his drink, set the glass back down. "There's no good way to say this, so I'll just begin. Two weeks ago, a Phoenix woman went missing. Disappeared from a bar in Carefree after her shift one night. Two days ago, her body was found in the desert."

Josh shifted in his chair. Tory caught a flicker of something in his eyes that put her on alert. "You knew about this?" she asked.

"Ham called when she went missing. He thought I'd want to know."

"Brown's been calling me for updates," the detective said. "He's working for you?"

Josh nodded. "After what happened to Lisa Shane, I asked him to keep me updated on the investigation. He called, told me about the girl. I was hoping she took off with her boyfriend. I didn't know you'd recovered her body."

"Information hasn't been released pending notification of next of kin."

Tory zeroed in on Josh. "You should have told me when it happened. Why didn't you?"

"Like I said, I was hoping the girl had just left town."

Larson's gaze remained on Josh. "Or maybe you didn't want to worry her."

Josh looked away.

The detective turned back to Tory. "The thing is, there are similarities between the Shane abduction and what happened to the waitress, Patty Daniels. The coroner puts the time of death about a week after Ms. Daniels went missing. The ligature marks on her wrists and ankles indicate she was restrained during the time she was missing. Before she was killed, she was violently beaten and raped."

Tory thought of Lisa and swallowed against a wave of nausea.

"What was the cause of death?" Josh asked.

"Strangulation."

Josh's hand tightened around his frosted glass. "Bastard wanted to enjoy it."

"That's right," the detective said. "I've seen this kind of behavior in certain types of killers."

"What type?" Josh asked.

Larson flicked a glance at Tory, but spoke to Josh. "Serials. Men who are sexually aroused by torturing their victims before they kill them."

Tory trembled. Could Damon be a serial killer? It didn't seem possible. But she had read about killers, men like Ted Bundy who seemed to live completely normal lives.

She took a breath for courage. "Why are you here, Detective Larson? What do you want from me?"

"I want you to tell me about Damon Bridger. So far Lisa Shane hasn't remembered anything about the attack on her. The doctors think there's a good chance she never will."

Tory had spoken to her friend several times since she had moved from Phoenix. Lisa sounded upbeat, glad to be back in Cooperstown, grateful for the chance to rebuild her relationship with her parents.

She'd been a wild teen, her parents overly strict and determined she marry a man they approved. Now they were getting to know the responsible, successful career woman their daughter had become.

In a way, it was good Lisa didn't remember what had happened during those terrible days in captivity somewhere in the mountains.

"When we spoke at the hospital," Larson continued, "you were convinced Bridger was the man who abducted Ms. Shane. You thought he might have been looking for information about where to find you."

Tory's hand trembled where it rested on the table. "I don't know, I . . . I thought it was possible, but you said he had an alibi. I don't know Patty Daniels. Why do you think she's connected to me?"

Larson looked at Josh, who reached over and caught her hand, quieting the tremors. "She was your size, honey. And she had your same red hair."

Her breath froze. For a moment, she couldn't breathe. "Oh, my God. You think Damon murdered that girl because she looked like me?" She shook her head. "I know Damon's crazy, but surely he wouldn't . . . wouldn't . . ."

"You use the word 'crazy,'" Larson said. "You think he's mentally unbalanced?"

She dragged in a shaky breath and fought to collect her thoughts.

Josh squeezed her hand. "Just take your time, honey."

"Damon wasn't . . . he wasn't that way at first. He seemed like this really great guy. I don't know how he fooled me so completely."

For the next twenty minutes, she told the detective how Damon had changed, how he had abused her, beaten her, and stalked her. How he had threatened her until she'd had no choice but to run.

"The police did their best, but there are laws they have to follow and Damon is smart." She told him about the kitten he had murdered and the dog he had killed.

"He seemed to get some kind of sick pleasure out of it. He seemed to enjoy inflicting pain. All the time he was beating me, he was grinning."

"My captain didn't want me coming out here," Larson said. "There's no evidence, nothing except for his attack on you to make Bridger a person of interest. But I have a feeling about this guy. I wanted to hear what you had to say."

"Bridger's obsessed with Tory," Josh said. "They were engaged, which he seems to believe gives him ownership. There's a good chance he hired a group of bikers to vandalize the ranch. He's probably behind the identity theft I just had to deal with. If it was Bridger—and I'm betting it was—he hasn't given up. He still wants Tory, and he'll do anything to get her."

"He may have substituted another victim for the woman he wants," Detective Larson said. "If you're right, Damon Bridger is a very dangerous man."

Larson left the ranch determined to find out if Bridger was the man behind the attack on Lisa Shane and the red-haired woman who had been murdered. According to Larson, Damon had no alibi for the night the girl had gone missing. He was home in bed that night, he'd said.

But there was nothing illegal about him sleeping in his own bed and no evidence he had left the house anytime before morning, so he remained in the clear.

Aside from Tory's suspicions and Detective Larson's hunch, the police had no reason to believe Damon was involved. Add to that, his father's money and powerful position in the community made him a formidable opponent. Without some kind of evidence, there wasn't anything the police could do.

Josh was worried. The quagmire they were entangled in

was getting deeper and stickier. When Cole and Noah rode their ATVs up in front of the barn at the end of the day, Josh walked over to speak to them.

"What's going on?" Noah asked at the solemn look on his face.

"A detective named Larson flew in from Phoenix to talk to Tory. You remember that girl I told you about who went missing?"

Noah nodded. Cole's features darkened. "The waitress who looked like Tory?" he asked.

"That's the one. She turned up dead. Good chance it's the same guy who abducted Tory's friend Lisa."

"Cops think it's Tory's ex?" Noah asked.

"Cops don't know what to think. Larson's gut says it's Bridger. He thinks Tory could be in danger. So do I."

Cole lifted his baseball cap and scratched his blond head. He surveyed the vast grasslands around them, the ravines overflowing with thick dark green shrubs, the deep woods, and thickets of trees.

"Lot of land to cover. We can keep watch for Bridger, but there's still a guy out there who murdered two soldiers and might be coming after you. Until the feds make an arrest, maybe you should put on a few more men."

"I plan to," Josh said. "Just wanted to bring you up to speed."

"We'll stay alert." The men put up their gear and headed home for the day.

Mrs. T. brought Ivy home and Tory worked on supper. When Josh walked into the house, the smell of roast beef hit him and his stomach growled. He heard small feet and looked up to see Ivy running toward him.

"Look, Josh! I you made a picture! It's you and me and Mama and Star!"

Josh swept the little girl up against his chest and took the sheet of paper from her hand. In a crayon drawing colored in red, yellow, and green, he was as big as the stallion. He had a hand on each of the females' shoulders. Clearly, he was protecting them.

His chest clamped down. He wasn't ready for this. He still had nightmares about the men he hadn't been able to protect. He would never forget a single soldier's face. He'd come back to Texas to escape that kind of responsibility.

How had he gotten in so deep? More important, what was he going to do about it?

"It's beautiful, sweetheart," he said. "We'll put it up on the fridge." Setting Ivy back on her feet, he walked over to the refrigerator, took down a magnet that looked like a cowboy hat, and used it to hold up the drawing. "There. That looks nice."

Ivy grinned, turned, and raced back into the living room just as Tory walked in, her gaze following the path her daughter had taken directly away from him.

"You saved her," she said softly. "I was afraid she would never be able to trust a man again, but she trusts you. You saved her." She looked up at him. "You saved us both."

His chest tightened. He felt as if the walls were closing in. "I don't want to be your savior, Tory. I don't want to be anyone's savior." Turning, he walked out of the kitchen, crossed the living room, and walked out of the house.

Josh didn't come over that night. Tory could sense his restlessness, his frustration. He felt boxed in, a man at the end of a chain. Two of his friends had been murdered. There was a chance he was on the killer's hit list. Add to that, he felt responsible for her and Ivy.

Detective Larson believed Damon had murdered Patty

Daniels because she looked like Tory. Now that Damon knew where to find her, how long before he came after her?

As she lay in bed staring up at the ceiling, she tried not to think of Lisa and what she had suffered, tried not to think of the girl who had been tortured and killed.

Was it Damon? And if so, was Tory the woman he really wanted to murder?

She was exhausted when she crawled out of bed the next morning. She fed Ivy, then they went over to fix Josh's breakfast. He was gone when she arrived, already outside hard at work.

She made French toast and stuck it in the oven, made him a sack lunch, then took Ivy back to the trailer. With so much worry, it was hard to concentrate on the little girl's morning lesson, but Ivy was smart and she loved to learn. Tory somehow managed to get through it.

Later in the morning, she drove Ivy over to Mrs. Thompson's. She knew Josh didn't like her going even that far from the house, but it was only the end of the road and according to Hamilton Brown, Damon was still in Phoenix.

"Let's work in the garden before it gets too hot," Clara Thompson said to Ivy. Inside the big old white house it was cool, but outside the sun beat down fiercely. They might work outdoors for a while, but Tory figured they wouldn't last long.

"After lunch, we can have fun with letters and numbers, and I checked a book out of the library for us to read."

"A cat book or a dog book?" Ivy loved dogs. She asked for one every year for Christmas but it wasn't going to happen anytime soon.

"It's a dog book. *Doozy Hound Goes to the City.*"

Ivy grinned. "*Doozy Hound.* That sound good." Ivy ran into the living room while Mrs. Thompson walked Tory to the door.

"I'll never be able to thank you enough, Clara, for everything you've done."

"Don't be silly. I can use the extra money and having your daughter here is the highlight of my day."

Tory had mentioned the possible threat against Josh, but said the FBI hoped to have the man in custody very soon. She had also told Mrs. Thompson about Damon, though she hadn't mentioned the murder since there wasn't any proof.

"I hope you and Josh are being careful."

"Everyone's on alert. I'm sure it'll all get straightened out soon."

But she couldn't help wondering what would happen once things went back to normal. Would Josh still want her to stay on the ranch? Or would his restlessness continue to grow? Would he still desire her the way he always seemed to? Or would he be ready to move on?

And what about what she wanted? She was in love with Josh, but she would never be satisfied with a man who thought of her as little more than a friend. Better to end things, make a home for her and Ivy somewhere besides the ranch. Make a life that didn't depend on a man.

Her eyes stung. She refused to give in to tears, but her mood was dark when she returned to the house.

It wasn't time for her riding lesson, but feeling strangely claustrophobic, she wandered outside anyway. Josh was training a red roan horse named Woody. On a horse, he looked even more impressive than he usually did.

Tory loved watching him, the way he kept his shoulders so straight and yet moved in perfect rhythm with the animal beneath him. The way the horse understood his slightest command.

He glanced over and saw her, drew rein on Woody and swung down from the saddle, tied the roan to a ring in the fence and walked toward her.

"Sorry about last night," he said. "I should have let you know I wasn't coming over."

"I had a feeling you weren't coming." She looked up at him. "It's all right, you know. I'm not your wife. I'm not even your girlfriend. You don't have to answer to me."

A muscle tightened in his jaw. "That right? What about you? You don't have to answer to me, either?"

"There's no reason I should. We're friends who enjoy having sex. That's all we ever have been."

"Just friends? That's it?" He reached out and caught her shoulders. She gasped as he dragged her hard against him, angled his head, and his mouth crushed down over hers. Heat scorched through her as he walked her backward till his hard body pressed her against the wall.

Josh kissed her and kissed her, kissed her until she was making little noises in her throat and clinging to his shoulders.

Then he broke away.

"Dammit, you make me crazy." He stalked off, stared out through a newly replaced window, then walked back and stopped right in front of her, propped his hands on his hips.

Tory looked up at him. "You make me pretty crazy, too," she said softly.

Josh sighed. Reaching out, he gently touched her cheek. "We'll figure it out," he said.

But Tory wasn't so sure. She opened her mouth to say so when the sound of an engine reached them. "Someone's coming."

Since it was doubtful someone who wanted to kill either one of them would drive right up to the house, Josh headed for the barn door and Tory fell in beside him.

"It's Taggart," Josh said, recognizing the big black SUV and the blond man with the buzz cut behind the wheel.

The vehicle pulled to a halt and Quinn Taggart straightened and came out of the driver's seat. Josh walked up and the men shook hands.

"You want to go into the house out of the heat?" Josh asked.

Taggart shook his head. "Don't have time. Let's go stand in the shade."

They walked into the shade of the barn. It smelled like dust and hay. "What's going on?" Josh asked.

"We caught a break in the case. Our interrogators are some of the best. One of the men we arrested during the attack on the capitol started talking. We'd already connected the dots about Saldana and Whitmore both being in Afghanistan at the same time, but apparently the threat is more specific than we thought."

"How's that?" Josh asked.

"Turns out both men were involved in the fighting that took place in the Bala Murghab River Valley."

Josh nodded. "That's right. Special operations took on a large insurgent force near the ruins of an old medieval town."

"Marw al-Rudh."

"Seems you're well informed."

"Well enough to know your team was also engaged in the fighting there."

"That's right."

"The thing is, Josh, the man we swept up in the raid is an Afghan named Ahmad Bijan. He came from the village of Bala Murghab. His father is from the Buzi tribe, Mullah Ramazan, a spiritual leader in the region. He's extremely influential."

"What does any of that have to do with the murders?"

"According to Ahmad, his brother was killed by marine special ops soldiers who fought in that battle. Their father vowed revenge."

"You think this guy, Mullah Ramazan, would go to that much trouble?"

"He sent his son over here. Couldn't have been easy smuggling him into the country."

Josh grunted. "Good point."

"Two men are dead. The rest of the special ops marines involved are still on active duty, most deployed out of the country. That leaves you. If the killer is carrying out Mullah Ramazan's revenge, you could very well be his next target."

Chapter Thirty

Night sounds reached him through the darkness, crickets in the grass beneath the window, the hoot of the barn owl he'd spotted a couple of days ago.

Josh eased out of Tory's bed, careful not to wake her. Lately, after he came over and they made love, he'd been sleeping on the sofa. He hadn't had any more nightmares, but he wasn't taking chances.

Grabbing his jeans and boots off the floor, he went into the living room to put them on, then walked out on the porch. One of the vets he had hired for night guard duty stood near the barn smoking a cigarette, the red tip glowing in the dark. Josh headed in that direction.

Turley spotted him, snuffed his smoke, and met him halfway. At forty, Wes Turley was whipcord lean and rock-hard, his skin darkly tanned and leathery. He wore camouflage pants and a black T-shirt. A Nighthawk .45 rode in a holster tied down around his thigh.

"How's it going?" Josh asked.

"Been quiet. Aside from the horses and cattle, nothin' moving around out there."

"What about Ben?"

"Checked in half an hour ago. Hasn't seen squat."

"Good. You need anything?"

"We got a thermos of hot coffee and a couple of sand-wiches. We're good."

Josh scanned the grounds looking for Ben Rigby, the other vet he'd hired. It took a moment to spot the faint move-ment in the thick foliage down along the creek. He could just make out the shape of a man.

"That's him," Turley said.

Josh waved and Rigby waved back. "See you in the morning," Josh said, and started back to the trailer.

No trouble so far. Part of him wished something would happen. He could deal with a problem now easier than wait-ing for something down the road.

Restless, he walked back inside and stretched out on the couch. Thanks to his years in the marines, he could sleep damn near anywhere. The bad news was he also came wide awake at the slightest disturbance.

He slept fitfully that night. Too much on his mind. By the time the sun came up, the men were gone and he was back in his own house getting ready for the day. Tory came over and fixed him breakfast. He ate and headed outside to work.

The veterinarian was coming out this morning, Doctor Alejandro Nunez. One of the mares had come up lame and the foreleg seemed to be getting worse. Nunez was good. Unfortunately, he was a handsome devil and he clearly had eyes for Tory.

As Nunez pulled up in his dark brown GMC pickup, she came out of the house looking way too sexy in a clingy little blouse and those jeans with the rhinestones on the pockets.

Nunez parked, got out, and headed straight for her, homing in like a man on a mission. Josh felt a sweep of ir-ritation.

"Good morning," the doctor said to her, flashing a set of pearly teeth that magnified his dark, Latino good looks.

"Dr. Nunez, I didn't know you were coming," Tory said, smiling.

No, she didn't. Because Josh had conveniently forgotten to mention it.

"You ready to look at that mare?" Josh asked the vet.

"I could use a cup of coffee first."

"Of course!" Tory said. "Come on in."

Nunez waved at him and smiled. The man walked into the house and Josh's irritation grew. He wanted to grab Nunez by the seat of the pants and drag him out of there, haul him out to the barn where he belonged.

Josh softly cursed. Jealousy wasn't in his nature. Or at least it hadn't been. He headed for the barn, determined to put an end to his petty thoughts.

He was almost there when his cell phone rang. Pulling the phone out of his pocket, he recognized the caller and pressed the phone against his ear. "Hey, big brother, what's up?"

"Got a call from Ross Townsend in Phoenix."

"Yeah, what'd he have to say?"

"Unfortunately, he hasn't come up with squat on Bridger, nothing to connect him to Lisa Shane, but apparently there was a second abduction. This one ended in murder."

"I know. Detective named Larson flew in yesterday from Phoenix. Wanted to talk to Tory."

Linc went silent. Josh could almost hear his brother's brain spinning. "That doesn't sound good. Townsend said the girl was a little redhead. She was kidnapped and held prisoner, beaten, and raped like the Shane girl. Only this time she ended up dead. Larson thinks Bridger could have killed her?"

"He's gathering information, following his gut. He wanted to hear what Tory had to say."

"I don't like it."

"Neither do I. The good news is Ham says Bridger's still

in Phoenix. Ham's been checking Bridger's office periodically, making sure he hasn't left town."

"I still don't like it."

"There's something you're going to like even less."

"Yeah, what's that?"

"Taggart came back out yesterday. Long story short, Saldana and Whitmore were revenge killings, probably payback for some Afghan Mullah's son who was killed by special ops soldiers in the fighting in the Bala Murghab Valley. The rest of the guys are still deployed. Of the three who got out of the marines and came back to Texas—including me—two are dead."

"That's it. I'm calling Deke Logan as soon as we get off the phone. I want men posted around your property. If this guy comes after you, he won't get past them."

"I've got Cole and Noah, a couple of vets working nights. You don't need to do that."

"Too bad, little brother. I only found you a few years back. You made it home alive from the war. I'm not standing by and letting some bastard kill you."

He probably should have been angry at his brother's high-handedness, but he was getting used to Linc. Besides, it felt good to have family, someone who cared if you lived or died.

He thought of Tory, remembered the tears in her eyes, how worried she was about him, and his chest felt tight. He thought how worried he was about her, and silently cursed.

"All right, I won't argue. I've got other people's safety to think of besides my own. I don't want any of them ending up as collateral damage."

"Then it's settled. With luck, Logan should be there this afternoon." The call ended.

Since he had plenty to do besides worry, Josh went back to work.

* * *

The evening was balmy, stars poking through the blanket
of darkness, a light breeze in the air. Cole pulled his silver
Chevy pickup over to the curb across the street from Brittany's
little gray house. With its white shutters and flowered walkway, it had an old-fashioned charm that perfectly suited her.

Sitting there with the engine off, he could see her through
the living room window, sitting on the sofa, holding a book
in her hands. He'd been parked there last night, too, like
some idiot voyeur, trying to work up the courage to knock
on her door.

He should have just called, asked if he could come over,
but he was afraid she'd say yes. He kept thinking about what
had happened the last time, how he had humiliated himself,
how he'd acted like a callow teen with his first woman, instead of a battle-hardened soldier who'd stared death in the
face.

A battle-hardened soldier who'd come home without his
legs.

He scrubbed a hand over his face. Britt had said it didn't
matter. Was he brave enough to find out?

Clenching his jaw, he cracked open the door and slid
down from the seat. These days, he rarely noticed the hitch
in his stride as he walked, but he noticed it now, felt gangly
and awkward as he crossed the street, walked up the path,
and knocked on the front door.

He could hear footsteps on the carpet. She paused to
check the peephole, then pulled the door open.

"Cole!" He hadn't expected the warm smile that broke
over her face. It made his chest clamp down.

"It's so good to see you," she said, stepping back to welcome him. "Come on in."

He took a deep breath and crossed the threshold. He
almost couldn't believe he was there, ready to conquer his

demons. He was ready. But what if Britt had changed her mind?

"Would you like a drink? I have a bottle of scotch and a bottle of vodka, stuff my ex kept in the house."

Her ex-fiancé, Avery Kaplan. Callous sonofabitch. Cole had been engaged to a girl like that, always out for herself. Heather and Avery would make a perfect pair.

"Thanks," he said. "I'm okay for now." Though he could certainly use a little false courage. "I just . . . I wanted to talk to you about what happened last time."

Her cheeks flushed prettily. With her dark hair and big blue eyes, Brittany was a beautiful woman. Sweet, too. A schoolteacher. He had known her since college, had always liked and respected her.

"Would you like to sit down?" she asked.

He couldn't look away from those pretty blue eyes. He opened his mouth and his brains fell out. "I'd like to take you to bed. That's what I wanted to do the last time I was here. I haven't thought of anything else since I walked out the door that night."

"Oh," she said, and suddenly he felt like a fool.

"Damn, I'm sorry. Really. I don't know why I said that. I shouldn't have come. I apologize for being so forward. I hope you'll forgive—"

Her kiss cut off his words. Britt looped her arms around his neck, went up on her toes, and just kept kissing him.

A low groan escaped as Cole hauled her against him and deepened the kiss, tasting the sweetness that seemed to pour right out of her. The smell of spring flowers drifted up and his arousal strengthened. He'd been a fool to leave before. No matter what happened, he wasn't leaving again.

Lifting her into his arms, he carried her into the bedroom and set her on her feet next to the bed. "I want you, honey. I want you so damned much."

"Oh, Cole, I want you, too."

"Are you sure? If . . . if it bothers you, I'll understand."

She cupped his face between her hands. "You have no idea, do you? You have no idea what an incredible man you are. Take me to bed, Cole Wyman. Put me out of my misery."

Cole felt his mouth edging into a smile. It was the last thing he'd expected. "You sure?"

"Are you kidding?" She kissed him again and he kissed her back until both of them were breathing fast and he was so hard he ached.

After that, everything just seemed to fall into place. Two cogs fitting perfectly together, two people made just for each other.

Everything is going to be okay, he thought as he lay beside her, words that hadn't entered his head since that terrible explosion in the desert. *Everything is going to be okay.*

And as Brittany snuggled against him as if she belonged there, Cole believed it.

Chapter Thirty-One

Linc was worried. His brother was in considerable danger and there wasn't a lot more he could do. He'd called Quinn Taggart and pressed him for details on the murders of Josh's two marine buddies. Quinn had broken protocol and reluctantly filled him in.

Linc had also talked to Deke Logan. He had used the spec ops soldier turned security pro when he and Carly had been threatened by a drug lord. Linc trusted Deke, hired him to set up a security team around the property twenty-four/seven. But two thousand acres was a big chunk of land. There was always a chance the killer could get through.

He couldn't do much more about protection, but he could do something about Damon Bridger. This morning he'd phoned Ross Townsend, the PI he had working in Phoenix.

According to Ross, Bridger's alibi held up. There was nothing to connect Damon to the abduction of Lisa Shane or the murder of the redheaded waitress, no reason to believe he had anything to do with either of them.

But as Linc suspected and Townsend was soon able to confirm, Tory Bradford wasn't the first woman Damon had abused.

Townsend had convinced one of Bridger's victims to

come forward, a cocktail waitress who had met Damon at the nightclub where she worked, a place called the Peacock. Suzy Solomon had agreed to talk to Aaron Guinness, the attorney Nate Temple worked with in Phoenix. Guinness was filing a civil suit for assault and battery on her behalf.

According to Suzy, Damon had seemed like the man of her dreams when they'd started dating, but after the first few weeks, he'd grown more and more possessive—and more and more violent.

Then late one night he'd shown up at her apartment. They'd argued and Bridger had used his fists to prove his point.

Suzy had refused to see him again and Damon had written her a five-hundred-dollar check to keep quiet. Afraid to go against him, Suzy had let the matter drop.

Apparently, she regretted her decision. With assurances that she would be provided with protection, she had agreed to the lawsuit. Townsend had found another woman who could probably be convinced to file charges, as well.

If things went according to plan, she wouldn't need to bother.

Linc smiled as he leaned back in the chair behind his teakwood desk in the Dallas office.

Damon Bridger wanted trouble?

Lincoln Cain was just the man to give it to him.

Tory was eager to finish the webpage. She needed those ranch pictures badly. But Josh was determined to put off their photo safari until the FBI had the terrorist in custody.

"What if they don't catch him?" she asked as she carried his dinner, leg of lamb with mint sauce, mashed potatoes, and brussels sprouts, over to the table and set the plate down in front of him.

Josh had worked late, not unusual for him. Tory had already fed Ivy and herself. The little girl was in the living room now, playing a video game on the Fire tablet Josh had bought for her on the Internet.

Tory didn't think he was ready for all of them to sit down like a family at the dinner table. She didn't want him to feel even more trapped than he did already.

Tory wasn't ready for that, either. Ivy was growing more and more attached to Josh. If things didn't work out and they had to leave the ranch, it was going to be hard on her daughter. She didn't want to make things worse.

"We need those pictures," she continued. "Your brother has armed men running all over the ranch on four-wheelers. I'm not the target. How about letting me go out on one of the ATVs and take some photos?"

Josh cut into the slice of lamb on his plate. "No way are you going out there by yourself. Besides, my camera is an old piece of crap. You said as much yourself."

"I didn't say it like that, and I can probably make do with it for a while. How about bringing the horses in one at a time? We could get the individual photos completed, get that part of the webpage done."

He nodded. "That could work. But we still need a decent camera." He downed a bite of lamb and groaned in pleasure. "Maybe by the time we get the preliminary photos done, the FBI will have the terrorist in custody."

"Maybe." Though it seemed like a long shot to her.

"We'll head into Dallas tomorrow," Josh said between bites. "Pick up a camera and whatever gear you need. You know more about this kind of thing than I do."

"You think it's safe to leave the ranch?"

"I can't hide forever, and I'll keep my eyes open."

Since she really wanted to go, she didn't argue. "I wish I still had my old Canon," she grumbled. "I got low on money in Albuquerque and hocked it. I don't even have a cell phone camera anymore."

Josh took another bite of lamb. "Go on the Internet, find a good-quality camera shop in Dallas."

"All right." She went over to the counter and cut him a slice of carrot cake, walked back and set the plate down on the table. "Star would be fantastic on the front page of the website. I think we should start with him."

"Good idea." Josh eyed the cake with anticipation. "We'll buy everything we need, get set up, then bring the stallion in and do the photos."

He finished the pile of mashed potatoes he'd drenched in butter. "This is so freaking good." He looked up at her and grinned. The shadow of beard along his jaw made him look like an outlaw. "Best deal I ever made. Hiring you to cook."

She just smiled. One thing about Josh Cain, he appreciated a home-cooked meal. Good thing he burned off a jillion calories every day.

The evening slipped away. The following morning, Tory dressed with special care, choosing a flirty little yellow sundress with a swingy skirt and wide self-belt, one of the few summer dresses she owned.

A pair of strappy white open-toed sandals had survived the journey from Phoenix. They looked pretty with the tiny white daisies in the yellow fabric and the big white hoops in her ears.

"Wow," Josh said when he arrived at the front door to pick her up. "Baby, you look gorgeous." Those hot blue eyes traveled over her, head to foot. She thought that if Ivy hadn't been there, they might not have made it to the truck without a trip back to the bedroom.

"Umm . . . thank you."

She was surprised to see Josh in a pair of tan Wrangler dress jeans and a short-sleeved yellow print shirt. Clean-shaven, he wore polished lizard boots the color of whiskey, and apparently, he was leaving his cowboy hat behind. They were, after all, going into the big city.

He looked delicious.

The only hitch in what was starting as a very special day was the glimpse of a small semiautomatic pistol beneath his shirt in a holster clipped to his belt.

He was licensed to carry. He was a skilled marksman. Tory decided to pretend it wasn't there.

"You ready?" Josh asked.

Ivy ran up to him. "I'm ready, Josh!" She lifted her arms so he could pick her up and Josh obliged, propping her against his shoulder as he walked her out to his truck and set her in her booster seat.

"Pretty soon you'll be too heavy for Josh to lift," Tory said, blushing at the thought of how easily he carried her into the bedroom whenever it suited his fancy.

They dropped Ivy off at Clara Thompson's and headed the pickup toward Dallas. For the past few days, the weather had been in the nineties. Today was even hotter, the sun burning down so that mirages formed on the asphalt in the road ahead as the truck rolled along.

The camera shop, McFarland's, was in a strip mall on Northwest Highway in Garland. They took I-30 toward Dallas, turned onto 645 north, exited the freeway, and a few minutes later, the pickup pulled into the lot and parked in a space right in front of the shop.

The stores were all glass-windowed, and a grassy, treed meridian bordered the opposite side of the parking lot.

McFarland's appeared to sell high-quality equipment and be as professional as Internet reviews suggested. Tory started looking at low-priced cameras, but Josh insisted on purchasing something better.

"We'll be changing the photos as horses come and go and the ranch continues to grow. We'll be using the camera a lot more than once."

She loved it when he said *we*, as if they were a team, as if she were important to him. It was stupid. She had no idea how long she would be staying on the ranch, how long before he grew tired of her and was ready to move on.

He'd made no promises, never hinted at a long-term relationship. Whatever happened, she'd do a good job for him while she was there.

She ended up choosing a Canon EOS Rebel DSLR camera, which came with an extra lens. They also purchased a sturdy tripod, flash attachment, a light boom arm stand, filters, memory cards, additional batteries, and a canvas gadget bag.

They were walking out of the shop, their arms full of merchandise, when one of her white hoop earrings fell off and bounced on the sidewalk. As Josh bent down to pick it up, a gunshot echoed and a chip flew out of the stucco building exactly where his head had just been.

"Get down!" Camera gear went flying, hitting the sidewalk and scattering all over as Josh shoved her to the ground, shielding her with his body. Moving together, they crab-walked, scrambled, and crawled to reach cover behind the front wheel of the closest vehicle, a silver SUV parked next to the truck.

"Stay here!" Josh pulled his pistol from the holster at his waist. "Call 9-1-1!"

Her purse, which had survived the fall, still hung from the strap over her shoulder. Her hands shook as she dug out her disposable phone and hit the emergency call number she had programmed into her cell.

Staying low, Josh peered around the front of the vehicle. Another shot echoed, slammed into the hood, and he moved, firing off several rounds, running hard to a new location.

The dispatcher answered. "Nine-one-one. What's your emergency?"

Her heart was hammering, her palms sweating. "Someone is . . . is shooting at us. We're in front of McFarland's Camera store in Garland. We need help!"

Shots echoed. Josh returned fire and moved again, rolled behind a sturdy trash can, popped up, fired, and moved.

"Stay on the line, ma'am. I've got help on the way."

She was trembling. "I think the man shooting at us is . . . is wanted by the FBI. Could you call Agent Quinn Taggart? Tell him it's Victoria Bradford and Joshua Cain."

"All right. Please, stay on the line, ma'am."

Tory gripped the phone tighter as Josh fired again and ran toward the assailant, rapidly closing the distance between them. Tory couldn't breathe. She thought of the soldiers who had been killed and said a silent prayer for Josh. Then she prayed the police would get there quickly.

"Please, God . . . please . . ."

Josh crouched low. He knew exactly who the shooter was—the same man who had murdered Pete and Coy. The terrorist who wanted vengeance for the death of the mullah's Al-Qaeda son.

Josh fired toward the spot where the last shot had come from. The shooter was on the move, searching for a new position, but he hadn't given up yet. Josh caught a flash of color between two parked cars on the opposite side of the parking lot near the grassy meridian. He fired off two rounds and started running, managed to skirt some cars and flatten himself behind the trunk of a tree.

A low hedge ran in front of the vehicles on that side of the lot. Staying low, he ducked behind the hedge. Running along beside it, moving quietly now, he circled around, working to get behind the shooter.

He spotted the man up ahead, tall and thin with a heavy beard, his attention still fixed on Josh's last position. Josh eased closer. The hedge provided visual cover, but it wouldn't stop a bullet.

As the shooter prepared to move again, he spotted Josh, whirled, and fired, the bullet tearing through the shrubbery, missing him by inches. Josh fired back, hitting his target in the chest, knocking him backward into the parking lot, his head slamming against the pavement.

It took sheer force of will not to pull off another round, but he wanted the man alive, knew the feds needed the information the terrorist could provide.

Sirens wailed as Josh ran up to the unconscious man lying on his back on the asphalt. Blood poured from a wound in his upper right chest. His breathing was ragged, his mouth open and slack, but he was alive.

Josh kicked his pistol away, crouched and ripped open the man's white shirt, tore off a strip of fabric, and stuffed it into the wound to slow the bleeding. Sirens wailed. People were pouring out of the shops in the strip mall, beginning to form a circle around them.

Tory knelt beside him. "The police are on the way. The FBI, too. I told them to send an ambulance."

He nodded as he leaned over and put pressure on the bullet hole to slow the blood flow. Black-and-white patrol cars roared into the parking lot and the doors flew open. Uniformed officers spilled out and ran toward him, guns drawn.

"Dallas police! Put your weapon on the ground and your hands in the air!"

Tory took over, pressing hard on the man's chest while Josh raised his hands in the air.

"My pistol is holstered at my waist." A little .380. He wished he'd had his Beretta.

"Keep your hands in the air!" Three officers rushed forward and shoved him to the ground. One of them pulled the pistol out of his holster, then jerked his hands behind his back and locked a pair of cuffs around his wrists.

"My name is Joshua Cain. I'm former marine special ops. I've got a carry permit. The injured man is a terrorist wanted by the FBI."

The cop's dark eyebrows went up. "The feds are on the way," he said. He grabbed Josh's bound arms, helped him roll over and sit up cross-legged on the grass.

"That man tried to kill us," Tory said to the heavyset balding cop who was eyeing Josh like a criminal. "He murdered two other marines already. Josh was defending himself and me."

Another siren wailed as it drew near. Josh looked over to see an ambulance pulling into the parking lot. The doors swung open, EMTs jumped out and ran around to the back. In seconds, the paramedics had collected the gear they needed and were on the ground next to the victim, working to save his worthless life.

Tory backed away, her pretty sundress covered in blood. Josh wanted to go to her, comfort her, tell her she was safe and all of this was about to be over, but it wasn't going to happen right away.

The heavyset cop stayed with her while Josh remained cuffed a few feet away. When half a dozen FBI vehicles roared into the parking lot and slammed on their brakes, Josh breathed a little easier. The big blond man crossing the lot in his direction was a damned fine sight to see.

Taggart stopped to speak to the EMTs, then walked over to Tory. "You all right?" he asked.

"I'm okay. He tried to kill Josh."

Taggart nodded, continued on over to the officer who stood next to where Josh sat. "Take the cuffs off. Cain's the victim here." The cop bent to the task, the handcuffs clanking as they fell into the officer's hands. Rubbing his wrists, Josh rose to his feet.

"He going to make it?" he asked Taggart, tipping his head toward the man on the gurney being wheeled toward the ambulance.

"Fifty-fifty chance. He's lucky you only fired one bullet. Nice placement, by the way. Appreciate your restraint."

He grunted. "With any luck the bastard will live. You'll get some good intel and he'll spend the rest of his life in prison."

"With any luck," Taggart said grimly. "We're going to need a statement from both of you. Plenty of witnesses so you shouldn't have any problem."

Josh nodded. He headed for Tory, opened his arms, and she walked straight into them. He could feel her trembling and his chest clamped down. He drew her a little closer. "You okay?"

She swallowed. "I'm all right." But she nestled her head on his shoulder and a sob escaped, then another. "He almost killed you."

"Hey, it's over. Everything's going to be okay."

She tried to hold back tears. "I know. I'm sorry."

"It's all right, honey. This is a whole lot worse than a burned-up chicken."

Tory laughed. A shuddering breath escaped. "You're right. I can cry if I want to."

"Yeah, baby, you can."

But she filled her lungs with a deep breath of air and eased a little away, wiping the wetness from her cheeks. "You're safe. That's all that matters."

He wanted to tell her both of them were safe, but it wouldn't be true. Damon Bridger was still out there.

One problem at a time.

Josh bent his head and very softly kissed her. "We just need to give our statements; then we can go home."

Tory slid her arms around his waist and leaned against him. "I can't wait to get there."

"Yeah," he said. "Me either."

Chapter Thirty-Two

Damon crumpled the legal documents in his fist. How dare she! That bitch! What was she trying to do—dig him for more money? He'd given her five hundred bucks to keep her mouth shut; now she wanted more. She was a lying, cheating whore just like the rest.

It had been over a year since Damon had seen Suzy Solomon, a hot little brunette who worked at the Peacock. Petite. Small tits. Nice ass, though. And she gave a great blow job.

He'd gone out with her for nearly three weeks before she'd shown her true colors, the night he'd seen her leaving the club with one of the bartenders. He'd been furious, but he'd forced himself under control.

The next night, he'd gone to her apartment and accused her, but Suzy had denied it. He'd slapped her around, lost his temper and punched her a couple of times. No big deal. Besides, she'd had it coming.

He looked down at the crumpled documents gripped in his hand. Suzy wanted to make trouble? He'd give her more than she could handle.

He considered his options and excitement kicked his

pulse up a notch. His breathing grew faster, and arousal slipped through him.

He still had the car he'd rented using a fake driver's license and credit cards Izzy had gotten him on the Internet. The vehicle was parked in the garage of an empty rental property he owned. He could drive Suzy up to the cabin, teach her a lesson, show her who was boss. Show her the consequences of going against him.

His groin pulsed as he imagined the pain he would inflict, the way he'd make her beg, the feel of his hands running over her smooth skin, sliding up around her throat. He thought of the power he'd feel as he squeezed the life from her body, and a rush of sexual heat tore through him, making his blood run hot.

He swore softly. It was a fantasy he couldn't fulfill. When the bitch turned up missing, it would be too easy to make the connection.

Still, he couldn't let her get away with it. He'd talk to her, explain what was going to happen if she didn't drop the lawsuit. Give her a taste of what to expect.

His mouth watered in anticipation. He'd have to be careful, but he could make it work.

He tossed the papers on his desk, grabbed his sport coat off the back of the chair, and shrugged it on. He'd pay Suzy Solomon a visit, remind her exactly who she was dealing with. His hand tightened into a fist as he walked out of the office.

By the time he reached her apartment, he was in a dark fury. He had to control the rage burning through him or he would bring the law down on his head.

He started to slam his fist against the door, stepped back and took a deep breath, knocked softly instead. He was only a little surprised when Suzy saw him through the peephole and pulled the door open.

"Damon. I didn't . . . didn't expect to see you. You've been served with papers. You shouldn't be here."

"We need to talk, Suze. Straighten things out. I didn't realize you were still angry about what happened. I'm really sorry, you know. Please let me in."

"I probably shouldn't." But she opened the door wider and stepped back to allow him inside. "Last time you came over you hurt me."

Damon walked into the apartment, which had even more of those stupid cactus plants she liked sitting on the floor. Otherwise it hadn't changed. It was just as small and cluttered as he remembered.

"What did you want to say, Damon?"

"You got anything to drink? I could use a beer or something."

She disappeared into the kitchen and came back with a Bud, handed it over.

"Thanks." He cranked off the top and took a long swallow. "Why'd you file those papers, Suze? I told you I was sorry. I gave you money. You should have been satisfied."

"You hit me, Damon. You slapped me. You shouldn't have hurt me."

"You cheated on me, baby. You needed to learn a lesson." He set the beer down on the coffee table, walked closer. He could see the fear in those big blue eyes and just thinking about hitting her, slapping her, making her pretty mouth bleed made him hard.

"You should have learned your lesson the first time. Now I've got to show you what happens when you try to go against me." Anticipation seared through him as he caught a handful of her thick brown hair to hold her in place and drew back to hit her.

Suzy made a sound in her throat and the next thing he knew he was facedown on the floor, his arms cranked hard behind his back.

He grunted in pain, heard the metal clank of handcuffs, and swore foully. "You little bitch!"

"I'm Detective Jeremy Larson, Phoenix Police Department." The cop standing over him was tall and lean with curly brown hair. Another man stood a few feet away, same athletic build, short brown whiskers along his jaw.

"You're under arrest for attempted assault," Larson said. "You have the right to remain silent. Anything you say can and will be held against you in a court of law. You have the right to an attorney. If you cannot afford an attorney, one will be provided for you."

"Fuck you." Damon tuned out whatever else the cop had to say. He'd be out of jail in hours. He hadn't really done anything, made a few threats, no big deal.

One thing he knew. Once he was out, he wasn't waiting any longer. He'd had enough of his job at Bridger Real Estate, enough of being his father's lackey. He'd had enough pretending.

He was ending his charade, becoming the man he was meant to be, ending the waiting game he had been playing.

He was going after Victoria Bradford. Everything that had happened to him was her fault. He had to deal with her, end his obsession, and there was only one way to do that.

He thought of what he would do to her once he got her to the cabin, and sexual arousal burned through every cell in his body. It was time. He was going to make her pay.

And no one was going to stop him.

Night sounds seeped through the window, the light patter of rain. Lying in bed, Tory snuggled against Josh's side, their legs entwined, one of his arms draped over her middle. She was exhausted after the terrible day in Dallas that had almost gotten Josh killed, that could have ended with both of them dead.

She closed her eyes to block the memory, tired but content after Josh's incredible lovemaking. He was sleeping, his breathing deep and even. That he was still there, still in her bed, was a testament to the toll the day had taken on him.

She let him sleep but kept watch over him, knowing how upset he would be if he started to dream. He was afraid he would hurt her. Tory was convinced he would never do anything to cause her physical pain, no matter how deeply he slept, no matter how bad the nightmare became.

As if thinking about it had brought one of his dreams to the surface, he began to mumble softly. His head moved back and forth on the pillow, his body subtly shifted, and a mumbled curse slipped from his lips.

"Let go . . . of the . . . knife . . ." Just as before, his hand moved from where it rested beneath her breasts, slowly slid up around her throat.

He wasn't squeezing, just circling her throat with his fingers. She should wake him. He would be horrified if he realized what he was doing. His hand tightened, jerked a little, but he wasn't hurting her.

She didn't believe he would. She waited. She was taking a chance, she knew. Josh was a big man and strong. What if he truly believed she was his enemy, someone trying to kill him?

She steeled herself. Maybe it was a risk, but Josh was worth it. And he would never be free, never conquer his demons if he didn't get the chance.

He shifted on the mattress and perspiration broke out on his forehead. His fingers felt warm where they ringed her neck. A tremor ran through him, but his hand didn't tighten.

Tory refused to wake him. Instead she let the nightmare play out, praying she was right and that even in his sleep, Josh would recognize the familiar feel of her body and know she was lying beside him.

His muscles went rigid, and suddenly his eyes popped

open. He looked down at the hand still circling her throat, jerked away, and his gaze shot to hers. "Tory?"

"It's all right, honey. You were dreaming, but you didn't hurt me." She reached out and touched his cheek, felt the rough shadow along his jaw. "I knew you wouldn't, Josh. I knew it even if you were afraid."

He rolled toward her, buried his face in her neck. "I knew it was you," he said. "I was up on that roof, just like before. I was fighting for my life, but deep down, I knew it was you. I knew it was only a dream."

Tory slid her arms around his neck and held him. "It was a nightmare, honey. Just like other people have. You can trust yourself to know it isn't real."

He drew back and his eyes held hers. "The day you pulled up in front of my barn was the luckiest day of my life." And then he kissed her and he didn't stop.

He made love to her again and this time when they finished, he didn't leave. He spent the night in her bed, his body wrapped around hers, and they woke up together in the morning.

It would have been the best night of her life if it hadn't been for the uneasy look on Josh's face as he shoved the covers aside and got out of bed, as he realized the implications of what he had done.

By staying, he had taken their relationship to a new and deeper level, something she knew he wasn't ready to do.

As he headed back to his house, she watched him through the bedroom window. Now that the FBI had caught the terrorist, he didn't have to feel obligated to stay there and protect her.

She wondered if he would come over tonight after she put Ivy to bed or if he would stay away, try to put some distance between them. It made her heart hurt to think of it. Which told her how deeply she had fallen in love with him.

It told her how much it was going to hurt when he was gone.

* * *

The wind blew up a storm that Saturday morning. Dark, rolling clouds grew thick and heavy above the damp earth. The rumble of thunder and dull flashes of lightning in the distance made the livestock restless and uneasy. It perfectly suited Josh's mood.

He couldn't get the night he'd spent with Tory out of his head. No woman had ever affected him the way Victoria Bradford did. No woman had made him feel so protective, so possessive, so damned hungry. Her sweetness, her determination, her love for her little girl, combined with the raw sexuality that came to life whenever he touched her. They were impossible to resist.

What had started as lust had rapidly turned into something more, something he had no idea how to handle. He wanted her. Constantly. But he wasn't ready to commit to a permanent relationship and his uncertainty wasn't fair to either one of them.

He'd left the trailer at daybreak, though he'd wanted to stay in bed and make love to her again. Instead, he'd gone back to his house, showered and changed, gone out and started working the little two-year-old bay stud he'd brought in from the pasture a couple of days ago.

He wished he could get away. He longed to saddle Thor and ride out, just take off with no particular destination. If Cole and Noah were here, he would, but it was Saturday. The men were off for the weekend, and he didn't want to leave Tory and Ivy completely alone.

He hadn't forgotten the bikers. It was impossible to know what Bridger might do.

Yesterday after they'd returned to the ranch, he'd called Wes Turley and Ben Rigby, told them about the arrest the FBI had made, thanked them and said they would no longer be needed.

He'd phoned Deke Logan and relayed the news. He didn't miss the constant buzz of ATVs zooming around the property, the sight of armed men he'd hoped to leave behind when he had left Afghanistan.

He'd called his brother at the Tex/Am office. Linc had a meeting with the governor so the call had been brief, but his brother was relieved to hear the terrorist was in custody.

Still, Josh felt hemmed in, desperate for some time to himself. He was working the colt on a lunge line, running the horse in a circle, when Tory came out to the training ring.

"How's he doing?" she asked.

"Great. Buster's smart and eager to please. He's going to be a great horse."

"I was thinking maybe we could bring Star into the barn and get him settled, take some shots this afternoon." Fortunately, the camera gear had survived the shooting in the strip mall.

"Sounds good." He tugged the colt in, took hold of his halter, and led him out of the ring. Tory walked beside him over to the pasture behind the barn and waited while Josh turned the horse out to graze.

"Let's go get Star," he said and they headed for the pasture where the stallion was grazing. As soon as Star spotted Tory, his head came up, his ears shot forward, and he trotted over to greet them.

"How's my pretty boy this morning?" Tory scratched his topknot and he nickered softly. Looking at him now, it was hard to believe this was the same crazy-mean stallion who had been at the ranch when Josh first bought the place.

While Tory fed him half an apple in the flat of her hand, Josh slipped the halter over his head. "You like that apple, don't you, fella?" He ran his hand along the stallion's sleek neck, over his powerful chest, then down his back while Tory fed him the rest of the apple.

Together they walked the stallion out the gate back to the barn. Star walked into the stall without a moment's hesitation, turned around, and placidly stuck his head over the top, looking for another treat. Tory smiled and rubbed his head, which the stallion loved.

Josh had a hunch the horse had once been well-mannered, but the cruelty of his last owner had destroyed his trust in people. Tory was helping Star regain that trust.

Josh's stomach rumbled. He hadn't eaten anything all morning.

"Sounds like you're hungry," Tory said. "I'll have breakfast ready in ten minutes."

"Great, I'll be right there." He watched her walk away, trying to figure how a woman could manage to look sexy and feminine in a pair of work jeans and worn cowboy boots. As she disappeared inside the house, he felt the same tug of longing that had been pulling him in two directions for weeks.

The restlessness returned. He needed some space. Badly.

He was walking through the front door when his cell phone rang. Pulling the phone out of his pocket, he looked down and saw it was Linc, pressed the phone against his ear. "Hey, big brother."

"I've got news. Is Tory around? She needs to hear this, too."

"She's close. I'll get her and put the call on speaker." He walked into the kitchen and set the phone on the round oak table. "It's Linc. He's got news."

"Hey, Linc."

"Morning, Tory. Thought you'd both be happy to know Damon Bridger is in jail. The little party we planned for him last night went off without a hitch."

She looked up at Josh with those big green eyes he found so appealing. "What party was that?" she asked Linc.

"It's a long story. A waitress named Suzy Solomon filed

a civil suit against Bridger for assault and battery. He was served yesterday afternoon. Bridger wasn't pleased."

"I'll bet he wasn't," Josh said darkly.

"Damon showed up at Suzy's house last night and wanted to talk. Suzy let him in. Bridger started threatening her, pushing her around, getting more and more violent, but Suzy wasn't alone."

"You set him up," Josh said, smiling. "You got the woman to file charges. You figured Damon would show up and when he did, you had Townsend there to protect her."

"Townsend tracked her down and convinced her to file. He and that Phoenix detective, Jeremy Larson, were there when Bridger went haywire. Larson had him on the carpet in handcuffs before he could carry out his threats."

"I wish I'd seen that," Tory said.

"Everything he said was recorded. Larson arrested him for attempted assault. Since it happened Friday night, he figures Bridger won't get bailed till Monday."

"Couldn't happen to a nicer guy," Josh said.

Linc chuckled. "I've got protection set up for Ms. Solomon till things cool down. I figure Bridger's legal troubles will keep him busy for a while and out of your hair."

Tory smiled. "I can't tell you how much I appreciate your help, Linc."

"Believe me, it was my pleasure. Guys like that deserve all the bad luck they can get."

"Thanks, Linc," Josh said. "I owe you."

"Fine, you can barbecue the next time we're out at the ranch."

"Fair enough." Josh smiled as he hung up the phone.

"Your brother is the best."

Josh arched a brow. "Yeah? What about me?"

Tory grinned. "Next to you."

Josh bent and kissed her. The moment he felt the heat, he realized it was exactly the wrong thing to do. He needed to stay away from Tory. He couldn't let himself get in any deeper. He just wasn't ready for more.

Turning away, he sat down at the table and polished off the pancakes and eggs she'd fixed him. Ivy came over with a new crayon drawing, this one of her working with Mrs. T. in the garden. He put it up on the fridge next to the picture she had drawn before.

She was the cutest little girl. Sweet and loving. Well behaved and smart. Trouble was, he wasn't ready to take on the job of raising a kid. He'd just gotten out of the marines. As a sniper, he'd been responsible for the lives of dozens of men. He needed a break, time to himself, time to adjust.

His mood darkened again. He left the house and returned to the barn. He'd figure it out. He just needed a little more time.

An hour passed. Tory and Ivy were safe, at least for the time being, but Josh was still edgy. He checked on Star, then saddled Thor. Fetching his rifle out of a locked closet in the tack room where he had been keeping it, he slid it into the scabbard, pulled a lightweight rain poncho over his head, stepped into the stirrup, and swung up in the saddle.

Thunder rumbled overhead. A mist of rain cut through the humid air and the wind picked up. He had a little time before the storm hit in earnest. Tugging his hat brim low on his forehead, he gigged the buckskin and rode out of the barn toward the pasture.

It didn't take long to reach one of the main trails cutting through the grasslands. He nudged Thor into an easy lope, rode past a small lake, and headed north, off toward the river. No cell service this far from the ranch house. No one around but an occasional deer or rabbit, a wild boar shuffling through the underbrush.

Time slipped past. He wondered if Tory would have enjoyed the ride. He'd promised to show her the ranch, promised they would take photos for the webpage along the way.

He didn't like to think how close they'd come to being killed yesterday, that the shot that missed him could have hit Tory.

He didn't go to church often, but after yesterday's close call, he felt the need to give thanks. Maybe he'd take Tory and Ivy to church in Iron Springs tomorrow morning.

Then he thought how it would look like they were a family and scrapped the notion.

He drew rein, pausing on a knoll to survey the vast green landscape stretching in front of him. There were four ponds on the ranch, dark spots scattered in the vast stretches of green. A heavily wooded area full of wild game rose off to his left. A shallow ravine veered to the right and the river lay ahead.

The old hunting cabin wasn't much farther. The porch looked out over an oxbow in the stream. He'd head in that direction in case a thunderstorm blew in.

The wind felt good against his face as Josh leaned over the buckskin's neck and urged the big horse forward.

Chapter Thirty-Three

The afternoon was slipping away. With the bad weather, Tory was working in Josh's office, getting the webpage design finalized, preparing to post the photos she was ready to start taking.

She glanced at the time at the bottom of the computer screen. Josh had been gone for hours. Tory was worried about him.

Outside the window, the sky was the color of pewter, intermittent gusts of rain coming down, the wind tearing through the branches of the trees. Still, he didn't come home. Tory had sensed his dark mood that morning and tried to give him some space.

With everything that had been happening, she didn't blame him for seeking the solace of the vast, open spaces around him. Josh was a man's man. The ranch suited him perfectly.

She thought of his restlessness and couldn't help wondering how all of this would end. Clearly, Josh wasn't ready to settle down. When she had arrived six weeks ago, she would have said the same thing about herself.

Now everything she had ever wanted was right there in front of her, right there on the Iron River Ranch. She loved this wide-open country, loved the horses, loved the small community, the friends she and Ivy were making.

And she loved Joshua Cain.

Her heart squeezed. She knew he cared about her, knew he cared about Ivy. But he had just come home from the war, just gotten his life back, his freedom. She wished they had met at some later time. Maybe things would have been different.

She took a shaky breath. She could see where this was headed, see how much it was going to hurt when they parted, how hard it was going to be on Ivy. But she knew it was going to hurt Josh, too.

He was a good man. He had tried to do what was right, keep things professional. They had both known the dangers.

She wiped away a tear. Damon was in jail. He had legal troubles that might keep him there this time. She hadn't known about the other battered woman. Now that she did, she figured there were probably more.

Linc would find out. She had a feeling Lincoln Cain was a bad enemy to make. This time Damon wasn't going to get away with using his father's name and his family's wealth to escape the consequences of whatever he had done.

She could leave without fear, make a new start somewhere else. She knew deep down that no matter where she ended up, Josh and Linc would both be there to help her if she needed them.

It was time to start planning in earnest. She would talk to Josh, tell him the truth. This time she had a feeling he would agree.

An ache throbbed in her chest. She loved him. Deeply and without reservation. She would do anything for him. She thought that on some level he knew.

Timing was everything. This thing between them, it was just wrong place, wrong time. Maybe someday they would meet again. Things like that happened, didn't they?

Her throat closed up. She had known for a while it was time to leave. She felt safe enough now to go. When Josh came home, she would talk to him, convince him that leaving was best for both of their sakes.

The landline phone on the desk rang, jarring her out of her mournful thoughts.

Tory picked it up. "Iron River Ranch."

"Tory, it's Agent Quinn Taggart. I need to speak to Josh."

"I'm afraid he isn't here, Agent Taggart. He went riding this morning. He hasn't come back."

"Do you have a way to reach him? A problem's come up. I need to get word to him as quickly as possible."

The urgency in Taggart's voice alerted her. "What is it, Agent Taggart? What's wrong?"

He hesitated a moment, not long. "The man we arrested yesterday at the camera store?"

"Yes?"

"The pistol he was using matched the weapon used to kill Pete Saldana, but when we searched his apartment in Dallas, the rifle that killed Coy Whitmore wasn't there. There were two men using the apartment. Two men, Tory, not one. That means there's another terrorist still out there."

A heartbeat of silence fell. "Oh, my God."

"Can you get word to Josh? His life could be in danger."

"I'll find him, don't worry."

"Have him call me as soon as he gets the message."

"I will. I've got to go!" Tory hung up and quickly phoned Mrs. Thompson. "Clara, I've got an emergency. I need you to come and sit with Ivy."

"Of course. I can be there in five minutes."

"Thank you. Thank you so much."

"What is it, Tory?"

"Josh is in danger. I have to go." The call ended. She ran into the living room. "Ivy, honey, I need to find Josh.

Mrs. Thompson is coming over. Come out to the barn while I saddle Rosebud."

"It's raining, Mama."

"Not that hard." She tugged the little girl out the front door and they ran to the barn. Only a smattering of rain was falling, but it was sure to get worse. Tory finished saddling the sorrel just as Clara Thompson drove up and got out of the car.

Tory led the horse up to Clara. "Hold Rosebud for a second. I have to get something."

Standing under the covered porch, Mrs. Thompson held the horse's reins while Tory ran back to the trailer, down the hall to her bedroom. After he'd found out she knew how to shoot, Josh had insisted she take his .38 revolver and the portable gun safe and keep them next to her bed.

She unlocked the safe and grabbed the holstered revolver, took a belt out of the drawer, slid the holster onto the belt, and strapped it around her waist. Couldn't stop a smile as she caught a glimpse of herself in the mirror looking like Annie Oakley. Her life had surely changed.

But the FBI had just phoned. She wasn't taking any chances.

Hurrying back to the main house, she took the reins from Clara and swung up on the little mare's back.

"Be careful," Clara Thompson said.

"I will. I'll be back as soon as I can." Nudging Rosebud into a trot, then a gallop, she headed for the gate that led into the big, open pasture and the woods and ponds beyond.

There was a lot of land out there, but much of it was wide-open country. Sooner or later, she would spot Josh or he would spot her. The thought occurred that if she could find him, so could the man who was hunting him.

Tory urged the mare faster. Josh could be in very grave danger.

She wasn't coming home until she found him.

* * *

Josh rose from the wooden bench he'd been sitting on beneath the covered porch of the dilapidated old cabin. He'd been there awhile, staring out at the muddy river. During the hours he'd been there, the wind had picked up and so had the rain, but it had slowed to a stop now. It was time to go home.

He swung back up on Thor and headed out, took the main trail, the fastest, most direct route back. The restlessness he'd been feeling had passed. The storm seemed to have cleared his head, leaving his mind razor-sharp, everything in perfect focus.

He'd been thinking of Tory ever since he'd left the house. Victoria Bradford was everything he had ever wanted in a woman. She was smart, beautiful, and sexy, and her desires stood up to his own. He hadn't wanted another woman since the day she'd driven up in front of his house.

Tory was strong and brave and loyal. He would cut out his heart before he would let anything happen to her or Ivy. *His heart*. That, he'd discovered, had been the source of his troubles all along. He'd fought it, tried to ignore it, tried to deny it, but the straight truth was, he had lost his heart to Tory Bradford.

He was in love with her. The day she drove up in front of his barn was the luckiest day of his life.

At thirty-one, he hadn't planned on having a family—at least not for a few more years. But sometimes good things came along when you least expected them. As Linc had said, sometimes you had to make adjustments.

Josh found himself smiling. He wanted Tory with him. He wanted to marry her.

The rightness of it poured through him, settling deep in his bones. Tory was his woman. She and Ivy were his family. He'd been a fool not to see it a long time ago.

He was a little over halfway back to the house when he spotted a lone rider coming from the other direction, riding at a fast clip across the grass. He recognized the size and shape, knew that fiery red hair. She was riding like the wind, in perfect rhythm with the animal beneath her. A feeling of pride slipped through him.

Another feeling arose, this one deep and frightening. Something was wrong. Tory needed him or she wouldn't be out there.

Josh tugged the brim of his hat down, dug his heels into the sides of the buckskin, and the horse leaped forward. The gelding ran full tilt across the open grassland, flinging mud from its hooves.

Tory spotted him, turned the sorrel, and raced toward him. They met near a dense copse of trees along the bank of a pond and both of them drew rein. The buckskin slid to a halt and so did the sorrel, the animals dancing and blowing, still high from their run.

"Josh! Thank God, I found you!"

"What is it? What's going on?"

"Taggart called. There were two men—two terrorists, Josh, not just one. The man who killed Coy is still out there."

The words solidified in his brain. Pete had been killed with a pistol. A rifle shot had killed Coy. His anxiety seeped into the buckskin and the horse sidestepped beneath him. At the same instant a muffled thud sliced the air and a searing pain burned into his chest.

"Josh!"

"Get down!" Jerking his rifle from its scabbard as he leaped off the horse, he launched himself at Tory the instant her feet hit the ground and both of them went down.

Pain shot up his arm and his hat went flying. The horses bolted, scattered. Ignoring the blood soaking his shirt just inches away from his heart, he hauled Tory behind the trunk of a big oak tree and settled her on the ground out of the line of fire.

"Oh, my God, you're hit!" As he crouched beside her, Tory dragged his rain poncho over his head. She unbuttoned his shirt with shaking hands and he could hear her rapid breathing. "We need to stop the bleeding. Oh, God, Josh."

It was meant to be a heart shot. If Thor hadn't moved . . . He looked down to see that the bullet had torn through the flesh on his upper left chest but had missed a rib and continued on through. "It's not as bad as it could have been."

"It's him—oh, my God, it's the terrorist."

He nodded. One thing he knew. The shooter was no amateur. Not firing a sniper rifle with a sound suppressor.

"We need . . . need to put pressure on the wound," Tory said, her voice shaking. The bullet had hit on his left side and gouged through the flesh beneath his arm. The shot hadn't broken any ribs, but he was hurting like a mother-grabber and losing a lot of blood.

He didn't have time to worry about it. He needed to end this bastard. Now.

Propping his elbow on the ground, he rested the rifle stock in his palm, gritted his teeth against the burning pain, and sighted through the scope, scanning side to side through the trees until he spotted movement three hundred yards away.

Hidden deep among the foliage, the shooter, heavily camouflaged among the thick green leaves, would have been impossible for any but a trained eye to see.

He glanced back to see Tory whipping off her lightweight rain jacket, then unbuttoning the soft cotton blouse she wore underneath. She tore the fabric into pieces, made a pad, reached beneath him, and stuffed the fabric into the wound.

"I wish there was more I could do."

"It's fine." Josh sighted down the barrel as Tory pulled

her lightweight jacket back on over her lacy white bra and he couldn't resist a quick glance at her pretty breasts.

He checked his quarry through the powerful Sightron scope on the .308. The sniper lay deep in his nest, ready for the first mistake Josh made.

His stomach clenched to think the man had to have been watching the house, must have seen Josh ride out and followed. He shifted and blood dripped onto the leaves beneath him. If he lost too much, he'd be useless.

Taking careful aim down the barrel, he waited. A sniper was trained to hold a position for hours if he had to. With the blood he was losing, he didn't have that kind of time.

Come on, you bastard. Through the crosshairs, he watched a cluster of leaves tremble and caught a glimpse of the shooter's face. Josh pulled the trigger, the shot echoed, but the target shifted at the exact wrong moment and the bullet whizzed harmlessly out of sight.

Another muffled thud sounded in return, the bullet slamming into the tree trunk just inches from his head. The guy was good.

"Stay here. I need to find a better angle." Smearing a handful of mud on his cheeks and across his forehead, he slid down into the wet green grass and disappeared into the heavy shrubs and foliage at the edge of the pond.

He didn't need to get any closer to the target. He just needed to find a line of sight that exposed the shooter to a single well-placed shot.

He crept forward, ignoring the pain and the blood leaking down his chest, crawling on his belly through the mud puddles, twigs, and wet leaves.

Josh figured the sniper was doing exactly what Josh would be doing—waiting. Figuring, sooner or later, his target would have to move. As soon as Josh gave the shooter an opening, he would be dead.

He dropped down behind a fallen log covered in muck

and branches and rested the rifle barrel on top, pausing to scan the distant woods through the scope. The sniper's nest came into focus and he prepared to take the shot.

He couldn't afford to rush the shot again. If he missed, the killer could take him out and then come after Tory.

As he watched his opponent, everything inside him went still, his mind congealed into a single thought. *Make this one count.*

Josh sighted down the barrel through the scope. The target's camouflaged body shifted. Josh waited. The shooter moved a fraction, bringing the side of his head into the crosshairs, and Josh gently squeezed the trigger.

The rifle shot echoed and the man was dead, his body slumping forward, into the tall, wet grass.

Josh closed his eyes and his tense muscles relaxed. A slow breath seeped from his lungs. He searched the surrounding area through the scope, scanning carefully, checking with his well-trained naked eye, but didn't see any other threat.

From the start there had been two shooters. Pete and Coy were dead. Now both of their killers were dead, too.

Gritting his teeth, he pushed to his feet, and started toward Tory. She was still behind the tree, but she was holding her .38 revolver in her hand, pointed in the direction of the shooter.

His heart squeezed. She was amazing. And she could have been killed.

Tory shoved her pistol back into the holster at her waist, shot to her feet, and raced toward him. Careful of his wound, she ducked under his good arm, propping him up on her shoulder, helping him walk back to the oak. She set him down and leaned him back against the trunk of the tree.

Josh smiled up at her. "It's over, baby. This time it's finished."

She glanced around. "Are you sure there aren't more?"

"None here. We'll talk to Taggart, but I'm thinking this was the last member of the cell."

"You need a doctor, Josh. We've got to get you home."

"We'll have to catch the horses."

"Rose is just over there. I'll ride back and get help."

He didn't argue. The blood loss was beginning to make him lightheaded. Tory started for the mare, but as she grabbed the reins and tugged Rosebud forward, he heard the whop of helicopter blades pounding through the air in the distance.

Josh looked toward the west and saw a chopper heading in their direction. As it circled the open pasture, Tory ran into the open and started waving her arms. The chopper spotted her and began to descend. It settled in the wet green grass just a few dozen yards away.

The letters FBI on the side of the aircraft couldn't have been a more welcome sight. Josh shoved himself to his feet and started toward them. He had only taken a couple of steps before he passed out cold in the grass.

Chapter Thirty-Four

Tory sat next to Josh's hospital bed. They had kept him at Iron Springs Medical overnight. He had lost a lot of blood, plus he needed antibiotics to protect against infection.

He was cranky and anxious to go home. According to the doctor, the bullet had missed his ribs and hit soft tissue instead of bone. Nice and clean, the doctor had said. Josh had been lucky.

Tory thought they had both been extremely lucky.

The shooting had been a huge story on the eleven o'clock local news last night. It had been picked up by the wire service and spread all over the country. Josh was a hero once more. He wasn't happy about it but there was nothing he could do.

She reached over and fluffed his pillow, helping him get more comfortable, then looked up to see Agent Quinn Taggart pushing through the door of the private room Josh had been assigned, probably thanks to Linc.

According to Taggart, when he hadn't heard from Josh, he had phoned the ranch again. Mrs. Thompson had told him Tory had ridden out to find Josh, but they hadn't returned. She was worried, Clara had said.

Nervous about the second shooter, who so far hadn't

been located, Taggart and several other FBI agents had helicoptered out from the Dallas office, arriving just in time to whisk Josh off to the hospital.

Other agents had been called in to handle the crime scene, bring the horses in, and remove the body of the terrorist who had killed Coy Whitmore and tried to kill Josh.

"How's he doing?" Taggart asked Tory.

"I'm doing fine," Josh answered grumpily. "I'll be better when I get out of here."

"They're letting him out this afternoon," Tory said.

"They're letting me out this morning," Josh grumbled.

Taggart's gaze swung back to her. "I can see he's doing okay. How are you doing?"

She glanced away. Her jeans were still spotted with Josh's blood, her boots crusted with dried mud. She was wearing a clean pink T-shirt with a butterfly on the front that Carly had bought her in the gift shop.

"I'm okay. We were lucky." They had been lucky, but her mood was glum. Josh would need her for a while during his recovery, but after that, it was time for her to get on with her life.

She thought she might stay in Iron Springs, at least for a while. *Maybe.* Unless seeing Josh around town hurt too badly.

Taggart ran a hand over his short blond hair and straightened his tie, back to his more formal FBI persona.

"You'll both be happy to know every shred of intel we have confirms we've rounded up the last member of the cell. Josh won't have to be looking over his shoulder for the rest of his days."

"That's good news," Josh said.

"I'm sorry we didn't figure it out sooner," Taggart said, "but we did the best we could."

"We appreciate everything you've done," Tory said.

"You can pick up your weapons in the Dallas office whenever you're ready." Taggart checked his wristwatch.

"I've got to run. Just wanted to make sure you two were okay. If you need anything, you know where to find me." The agent turned and walked out the door.

Josh gave Tory a too-sweet smile. "How about seeing if you can find that doctor, honey, get him to sign my release papers."

She laughed. "You are such a con man. I'll tell you what. I'll take the truck, go home and change, get you some clean clothes while I'm there. You can hardly leave here covered in dried blood and crusted mud. If the doctor hasn't released you by the time I get back, I'll hunt him down like a dog and convince him to let you go home."

Josh laughed. Then the smile slid off his face. "We need to talk, baby. It's important."

Her stomach knotted. "I know . . ." she said softly.

He relaxed back on his pillow. "Don't be too long."

She just shook her head. Last night, as soon as the helicopter had landed at the hospital and Josh had been whisked into the emergency room, she had phoned Linc and Carly.

They had immediately helicoptered in to Blackland Ranch, then driven both Linc's and Josh's pickups to the hospital so Tory would have a vehicle to use and a way to get Josh home.

They had stayed for several hours, until they were satisfied Josh was going to be okay and he had succumbed to the drugs and exhaustion and fallen deeply asleep. Tory had spent the night in his room. She wanted to be there when he woke up in the morning.

At dawn, he'd awoken, his beautiful blue eyes immediately searching for her. His shoulders eased when he saw her.

"I knew you'd be here," he said, still groggy from the meds they had given him. "You're . . . amazing." He'd drifted back to sleep, slept a few more hours, but now he was awake, restless, and anxious to leave.

"I won't be long," she promised as she pushed through the door and stepped out into the hall. Taking the elevator down, she crossed the lobby and headed out to the parking lot.

With all the turmoil, Clara Thompson had stayed in the trailer with Ivy. She was staying till Tory got Josh home and settled.

Driving the pickup down the highway, Tory had just reached the edge of town when the disposable phone in her purse started ringing. Very few people had that number, just Josh, Mrs. Thompson, Lisa and Shelly, now Carly and Linc.

Normally, she didn't talk on the phone while she was driving, but with all the trouble lately, she pulled over and dug it out of her purse. She didn't recognize the caller ID.

Hoping it was just a wrong number, she pressed the phone against her ear. "This is Tory."

"Well, hello, sweetheart. Have you missed me?"

Her stomach convulsed, instantly knotted. *Damon*. Her hand shook. How had he gotten this number? She started to hang up, but remembering the redheaded waitress, she was afraid of what he might do to someone else if she did.

"What do you want, Damon?"

"What do you think I want? I've missed you, Victoria. I want to see you. Since I have your little girl, I bet you want to see me, too."

A wave of nausea hit her, making the bile rise in her throat. *Oh, my God! Damon is here! He has Ivy!* She took a deep breath. She couldn't let him know how terrified she was. "I don't believe you. Where are you?"

"I'm waiting for you at the ranch. Ivy's with me. Mrs. Thompson gave me your number. She was very cooperative."

She held back the sob in her throat. "You haven't . . . haven't hurt them? You haven't hurt Clara or Ivy?"

"What, that nice old lady and your little girl? Why on

earth would I want to hurt them? You're the one I want, Victoria."

She cranked the engine and pulled the pickup back onto the highway. "How did you know where to find them?"

"You really thought I didn't know where you were and what you were doing? I've had someone watching you since you left Phoenix. People are such scum. Nothing they won't do for money."

The inside of her mouth felt bone-dry and her mind had gone numb. She couldn't think straight. She was terrified she would say the wrong thing.

"I heard about your boyfriend," Damon continued matter-of-factly. "Too bad he's in the hospital."

Oh, God.

She gripped the steering wheel, passed a car a little too fast, took a shaky breath, and prayed her voice would come out even. "If you have Ivy, I want to talk to her."

"All right." She heard him moving around. "Ivy, sweet-heart, come over here. Your mama's on the phone. Ivy's a little upset," he said to Tory, "but she's okay."

Ivy was not okay. She was terrified of Damon. And what had happened to Clara Thompson? *Oh, God.*

She passed another car, driving one-handed, slowing just enough to be sure she wouldn't crash. "Ivy?"

"Mama, I'm scared. Damon's here." Ivy started crying.

"It's all right, baby. Mama's almost home. Just be a good girl till I get there, okay?"

"I'm afraid he'll hurt you."

"I'll be all right. Just do what Damon says, okay?"

"'Kay."

"Is Mrs. Thompson there?"

But the phone was jerked away. "The old lady's here, but she's resting."

Her throat ached. "Did you hurt her?"

324   *Kat Martin*

"She'll be fine. Turns out chloroform is a lot more effective than a stun gun."

"I'm on my way, Damon. Don't do anything to hurt them."

"If you call the police . . . if you tell anyone I'm here, you won't ever see your daughter again. Do you understand?"

She understood. She had known since she'd awoken in that hospital in Phoenix that Damon would find a way to destroy her. She didn't care what happened to her, but she couldn't let him hurt Ivy.

"I'm not far away. I'll be there in just a few minutes."

"I'll see you soon, sweetheart." Damon hung up the phone and Tory stepped on the gas.

Josh was tired of waiting. Where the hell was Tory? She was supposed to be bringing clean clothes. Hell, he didn't give a rat's ass if he went home buck naked. He just wanted the hell out of there.

He fiddled with the TV tuner, trying to find something to watch, finally gave up and turned it off. His cell phone rang. He reached over and snatched it off the tray table, recognized Ham's number.

"Hey, Ham. What's up?"

"Saw you on TV. Glad you're okay."

"Thanks. I'm supposed to be getting out of here today, but—"

"We got a problem, Josh. I just found out a few minutes ago that Bridger's old man pulled some strings. Damon's been out of jail since Saturday morning. He's not at work and he isn't at home. We got Suzy Solomon covered, but I'm worried about Tory, Josh."

"Jesus, I gotta call her. Thanks, Ham. I'll call you later." Josh hung up and quickly dialed Tory's cell, but it rang and rang and she didn't pick up.

His nerves stretched taut. He ended the call and carefully

eased out of bed, disconnecting himself from wires and tubes as his feet hit the cold linoleum floor. He carefully moved his arm. He was stiff and hurting like hell, but he'd live.

Dragging off the hospital gown, he tossed it away and walked naked to the small locker where his clothes were stored. As he reached inside, a little blond candy striper walked into the room.

Her eyes rounded and her gaze ran over him from head to foot. "Oh, my."

"If you don't mind, I need to get dressed."

"Yes . . . I can see that. Sorry." Cheeks red, she hurried out of the room.

Putting on his clothes with a hole in his chest wasn't easy, but he managed. His denim shirt was stiff with dark blood but at least it covered him up. With only a hiss of pain, he sat down carefully and pulled on his jeans and boots.

He phoned Tory again, but still got no answer. He needed a ride. His brother and Carly had already gone back to Dallas. He'd call Noah or Cole. Both had come down to the hospital last night. He recalled Cole being with Brittany and smiled. If he'd ever seen two people in love, they were it.

Which made him think of Tory, and his smile quickly faded. He reached for the door just as it opened and Noah walked in.

Noah's dark eyebrows shot up. "Didn't expect to see you up and about. I guess you're feeling better."

"I was just going to call you. Bridger's out of jail. Tory could be in trouble. I need a ride back to the ranch."

Noah's features hardened. "Let's go."

They hurried down the hall past a couple of nurses and the doctor who was supposed to release him.

"Hey, where are you going?" The doctor, a good-looking Asian, seemed too young to have a medical degree. "I need to check your wound and get it rebandaged."

"I don't have time. I'll come back later." Like hell he

would. He'd had enough of hospitals to last him a lifetime. He didn't wait for the doctor's reply, just hurried on to the elevator and pushed the button, walked in as soon as the doors slid open.

Noah's Dodge pickup was parked in the lot. They climbed inside and Noah started the engine. Josh tried calling Tory again, still got no answer. The side of his chest ached, throbbed clear down his leg, but he didn't have any pain pills and he wouldn't have taken them if he'd had them. Not until he was sure Tory was safe.

"Hang on," Noah said, and fired out of the lot.

Chapter Thirty-Five

Mrs. Thompson's Honda Civic sat where she had parked it yesterday afternoon. Tory glanced around, searching for Damon's BMW, but it wasn't there. He had probably flown into Dallas and rented a car. She noticed the barn doors had been closed, figured the rental car must be parked inside out of sight.

She drove the truck up in front of the house and turned off the engine, took a deep breath, and cracked open the door. Too bad the FBI still had the .38 revolver she'd been carrying yesterday. At the moment, she could shoot Damon Bridger without the slightest qualm.

Instead, she steeled herself and walked up on the porch of the double-wide, turned the knob, and pulled open the front door.

Damon sat on the living room sofa, with Ivy statue-still beside him. Her blue eyes were round and glazed with tears. She looked terrified.

The moment she saw Tory, she jumped up and ran toward her. "Mama!" she squealed, throwing her arms around Tory's waist.

"It's okay, sweetheart. Mama's here now. Everything's going to be okay." *Somehow*. She smoothed her little girl's blond hair back from her face, brushed away the wetness on her cheeks. "I want you to go into your room and stay there till I tell you to come out, okay?"

Ivy turned to look at Damon.

"Do what your mother tells you," he said.

Ivy clung to her a few seconds more, then ran down the hall to her room.

"Close the door," Damon called after her. The door clicked softly behind her.

Damon rose from the sofa. Tory swallowed as he approached but firmly held her ground. Whatever happened, she would never cower in front of him again. "Where's Mrs. Thompson?"

"She's in your bedroom. She's still out. Aside from a headache, she'll be fine."

"What are you going to do to them?"

"Nothing. As long as they stay in there out of the way, they'll be okay. You're the one I came for. I think we both know that." He walked up to her, reached out, and ran a finger over her cheek. She managed to hide a shudder of revulsion.

"Just like old times, isn't it? You and me together?"

"If you hurt me, this time they'll put you in prison. Josh won't let you get away with it. Even your father's money won't be enough to stop him. His brother's a very powerful man." She smiled grimly. "But I think you found that out already."

He backhanded her across the face so hard she stumbled and nearly fell. Her lip throbbed. Her hand trembled as she wiped away a trace of blood.

"What do you want, Damon?"

"We're going to take a little road trip, you and me. Get to know each other all over again. Doesn't that sound like fun?"

Oh, God. Damon surprised her by pulling a pistol, a big black semiautomatic. She hadn't even known he owned a gun. She thought of Lisa. She'd been shot as she'd tried to escape. Was it him?

Deep down, she believed it was, believed she'd been right all along. The thought that he might have murdered the red-headed waitress made her stomach roll with nausea.

"Give me your phone."

She handed it over, watched as he took out the battery and stuck it into his pocket. She knew Josh had been calling her cell. She had seen his number come up on the screen. She'd ignored the calls, afraid he would know by the sound of her voice that something was wrong, afraid of what Damon would do to Ivy and Mrs. Thompson if Josh interfered.

Now that she was there, at least for the moment they were safe.

She had to stall for time. "I-I need to change my clothes." She looked down at the dirty garments she had been wearing since yesterday. "I spent the night at the hospital."

Damon's dark eyes ran over her. "You're right. You look like hell." He motioned with the barrel of the pistol. "I'll go with you. Not like it's anything I haven't seen before."

She bit back a sob of despair. She had to be strong. Sooner or later, Josh would figure out something was wrong. She just hoped it wasn't too late.

Damon sat on the edge of the bed, cradling the pistol like a favorite toy while she stripped off her dirty clothes.

"You need a shower," he said. "You smell like blood. We'll get a room somewhere tonight. You can shower when we get there." His lips edged up in a smirk. "After that, I have plans for you."

Her throat tightened and her eyes burned. She blinked. She didn't have time for tears. She had to plan, find a way to get the gun away from Damon.

"Hurry up, or we'll leave the way you are."

He meant it. He'd drag her out of there naked if she didn't do what he said.

Fighting not to tremble, she finished dressing in clean jeans and a navy blue T-shirt, grabbed a jacket in case she needed it wherever they were going. Damon motioned with the pistol for her to precede him out of the bedroom.

"The car's in the barn. Move your ass."

"I need to check on Ivy before I leave."

"She'll be fine. The old lady's here. She'll be waking up pretty soon. She's tied up so we'll have some time before she calls the police."

"You aren't worried about that?"

"I could kill them, I guess, but what's the point? Your boyfriend would know who did it, so it really wouldn't do any good. I cut the phone line and disabled the cell phones. Nobody's seen the car and I'll take back roads, so finding us won't be easy. Let's go."

Tory steeled herself. Since getting Damon out of the house would be safest for Ivy and Clara, she walked in front of him away from the double-wide while he pointed the gun at her back.

The barn loomed ahead. Stuffing the gun into the waistband of his jeans, Damon paused outside to slide open the doors and she saw a silver Ford Fusion with a rental plate parked inside.

Damon walked back, grabbed her arm, and jerked her forward, shoving her so hard she stumbled and went sprawling in the dirt. Damon jerked her up and slapped her, then shoved her again, pushing her roughly through the open barn door.

As they walked into the interior, she heard a sound like a hammer slamming into boards. Following the sound, she saw Star, his ears laid back, his teeth bared in fury. The stallion kicked the boards of the stall and screamed as if he were in pain.

"What the hell's wrong with that horse?"

But Tory knew. Her heart began to pound as an idea

formed in her head. It was risky, but it was the best chance she had.

"You really think I'm just going to get in that car and let you drive me away?" She moved closer to the stall and Damon followed, a look of fury on his face.

He backhanded her with his fist and pain exploded in her jaw. "You're going to do exactly what I tell you." Damon grabbed a handful of her hair and dragged her closer. "Get in the fucking car!"

Tory twisted, drew back and punched him in the face as hard as she could, and Damon went insane. She turned to run but he grabbed her and she started to struggle.

"You little bitch!" He slapped her so hard her ears rang. Tory stumbled forward, closer to the stall, near enough to slide the latch open on the door.

She swung the stall door open, screamed at the top of her lungs, and Star shot out of the stall like a wounded wild beast.

Damon pulled his pistol as the stallion charged, the horse knocking him backward into the side of the car. The pistol fired as it sailed out of Damon's hand and he went down hard, his hands coming up to ward off the big black horse bearing down on him.

"Get him off me!" Damon screamed. Rearing up on his hind legs, Star brought his sharp hooves slamming down, landing with twelve hundred pounds of force on the man on the concrete floor.

Star reared again. Tory ran for the pistol, picked it up, whirled, and pointed the gun at Damon, but it was too late. The horse pounded down, a crushing, killing blow that exposed gore, flesh, and bits of skull. The bile rose in Tory's throat and she glanced away from the grisly scene.

She was trembling, barely able to breathe, her heart thundering. When she looked back, Star stood over Damon's body, legs braced apart, shaking all over, dark eyes wild. Blood oozed from a bullet hole in the horse's left shoulder.

The sound of slow, careful footsteps reached her. "It's okay, honey," Josh said softly. "Put the pistol down and just take it nice and easy." His deep voice echoed through the barn, calming her as nothing else could. She hadn't heard a vehicle drive in.

Her hand shook as she set the pistol down on the floor and the tears she'd been holding back flooded into her eyes.

"Everything's going to be okay," Josh said, closer now, soothing her as much as the horse. "Just take it easy."

"Ivy's . . . Ivy's in the house."

"Noah went inside to find her. She'll be okay. He's calling the sheriff."

"Damon drugged Clara."

"Noah will take care of her. You need to focus on Star."

Tory swallowed, turned back to the stallion, who stood over Damon's limp, blood-soaked body. Star nickered wildly, tossed his head, and stomped his front hoof, sending a rush of blood down his injured leg.

"It's . . . it's okay, boy. It's all right, Star."

"Star's just afraid," Josh said softly. "He needs you to stay calm, show him everything's okay."

She took a deep breath. "It's all right, boy. Everything's okay." Moving slowly, she made her way up next to the stallion, ran her hands along his sleek neck, felt him trembling. "Easy, boy. You don't have to be afraid."

"See if you can get him to follow you."

She kept talking to him, soothing him. Just standing next to the horse eased his trembling, seemed to ease his fear.

"Can you lead him away from Bridger?" Josh asked.

Tory wiped tears from her cheeks. "I think Damon's dead." She knew he was. She just couldn't make herself say it. She pressed her lips together and tried to hold on. "He shot Star."

"We'll take care of Star. Can you get him back in his stall?"

It was dangerous and both of them knew it. She silently thanked Josh for having enough confidence in her to let her handle the stallion.

She returned her attention to the horse, rubbed his top-knot, rubbed his ears, spoke to him and stroked his neck. Star took a big, deep breath and let it out slowly. When his head drooped down, she took hold of his mane and backed him away from Damon, very slowly turned him around, and led him back into his stall.

Fresh blood oozed down the stallion's front leg, but the shot had gone wild. A piece of torn flesh hung down, but the injury didn't look too serious.

"The vet's on his way," Josh said, ending the call he'd just made and stuffing the phone back into his pocket.

Tory closed the stall door and walked toward Josh and he enclosed her in his arms. His jaw clenched as he took in the bruise on her face and her swollen lip. He gently wiped a trace of blood from the corner of her mouth.

"Bridger's dead. If he wasn't, I'd kill him myself."

A sound escaped from her throat. There was no doubt Damon was dead. His skull had been crushed into bloody bits and pieces.

She wanted to grab onto Josh, hold on for all she was worth, but she knew he had to be hurting.

"Everything's going to be okay," he said, his arms still around her. "You're safe. Ivy and Clara are with Noah."

She managed to swallow. "What . . . what about Star?"

"Nunez is bringing something to sedate him. He's still pretty shook up. We don't want to take any chances."

No. Though she didn't believe the horse would hurt her or Josh, he was injured and upset. They couldn't afford to take chances.

"Why don't you go on inside, honey? Ivy needs you. Let me take care of this."

The lump in her throat ached. She had to go into the house. Her little girl needed her. She looked at Damon and couldn't make herself move.

She watched Josh disappear into the tack room. He brought out a blue plastic tarp and spread it over Damon's lifeless body.

He returned to her, eased her back into his arms. "Come on, honey. Let's go inside." He glanced over at the lump beneath the tarp. "It's over, baby. You'll never have to be afraid of Damon Bridger again."

Chapter Thirty-Six

Noah had called the sheriff and freed a groggy Mrs. Thompson. She sat next to Ivy on the sofa. Noah was on his way out to the barn when Josh led Tory into the house.

"Mama!" The reunion was tearful. Josh was just grateful that everyone was going to be okay.

Dr. Alejandro Nunez showed up right away and for once Josh was glad to see him. The vet gave the stallion something to calm him, then cleaned and stitched up the wound in the horse's front leg.

Josh still had a hard time believing what he had seen in the barn. The stallion had been willing to die for Tory. Josh thought that he and Star shared something in common.

The sheriff arrived with the medical examiner and an ambulance. Josh gave Howler his statement, then made phone calls while the sheriff spoke to Tory and Clara Thompson. Josh called Detective Larson and Hamilton Brown in Phoenix, then phoned his brother.

"It's over," he said to Linc. "Bridger's dead out in my barn."

Linc's voice roughened with worry. "You kill him?"

"Star killed him. The stallion didn't take kindly to Bridger manhandling Tory."

"Christ."

"Hard to believe, I know."

"Suzy Solomon will be relieved. Maybe the Shane girl, too, if he's the one who abducted her."

"For Lisa's sake, I hope the cops find the connection they've been looking for so she won't have to be afraid anymore." Standing on the front porch with the phone pressed against his ear, Josh looked up as Howler walked out of the house.

"Sheriff's still here. I gotta go."

"Be sure to give the good sheriff my regards," Linc said dryly.

"Yeah, I'll do that." Josh hung up the phone.

"I got what I need from the Bradford girl and Clara Thompson," the sheriff said. "EMTs checked everyone out and they all seem okay. Little girl's fine and Clara refused to go to the hospital. Anything you want to add before I leave?"

"If you're interested, there's a chance this guy tortured and killed a woman in Phoenix. A detective named Jeremy Larson handled the case."

"I'll give him a call. You got that horse locked up good and tight?"

"He's in the barn," Josh said.

"I'll be out with the vet in the morning. I saw a skip loader parked out back. Ought to do to bury the animal."

Josh froze. "What are you talking about?"

"That horse is a killer. He's got to be put down."

"No way," Josh said. "That horse saved Tory's life. He killed a man who likely meant to torture and murder her. The stallion's a hero. No way are you putting him down."

Something that resembled payback gleamed in the sheriff's eyes. "I'll get a court order if I have to, Cain. That horse is a menace. He's got to be dealt with."

"Try it and I'll fight you all the way."

The door opened just then and Tory walked out on the porch. She took in the sheriff's puffed-up posture and Josh's angry stance.

"What's going on?"

"Why don't you explain it to her, Cain? As soon as I get that court order, I'll be back." The sheriff swaggered off to his truck, climbed in, and slammed the door. The vehicle rolled off down the road. The ambulance would be leaving with Bridger's body as soon as the medical examiner was done.

"What's going on?" Tory repeated.

"Howler's getting a court order to have Star put down."

"What?" Her gaze shot to the barn. "He can't do that! We have to stop him!"

Josh caught her shoulders. "Take it easy. We aren't going to let it happen."

"What can we do?"

"I'll call Nate Temple, see if he'll take the case or recommend someone who will." He drew her into his arms. "It's going to be okay."

Tory pulled away. "Is it? It seems like no matter what we do, nothing is ever okay." Turning, she went back inside the house.

Clara Thompson came out, said good-bye, and headed for home. A few minutes later, Tory and Ivy came out and went over to their trailer.

Josh wanted to follow them, make certain they were okay, but he wasn't sure it was the right thing to do. Ivy had been terrified of Bridger. She had to be traumatized by what had just happened.

And watching a man be stomped to death had to have been terrible for Tory.

He wanted to give her the space she needed, the time she needed to heal.

The good news was when Josh called Nathan Temple, he agreed to take the case. Temple immediately filed a petition for a hearing to stop the sheriff from executing the stallion. It was scheduled for the beginning of next week.

Josh figured Tory would shoot the sheriff herself if he

continued to insist on destroying the beautiful horse that had saved her life.

In the meantime, Josh needed to talk to her, straighten things out between them. Unfortunately, it didn't look like that was going to happen anytime soon.

The day of the hearing arrived. Tory dressed in the black suit and peach silk blouse she had worn to Coy Whitmore's funeral in Gainesville.

Before they left for town, Josh walked her out to the barn to say good-bye to Star, who nickered softly as she approached, then stood quietly as she fed him an apple, his leg already healing.

"Good boy." Her throat tightened as she rubbed his ears and patted his glossy black neck.

Every day since the sheriff had made his threat, she had worked to gain support for their cause. She had talked to people, explained what had happened, asked them to write a letter in support of the stallion or at least sign her petition. She had even done an interview on KTEF, *Channel 6 Evening News*.

She wasn't sure any of it would work. She slid her arms around the stallion's neck and nuzzled his velvety nose. She couldn't imagine the authorities killing such a magnificent creature. Not when she had deliberately incited him and he had only been trying to protect her.

Finally it was time to leave. Josh and Ivy waited for her next to the pickup. Tory had taken her daughter to see a child psychologist in Iron Springs, a doctor named Sharon Melrose. Ivy had liked the woman right away. The little girl was scheduled for a few more sessions, but the doctor had been confident Ivy would be okay.

Josh lifted the little girl into her booster seat and belted her in, then helped Tory into the passenger seat. Ivy was staying with Clara. Tory was happy to see the older woman had recovered well from Damon's brutal assault.

Like most Texas women, Clara Thompson was tough and she was strong. It took more than a monster like Damon to defeat her.

"Good luck," Clara said once she had Ivy settled and drawing at the kitchen table. "I'll be holding good thoughts."

"Thank you," Tory said. "For everything."

It was a quiet ride into town with both her and Josh worried. "You think we have a chance?" Tory asked.

"Temple's one of the best. If anyone can win, he can."

But the attorney had warned them that cases like this weren't easy. Family members of the deceased were determined to make someone pay. In this case, Montgomery Bridger, Damon's father, was adamant that the horse be destroyed.

The senior Bridger refused to believe his son had meant any harm. Damon had loved Tory, he said. His son just wanted to win her back, that was all. He didn't deserve to die.

The ridiculousness of the statement infuriated Josh even more than Tory.

The pickup had almost reached its destination when she spotted the first group of people walking toward the big pink stone courthouse. Whimsical arches and towers made the structure, surrounded by manicured lawns, look like something out of a Harry Potter movie.

Another group of people walked past. Tory's eyes widened as she realized what was going on. "Oh, my God, Josh!"

More people got out of their cars and started toward the courthouse, all of them carrying signs. SAVE STAR. SAVE THE HERO STALLION. WE DON'T KILL THOSE WHO PROTECT US. There were dozens of signs and even more people. The residents of Iron Springs had turned out in full force.

Tory's eyes burned. She loved the town almost as much

as the beautiful horse that its people were fighting to protect. Almost as much as she loved the man sitting beside her.

She didn't want to think about Josh, didn't want to think of the way he'd been avoiding her, how he'd begun to pull away from her, now that she was safe.

Josh parked the truck and helped her down. He took her hand and started toward the courthouse. Making their way through the milling crowd, they climbed the wide front steps and went inside.

Nate Temple stood in front of a long mahogany table looking polished and perfectly groomed, silver glinting in his light brown hair. Carly and Linc sat on the bench behind the railing. Noah and Natalie, Cole and Brittany sat farther down the row. Ty Murphy was doing his part by keeping an eye on the ranch.

Tory spotted Ben Rigby and Wes Turley, the vets from Pleasant Hill who had guarded the ranch at night. Billie Joe Hardie, the waitress from Jubal's, was there; Cathy Miller and her husband from the mercantile; and Dr. Alejandro Nunez, the veterinarian. Howler and one of his deputies sat in the back row.

Tory and Josh took seats at the table next to Nate Temple, and the bailiff announced the arrival of the judge, a short, stout man with a fringe of hair around his bald head. The audience stood as he walked in, his long black robe fluttering around him as he took a seat behind his massive desk.

When the judge rapped the gavel, bringing the courtroom to order, everyone sat back down, and Josh squeezed Tory's hand.

"Let me begin by saying this is an informal hearing. In this case, we have received testimony ahead of time from both parties." He rifled through a stack of papers sitting on top of the desk. "As you can see, there's been a great deal of local participation. I've received dozens of letters from all over the state."

Representing both sides, she would imagine. Not everyone believed a horse who had killed a man should live.

"With so much input, I'm waiving the need for additional testimony. I have also received additional information from Phoenix that just came to light."

The audience shifted and mumbled.

"Late last night evidence surfaced linking Damon Bridger to the brutal kidnapping and murder of Patricia Daniels, as well as the kidnapping, assault, and attempted murder of Lisa Shane."

The courtroom erupted in complete pandemonium. The judge sharply rapped the gavel and eventually everyone quieted.

Tory felt Josh's hand tighten around hers. Her heart was squeezing. She had always believed Damon was guilty.

"Under the circumstances and considering the testimony Ms. Bradford gave that she incited the horse to violence as a means of self-defense, the court has decided, with certain safety precautions which must be agreed on, the life of the stallion, Satan's Star, shall be spared."

He rapped the gavel. "Case dismissed."

The courthouse went wild. Tory threw her arms around Josh's neck and just hung on. She might not be there to see the great colts the stallion would produce, but the magnificent horse would live.

She smiled through her tears. It was enough.

Chapter Thirty-Seven

It was evening, one of Josh's favorite times of day. Supper was over. The ranch had settled into a quiet peace.

Taking extra care, he showered and shaved, dressed in a white western shirt and a pair of dark blue jeans, pulled on his good boots, and headed over to the trailer. Ivy would be asleep by now. It was time to have that talk with Tory he had been putting off far too long.

As he walked up on the porch, he took a deep breath. He wished he'd gone to town and bought some flowers, maybe a bottle of champagne.

Tonight wasn't going to be an official proposal—he wanted to do that right. But he needed to clear the air, get his feelings out in the open, let Tory know his intentions.

Pray she felt the same way he did.

Even if she did, ranch life wasn't easy. Maybe she'd want to go back to the city, return to the more sophisticated life she'd led before. His stomach churned with nerves.

He knocked, waited a moment, then turned the knob, and stepped into the living room. They'd done away with formality a long time ago. Tory was just coming out of her bedroom. She was wearing a short cotton nightgown with tiny sprigs of lilac scattered over the front, her legs and feet bare, her fiery hair a halo of curls around her shoulders.

She always looked so damned pretty, always made him want her. Tonight he wanted more from her than just her sweet little body. Tonight he wanted her heart.

Her eyes widened when she saw him. Something shifted in her features before it disappeared. "Are you . . . are you going out?"

He frowned. "Hell, no. Why would I want to go out when the prettiest girl in Howler County is standing right here?"

"You're all dressed up. I just thought . . ."

"Clean jeans and a white shirt isn't exactly a tuxedo."

She smiled. "I guess not. So what's the occasion?"

"It's a nice night. I thought we might sit outside for a while and talk."

Her smile faded and she glanced away. In the moonlight, her lips trembled, and the knot returned to his stomach.

She sat down on the bench beside the door and Josh sat down beside her. He could hear crickets chirping in the grass, and the barn owl was hooting again.

"I've been thinking," he said, trying to figure where to start. "This trailer . . . eventually the ranch will need a couple more hands. The trailer might make a good bunkhouse."

He was shocked when her eyes welled with tears.

"I know this must be hard for you," she said. "You don't have to worry, Josh. It's okay. We can be honest with each other. I know it's time for me to go. Now that Damon is no longer a threat, there's no need for me to stay. I can finish out the week and—"

"Wait a minute! I don't want you to leave! I want you and Ivy to stay. I want you to move out of the trailer into my house. This whole thing . . . having two places. It doesn't make any sense."

She just shook her head. "I can't do it, Josh. I can't handle it anymore. When I was in town yesterday, I looked at apartments. I found one I think will work. I'd like to stay in Iron Springs . . . if . . . if it isn't a problem for you. It's a great little town, a good place to raise Ivy, if—"

He caught her shoulders to silence her words, feeling as if someone had stabbed a hot poker into the wound in his chest. He was making a mess of this. He had to fix it—before it was too late.

"I'm getting this all wrong. I'm trying to tell you how I feel, but I'm not good at this kind of thing."

He glanced away, took a shaky breath, and turned back. "That day you and Ivy showed up in front of my barn, I didn't know what to think. I saw you as a burden. You know— a woman with a kid? A woman on the run from trouble? You didn't figure into my plans. I thought you were the kind of problem I didn't need."

He caught her chin with the tip of his finger, forcing her to look at him. "But you were never a burden, Tory. You were a gift. I'm thankful every day to have you here."

The tears in her eyes spilled onto her cheeks. "I can't just be your friend, Josh. Not anymore."

He cupped her face in his hands. "Don't you understand, baby? You aren't just my friend. You're my heart, Tory." He kissed her then, feeling desperate, trying to show her how he felt when his words didn't seem to be enough.

He kissed her and kissed her and didn't stop until he felt her body soften, her arms slide up around his neck, and she kissed him back the way he was kissing her.

Josh eased away. "I need to know, baby. Do you love me? That's what it comes down to. Because I love the hell out of you."

Her lips trembled. Her hand came up to his cheek. "Josh . . ." Fresh tears welled. "I love you so much."

Relief made his muscles feel weak. "Enough to marry me?"

The tears in her eyes rolled down her cheeks but she was

smiling. "I love you. I love everything about you. I'll marry you anytime you say."

Josh blew out a breath, his worry slipping away. "Okay, then. We're getting married."

Tory threw her arms around his neck. Even the twinge of pain that shot down his side couldn't wipe the smile off his face.

Epilogue

Four Months Later

The late October day broke clear and bright. Yesterday's storm had cooled the grasslands. Dressed in a dark blue pencil skirt, yellow print blouse, and a pair of navy sandals, Tory was returning home from church with Josh and Ivy.

They'd taken Clara Thompson with them, then left Ivy with her for a few hours in the afternoon. Tory and Josh were going out riding, taking new photos of the ranch for the website, pictures of some of the new horses he had purchased, as well as more shots of the lush green landscape, ponds, and the river that ran along the northern border.

Tory was really looking forward to the outing.

She changed into a pair of jeans and a lightweight sweater, then went in and made a picnic lunch, adding a nice bottle of white wine.

A lot had happened in the last four months. It turned out the ballistics from Damon's .45 caliber pistol had matched the bullet taken from Lisa's back, which had given the police all sorts of new information.

Izzy Watkins had been arrested on charges of aiding and abetting. Izzy had admitted he had lied about Damon's alibi, that he hadn't been with Damon the night Lisa had been abducted.

He'd also admitted to helping Damon acquire false identification, been complicit in hiring motorcycle vandals to destroy private property, and committed identity theft. Izzy's lawyers had managed to cut a not-so-great deal that would put him in prison for at least the next few years.

Though Lisa's memory of the terrible days after her abduction had never returned, the cabin Damon had used to hold her prisoner had finally been found. The property was still in the name of Damon's deceased mother's father, who suffered from Alzheimer's and lived in a retirement home, the reason finding the property had been so difficult.

All kinds of evidence had turned up in the basement. CSIs really knew their stuff.

With Montgomery Bridger such an important man in Phoenix, a lot had been written and broadcast about his son. According to local area shrinks, Damon Bridger was a man on the edge who had been sliding further and further toward the dark world of a serial killer.

There was nothing in his past to explain it. Apparently, sometimes it just happened. They didn't know what had turned him into the sadistic killer he had become, but if he hadn't been stopped, it would only have been a matter of time before he tortured and killed again.

Tory shuddered to think that if it hadn't been for Star, she would likely have been his next victim.

Another interesting event had occurred. According to FBI agent Quinn Taggart, the billionaire terrorist from Houston, Jamal Nawabi, had been killed in prison. His Middle East connections had at last come to an end.

A lot of people felt a whole lot safer.

"You ready to go?" Josh led Thor and Rosebud up to the front porch. In his faded jeans, boots, a snug T-shirt stretching over his gorgeous muscles, and a battered straw cowboy hat, the man was total eye candy, a sight Tory never grew tired of.

She handed him the lunch she'd prepared and Josh stuffed it into Thor's saddlebag. "You bring a blanket?" The hot gleam in his eyes made her stomach float up.

"I've got it ready to go. I just need to grab it." No way would she have forgotten. She ran back in and got the rolled-up blanket, which Josh tied behind Rose's saddle.

"The crew will be starting again in the morning," he said. He was remodeling the kitchen and bathrooms, determined to fix the house up the way he thought she would want it. He'd bought her a sweet compact SUV as a wedding gift and Ivy now had a little spotted puppy.

Tory didn't really need anything as long as she was with Josh.

They had been married two months, the best two months of her life. As he grabbed her, hauled her close, and very thoroughly kissed her, she thought he felt the same.

"Kitchen's almost finished," she said. "I can't wait to see how it turns out."

He grinned. "No more burnt chicken."

"Absolutely not." She swung up on Rosebud at the same time Josh swung up on Thor. He looked at her with those beautiful blue eyes and everything inside her settled.

"You ready?" The buckskin danced beneath him.

Tory grinned. "I'll race you to the gate." She laughed as Rosebud leaped forward, hooves thundering, leaving her cowboy husband behind.

But not for long.

Have you read all of Kat Martin's Texas Trilogy?
Read on for excerpts from *Beyond Reason*
and *Beyond Danger*, available now!

BEYOND REASON

**New York Times *bestselling author Kat Martin
raises chills as danger stalks a woman
determined to make it in a man's world . . .***

Five weeks ago Carly Drake stood at her grandfather's
grave. Now she's burying Drake Trucking's top driver,
and the cops have no leads on the hijacking or murder.
Faced with bankruptcy, phone threats,
and the fear of failure, Carly has to team up
with the last man she wants to owe—Lincoln Cain.

Cain is magnetic, powerful, controlling—and hiding
more than one secret. He promised Carly's granddad
he'd protect her. The old man took a chance on him
when he was nothing but a kid with a record,
and now he's the multimillionaire owner of a rival firm.

But Linc's money can't protect Carly
from the men who'll do anything to shut her down,
or the secrets behind Drake Trucking.
If she won't sell out, the only way to keep her safe
is to keep her close . . . and fight like hell.

Iron Springs, Texas

For the second time since her return to Iron Springs, Carly Drake stood in a graveyard. A harsh Texas wind whipped the blades of grass around her legs as she waited in front of the rose-draped casket.

Between the rows of granite headstones, the Hernandez family huddled together, a wife weeping for her husband, children crying for their father.

Carly stood with her head bowed, her heart aching for the loss of a man she had known only briefly. Still mourning her grandfather's recent passing, she understood the pain Miguel's family was feeling. Joe Drake, the man who had raised her, the only father Carly had ever known, had died just five weeks ago.

But unlike her grandfather, whose heart had simply worn itself out, Joe Drake's number one driver had been shot in the head, and the criminals who had committed the truck hijacking were still on the loose.

In the weeks since her grandfather's death, Carly had been doing her best to run Drake Trucking, to keep the company afloat and its employees' checks paid. She was doing the best she knew how, but Miguel had been killed on her watch and Carly felt responsible.

The wind kicked up. The end-of-September weather was fickle, hot and humid one day, rainy and overcast the next. The breeze plucked fine blond strands from the tight bun fashioned at the nape of her neck. As she smoothed the hair back into place, her gaze came to rest on a man on the far side of the mourners, a head taller than Miguel's Hispanic family, taller than most of the other men in the crowd, big and broad-shouldered, with dark brown hair and a strikingly handsome face.

Carly leaned over and spoke quietly to the woman beside her, Brittany Haworth, a willowy brunette who had been her best friend in high school, a friendship that had resumed the day Carly had returned to Iron Springs, as if they had been apart just days instead of years.

"That man across from us," Carly said. "The tall one? He was also at Joe's funeral service. I remember him going through the line to pay his respects, but I was so upset I barely paid attention. Do you know who he is?"

Brittany, a little shorter than Carly's five foot seven inches, looked up at her. "You're kidding, right? You don't recognize him? Obviously, you don't read the gossip rags. He's in the newspapers all the time. That's Lincoln Cain. You know, the multimillionaire?"

Carly's gaze went across the casket on the mound above the grave to the big man in the perfectly tailored black suit and crisp white shirt. "That's Cain?"

As if he could feel her watching him, his eyes swung to hers, remained steady on her face. Carly couldn't seem to look away. There was power in that bold, dark gaze. She could actually feel her pulse accelerate. "So what's Cain doing in Iron Springs?"

"He owns a ranch here. He was born in Pleasant Hill, left

to make his fortune, came back a few years ago mega-rich. It's a fascinating story. You'll have to Google him sometime."

"I still don't understand why he was at Grandpa Joe's funeral, or why he's here today."

"For one thing, he was Joe's competition. Texas American Transport is one of the biggest trucking companies in the world."

She nodded. "TexAm Transportation. I know that, but—"

"Cain credits Joe Drake as one of the people who put him on the path to success. The Iron Springs *Gazette* published a couple of articles about him and Joe."

Guilt swept over her. She'd been away so much. Off to college at the U of Texas in Austin ten years ago, which her grandfather had paid for, then a job in Houston as a flight attendant.

She had always wanted to see the world so instead of coming home to help Grandpa Joe, she'd gone to work for Delta. She'd been transferred here and there, worked out of New York for a while, came back to Iron Springs a couple of times a year, but her visits never lasted more than a few days; then she was gone again, flying somewhere else, off on another adventure.

Five weeks ago, she'd quit her job, given up her apartment in Seattle, and come home to stay. Joe's heart condition had worsened. She'd started worrying about him, decided to come back and help him run Drake Trucking, take over some of the responsibilities and lessen the stress he was under.

She'd only been in Iron Springs a week when Joe had suffered a massive heart attack. He'd died in the ambulance on the way to the hospital. By the time she'd received the call, rushed out of the office, and driven like a maniac to Iron Springs Memorial, Joe was gone.

She hadn't been there for him when he needed her.

Just as she had so many times before, Carly had failed him.

"Carly . . ."

She glanced up at the sound of Brittany's voice. The service had ended, the mourners breaking up, people walking away.

"He's coming over," Britt whispered. "Lincoln Cain."

Carly homed in on him, about six-five, a man impossible to miss. She straightened as Cain approached.

"Ms. Drake? I'm Lincoln Cain." He extended a big hand and she set hers in it, felt a warm, comforting spread of heat. Since being comforted only made her feel like crying, she eased her hand away.

"We met briefly at your grandfather's service," Cain said, "but I doubt you recall."

His eyes weren't brown, she realized, but a sort of dark gold. He had a slight cleft in his chin and a jaw that looked carved in stone. "Yes, I remember seeing you there. I don't recall much else. It was a very bad day."

"Yes, it was."

She turned. "This is my friend Brittany Haworth."

He gave a faint nod of his head. "Ms. Haworth."

"Nice to meet you," Britt said. She'd always been shy. The way she was looking at Cain, as if the sexiest man alive had just dropped by for a visit, Carly was surprised her friend was able to speak.

Cain's gaze returned to Carly. "I realize how difficult it must be, going through all of this again so soon. Once more you have my condolences."

"Thank you. It's been difficult. But my grandfather lived a long, full life. I can only imagine how painful this has been for Miguel's family."

A muscle in Cain's jaw tightened. "Maybe catching his killers will ease some of their pain."

"You think the police will catch them?"

"Someone will."

There was something in the way he said it. Surely, he didn't intend to involve himself in catching the men who'd killed Miguel.

"I didn't realize you were a friend of my grandfather's."

His features relaxed as if a fond memory had surfaced. "Joe Drake was a good man. One of the best. He gave me my first job. Did you know that?"

Her eyes burned. That sounded so like Joe. Never a handout but always a hand-up whenever one was needed. "I wasn't around much after I got out of high school. I should have come home more often. You'll never know how much I regret that."

His expression shifted, became unreadable. "We all do things we regret." Up close he was even better-looking than she had first thought, his dark hair cut a little shorter on the sides, narrow brackets beside his mouth that only appeared once in a while, not dimples, but something more subtle, more intriguing. "Your grandfather loved you very much."

A lump swelled in her throat. She had loved him, too. She'd never realized how little time they would have. "Thank you for saying that." She needed to leave. She was going to cry and she didn't want to do that in front of him. "I'm sorry, but if you'll excuse me, I need to say good-bye to Conchita before we go."

He nodded. "There's something I need to discuss with you. After Joe died, I waited. I wanted to give you time to grieve, but after what happened to Miguel, it can't wait any longer."

She tried to imagine what Cain wanted. Something to do with Joe, she thought. "All right. You can reach me at the office. I'm there every day."

"I know the number. I'll be in touch."

She watched as he turned and walked away, wide shoulders, narrow hips, long legs striding across the grass as if he had something important to do. What could one of the wealthiest men in Texas possibly want to talk to her about?

Carly watched as Cain slid into the back of a shiny black stretch limo waiting for him at the edge of the graveyard.

"I wonder what he wants," Brittany said, voicing Carly's thoughts.

"He's in the transportation business, so it must have something to do with Drake Trucking."

"Cain owns half of Texas American. It's a huge corporation, so you're probably right. Or maybe it's something personal, something to do with your grandfather."

"Maybe. I guess I'll be finding out." Carly started making her way through the tombstones. Up ahead, the family stood on the church steps, accepting condolences. Carly squared her shoulders and kept walking.

She wasn't what he'd imagined. Oh, she was as beautiful as the pictures her grandfather had proudly shown him: late twenties, taller than average, with big blue eyes and golden blond hair past her shoulders. Joe had shown him a photo of her playing volleyball on the beach so he knew what she looked like in a bikini, knew she had a dynamite figure.

She didn't seem concerned with her appearance the way he'd expected. He'd thought she'd be more aloof, more self-absorbed. He hadn't expected her to be grieving her grandfather so deeply.

He'd been sure he wouldn't like her. Not the young woman who had accepted so much and returned so little.

And yet as he had watched her with Miguel's family, as he read her sorrow, the depth of her concern, he had been surprisingly moved. She felt responsible in some way for her employee's death. She blamed herself and he couldn't allow that to happen.

Linc had made a vow to her grandfather. He'd promised Joe Drake that if the worst happened and his heart gave up, he'd look after Carly, make sure she was okay.

Linc planned to do just that.

And the best way he could take care of her was to buy her out of Drake Trucking. The best thing he could do for Carly was to send her packing—before she ended up as dead as Miguel Hernandez.

BEYOND DANGER

*New York Times **bestselling author Kat Martin
brings page-turning suspense to a tale of secrets
and passions turned deadly* . . .**

Texas mogul Beau Reese is furious.
All six feet three obscenely wealthy, good-looking
inches of him. His sixty-year-old father, Stewart,
a former state senator no less, has impregnated a
teenager. Barely able to contain his anger,
Beau is in for another surprise.
It appears that Stewart has moved an entirely
different woman into the house. . . .

Beau assumes that stunning Cassidy Jones is his
father's mistress. At least she's of age.
But those concerns take a sudden backseat
when he finds Stewart in a pool of blood on the floor
of his study—and Cassidy walks in to find Beau
with his hand on the murder weapon.

The shocks just keep coming. Someone was following
Stewart, and Cassidy is the detective hired to find out
who and why. Now she'll have to find his killer instead.
Her gut tells her it wasn't Beau.
And Beau's instincts tell him it wasn't Cassidy.
Determined to track down the truth, they form an
uneasy alliance—one that will bring them
closer to each other—
closer to danger and beyond. . . .

Pleasant Hill, Texas

Beau could hardly believe it. His father was sixty years old! The girl sitting across from him in a booth at the Pleasant Hill Café looked like a teenager. A very pregnant teenager.

"Everything's going to be okay, Missy," Beau Reese said. "You don't have to worry about anything from now on. I'll make sure everything is taken care of from here on out."

"He bought me presents," the girl said, dabbing a Kleenex against the tears in her blue eyes. "He told me how pretty I was, how much he liked being with me. I thought he loved me."

Fat chance of that, Beau thought. His dad had never loved anyone but himself. True, his father, a former Texas state senator, was still a handsome man, one who stayed in shape and looked twenty years younger. Didn't make the situation any better.

"How old are you, Missy?"

"Nineteen."

At least she was over the age of consent. That was something, not much.

Beau shoved a hand through his wavy black hair and took a steadying breath. He thought of the DNA test folded up and tucked into the pocket of his shirt. He had always wanted a baby brother or sister. Now at the age of thirty-five, he was finally going to have one.

Beau felt a surge of protectiveness toward the young woman carrying his father's child.

He looked over to where she sat hunched over next to her mother on the opposite side of the pink vinyl booth. "Everybody makes mistakes, Missy. You picked the wrong guy, that's all. Doesn't mean you won't have a great kid."

For the first time since he'd arrived, Missy managed a tentative smile. "Thank you for saying that."

Beau returned the smile. "I'm going to have a baby sister. I promise she won't have to worry about a thing from the day she's born into this world." Hell, he was worth more than half a billion dollars. He would see the child had everything she ever wanted.

When Missy's lips trembled, her mother scooted out of the booth. "I think she's had enough for today. This is all very hard on her and I don't want her getting overly tired." Josie reached for her daughter's hand. "Let's go home, honey. You'll feel better after a nap."

Beau got up, too, leaned over and brushed a kiss on Missy's cheek. "You both have my number. If you need anything, call me. Okay?"

Missy swallowed. "Okay."

"Thank you, Beau," Josie said. "I should have called you sooner. I should have known you'd help us."

"I'll have my assistant send you a check right away. You'll have money to take care of expenses and buy the things you need. After that, I'll have a draft sent to Missy every month."

Josie's eyes teared up. "I didn't know how I was going to manage the bills all by myself. Thank you again, Beau."

He just nodded. "Keep me up to date on her condition."

"I will," Josie said.

Beau watched the women head for the door, the bell ringing as Josie shoved it open and she and Missy walked out of the café.

Leaving money on the table for his coffee, he followed the women out the door, his temper slowly climbing toward the boiling point, as it had been ever since he'd first received Josie's call.

His father should be the one handling Missy's pregnancy. He'd had months to step up and do the right thing. Beau figured he never would.

As he crossed the sidewalk and opened the door of his dark blue Ferrari, his temper cranked up another notch. By the time the car was roaring along the road to his father's house, his fury was simmering, bubbling just below the surface.

Unconsciously his foot pressed harder on the gas, urging the car down the two-lane road at well over eighty miles an hour. With too many tickets in Howler County already, he forced himself to slow down.

Making the turn into Country Club Estates, he jammed on the brakes and the car slid to a stop in front of the house. The white, two-story home he'd been raised in oozed Southern charm, the row of columns out front mimicking an old-style plantation.

Climbing out of the Ferrari, one of his favorite vehicles, he pounded up the front steps and crossed the porch. The housekeeper had Mondays and Tuesdays off so he used his key to let himself into the entry.

On this chilly, end-of-January day, the ceiling fans, usually rotating throughout the five-thousand square-foot residence, hadn't been turned on, leaving the interior strangely silent, the air oddly dense. The ticking of the ornate grandfather clock in the living room seemed louder than it usually did.

"Dad! It's Beau! Where are you?" When he didn't get an answer, he strode down the hall toward the study. He had phoned his father on the way over. Though he'd done his best to keep the anger out of his voice, he wasn't sure he had succeeded. Maybe his father had left to avoid him.

"Dad!" Still no answer. Beau continued down the hall, his footsteps echoing in the quiet. As he reached the study, he noticed the door standing slightly ajar. Steeling himself for the confrontation ahead, he clamped down on his temper, rapped firmly, then shoved the door open.

His father wasn't sitting at the big rosewood desk or in his favorite overstuffed chair next to the fireplace. Beau started to turn away when an odd gurgling sound sent the hairs up on the back of his neck.

"Dad!" At the opposite end of the desk, Beau spotted a prone figure lying on the floor in a spreading pool of blood. "Dad!" His father's eyes were closed, his face as gray as ash. The handle of a letter opener protruded from the middle of his chest.

Beau raced to his father's side. "Dad!" Blood oozed from the wound in his chest and streamed onto the hardwood floor. He had to stop the bleeding and he had to do it now!

He hesitated, praying he wouldn't make it worse, then with no other option, grabbed the handle of the letter opener, jerked it out, gripped the front of his dad's white shirt, and ripped it open.

"Oh, my God! What are you—"

Beau glanced up at the shapely brunette standing in the doorway. "Call 9-1-1! Hurry, he's been stabbed! Hurry!"